q

"I'm sorry, l_____ where else to go. There was no one else I could turn to and—"

"Shh. 'Tis all right. It's glad I am you came to me." Caitlin leaned forward and placed her hand on Michael's broad shoulder. "You musn't worry. I'll tend to your poor hands."

With infinite care she smoothed the salve over the red and blistering flesh. Her gentle hands caressed his with a healing touch that was more intimate than a lover's.

"How did you do this, Michael?" she asked cautiously.

"It was the horse. Princess Niav's enchanted stallion . . ."

His voice trailed off and he closed his eyes. She moved her palms slowly up his hard thighs, and he shuddered at her touch. She thought she had hurt him. But when he opened his eyes, she saw a different pain in those emerald depths, the ache of unfulfilled desire, and desperate need that mirrored her own.

She gently caressed his cheek and turning his head, he pressed his warm lips into her palm. They would be lovers again someday. Every time she touched him, she felt it, knew it. It was only a matter of time. But this wasn't the time. Michael's greatest hurt was yet to come and her tender care couldn't shield him from that. . . .

DREAM CARVER

SONJA MASSIE

PINNACLE BOOKS
WINDSOR PUBLISHING CORP.

PINNACLE BOOKS

are published by

Windsor Publishing Corp.
475 Park Avenue South
New York, NY 10016

First printing: May, 1989

Printed in the United States of America

Dedicated to my mother
Peggy Ann McGill
An Irish rose whose blossom faded too quickly, but her sweet
fragrance remains with those of us who loved her.

The author would like to thank people on both sides of the Atlantic for their contributions to this novel.

In the United States: Charlotte Dinger and William Dentzel for generously sharing their knowledge of the carousel. And Brian Nolan, whose gentle brogue bridged the lonely gap between California and Ireland.

In Ireland: Martin and Agnes O'Dwyer, owners of the wonderful Cashel Folk Village in Cashel, County Tipperary.

Frank Lewis of Killarney, who helped me find the perfect setting for the book and my own family roots in the shadow of Carrantuohill.

Morgan Llywelyn, who told me that I was a druid, something I had always suspected.

The Faul children: Frances, Martina, Andrew, Gerald, and Joseph, who sang to me in a lovely green meadow on my first day in Ireland.

And Michael Quirke, the woodcarver of Sligo, whose stories and carvings revealed the true spirit of Eirinn's land to me in a way that no textbook could.

Chapter One

A blast of pungent sea air swirled through the tiny village of Lios na Capaill, scattering dry leaves in the school yard, which was now curiously silent, deserted by children who had been sent home early because weather was on the way. Foul, dodgy weather.

As the wind swept a path between the gravestones in the church cemetery, it sounded for all the world like a tortured banshee, prophesying imminent death and destruction.

Inside their cottages the villagers shivered, crossed themselves, and whispered prayers to send their departed relatives back into their graves where they belonged. Those who had shutters closed them against the wind and any malevolent spirits who might be riding the wings of the hurricane.

Still wailing, the storm whipped down the village street, past the three pubs, the police barracks, the tailor's cottage, and the forge with its horseshoe-shaped door. At the end of the street the carpenter's shop

9

caught the brunt of the blast, as the wind buffeted the shop's one window, rattling the pane in its casement.

"Saints preserve us. Have you ever heard such a frightful sound, Michael?"

Young Michael McKevett looked up from his carving and blinked his green eyes, as though seeing the girl for the first time. "What? Were you talking to me, Annie?"

"No, I was talking to my wee brother here," she replied, pushing out her lower lip in a pout. If there was anything Annie couldn't bear, it was to be ignored. She looked down at the baby in her arms and caressed the soft red fuzz on his head. "At least baby Daniel looks at me when I talk to him," she said, "though he hasn't much to say."

Unlike his sister who can talk the hind leg off a mule, Michael thought, but he held his tongue. If he said anything so unkind to Annie, she would surely cry. And Michael remembered the last time he had made her cry. It had been ten years ago when they had been mere garsoons five years old. He had tied her long braids into a knot, and her mother had been forced to cut her hair, her beautiful golden hair.

Annie's father, the burly village blacksmith, had thumped Michael soundly on the head, Michael's own father had beaten him senseless with the harness leather, and Annie had cried for four days until her eyes had swollen shut. She had been a fearsome sight with red, puffy eyes and her beautiful hair chopped off like a lad's.

Michael had vowed that he would never be unkind to her or make her cry again, and after ten years he had kept his promise.

A chilly gust funneled down the chimney and scattered the fine white ash and glowing embers of the peat

10

around the open hearth where Michael sat on a three-legged stool. " 'Tis a bad wind, for sure, Annie," he said. "And I believe it's gettin' worse."

Michael stood and stretched to ease the knots that hours of carving had tied in his back. He was exceptionally tall for his fifteen years, his limbs sprouting long and lean, a young oak without mature foliage.

He laid the miniature horse that he was carving on the floor beside the stool and joined her at the window. He squinted through the mist-fogged glass, looking for the familiar sight of his father stumbling down the street, coming from O'Leary's pub. A wave of giddy relief swept over him when he saw the empty street.

The pub door flew open, and Michael tensed, expecting his father to stagger out. But his heart leaped when he saw that it was Caitlin, John O'Leary's lovely, red-haired daughter, hurrying outside to shutter her father's windows. Michael's green eyes glittered with youthful interest when the wind whipped Caitlin's dress taut across her maturing body, her copper curls swirling around her pretty face. Memories of last Sunday afternoon caused his blood to rush to his cheeks. After Mass, he and Caitlin had sat beside the river, holding hands, talking of everything and nothing. Hours later he had summoned the courage to kiss her. And what a kiss it had been. He was still overcome with gratitude that she had allowed him such sweet liberties.

Ah, Caitlin, he thought and wished that it was she standing beside him and not Annie, who scowled up at him, her blue eyes narrowed with suspicion and disapproval.

"That Caitlin is a bad one," she said with a self-righteous lift to her dimpled chin. "She'll come to no good in the end."

"Caitlin's a fine person, and I'll ask you not to speak

11

ill of her in my hearing." From the corner of his eye he saw Annie push out her bottom lip, but he ignored her pout. "Da's still there at the pub, tiltin' his glass," he said, eager to change the subject. "O'Leary's tap must have been open when it rusted. If he stays there another hour, I'll finish my horse. He'll be drunk and complaining like a disappointed weasel when he comes home. But it'll be worth it, it will, if I can finish the horse."

Michael was carving the horse for his mother, to brighten her mood. Patrick McKevett had come home drunk the night before and had beaten his wife from head to toe, but Michael didn't want to tell Annie that. Annie had a gentle father who never raised his hand to his loved ones; she wouldn't understand such things.

Turning away from the window, Michael surveyed the shop, making sure that everything was in order. The work benches had been swept free of curled shavings and every speck of sawdust. On the lime-washed walls the tools hung in their proper places: the scorp beside the well-worn mallet, the awl next to the hammers and the saws. The planking was stacked uniformly, and the templates were sorted and filed.

But it wouldn't matter how well Michael had done his job if his father came back to the shop drunk. It never mattered.

The lad returned to his stool and picked up his carving. Annie followed him, sat on a stool beside the fire, and stuck her little finger into baby Daniel's mouth to keep him from whimpering.

"You shouldn't be carvin' today, it bein' Little Christmas. You should have more respect for holy days. I bet you didn't even go to Mass this mornin'."

Accustomed to Annie's sermons, Michael ignored her and continued to whittle.

"I don't know why you're always sneakin' around carving like you do, Michael," she said. "Your father beats you for it every time he catches you. Why don't you just build the settle beds and dressers the way he wants you to?"

Michael looked down at the horse in his hand. With the last sweep of his tiny carving chisel he had given the stallion a bridle, a fine bridle fit for Brian Boru himself. Lovingly he ran his forefinger over the horse's delicate legs. "It's a wonder, Annie," he said, trying to put his feelings into words that she would understand, "to take a piece of wood, to feel it alive in your hand, to carve a dream that was inside your head and make it something that you can see with your eyes and touch with your fingers. . . . It's a wonder."

Annie's wide blue eyes searched his and he could see that she didn't understand. Nobody understood.

"It's just a wooden horse, Michael," she said quietly. "A fine horse, but . . ."

"It's an enchanted horse. It's Princess Niav's stallion. Here, take him in your hand and you can feel his magic."

He placed the horse in her palm and closed her fingers around it. "Use your fancy, Annie," he whispered. "Close your eyes. Can't you see the stallion, glowing white in the moonlight as he rises up from the black waters of Killarney Lough with Princess Niav on his back? Look, you can see Oisin standing there on the shore. She beckons to him and he follows her. Then she leads him away to the Land of the Ever Young. Can't you see it all, Annie? Isn't it a splendid sight?" He waited breathlessly as he watched her face, her tightly closed eyes, golden lashes sweeping her pale cheeks. Her forehead wrinkled with concentration.

Finally her eyes snapped open and she shook her

head sadly. "Didn't see it," she said. "Didn't see a thing. Are you sure it's a white horse, Michael? Maybe it's a black horse and ye can't see him in the dark. Are ye sure he's white?"

"Yes, Annie, he's white for sure, but it's all right if you can't see him. Nobody sees such things except meself." Michael sighed deeply. He had really wanted Annie to see that vision with him. He had wanted someone to understand how beautiful these dreams were that played through his mind as freely when he was awake as when he was asleep. Delicate, gossamer dreams spun with the fragility of a spider's web. Again and again Michael found his fancy snared by that glittering web, lured by his own imagination into the Land of the Ever Young where there were no drunken fathers, and where everyone saw visions like his own.

"Do ye think I'm daft, Annie? Tell me truly," he said, his heart in his voice. A childish vulnerability showed in the tremulous set of his jaw, which was covered with the first sprinklings of a heavy beard.

"Aye. Yer daft as a goose. Touched by the fairies, they say around town. But I like you anyway."

"Thank you, Annie," Michael replied dryly. " 'Tis a kind and generous heart ye have."

Michael wished that Annie would leave him alone to carve in blissful solitude and revel in the memories of his afternoon with Caitlin. Lying there in the grass, her copper curls sparkling in the sunlight, her amber eyes warm with affection, Caitlin had looked like Princess Niav herself.

Michael sighed and took the horse from Annie's hand. With the sharp edge of the chisel he put the finishing touches to the bridle. Annie seemed to sense that she had offended him and, for once, she sat quietly, saying nothing.

The shop faded from Michael's perception as his mind soared on a flight of fancy. With his dream taking form in his hands, he no longer resented Annie's intrusion. He didn't feel the cold bite of the wind as it swept down the chimney and swirled smoke and dust into the room. He didn't hear the ring of the blacksmith's hammer in the forge next door. He paid no mind to the scraping of heavy brogues just outside the shop. By the time he and Annie heard the halting, uneven footsteps, it was too late. The door flew open and Patrick McKevett stumbled inside.

McKevett was a dark little gnome, long of arm, short of stature, and slightly built. But small as he was, an enormous evil radiated from the man, a pervasive blackness that penetrated Michael's heart and ripped away the fragile, glimmering web of imagination. Princess Niav and Oisin fled on their enchanted stallion to the Land of the Ever Young, leaving Michael behind, shaken and empty.

With a trembling hand the lad thrust the horse and chisel into a basket full of turf bricks. There was nothing he could do about the scattering of wood shavings around his feet. It was too late now. He should have been listening for his father's return.

He glanced over at Annie and saw the fear in her wide blue eyes as she shrank beneath Patrick McKevett's drunken glare. "Take baby Daniel and go home, Annie," Michael told her.

"But—"

"I said go along home. Now."

An unexpected surge of protectiveness swept through Michael and he liked the feel of it. It made him stronger, somehow, if he had someone weaker to shield from this malevolent presence that was his father.

Annie seemed to sense Michael's newfound authority. She gathered her woolen cloak and her baby brother, and scurried out the open door into the wind and weather.

McKevett slammed the heavy door behind her and shuffled across the hard-packed dirt floor to stand on unsteady legs beside his son's stool.

"What is it you're doin' there, lad?" he asked, his deep voice raw and slurred from harsh liquor.

"Nothing," Michael replied as he stared down at a twisted crack in the floor.

"I can see that with me own eyes." Patrick squinted owlishly through red-rimmed lids. With drunken deliberation he stuck his hands into the pockets of his baggy flannel breeches and rocked on his heels, nearly toppling over backward. "You're sitting there, warming your arse by the fire when there's work to be done. It's an idle one you are, lazy as a piper's little finger, and good for nothing in this world or the next."

Michael ventured a peep at his father and melted under the hatred that glittered in those black eyes with their thick eyebrows drawn together over the bridge of a flat nose. An eye from Patrick McKevett could wither grass—or scald a tender lad's heart.

Michael wondered, as he had all his life, what he had ever done to deserve all that hate.

"I finished the sideboard for his honor Lord Seawright," he offered, "and I swept up."

"Swept up, you did? If this looks clean to you, you're as blind as a bush." McKevett pointed to the shavings at Michael's feet. "You'd best be looking lively or I'll cut a hazel switch to put some life into those two legs of yours."

Michael shot off his stool as though the devil had pricked his backside. He grabbed a broom and quickly swept the shavings into a neat pile. As he worked he

16

felt those red eyes bore into him, appraising him as an eagle studies a mouse.

Michael replaced the broom and stood in meek submission as he awkwardly waited for his father's next command. But the man simply watched him, his thin lips pressed together in a mirthless smile.

The silence and the tension grew thicker and heavier by the moment as they stood, Patrick staring at Michael, Michael staring at the floor until the sight nearly faded before his eyes.

A sudden gust of wind ripped the sign outside the door off its chains and slammed it against the wall. Michael's taut nerves jerked as though he had been struck. The smirk on McKevett's face widened.

Confusion swept over the lad as he tried desperately to determine his father's intentions. What could he say to break the awful silence? What did the man want to hear? Michael's instincts told him that there was nothing he could say that would help.

"What were you carving before I came in?" McKevett asked, walking closer to the stool where the boy had sat, his bleary eyes scanning the immediate area.

"Nothing." The lie escaped Michael's lips before he had time to censor it. He had learned years ago that lying was the worst transgression on his father's long list of offenses. Patrick McKevett was not known for his forgiving nature, and lying was the unpardonable sin. Besides, Michael had learned through painful trial and error that his father always knew when he was lying. Like the good God above, the devil below and all the saints in between, Patrick McKevett could see inside your soul ... and he always knew.

But Michael had to take the risk this time for the horse. If his father found it ...

Michael watched the man's work-gnarled hand reach

into the basket of turf sods and pull out the horse, his horse, Princess Niav's enchanted stallion.

Retribution was swift and sure. McKevett walked across the floor and cuffed Michael's right ear with a resounding whack. "You're a liar and a scoundrel," he hissed. "Damn your lazy hide into hell and out of hell."

Michael hardly felt the sting of the time-worn curses or the pain in his ear as his heart burst against his ribs. The horse was gone now; he knew it as surely as he knew that he would be beaten.

With a sardonic grin crinkling McKevett's craggy face, he walked over to the fire and, still holding the horse in one hand, he took three turf sods from the basket, laid them on the ashes and stirred the pile with an iron poker. As the embers flickered into flame, Patrick's twisted smile widened, showing a row of broken, yellowed teeth. Carefully, deliberately, he laid the horse on the stool where Michael had been sitting.

For a moment Michael allowed himself to hope that maybe ... just maybe ...

But McKevett picked the horse up with a pair of long-handled tongs and held it by one delicate hoof over the crackling fire.

A puff of cold, wet wind blew down the chimney, sending a choking cloud of smoke into the room. The blaze flared beneath the horse.

A long-asleep beast named Rage woke deep inside Michael's soul. It reared on its haunches, filled his chest and burst out through his throat.

"No!"

The roar could have been heard as far away as Dublin City. Its ferocity startled them both.

Michael's fists clenched at his sides and his body shook violently as though buffeted by the gale outside. "Don't!"

18

Patrick McKevett hooked one thumb through his galluses in a gesture that was supposed to appear casual, but his black eyes reflected his uneasiness at this change in his son. "You'd better hold the clapper of your tongue, lad. Don't show all your teeth until ye can bite." His thin whiskers twitched with a smile. "You'd best be making amends. Tell me that it's sorry you are for bein' so disrespectful to your lovin' father."

Michael's throat constricted and tears filled his eyes. *It's little reason I have to respect or love the likes of you,* he thought. But he kept quiet and didn't speak his mind. There was no point. The horse was lost, but the game had to be played through to the end.

"I'm sorry, Da, that I was so disrespectful," he said, the words tasting as bitter as thick milk. The fury and despair in the boy's voice belied his apology. He took two steps toward his father.

Father and son stood toe to toe, but no longer eye to eye. Michael towered almost a head above his father, a fact that neither had fully realized until that moment. Michael's eyes met Patrick's, and in that instant the boy saw something that he could scarcely believe, something that he had never thought he would see in those cold black depths. Fear.

His father. Afraid. Of him.

The knowledge filled him with courage and fueled his wrath. "You'll give me what's mine, and you'll be giving it to me now," Michael said, his voice quivering with anger instead of its usual timidity.

McKevett's eyes widened slightly and the sneer disappeared from his face. His wispy beard trembled ever so slightly and his pointed tongue darted out to wet his lips. "Say please," he said. His words taunted, but his voice shook even more than his son's. "Say please and I'll give it to you."

"Pl—" The word rushed to Michael's lips; a long-standing habit was hard to break. But it stopped there, held tightly between his clenched teeth. Michael had finally gained some ground in a lifelong battle. He wouldn't give up so easily.

But as he looked at the horse that dangled over the fire, its dainty legs, the fine details of sinew, muscle and mane, his heart turned over as a mother's would for her child. He thought of all the months of secretive, painstaking carving. He thought of his mother's sad brown eyes and how they would glow with joy when he gave her the horse. He thought of Princess Niav of the Golden Hair.

"Please, Da," he whispered. "Please . . . don't burn my horse."

In an instant the mocking grin returned to split McKevett's whiskered face. Laughter mixed with a snarl barked out of him as he dropped the horse into the flames.

Michael stood, shocked by the expected. His father's coarse laughter assaulted his ears and pierced his soul.

Then he heard another sound. The horse's death screams. No one else could hear them, but Michael could. He had created the horse, coaxed it from the depths of his imagination. It was his, and it was dying.

Michael lurched toward the fire and grabbed at the horse. He heard, more than felt, the cracking of his jawbone when his father's fist slammed into his face.

Fifteen years of torment exploded inside the boy. He lowered his head, ran full force, and butted his father in the stomach. His breath left him in a whoosh as he doubled over and held his belly, fighting for air.

Again Michael dove toward the hearth and thrust his hand into the fire, retrieving the horse, which was already ablaze. The flames seared the palm of his hand.

Michael cried out and let the horse drop to the floor. He watched in horrified fascination as the orange tongues of flame curled around the slender legs and licked at the delicately carved saddle ornamentation. The scattered sparks sought fuel, the small pile of wood shavings, where they flared into full blaze.

Then it struck him, a blow across his back with the heavy iron tongs, sending Michael, sprawling, onto the floor amid the flames.

In an instant his father was over him, his face a lurid red from rage and the glow of the fire, which was spreading from the shavings to a stack of dried planks.

Michael choked as his lungs filled with the smoke from the burning wood and with a more pungent, rancid smell, the stench of his own hair burning. He looked up into his father's hate-distorted face and knew as blows rained down on his face and body that this was no ordinary beating. The moment that Michael had feared since birth had arrived, as he had known it would. His father was going to kill him—as surely as he had killed the horse.

So, this is what it's like to die, Michael thought in a strangely detached part of his mind. There was no way out of this one. No way except ...

The boy's searching fingers closed instinctively around the iron tongs. The beast inside howled its fear and rage, and Michael swung with all his might at the face above him.

A half second later, the sneer was gone. So was part of his father's nose and cheek.

Then a deluge of blood obliterated what remained of Patrick McKevett's face.

* * *

The blacksmith's hammer hovered in midair before crashing down and missing the horseshoe. Kevin O'Brien never missed unless his attention was elsewhere, as it was now. With his next stroke the hammer struck the shoe and sent a shower of glittering red-orange sparks into the air to settle and blacken on the floor of the forge.

As O'Brien pounded away at the glowing iron, he pretended, not for the first time, that it was his neighbor's face.

"That bloody, yellow-backed devil. May the curse of Cromwell be on him, and may he die the death of a kitten," he muttered through his bristly red beard as the wind bore yet another cry of fear and pain from the woodshop next door. O'Brien's hammer missed its mark again.

What he wouldn't give to have a go with his neighbor, man to man and fist to face. Patrick McKevett was no great prayer in any of his fellow townsmen's beads, but Kevin O'Brien despised the man. Nothing would have pleased O'Brien more than to grab Patrick by the seat of his breeches and land him on the back of the Old Man in the Moon above.

On several occasions Kevin had challenged Patrick to a tussle in the small field that separated the woodshop from the forge. But, every time, the bully who took his pleasure in beating his wife and son had found a way to wiggle out of an honest fight with the burly blacksmith.

Patrick McKevett may have been a coward, but he was no man's fool. Most men in the village of Lios na Capaill would have politely declined such a challenge from Kevin O'Brien. The blacksmith brooked no guff from any man. He didn't have to. Kevin O'Brien stood head and shoulders above the tallest of the villagers, and his muscular arms and barrel chest were the result of the backbreaking labor of his trade.

Few men were foolish enough to incur his wrath, and fortunately, the blacksmith was slow to anger, a decent, Christian man. With patience and charity Kevin looked for the good in all men—except his neighbor, Patrick McKevett. Some men were evil all the way through; there was no point in looking. The Man of Horns was active in that one to be sure, always had been. As a lad Patrick had been a heartache to his parents, and a lifetime of drink hadn't improved his disposition. McKevett just got more wicked year after year.

As O'Brien picked up the horseshoe with tongs and plunged it sizzling into the dark water, another cry drifted over to be heard above the bubbling of the hot shoe.

"Don't!"

There was a different tone in the lad's voice this time, a note of defiance. O'Brien noticed the difference and nodded approvingly. So, the cub finally roared back. Perhaps there would be an end to this matter after all.

For fifteen years Kevin had watched the rage building and simmering in the young Michael. O'Brien had thought as he watched Michael grow taller and broader of shoulder every year that he wouldn't want to be in Patrick McKevett's brogues when the lad reached manhood with all that pain boiling inside. Someday there would be the Devil to pay, and Patrick would pay dearly; O'Brien was sure of that.

The door to the forge blew open and O'Brien's oldest daughter, Annie, hurried inside, her long blond hair swirling around her shoulders. In her arms she held her baby brother, Daniel, Kevin's only son. A son was the only thing that O'Brien had desperately wanted, a strong, healthy son to carry on Kevin's blacksmith trade. Kevin had spent countless hours on his knees before his fervent prayers had finally been answered and Daniel O'Connell O'Brien was born, a strapping red-haired boy with the sturdy limbs of a fine smith. But in answering his prayers God had taken the one Kevin loved best, his dark-eyed Deirdre.

Now fifteen-year-old Annie was mother to her infant brother and mistress of Kevin's household.

O'Brien left the shoe and tongs in the bath, took the baby in his heavily muscled arms, and cradled him tenderly against the bib of his work-blackened leather apron. "What is it, love?" he asked his daughter. "You shouldn't have brought the wee one out in this storm. It's an evil wind that's brewin' out there. The fairies might have swooped right down and snatched the babe out of your arms. They have a fancy for red-haired garsoons, you know."

Annie's fair skin was pink from the sting of the cold and her blue eyes were wide with fear. "Oh, Da, I'd never let the Good People snatch Danny, you know that. I came to fetch you on account of Mr. McKevett. He's beatin' Michael again."

"Aye, McKevett is a bad one all right," O'Brien said, clucking his tongue sadly. "You could scrape the meanness off him, so thick is it on that tough hide of his."

Annie shook her head impatiently, sending her blond curls bouncing. "But I heard Mr. McKevett give Michael a terrible thump. And this time it's Michael who's yelling back at his father. I'm afraid something dreadful's going to happen, Da."

With one calloused finger the smith smoothed his daughter's tousled curls back from her forehead. "Ah, Annie, my pet. What am I to do with you? Your ears have been on the stretch again, hearing what's no business of your own. Many times I've told you—don't see all you see, and don't hear all you hear."

Annie blushed beneath her father's gentle criticism, but continued her persuasion. "Can't you help Michael, Da? Can't you make Mr. McKevett stop?"

"No, love, I can't," he said.

"Why not? You're bigger than he is."

The blacksmith's heart twisted as he watched the tears roll down his daughter's rosy cheeks and her dimpled chin quiver. He brushed the glittering drops away with his fingertips. "Because we mustn't interfere with another man's family. Never scald your lips with another man's porridge, I always say."

But Annie had no patience with her father's oft-repeated platitudes. "If you don't help him, Da, who will?" she asked plaintively.

It was such a simple question, asked with the sincerity of innocence. A simple question that demanded an honest answer.

Kevin looked down at his infant son asleep in his arms. He couldn't imagine striking this tender babe, now or in the years to come, and he would kill any man who dared raise his hand to a child of his. Kevin O'Brien protected his own with a fierce paternal love.

But who would protect young Michael McKevett? The same person who had defended the poor lad for the past fifteen years. No one.

The blacksmith handed his son into Annie's arms, squared his broad shoulders, and marched out the horseshoe-shaped door of the forge into the driving wind. He strode past his livery where Lord Hussey's two hunting stallions awaited shoeing. They could wait a bit longer. This situation had waited too long already.

Annie followed at the heels of her father's heavy boots, sheltering baby Daniel from the wind and mischievous fairies beneath her woolen cloak. She had to run to keep up with his long strides as he crossed the small grassy knoll separating the forge from the woodshop. The wind tore at her cloak, whipping it around her and tangling her long blond curls.

As they neared the building, the blacksmith stopped and sniffed the air. The wind carried the unmistakable scent of smoke, and it wasn't the smell of a simple turf fire.

O'Brien raced toward the shop and tore open the door. Black smoke billowed out, confirming his worst suspicions. "A fire! Annie, go alert the fire brigade. Hurry!"

The blacksmith bolted through the doorway and stood, paralyzed by the assault on his senses. The swirling, acrid smoke stung his eyes and choked his lungs. He wheezed and sputtered and bent double, gasping for breath.

A half-dozen small fires blazed along the shop floor, and the front of the room was already consumed by the flames that licked hungrily at stacks of lumber and the timber beams of the ceiling.

With one hand he held his shirt collar over his nose and mouth, and with the other hand he groped through the murky darkness of eery, dancing shadows.

He had walked only a few feet when his foot struck something—someone—lying sprawled on the floor. Bending over, the blacksmith recognized the body and the clothes, not the face, of Patrick McKevett. "Jesus, Mary and Joseph," he whispered and quickly crossed himself. His stomach churned as he stared at the gory mass that had been his neighbor's stern features. Beside the man's head lay the bloody iron tongs.

Even in his dazed state, the blacksmith knew what had happened . . . and why.

O'Brien thought of the times he had pretended to do this very thing to McKevett's face, and he felt a sharp stab of guilt, as though his fantasies had somehow become reality, a reality far more grim than his imaginings.

Could the man possibly be alive with his face torn like that? he wondered. O'Brien knelt beside the body and laid his hand on the front of McKevett's shirt to check for a heartbeat.

"He's dead."

The quiet voice came from behind him. The blacksmith spun around and saw the lad huddled in a smoke-filled corner, his arms wrapped tightly around his knees, which he had drawn up to his chin. He was trembling violently. His green eyes stared from hollowed sockets, oblivious to the flames that snaked through the pile of shavings at his feet.

O'Brien left the fallen man and hurried over to Michael. With one hand beneath each of the boy's arms, the smith lifted him from the floor and pulled him toward the center of the room, away from the flames. The lad was heavier than O'Brien had expected, and when he released him, he sagged against his chest.

Kevin's eyes traveled over the boy's battered face, the swollen eyes, the split lips, and stopped on the bloody, torn shirtfront. He ripped the shirt open to discover the wound that had caused such terrible bleeding, but he found only bruised ribs.

He looked back at the father's torn face and into the boy's haunted eyes. The full horror of the situation smote O'Brien, adding to his burden of guilt. If he had only interfered minutes earlier, maybe ...

The loud crackling of a burning beam overhead jarred Kevin back to reality. The fire had nearly surrounded them. Soon the path to the back door would be blocked.

O'Brien glanced back at the body on the floor with its ever-spreading black pool of blood. Had he felt a heartbeat when he had laid his hand on the man's chest? Yes, he had. There was no denying it. Death had not yet visited Patrick McKevett.

O'Brien looked down at the boy, his battered face, his bloody shirt. The blacksmith was torn with indecision. Could he live with his conscience?

Kevin O'Brien decided that he could.

With an effort he lifted the lad into his arms, tossed him over his broad shoulder, and carried him from the burning building.

"Here, Annie." Kevin lowered the boy onto a straw pallet next to his fireplace. "You and your sister tend to the lad's wounds, and don't let anybody see him until I say."

Annie and her younger sister, Judy, knelt beside Michael, clucking over him like two hens with a single chick. "Saints have mercy,' Judy breathed, pity shining in her dark eyes as she touched the purple swelling beneath his eye. "What happened to him? Did the wind bring the chimney down and him there to meet it?"

The blacksmith hurried to the door. "Don't ask questions now, girl," he said. "Just peel that shirt off his back and burn it. Keep him here and don't let a soul into the house. I'll tell you both all about it when I get back."

But as Kevin left his house and fought his way through the wind toward the burning workshop to help his fellow villagers fight the fire, he knew that he would never tell his daughters what he had seen. Or what he and Michael McKevett had done.

He would never tell anyone.

"Hail Mary, full of grace, the Lord is with thee . . ."

A chunk of sodden turf and straw tore loose from the roof and fell to the floor, narrowly missing Annie and her sister where they knelt in frantic prayer beside their bed.

"Blessed art thou amongst women . . ."

Thirteen-year-old Judy clasped her baby brother tightly against her small breasts, despite his wailing protests. Annie gripped her rosary, her eyes squeezed closed, her cheeks deathly white.

"And blessed is the fruit of thy womb—"

"Jaysus Christ!" O'Brien exclaimed from the loft of the three-room cottage as yet another hunk of his thatched roof took wing and soared into the night. Rain and sleet poured through the open hole, soaking him from his copper hair to his heavy leather brogues. He hurried down the ladder and stood in the kitchen as water ran from the loft down the lime-washed walls to the flagstone floor of the cottage. "God Almighty," he said, shaking his head, "Have you ever seen such a night as this? Pray faster, girls, or we'll all perish for sure, for sure."

Annie and Judy complied, but with no immediate result. As though to mock their prayers, the wind smote the cottage window and shattered it, spraying glass across the room.

Judy screamed and hunched over, curling her slender body around the babe in her arms. Annie prayed louder and faster.

Kevin hurried over to young Michael who sat motionless on the bare hearth. Shards of glass sparkled in his chestnut hair and a thin line of dark blood trickled down his pale cheek where the glass had cut him.

"Are ye all right, lad?" Kevin asked as he bent over and placed a beefy hand on the boy's shoulder. Kevin could feel the frail body tremble beneath his touch. He quickly removed his hand. "Are ye daft and your senses fled entirely? I asked if you're all right," he repeated as he knelt on one knee beside the boy.

Michael said nothing, only stared at him with enormous green eyes that made Kevin's heart turn crossways in his chest.

The wind shrieked through the broken window, sounding like the wail of a tortured soul. Kevin felt the hackles rise along his nape, a fear that had little to do with the fact that his house was falling apart over his head.

"It's him," the boy whispered, his voice as dry as a dead oak leaf. "It's my father. He's going to kill me because I murdered him."

O'Brien shuddered, then gripped the boy by the shoulders. "You'll not say that ever again, lad. Do you hear me?" he said, scolding the boy for echoing what had already crossed his mind a dozen times that evening. The wind did, indeed, sound like the crying of a lost soul, and Kevin O'Brien didn't need any priest to tell him whose soul it was crying out for vengeance. Patrick McKevett wasn't a man likely to forgive . . . on either side of the grave.

The wind shook the house again, rattling the china in the dresser. Judy quickly rose from her knees, handed the baby to Annie, and hurried to the dresser. "I'll take Ma's china down and wrap it in a blanket," she said.

"Come back here and get down on your knees, Judy O'Brien," Annie rebuked her sister with righteous indignation. "Imagine, you worrying about dishes when all heaven and earth's comin' together."

"Leave her alone, Annie," Kevin said as he watched his youngest daughter wrap the family china lovingly in an old quilt. "Those dishes were her ma's and they're Judy's treasure."

"Our treasures should be in heaven, not here on earth," Annie protested, repeating the message of last Sunday's sermon. To illustrate her point, she laid baby Daniel in his cradle beneath the pictures of Christ and the Virgin, then she knelt before the cradle and resumed her prayers.

Judy stowed the dishes beneath a heavy table, then turned to her sister and baby brother. She shook her head in dismay and snatched the holy pictures from the wall.

"What are you doing?" Annie demanded. "What kind of blasphemy is this, ripping the Virgin's picture from its place of honor over the babe?"

"Use the mind the good God gave you, Annie," Judy snapped. "The wind could blow the pictures down on the baby's head and where would we be then, I ask you? In the cemetery burying the poor wee one next to his mother."

Another shattering blast silenced the disagreement, sending both girls to their knees in rapid prayer.

O'Brien whispered a prayer of his own, though he feared that God wouldn't listen to him after the mortal sin he had committed this day.

Young Michael shivered and ducked his head into the thick guilt that Kevin had wrapped around his shoulders. "Ma," he cried, his voice broken with sobs.

Kevin took the lad in his arms and cradled him as though he were his own child. "Hush now, Michael," he said. "Don't worry about your ma. I checked on her

31

earlier and she's at the church with Father Murphy and some of her friends. They're giving her comfort in the hour of her sorrow."

"Does she hate me for what I did?" the boy asked. "Is she glad that he's dead and won't hurt her again, or does she hate me?"

Kevin cast a furtive look toward his praying daughters. "She doesn't know, lad. Nobody knows. They all believe he died in the fire. You must never say that you kilt him. Never say it again."

"But I did—"

The sharp pain in the boy's voice pierced O'Brien's conscience. He couldn't let this child go on thinking that he'd murdered his own father, but he couldn't tell the lad the truth . . . that he himself had allowed Patrick McKevett to burn to death. No one must ever know. Even if it meant that Kevin must add lying to his sin of murder.

The smith's soul felt as black as bog oak. God would punish him somehow. There would be a frightful price to pay. And if, by some miracle, God had mercy on him, Patrick McKevett wouldn't. McKevett would see to it that he paid.

Outside a terrified horse whinnied and a cow bellowed. The old oak beside the cottage groaned, its mighty limbs creaking as the wind twisted them with a ruthless hand. Wet straw, sodden clumps of turf, and splinters of lath rained down on Kevin and the children as the gale ripped away the remainder of the roof.

Icy rain sliced through the decapitated cottage. The glow of the candle lantern was snuffed out, plunging Kevin and his family into a wet, shrieking blackness.

"Da!" Annie screamed. Baby Daniel wailed.

"Be still, love. I'm coming!" Kevin shouted as he stumbled through the dark. "I'm coming."

32

Then he heard it. A tearing, rending crackle. The moan of the giant oak as it was ripped from the ground by its roots.

"No!"

Kevin's scream was lost in the roar of the wind and the death groan of the tree as it plunged downward, crumbling the south wall of the house.

In the darkness Kevin couldn't see but he heard the screams of his children. And he knew that he had paid the ultimate price for his sin.

Chapter Two

January 6, 1845

O'Leary's pub was cozy and comfortable, like the woman who ran it. The room itself was no different than any other Irish pub with its low, timbered ceilings, the rough-hewn tables and benches, and the rush-lights flickering in the dim, smoky corners. But the fire on Caitlin O'Leary's hearth always seemed to burn a bit brighter, and her ale slid down the throat a little smoother. Besides, Caitlin was a red-haired beauty whose pretty face and well-rounded body had caused many of her patrons to entertain thoughts they later had to confess to old Father Murphy.

A dozen male eyes watched the sensuous sway of her shapely hips as she moved from table to table, refilling mugs and slipping coin after coin into her pocket. Having temporarily quenched their thirst, she returned to the bar and began to rub its highly-polished oak with a soft cloth, the money jingling in her apron pocket. The bar had seen better times. Its surface bore the scars of the countless mugs of ale that had been slammed down over the years. But like everything else in Caitlin's pub, including the woman herself, the bar glowed with O'Leary pride.

Here in her pub the men of Lios na Capaill raised their cups of cheer to celebrate their joys. And when sorrow crossed their paths, they sought the amber liquid's solace and the sympathetic companionship of their neighbors. Tonight, on the fifth anniversary of the Night of the Big Wind, the villagers remembered . . . and wallowed like contented boars in the sorrow their memories evoked.

"If we live to be as old as a bush in a fairy fort we'll never see the likes of that tempest again," William O'Shea, the piper, prophesied with his long, thin nose buried deep in his mug of ale. Will's two companions tilted their mugs, joining him in drink and reminiscence.

"Aye, this village looked as though Cromwell himself had called on her. Sacked and ruined, she was," Seamus Quirke said, stroking his scraggly ginger beard that bore the rusty stains of ill-aimed tobacco squirts. " 'Twas the saddest thing me eyes ever had the misfortune to look upon." Quirke blinked back the salt tears and wiped his nose on the sleeve of his heavy seaman's coat with a long liquid sniff.

"Ah, well, the old ones were mumblin' in their gray beards back then that there'd be seven years o' rotten luck comin' our way, what with the storm blowin' as it did on Little Christmas. The Lord only knows what calamities He has planned for us these next two years," William said.

"Instead of borrowin' trouble from tomorrow, we should be thankin' the good God for His blessings in the past," exhorted Cornelius Gabbit, the round-faced little tailor, as he fingered the shiny brass buttons on the jacket that strained across his rotund belly. "Our homes were ruined, surely, but our lives were preserved. Some weren't so fortunate five years ago this very night," he added.

Drawing William's fifth pint of the evening, Caitlin cast a long, sympathetic look across the pub's dark interior to the other side of the room where Michael McKevett sat beside the fire, a giant hulk of a man bent intently over a piece of wood that he was carving. Firelight glittered in his dark chestnut waves, and deep lines of concentration furrowed his ruggedly handsome face.

He must have heard their conversation, but he continued to carve without raising his head. A miniature horse was rapidly taking form in his hands, huge, callused hands stained black from the smith's craft. Yet his long fingers were nimble and patient as he guided the sharp tip of the knife into the soft wood, coaxing a living horse from a chunk of pine.

William licked the thick foam from his wispy brown moustache. 'Aye, many a good man lost his life the Night of the Big Wind.''

"And some who were not so fine," Seamus replied in a voice that was permanently hoarse from bellowing into the winds that swept the coasts from Galway to Kinsale. "If you ask me, the Lord above delivered some into the hands of the devil whom they'd served all their days."

Caitlin winced and cast another sideways glance at Michael. When she saw the pain reflected in his green eyes, her heart reached out to him across the smoke-filled room. Silently she willed the threesome to be quiet, but the free-flowing ale had loosened their tongues.

"Nobody, saint or sinner, got away that night with-

36

out paying some price," Will said. "Just look at what happened to poor Kevin O'Brien's baby boy, and Kevin being one the finest lads who ever walked the green earth."

Seamus and Cornelius shook their heads sadly and buried their faces, along with their sorrows, in their mugs.

"Then there was Mr. Guinness's misfortune," William continued, "and heaven knows, the devil would have no reason to knock upon his door, considering the quality of his brew."

They all nodded in complete agreement on that count. "I can see it all as though it were happening this very moment," Will said. "That mighty wall of his stable crashin' down onto those twenty fine horses and crushin' every bone in their noble bodies."

Caitlin knew that it had been nine horses, not twenty, but far be it from her to call a man a liar just because he embroidered the truth a bit to enhance his story.

At the mention of horses, Michael looked up from his carving, his face glowing with keen interest. Caitlin's eyes met his, and she felt the tug of the bond between them.

Caitlin O'Leary could have had any of the men who walked through her door. There was hardly a male in Lios na Capaill, with the possible exception of old Father Murphy, who would have refused an invitation to her bedchamber. There were many nights when Caitlin needed to feel the warmth of a male body next to hers, to hear the hushed whispers of a deep voice. But there was only one masculine voice she wanted to hear, one hard, muscular body she wanted to touch. And Michael McKevett seemed always just beyond her reach.

She and Michael had been friends all their lives, growing up together in the tiny village. And one summer they had been more than friends. That summer had been the happiest of Caitlin's life. But five years had passed, and so much had happened to them both since then.

A hurricane had swept over Ireland, and when it was gone, Michael's father was dead, their woodshop had burned to the ground, and Michael was changed forever. Five years later Caitlin still didn't know what had happened to her friend that night.

After the storm Michael had retreated behind a wall as thick as those of Kenmare Abbey, and he allowed no one, not even Caitlin, inside his fortress. But sometimes when he sat, carving beside her hearth, his profile silhouetted against the light of the turf fire, she saw him watching her. With those compelling green eyes, he studied her through a tiny chink in the formidable masonry that surrounded him.

Caitlin hung the polishing towel on a hook and walked over to him. She felt his awareness of her even before he acknowledged her presence with a nod. "Shall I fetch you another ale?" she asked.

He laid the carving knife on the floor beside his stool, flexed his fingers, and rubbed his palm over his heavily-muscled thigh that swelled against the flannel of his trousers. Caitlin watched the gesture and felt an aching shiver of desire. It was a familiar feeling, one she experienced every time she was near Michael.

"I'll have another drop o' the pure, if you would be so kind, love," he said, lifting his empty mug from the hearth and placing it in her hand. His voice was deep and husky, tempered with a gentle Kerry brogue. The sound went through her like hot, honeyed mead.

She felt his eyes caressing her as she turned and walked across the rush-strewn floor to the bar, the hem of her red wool skirt brushing her shapely ankles. In a moment she returned with his ale. When she placed the mug in his hand, her fingers brushed his, and a flood of memories washed over her. Memories of his strong, gentle hands and the innocent pleasures his fingertips had imparted on those long, sultry, summer evenings.

Now Michael's hands were always busy carving— carving as though his life depended on it.

"And what lovely thing is it you're making tonight, Michael?" she asked, bending over him.

His eyes trailed down her throat to the curves of her full bosom that spilled over the top of her low-cut bodice. Modestly, he glanced away, but a half-smile curved his sensuous mouth.

He picked up the carving from his lap and held it out to her. " 'Tis Princess Niav's enchanted stallion," he said with a teasing grin. "Surely you haven't forgotten the story of the flying horses . . . though 'twas a long time ago I told it to ye."

"I remember every story you ever told me, Michael," she said, "every word." She remembered much more than his stories, and the emerald gleam in his eyes made her think that perhaps he was remembering, too.

"I was carving a horse just like this one five years ago tonight," he said, his voice raspy as though touched by an unspoken emotion. The chink in his wall had widened to a window, and she could almost see inside. This was the way, she realized, to breach her friend's defenses. He could be touched through his carving.

She ran sturdy, work-roughened fingers over the horse's delicate legs. "What happened to the other horse?" she asked, her whiskey-colored eyes gently probing his.

"It died . . . in the fire. This is the first time I've carved him since that night."

She nodded solemnly. "I understand," she said; and

39

she did. As her fingers curled around the tiny wooden horse she could feel a vitality in the wood, the same power that radiated from the man who had carved it and given it a bit of his own life. If this horse were burned, it would, indeed, die along with a part of Michael.

He searched her face to see if she truly understood, and she saw his amazement when he realized that she did. But she had gotten too close. The guarded look returned to his eyes, and she felt the stones of his wall slide into place again, shutting her out.

With a little sigh she handed the horse back to him, "Thank you for showing him to me, Michael. He's a treasure to be sure."

He reached into his pocket and produced a coin which he pressed into her palm.

"You don't owe me anything, Michael," she said. "You'll have free ale here for years before I've repaid you for the fine sign you're carving for me to hang over my door."

"But I'm not intendin' to be paid for that," he protested. " 'Tis my pleasure, indeed, to be carving it for you."

She shook her head. "No. Business is business, and Caitlin O'Leary pays her debts to any man ... even if he is a friend."

Michael smiled at her, and in his eyes she saw his admiration for her strength and spirit. Caitlin's unusual, independent streak both intrigued and frightened her male customers who were accustomed to subservient womenfolk. She was the only woman in the village who owned a business, and a thriving enterprise at that. John O'Leary had died three years before, leaving the pub to his only child. She ran the same friendly, efficient pub as her father ... except that Caitlin was much more pleasant to behold.

Not only was she a pretty, well-balanced lass, but she was healthy, stout, and hardworking. And the pub was a jewel of a dowry. Caitlin O'Leary would have been a prize catch for the bachelors of Kerry, if she had only been a little meeker, and a tad more shy-eyed, like a woman should be.

But Michael had always accepted Caitlin as she was, strong-willed, ambitious, and fiercely self-reliant. As she pressed his coin back into his palm, she silently blessed him.

Before he had time to argue with her, the pub door swung open, and his fellow blacksmith, Sean Sullivan, stomped into the pub, followed by one of Caitlin's least favorite people, Rory Doona. Sean and Rory were as different as a golden summer morning and a black winter night. Sean was tall, slender and cornshock fair, his broad smile easily offered to any man, woman or child. Rory was a short stub of a fellow with hair that was boot black and a disposition to match.

Caitlin hated seeing the two of them together. Rory was a rotten pratie who spoiled the rest in the pit. He was a man who lived by violence and was seldom seen without a black eye in his head. As she watched Rory storm into the pub and join his friend in the corner, Caitlin sensed some new mischief brewing with Rory in the thick of it.

"May the Lamb of God himself stomp a hole in heaven's floor and kick all landlords up their arses and into the fiery furnace of hell," Rory swore as he hoisted a mug of ale. Mugs were raised and the eloquent curse was seconded all around. Caitlin withheld her approval. Though Rory Doona blithely cursed everyone and everything in his sight, Caitlin reserved her curses for

41

those who were truly deserving. Calling evil upon a man's head was a serious matter, indeed. She noticed that Michael refrained as well.

With a wistful glance toward the crowded table in the corner, Sean pulled up a three-legged stool next to the fire, sat down beside Michael, and pulled a clay pipe from his pocket. Caitlin watched Sean grapple with this decision every evening, whether to join the rowdy crowd in the corner, or sit with his friend beside the fire.

As Caitlin hurried to draw the two men's customary pints of ale, Sean plucked an ember from the fire with a pair of tongs and lit his pipe. He inhaled deeply and closed his eyes, deliciously satisfied. " 'Twas a hard day we had at the forge," he commented to Michael, squinting through the cloud of smoke and the thatch of straight blond hair that always dangled in his eyes.

"Aye, but we made old Kevin the happy one with his pockets full of coin," Michael replied as he resumed his carving. "So, what bee is it that Rory's got a buzzin' round his arse tonight?"

"Ah, he had a bit of a disagreement with Lord Armfield on the road awhile ago." Sean gratefully accepted the mug from Caitlin's hand and gave her the full benefit of his smile, a smile with all its teeth, the smile of a peace-loving man. But Michael wasn't smiling. His square jaw tightened, and it occurred to Caitlin that, perhaps, he resented Sean's attention to her. But she quickly cast the thought aside. There was nothing between Michael and herself any longer except friendship. Why should he care who smiled at her?

As she returned to the bar, she heard Rory slurp the foam off his ale, and she felt the usual twinge of irritation toward the uncouth, arrogant little weasel.

"That damned Armfield cost me the life of my good

mare," Rory bellowed, wiping his mouth with the back of his hand. "She's dead and stiff and cold as a frog on a mountain, and it's his fault entirely."

Outrage boiled up inside Caitlin, along with disbelief. She knew Mason Armfield well, and she couldn't believe that he would kill an innocent animal. She looked over at Michael and saw her own anger reflected in his expressive eyes. Michael was a blacksmith with a great love for all animals, and especially horses. Landlords brought their finest steeds from many miles away to have Michael McKevett shoe them because he was strong and patient enough to gentle the most spirited animal.

She knew that Michael had a special liking for Rory's mare. She had been at the forge only three days earlier, collecting a mended kettle, when she had seen Michael shoeing the pony, taking extra care with her because of her condition.

Caitlin watched apprehensively as Michael laid his chisel and the wooden horse on the hearth and slowly stood. Her experienced barkeeper's eye saw a fight brewing.

"Lord Armfield killed your brood mare and her with foal?" Michael asked, his voice trembling with indignation.

"Not exactly," Rory replied into his brew. "I met up with him on the high road to Killarney this morning and he told me he was after buying her from me. Well, you lads know as well as I do that if a landlord decides he'll buy something from you it's as good as him stealing it. You're not allowed to tell him 'no' and he'll pay as little as he wants. Landlords are no better than the damned tinkers when it comes to horse thievin'— except the landlords aren't hanged for their crimes."

Michael stepped closer to the table and gripped the edge with his big hands. "Go on ..." he prompted.

Rory cleared his throat and continued. "So Armfield says, 'I'll give you three crowns for that mare of yours,' and I says, 'She's not for sale.' Then he says, 'You've no right to own such a fine horse, because you aren't caring for her properly.' "

"No, he didn't say that, surely!" exclaimed Cornelius, the tailor. Spots of red indignation appeared on his cheeks, giving some color to his usually pasty complexion.

Seamus spat explosively into the rushes on the earth floor. "Damned landlords. I suppose he'd be givin' his horses a drop o' sherry in the evening and laying them down to sleep on feather ticking."

"Were you riding the beast, Rory, and her about to foal any day now?" Michael asked. His voice was quiet and smooth, but his meaning was clear to all. Michael was insinuating that Armfield had been right about Rory's mistreatment of the pony.

"I had her hitched to a wagon. Deliverin' a load of turf, I was." Rory crossed his arms defensively over his chest.

"So, what happened then?" Cornelius asked, adjusting the lace cravat beneath his third chin.

Rory drew himself up to his full five feet, two inches. "I wasn't going to sell my mare to the likes of Armfield just because he took a fancy to her," he said. "I took my squirrel gun from under the wagon seat, and I shot her once through the ears. Pained me to do it, but it would have pained me more to see him leading her away. Then I turned to him and I says, 'There's your horse, Your Honor. May she give you many long years of service.' Then I threw his three crowns on the ground beside those fine polished boots of his."

"My, my, it's a brave one you are, Rory Doona," William exclaimed. "A brave one, indeed."

Rory basked in the admiration of his cohorts, preening like a peacock with two tails, until he looked up into Michael's fiery green eyes.

Michael held his fists at his sides, as though pulling back tightly on the reins of his anger. "You're a fool, Rory Doona," he said, echoing Caitlin's thoughts, "and a cruel fool at that. You destroyed that fine animal who had more grace and dignity than you'll ever know."

Michael moved a step closer to Rory, but Sean wedged himself between them. "Michael, watch that temper of yours," he advised his friend. "We all know how you feel about horses. But the mare belonged to Rory, and if he wanted to shoot her dead rather than sell her, it was his business and none of yours."

Rory jumped up from the bench and slammed his fist down on the table. "Don't hold him back," he told Sean. "If it's a fight Michael wants, I'll not deny him."

Caitlin shook her head in disbelief at Rory's lack of sense. No man in his right mind would challenge Michael McKevett to a fight. There was a fierce anger in Michael that frightened even Caitlin, a rage that seemed barely contained. Even the rowdiest characters in the village sensed that Michael was a man who was best left along. Besides, Rory was no physical match for Michael, a blacksmith journeyman with the hard, muscular body and tireless strength of his trade. Caitlin had seen him straighten a horseshoe with his bare hands and toss an anvil eight feet into the air during friendly competition in the forge yard. Any man who incurred his wrath was a fool, indeed.

But before either Michael or Rory had the chance to do each other harm, the pub door opened and, as though materializing out of their conversation, Mason

Armfield entered. The landlord's presence instantly chilled the heated atmosphere as his gray eyes surveyed the room and its inhabitants, taking in the charged situation.

Caitlin felt a strange mixture of emotions when she saw the Englishman come through the door: affection, apprehension, sympathy and fear. When Lord Armfield had arrived in Lios na Capaill three years before, he had changed Caitlin's life forever. Just as the hurricane had turned Michael McKevett into a man overnight, robbing him of his innocence, cutting short his childhood, Mason Armfield had ushered the pretty Irish lass into womanhood. And for Caitlin, there was no going back.

At first glance Mason Armfield was a handsome figure, tall and lean, with regal bearing. His hair, prematurely white, fell to his shoulders straight and perfectly combed. His face was gaunt and as pale as a monk's. But a closer look revealed the reason why Lord Armfield seldom left his Georgian mansion in daylight hours. His hollowed cheeks were crisscrossed with long white scars, puckered gashes that folded into one another, a hideous disfigurement that marred the classic profile.

"Well, speak of the Devil and he'll appear," Rory muttered without bothering to lower his voice.

Caitlin had the overwhelming urge to make Rory swallow his words along with his front teeth. But Lord Armfield didn't need a lowly barmaid to defend him. So she restrained her temper and watched tensely with the others to see what would happen next.

Rory and the landlord stared at one another for a few strained moments, Armfield's eyes glittering with undiluted hatred. Then the landlord turned his back to them and pulled his dove grey cloak from his broad

46

shoulders. He hung it on a peg on the wall and took his customary seat at a dark corner table.

Michael returned to his stool on the hearth and picked up his carving. As Caitlin walked to the private table in the corner, she tried not to think about that fine mare lying on the side of the road with a bullet through her noble head. Her death had been such a senseless waste. Damn Rory Doona.

"Good evening, your honor," she said. "What can I get for you tonight?"

The ice in those gray eyes melted ever so slightly as Armfield returned her smile. "I'll have a glass of your fine brandy, Miss O'Leary," he said, his eyes never leaving her pretty face. "It's a brisk night out there, and a man could do with something warm and smooth to chase away the chill."

The double meaning of his words and the low, intimate tone of his voice embarrassed Caitlin, and she cast a guilty glance around the room to see who might have overheard. The group in the corner were too busy grumbling among themselves to notice. But when her gaze met Michael's, her heart sank. A deep scowl creased his brow, and his green eyes darkened with suspicion.

Caitlin had always been afraid that Michael might discover what was between her and Armfield. She had already suffered the loss of Michael's love. She couldn't bear the thought of losing his respect as well. Irishmen expected their women to remain as pure as the Blessed Virgin until marriage, and no Irishman would forgive a woman for being with another man, especially an English landlord.

"Shall I get you another ale, Michael?" she asked him on her way to the bar.

"No," he said gruffly without looking up from his carving.

Caitlin winced inwardly, but her face showed no sign of her disappointment. The closeness they had shared over the horse was gone completely now, and she felt an acute sense of loss.

As she served Armfield his brandy, the mutterings from Rory's table floated in snatches around the smoky room. "Damned landlord ... raised the rent because my lady planted some posies in the garden." Caitlin watched Armfield's jaw tighten and his ashen complexion flush with anger.

"Steal a man's horse ... lower than a toad's belly."

"Aye, there's not a Saxon alive with a kernel of honor in him."

Finally, Armfield rose from his bench and slowly walked across the room to stand beside Rory's chair. "I believe that you and I have some unfinished business, Mr. Doona," he said, his voice clipped and resonant with the rolled vowels of the aristocracy. "If you have something to say, stand and say it to my face instead of mumbling in your ale like a coward."

Rory leapt to his feet, his fists clenched. "I'm no coward, Your Honor," he spat, "but if a poor Irishman were to insult an English gentleman face to face, he'd soon have a bullet resting between his ribs, shot from some fancy little silver pistol that you landlords carry inside your fine jackets."

A muscle in Armfield's scored jaw twitched as he stared down at the dark little man who bristled with insolent pride. Without another word the Englishman reached inside his finely tailored jacket and pulled out a tiny, engraved silver pistol and laid it on the table. The challenge was etched as clearly as the scars on his face.

Sean, always the peacemaker, started to rise from his stool to intervene, but Michael's hand shot out, grabbed his forearm, and pulled him back onto his seat. Seconds ticked by as Caitlin and the others held their breath. Their eyes darted between Doona and Armfield as they waited for one of them to make the next move.

Rory had never understood the wisdom of a graceful retreat. He stood, shoulders squared, be-whiskered chin held high, ready for the fight.

"Don't be a jackass, Rory," Sean said, despite Michael's warning grip on his arm. "You'll bring a heap of dung on your head if you raise your hand to his Honor and you know it. We'll all pay the price in the heel of the hunt."

But Rory was past reason or logic. His small black eyes flashed with anger as he stepped closer to Armfield, who stood like the Cliffs of Moher, tall, proud, and unmoving.

"Gentlemen, you'll not do this in my pub," Caitlin said in a quiet but authoritative voice as she left her place behind the bar and positioned herself between the men. "If the two of you want to crack each other's skulls, you'll do it outside where there's no glass or furniture to break."

Her words were for both of them, but she was facing Armfield, her eyes silently pleading with him. She could feel Michael watching them as waves of jealousy radiated from him, adding to the tension in the room.

After a long moment, Armfield quietly lifted his pistol from the table, replaced it inside his jacket pocket, and returned to his table. Everyone except Rory breathed a sigh of relief and settled down to drink away their anxieties. Sean left his stool by the fire and pulled Rory down onto the bench where he sat, disgruntled, but conversing in quieter tones. William O'Shea pulled a tin pipe from his hip pocket and played a melancholy tune, his long slender fingers coaxing clear, magical tones from the crude instrument.

The plaintive melody painted pictures in Caitlin's mind. The vivid image of Rory shooting that dainty mare. Her unborn colt dying inside her. The picture of Rory raising his clenched fist to Armfield and bringing the wrath of the English down on a village that had already seen more than its share of grief.

She ventured a look at Michael. He raised his head and their eyes met. In spite of his anger and jealousy, she felt that bond again, as though they were both seeing the same visions, feeling the same hopelessness and loss.

Michael stood, shoved his carving knife and the tiny horse into his coat pocket, and walked over to Sean. "I'm going along home now," he said. "I'll see you later at Kevin's."

"Till then." Sean offered his hand. "Safe home and around the fairy forts."

When they shook hands, Caitlin heard the faint rustle of paper. She saw a note slide from Sean's palm to Michael's, and a shiver went through her. Caitlin had sharp eyes and ears and nothing that happened in her pub went without her notice. She had seen such notes passed before, and she knew that before the night was over, something terrible would happen.

She looked over at Mason Armfield, quietly sipping his brandy in aristocratic solitude. Her love for Michael McKevett battled with her loyalty to the Englishman. Was there any way to warn Armfield without risking the lives of her fellow Irishmen ... and most importantly, without betraying the man she loved?

* * *

50

It was a still winter night without even the stirring of a breeze. *Not at all like the Night of the Big Wind*, Michael thought, as he walked down the road and through the village. Stars, like sparkling bits of ice, glittered in the frosty sky, and the smell of burning turf scented the moist night air. Through dimly lit windows Michael could see his neighbors settling down for a light evening meal, perhaps a story and a song, or a draw from their pipes. And of course, their nightly prayers.

As Michael walked down the quiet village street, he fingered the bit of paper in his pocket. He knew what the note was and, as much as he hated to admit it, he knew what he was going to do about it.

When he neared the edge of the village, he took a deep breath and puffed a small white cloud into the crisp air. He stuck his hand into his pocket and pulled out the note. With another sigh he unfolded it and turned it into the moonlight. The inevitable symbol was scrawled at the top, a crude drawing of an oak tree. A black oak. Below the drawing was printed in an unpracticed hand:

FAIRY FORT
MIDNIGHT

Michael would be at the ancient ringed fort at midnight to join his fellow Irishmen in their secret battle against tyranny. At least, he wanted to think that was why he would be there.

But Michael knew why he was joining the Black Oaks in the dead of the night to wreak havoc on Mason Armfield. And it had nothing to do with patriotism, or the fellowship of Irish brothers, or Rory Doona's dead mare.

It had everything to do with a beautiful red-haired barkeeper named Caitlin O'Leary.

The sound reached Michael's ears long before his feet touched the outskirts of town and the edge of the cemetery. The low, moaning keen sliced through the night air and filled him with dread and despair. His mother, Sorcha, was in the graveyard again, mourning her dead husband. He had already been to the rectory looking for her, but in his heart he had known that she would be here.

Michael no longer tried to figure out why she lamented the loss of a man who had made her life a misery. After five years Michael was numb. A man could only absorb so much guilt, so much regret, and Michael had finally reached his limit.

"Mama, what is it you're doing out here in the cold night, and your bones full of aches?" His voice barely concealed his irritation as he passed through the rusty iron gate.

Michael was thankful that it wasn't raining or sleeting as it had been five years ago tonight, because, rain or shine, Sorcha spent the better part of her evenings here in this dismal place beside Patrick McKevett's grave.

Michael knelt on one knee in the dew-damp grass and held out his hand to her. But she shrank away from him and leaned back against the cold stone slab of her husband's gravestone. Her fingertips traced the intricately carved Celtic cross and host of cherubim who adorned the monument's base. "It's a wonderful stone, isn't it, Michael?"

Michael looked down at his mother and thought that for a moment she looked as she had years ago with the moonlight muting the harsh lines that creased her face. "Yes, Mama, 'tis a fine stone. The finest in the entire graveyard, except for the Armfields' vault, of course." His voice lacked enthusiasm. He heartily resented the ornate gravestone which had cost his mother every pence she had in the world.

"He was a fine man, my Paddy was ... a godly man. Wasn't he, Michael?"

Something in Michael's belly twisted. He could taste hate welling up from his guts, bitter as bile. He was sick to death of this game they played, pretending that Patrick McKevett was a martyred saint. *No, Ma, Da wasn't a godly man!* his mind screamed. *He was the Devil himself and you know it. Everyone in the village knows it, and you're making fools of us both by lying here on his grave all these years.* But he didn't speak the words. He didn't know if she could bear to hear the truth. And if he ever allowed his heart to speak, he was afraid of what it might say.

When he didn't answer, tears flooded her eyes. Her pale thin lips trembled above her quivering chin, and as she turned her face full into the moonlight, the illusion of youth faded. Her skin which had once bloomed with health hung from her chin and around her neck like funeral drapings. A chilling premonition swept over Michael. He would be laying her beneath this grass soon. He could feel it.

It's this cursed graveyard, he thought as he surveyed the tumbled tombstones and the ancient round tower that glowed in the silvered light. How could anyone sit here night after night among the dead and not have the life drained from them?

A shudder ran down Michael's spine as a cold gust of wind brought a flurry of oak leaves down around them, the musty scent of decay filling the night air. One crumpled leaf settled in Sorcha's faded brown waves and Michael brushed it away with his fingertips.

53

"My Paddy died five years ago this very night," she said in a faraway voice. "Burned alive, he did, in that workshop of his. 'Twas the worst death a man can die, to feel the fires of hell here on earth. But he was a fine man, my Paddy. The best who ever walked the green earth. Wasn't he, Michael?"

Michael shook his head as he stood and pulled his great coat more tightly around him. "Come along with me, Mama, and I'll take you back to the rectory. Father Murphy and Father Brolin will be wanting their dinner and you not there to fix it for them. You mustn't seem ungrateful after them giving you a home and work to do."

He offered his hand again, but she shook her head and clung to the gravestone. "No, I'll stay here. I want to be with my Paddy."

Michael's thread of patience snapped. He considered throwing her over his shoulder and carrying her back to the rectory. That would certainly be the easiest way. But it seemed disrespectful somehow for a man to haul his mother around like a sack of praties, so he dismissed the idea. "Mama, if you don't come along now you'll catch your death o' cold, and you'll be joinin' your precious Paddy sooner than you're intending to," he said harshly.

Sorcha blinked and tears spilled down her hollow cheeks. "How can a son speak that way to the mother who bore him? You're a shame to your father's memory, Michael. You should be down on your knees this minute, praying for his eternal soul."

"If you haven't prayed his soul out of hell and into heaven by now, my prayers aren't likely to do him any good," Michael said wearily as he thrust his hands deeply into the pockets of his coat, which no longer seemed warm enough. The cold of the graveyard had seeped all the way to his bones. He hated this place, hated the smiling cherubs on his father's gravestone. He looked down at Sorcha's pouting face, her mouth drooping at the corners. *God help me,* he thought, *sometimes I even hate her.*

He could remember a time when his mother had been his whole world and he had loved her deeply. She had held him in her arms for hours and told him wonderful glittering stories of Erin's heros, of Oisin and Princess Niav. But now Sorcha was empty, with no more stories to tell. Those precious times seemed so long ago. Before the fire. Before the guilt. Before these graveyard vigils that never ended.

Sorcha shook her head sadly. "You're a disappointment to my heart, Michael, the way you handle the matters of God so carelessly. It's your soul I'll be praying for someday when it's wandering lost through purgatory. And it's a heavy burden of sin that you'll be carryin' into eternity." She sniffed and dabbed at her eyes with the fringed edge of her shawl. "Ye must go to confession, Michael," she sobbed. "Ye must cleanse your soul of his death."

Michael's heart froze in his chest. His death? What did she mean? Could she possibly know? He bent over her and placed his big hands on her shoulders. "Hush, Mama. You don't know what you're saying."

"Aye, I know. I know what you did to him." Anger glimmered in her weak eyes as she glared up at him. "Ye kilt him, Michael. Ye murdered yer own father, sure."

She knows. She's always known. The realization cut him deeply, making him even more ashamed and angry. In the past five years her haunted eyes had probed his, questioning, silently accusing. But she had never voiced her suspicions.

55

Michael had thought that his horrible secret was safe, known only to himself and Kevin. He should have known that murder was a secret buried in a shallow grave that would never rest until it was unearthed.

In the darkness behind them an iron gate creaked, and Michael's nerves jerked. He whirled around and his pounding heart sank at the sight of a young woman entering the cemetery. She must have heard. Now someone else knew, too. Someone who was always standing in the shadows, hearing what she shouldn't.

"Surely you don't mean that, Mrs. McKevett," the girl said as the wind fluttered the ends of her blue woolen cloak around her slender figure and whipped her golden hair across her face. She was a lovely sight, but Michael didn't notice her beauty. She was only Annie, his childhood friend and Kevin O'Brien's oldest daughter. After living with the O'Briens for the past five years, Michael considered Annie no more and no less than his sister, at times a nosy, bothersome sister.

Annie knelt beside Sorcha and took the woman's frail hand between her own. "Michael never hurt a soul, Mrs. McKevett," she said. "He's a treasure, the finest son a mother could want. And he loves you so. He just wants you to go back to your room at the rectory and get warm by the fire."

The reassuring sound of the young woman's voice and the touch of her small hand seemed to draw Sorcha back to reality. She looked around, as though surprised at her moonlit surroundings. "The poor priests," she said. "They must be wanting their evening tea."

Michael shifted his feet impatiently and kicked at a stone imbedded in the soil at the foot of his father's grave. Why was it that his mother never listened to him and yet Annie had always been able to soothe Sorcha's troubled spirit with her gentle ways? Annie had intervened many times on Michael's behalf, and yet he felt more jealous than grateful to her. He ached when he realized that his mother considered Annie perfect in every way, while he was only a thorn in her flesh.

Annie patted Sorcha's hand. "Don't worry about the good fathers. I took them a pot of stew that will keep them eatin' for a week. Why don't you come along home with Michael and me? You can have your tea with our family tonight."

"But Michael doesn't want me to come home with you," Sorcha said, looking up at her son. Michael couldn't meet her tearful gaze. She knew his secret. Somehow she had guessed, and he would never be able to look her in the eye again.

"Of course, I want you to have tea with us, Mama," he said without conviction. He held out his hand again, but once more she refused it.

"Annie will help me," she said. "Won't you, Annie? Annie understands what it's like to be a woman alone in this world, the poor motherless child."

Annie stood and helped Sorcha to her feet. She wrapped the edge of her long cloak around the woman's thin shoulders and guided her toward the gate. "We'll see you at home soon, Michael," she said. "And don't be long or the bread will be hard as the hobs of hell."

Michael watched them leave with a surge of relief and anger. How could Annie make his mother happy when he couldn't? Why did Sorcha shame him by talking about how alone she was when she had a grown son who wanted to take care of her, if she would only let him?

He looked down at the ornate tombstone, at the cherubim who seemed to mock him with their angelic, benevolent smiles. "You won't set her free, will you, you old limb of the devil?" he said. "You won't give up until she's there beneath the sod with you. I damned my soul by killin' you, and it did no good." Michael thought of all that murder had cost him: his innocence, his childhood, his self-respect. But most of all, it had cost him Caitlin O'Leary. After that day he had never touched her with his bloodstained hands. A murderer didn't deserve the happiness he had found in Caitlin's arms that summer.

In impotent rage he kicked at the rock that was half-buried in the grass. It came loose and struck one of the marble cherubs, chipping away part of its chubby cheek and pointed nose.

Michael threw back his head and laughed at the bitter irony, the mirthless echo disturbing the silence of the graveyard. He looked up at the full moon and saw yet another face laughing at him, mocking his pain and his memories.

Chapter Three

"Must you be goin' so soon, Your Honor? The night's still young, and everyone's gone but ourselves ..." Caitlin raised one eyebrow ever so slightly, conveying the rest of her message.

Armfield was reaching for his cloak that hung on the wall, but he withdrew his hand and looked down at her, a flicker of surprise in his gray eyes.

She moved closer to him, her pulse thundering in her ears. But her pounding heart had nothing to do with passion. Caitlin was afraid. Afraid that the plan she had concocted during the long evening wasn't going to work.

Armfield pulled a gold watch from his pocket and glanced at it. "The night isn't young, Caitlin, and I have a long day ahead of me tomorrow."

She laid her palm lightly on the front of his shirt and looked up at him through thick lashes. As she watched his eyes trace the outline of her lips, she took heart. Perhaps this would work after all. "Don't go, Mason," she whispered. Her hand trailed down the linen shirt and stopped at his waist. "You've never slept with me here in my pub. Please stay with me tonight."

He didn't answer, but she saw the familiar gleam leap into his eyes. Taking his hand, she led him to the door of her bedchamber in the back of the pub. But when she opened the door and stepped into the room, he didn't follow her. He stood in the doorway, his arms crossed over his chest.

She wasn't surprised that he was reluctant and suspicious. In three years she had never invited him into her bedroom. Her hands went to her bodice, and she slowly began to untie the lacings. "Come along now," she said with a playful grin. "I won't bite ye. At least, not too hard."

He watched her intently without saying a word or moving from the doorway. Finally, he pulled his eyes away from her and cast a quick glance around the room, taking in the old, wrought iron bed, the primitive nightstand and candle lantern, and the small dresser with its cracked mirror.

Caitlin saw the contempt on his face, and for the first time in her life, she looked at her home through aristocratic eyes. She saw the drab little room with its shabby furniture, and she was ashamed. But her shame quickly turned to anger.

"What's wrong, Mason?" she asked with an indignant lift to her chin. "You've never objected to bedding a peasant woman on your own fine feather mattress. Are you afraid you'll get lice from my poor, straw ticking?"

The fire in his eyes vanished. He turned his back to her and walked across the pub to retrieve his cloak from the wall.

Tightening her lacings, she followed him, her mind too clouded with anger to see any way that she could redeem the situation. He wouldn't stay with her now, even if she wanted him to. And she didn't. She wanted him out of her pub and out of her sight. She only wished that she were angry enough that she didn't care what happened to him tonight.

But she wasn't that angry.

"Mason, at least stay a while longer and have another brandy," she said, intercepting him at the door.

His eyes surveyed her coldly, and she knew that she had hurt him as well as angered him. "No, thank you, Caitlin. I'm going on a trip tomorrow, and I need a good night's sleep."

He opened the door, and she peered uneasily into the darkness. "Please, be careful, Mason," she said, trying to keep the fear from her voice. "And God be with you."

"I'll only be away for a few days, Caitlin," he said, studying her curiously. "I'm only going as far as Cork."

He mounted his white stallion and rode away. She watched him until he disappeared in the blackness of the night.

"Protect him," she whispered to any saints or benevolent spirits who might be listening. "Please send a guardian angel to sit on his shoulder tonight, and don't let him be hurt too badly."

The aroma of Annie's stew and fresh-baked soda bread greeted Michael when he opened the door of the O'Briens' cottage, the home which Kevin had built to replace the one the storm had destroyed. Michael had to duck his head to walk through the door even though Kevin had made it taller than usual to accommodate his own exceptional height.

Michael nodded to Kevin and Sean, who sat companionably close to the fire on three-legged stools.

"Good evening, Michael, my lad," Kevin greeted him

61

warmly, a smile splitting his grizzled red beard. "Come share a smoke with us. Sean brought us some good tobacco from Killarney. We mustn't let it go to waste."

Michael shook his head, hung his coat on a peg near the fire, and washed his hands in a porcelain basin of water that was set on a chair behind the door. With his damp fingers he smoothed his chestnut waves into obedience. "No, thank you, Kevin," he declined graciously. "You enjoy a pipeful for me."

Kevin nodded and pulled a thick black braid of tobacco from his pocket. "I will, indeed," he replied as he sawed at it with his knife.

Michael fingered the note tucked into his pocket and cast a questioning look at Sean. But Sean's eyes were trained on Judy, Kevin's youngest daughter, as she bustled around the table, laying out the evening meal. Judy looked up from her dishes long enough to catch Sean's bold smile and her rosy cheeks flushed, complimenting her dark coloring. She returned his smile with her eyes and ducked her head, her glossy black hair swinging down to cover her face.

Michael wasn't the only one to notice the exchange of glances. O'Brien cleared his throat and offered Sean a cut from his own braid of tobacco. But the gleam in the smith's narrowed eyes was less than cordial.

"I see that you've made it home at last," Annie said from the settle bed where she sat, attending to Sorcha's arthritic hands. She carefully wound strips of white cloth which had been soaked in poteen around the gnarled fingers and tied them securely.

Sorcha looked up at Michael, a reproachful expression on her wizened face. "It's about time you found your way home and us here waiting for you."

Michael ignored them both. "I'm sorry if I ruined your tea, Judy," he said gently. "The fine smell of your soda bread beckoned to me from the other side of the village. I heard the other women saying, 'There's no point in us makin' bread tonight, for sure we'll never bake any so fine as Judy O'Brien's.''

Judy's wide, wholesomely pretty face beamed under his praise as she lifted the heavy iron pot of stew from the crane where it had been suspended over the fire.

" 'Twas no harm done at all, Michael,'' she said. "The bread isn't baked just yet anyway.'' She tapped one of the four loaves on the skillet and frowned when the tone didn't suit her.

Michael turned his back on the room and its occupants and walked to the outshot bed in the corner. He pulled the small horse from his pocket and drew the curtains aside.

"Is there a Mr. Daniel O'Connell O'Brien at home?'' he inquired as he stuck his head into the alcove. "I certainly hope the lad's here, because there's a delivery for him from the postboy.''

"I'm Mr. Daniel O'Connell O'Brien, himself,'' the boy inside piped. His small face beamed a wide smile beneath a nose spangled with golden freckles.

The trials of the day melted away when Michael saw the smiling face. Daniel O'Brien's shining smile was the sun in Michael's life. Danny was the one person who loved Michael totally and unconditionally, as only a child could.

"Ah, and a fine lad you are, too,'' Michael replied. "A lad known far and wide for his acts of courage and valor in the defense of old Erin.''

"And known for havin' the bum leg that the tree fell on the Night of the Big Wind,'' Daniel added dryly as he pointed to his withered right leg that stuck out from beneath the quilt.

"Aye, that's true enough,'' Michael admitted as he

sat down beside the boy on the bed and wrapped his arm around the child's thin shoulders. "It's lucky you are that you're a lad and not a mule or you'd have been shot for sure. But then, a mule's not good for much unless he has four good legs, and a boy's worth at least a pound of gold with only one."

"You always say that." The boy's brown eyes glimmered with affection for his giant friend. A warmth flowed through Michael that thawed the chill of the graveyard.

"Because it's always true," Michael replied. "Aren't you after seeing what the postboy brought to you?"

"Yes, indeed. Show it to me before you're a minute older."

Michael pulled the horse from behind his back and held it out to the boy. Out of the corner of his eye he saw Kevin's disapproving scowl from across the room. Kevin didn't approve of Michael's carving. Kevin didn't approve of anything that took Michael away from smithing even for a moment.

Sometimes Michael wished that he didn't owe his life to Kevin. And after five years it seemed that his debt was no closer to being paid. Five years of toil and sweat, learning the blacksmith trade. He had loyally served Kevin, never denying him in any way. But sometimes Michael had to carve, had to express himself in warm, living wood instead of cold, hard iron. Would the day ever come when he would be able to carve without guilt?

Michael turned his face away from Kevin, refusing to allow the man's disapproval to rob him of the joy of giving the horse to Danny.

Daniel breathed a long sigh of admiration and reached for the horse. "Ah ... it's lovely to be sure. But the postboy didn't bring it to me. You carved it yourself, you did, with your knife."

The joy in the child's eyes was more than payment enough to Michael for the hours of work he had invested. Sometimes Michael forgot that Danny was Kevin's son and not his own. It hurt Michael to see how Kevin ignored the lad, seeing only his deformity and failing to see the bright and active mind behind those sparkling eyes.

Michael knew that when Kevin looked at his only son, he saw the death of his dream. Daniel would never be the strong, burly blacksmith who could carry on Kevin's trade. The Night of the Big Wind had destroyed Kevin's hopes along with his son's leg.

"I wish I could make something like this," Danny said as he ran his stubby fingers over the horse's mane and bridle. "But all I can carve are quare lookin' people who look like me, only twisted and lame all over." Daniel reached beneath the quilt and pulled out a small lumpy figure that could have been a man with very long ears, or a hare with very long legs.

Michael laughed and hugged the child and his carving to his chest. "You keep carving these quare looking folk today and tomorrow you'll be carving horses ... beautiful, glorious ponies that your fancy can climb upon and fly away to—"

"To the Land of the Ever Young," Danny supplied eagerly. Michael told him many stories, but this was his favorite by far.

"With Princess Niav of the Golden Hair."

"Where the horses wear bridles of silver—'

"And their saddles are covered with jewels and roses—"

"And lillies—"

"And the horses don't gallop."

"But they fly like the wind and you just barely hanging on to their golden manes," Danny breathed.

Michael knew by the way the child's eyes glimmered that he could see the enchanted land on the horizon of his imagination, and it filled Michael with joy to share his vision with someone he loved.

He gently ruffled the boy's curls. "And the angels play music so sweet and so gay and so loud that it hurts your ears to hear it."

"And there's not a twisted leg in sight," Danny added wistfully, "and it wouldn't matter if there was because all the boys and girls there don't walk, but they ride on the flying horses."

Michael and Danny sat quietly, their imaginations temporarily spent, and stared at the horse in Daniel's hand. "I wish I really could get on this magic horse and fly away to the Land of the Ever Young with Princess Niav," the boy said after a long silence.

"Don't we all, Danny, lad." Michael bent his head and kissed the boy's red curls. "Don't we all."

After tea, Sean and Kevin stood outside the cottage door, watching Michael frolic in the moonlight with Danny and five of the neighbors' children. "Do you think he'll join us tonight?" Sean asked as he tapped his pipe against the side of the house.

"He'll come along," Kevin replied. "Though I can't imagine how much help he'll be, considering how he feels about horses."

Kevin watched Michael lift Danny and the others up to a giant wagon wheel that he had mounted parallel to the ground on a pike. The children grasped the spokes, and Michael spun the wheel, sending them flying in a squealing circle of glee.

"He's a strange one, that Michael is," Sean said. "But the garsoons do love him, don't they? I've never seen a man so fond of children and horses as old Michael is."

Kevin shook his head solemnly as he watched his frail son fall off the wheel and into Michael's waiting arms. The children weren't the only ones who loved Michael McKevett. Kevin O'Brien loved him too.

God had taken the strength and health from Kevin's only son on the Night of the Big Wind. But God was merciful. That very night he had given Kevin another son, a son who was bigger and stronger than any man in the village, or in all of Kerry for that matter. Michael was a fine son, even if he did prefer to work with wood instead of iron and even if he did go a bit mental at times with his head full of myths and legends.

"Michael will be with us at midnight," Kevin said confidently. "He's a strange one in some ways, but he'll not let us down when we need him. And the Black Oaks surely need him with us tonight if we're to see the morning light with our souls still inside our bodies."

"Aw-w-w, Michael, just one more push. One more time," pleaded the trebled voices. The children surrounded Michael and tugged at the hem of his coat and his hands. "Push us one more time and then we'll go home sure. . . . We promise."

Michael dropped to his knees in the dirt and enveloped as many of them as possible in his long arms. "You'll be the death of me yet," he groaned, hugging them close.

Little Katrin, Will O'Shea's daughter, buried her face against his cheek and kissed him shyly. "Michael's all tired out, can't ye see?" she told her playmates. "He'll push us again tomorrow night. Won't you, Michael?"

He returned her kiss and squeezed the bundle of

them until they squealed for release. "Aye, tomorrow night I'll push you till we're all dizzy. Be off with you now before your mothers get worried about you."

He let them go with a sigh of regret. "Safe home," he admonished them as they scurried down the road toward their cottages.

Danny remained at his side until he reached down and ruffled the child's soft red curls. In the moonlight Michael could see the love on the small face and it went straight to his heart. Who but a child could love so purely? He wished to God that this boy was his son. He wished they were all his children, his to love, to teach, to protect in a way that he had never been protected and loved.

For some reason he thought of Caitlin, of her full, maternal breasts and her wide hips that were made to bear children. He could see her, sitting before the fire with a wee one in her arms, the babe suckling at that rounded white breast, while several others played on the floor around her skirt. The thought warmed him and at the same time made him ache with longing. Someday.

"What is it you're thinkin', Michael?" Danny asked, tugging at his sleeve.

"Why?"

"I just wondered 'cause you were grinnin' like a goat eating nettles."

Michael gently swatted the boy on his rear. "I was thinking that it's time you were off to bed. Annie will be out here yelling for you if you don't go inside."

"Daniel O'Connell O'Brien, come in the house this minute and get into bed," came a cry from the house.

Danny looked up at Michael, smiled, shrugged, and hobbled off toward the cabin.

Michael watched him go, then looked up at the stars

glimmering in the dark Kerry sky. He closed his eyes and whispered his first prayer in a long time. "A dozen like him, Father. If you give me nothing else in this life, please give me sons and daughters with gentle spirits and bright shining eyes like Danny's."

Michael waited, somehow hoping to hear a reply with his heart, if not with his ears. But the prayer bounced back at him from the black sky, unreceived. For a fleeting moment Michael had felt purified, cleansed by the love of the children. He had forgotten that he was condemned by his mortal sin of murder. He had forgotten that God no longer listened to his prayers.

Moments later, Michael stepped inside the O'Briens' barn, a candle lantern in his hand. The candle cast a cozy glow as he hung the lantern on a hook in the wall and walked over to the cow and calf stalled at the end of the byre.

The calf blinked sleepy, wide eyes at him. The cow lowed softly, but gave him no more notice than a swish of her tail. She was long accustomed to these late-night visits from this human being who couldn't seem to sleep with the rest of the world.

Michael walked to the far end of the byre where the mare was tied. Biddy was no longer the sassy little pony that she had once been. A bit swayed of back, she had hardly any teeth left. But on Sunday morning she pulled the O'Briens down the road to Mass, while Michael, the hopelessly damned, stayed home; and on occasion Biddy hauled a wagon half-full of turf from the bog to the cottage. For those reasons, as well as the fact that she was loved by the children, Biddy was kept warm and well-fed.

Michael ran his fingers over her flank and down her hind leg. He gently massaged the swelling in her hock that was getting worse day by day. They would have to put Biddy down soon, and that would be a sad day in the O'Brien clan.

He left the horse and sank down into a pile of straw. Leaning back against the wall, he released a long, tired sigh. His body ached with weariness, but his hands itched. They had to carve, and he couldn't deny the urge.

Michael pulled a chunk of maple from his pocket along with a couple of small carving chisels.

In only minutes the lump of wood was taking form. It was another horse. A mare. A mate for the stallion that he had given Danny.

So many nights this overpowering need had driven him here, to this quiet place to carve. Nothing would soothe that beast inside him except to sit here in the straw with the animal scents filling his lungs and the sounds of the night in his ears. To allow his mind to be still like Killarney Lough when there were no ripples on its glassy surface. To open his soul and allow it expression in the wood. To turn a worthless chunk of maple into a wonder. It was the only time that Michael felt at peace with God, with his fellow man, with the beast inside.

But no matter how many figures he carved, he was never fully satisfied. It wasn't right somehow. There was something locked deep inside him that never made it to the wood. Something that was wonderful, that only he could carve. Something that wanted to come into the world, but could come only through him.

Michael didn't know what it was. And it drove him to carve, more and more, hoping that someday he would discover it. Someday he would hold his creation in his hands and know that he had fulfilled that purpose which made every other in his life secondary.

"I've been lookin' all over for ye, lad." Kevin's voice filled the quiet and broke the blissful silence.

Michael's solitary peace dissolved when he looked up and saw Kevin standing there, a hurt look on his florid face. Kevin was always disappointed to see Michael carving. "Is it time yet?" Michael asked.

"Not just yet. Will you be going with us then?"

Michael gave a nod of resignation. "I'll go."

Kevin sat down in the straw beside him. With thick, permanently blackened fingers, he picked up a twig of hay, stuck it in his mouth, and chewed, his red-gold mustache twitching thoughtfully. His expression was one of forced nonchalance, and Michael knew that something was on his mind.

"Spinning the garsoons on that wheel . . ." he said, "it's a waste of time and muscle."

" 'Tis my time and my muscle," Michael reminded him gently. "And I don't believe a man wastes himself when he gives pleasure to little ones."

Kevin bit off the end of the straw and spit it out. His eyes watched Michael's hands as they guided the chisel along the wood that was already beginning to look like a horse. "I see you carved a pony for Danny," he said. " 'Twas a nice horse, but he didn't need another animal, what with all the dogs, chickens, cats, and birds you've carved for him."

"He didn't have a horse," Michael said. He knew where Kevin was headed. He just didn't know how long it would take him to arrive.

"Annie's not very happy about you giving him another one. She's tired of picking those animals up off the floor after he's played with them. She asked me tonight when you're going to carve a barn to keep them in."

Michael chuckled softly. He could imagine Annie saying that. Her tongue had a sharp edge to it from time to time. "I'll speak to Danny about it," he said. "I'll tell him to be sure they're out of Annie's way."

"You're not after teachin' him to carve anymore, after I asked ye not to?"

Michael could hear the irritation in Kevin's voice, and he felt his own anger stirring. "No," he said with a note of bitterness. "But if it's in him to carve, you won't be able to keep him from it."

"Apparently not," Kevin replied. "I can't keep you from carving. I'll never understand why a man would want to whittle wood when he can be a blacksmith. Smithing is the finest trade any man can have."

"I know you can't understand, Kevin," Michael said. "The Lord knows I've tried to explain it to you often enough. It's part of me, Kevin, the best part. Don't ask me to give it up."

Michael put down his chisel and looked Kevin in the eye with gentle but steadfast determination. He loved Kevin O'Brien dearly and always would. He would give his life for this man who had taken him into his home, kept him from starving, and taught him a worthy trade. And Michael knew why Kevin didn't want him to carve. Kevin had already lost the dream of having his son carry on his trade. Every time Kevin saw Michael carve, he was filled with fear that Michael would someday turn his back on smithing and take up the wood as a vocation.

"You owe me, Michael," Kevin said, his voice trembling with emotion. "I carried you out of that burning shop on my back. And I never told a soul that you . . ." His voice broke and Michael cringed inside. "I never told anyone what you did to your father. You owe me."

Michael's finger tightened around the chisel in his hand. Would he ever be free to carve without guilt?

First there had been Patrick McKevett's tyranny, and now there was his debt to Kevin O'Brien, which was even harder to fight against because of his love for the man.

"I'll serve you there in that forge all my days, Kevin," he said. "I owe you my life and my loyalty. But, please, don't ask for my soul. I'll not stop carving. I can't. Not even for you."

Caitlin saw the lantern light shining through the barn window, and she knew that Michael was carving again. Everyone in town knew that there were nights when Michael sat in the O'Briens' barn and carved until dawn. The villagers thought him touched by the fairies. Only Caitlin suspected that he was pursued by demons.

Often, the same devils drove Caitlin from her bed to roam the sleeping town. But her feet always led her here, to the barn, to stand outside and wonder what he would say if she were to invade his sanctuary. Would he welcome her company? Or would he shut her out? Caitlin, a woman known for her bravery, had never had the courage to find out.

But tonight she had a reason for being there besides loneliness. If she could only talk to Michael, perhaps she could prevent a tragedy.

She approached the barn quietly, her footsteps soft on the dew-damp grass. But she stopped at the door when she heard voices, Michael's and Kevin's. She listened only a moment, but it was long enough to make her furious with Kevin. The blacksmith owned Michael as surely as if he had bought him with a bag of gold, and he would always own him. Hadn't Caitlin's own father, John O'Leary, told her so himself before he had died?

She turned and hurried down the road back toward her pub. Pausing at the cemetery, she sought the matching Celtic crosses that marked her parents' graves, and she thought of her father's warning.

"You'd best forget about young Michael McKevett," he had told her that night three years ago when he had discovered her sitting on the stool before the pub fire, crying softly into her apron. "Kevin has taken the lad under his wing now. He'll turn him into a blacksmith yet—you mark my words. And ol' Kevin won't rest until he's married the boy to one of his daughters."

John O'Leary wiped his hands on his apron that was tied around his ample waist, a belly that had filtered too many pints of his own good ale. With a groan he knelt beside his daughter and poked her gingerly in the ribs with his forefinger. "Now stop that cryin', girl," he said. "You know I can't bare to see you weep, and me not knowin' how to comfort you. I wish to heaven your dear mother was here and not buried in yonder cemetery. She'd know what to say to you."

To put her father at ease, Caitlin dried her eyes and choked in her pain. She was instantly rewarded with a smile from John. "There, that's better," he said. "Ye've no reason to weep. I saw that new landlord makin' eyes at you when you served him this evening. And you didn't even notice."

"I noticed," she replied sullenly.

"Then why didn't you give him a twinkle of a smile, lass? If you play your cards right, you could live in a fine mansion like Armfield House."

She chuckled dryly and wiped her tears away with the hem of her apron. "I don't think 'twas marriage on Lord Armfield's mind when he was lookin' me over this evening."

" 'Twasn't necessarily marriage I was thinkin' of ei-

74

ther." John stood and pulled his daughter to her feet. Holding her by the shoulders, he looked her directly in the eye. "I'm going to tell you something now that I never thought I'd say to a daughter of mine. It's a hard life, the life of an Irishman, Caitlin. And it's even harder to be an Irish lass in times such as these. There'll come a day when I won't be here to protect you, and your life may depend on Lord Armfield's good will. So I'd make a friend of him, if I were you, and not an enemy. There are worse places to be than on the good side of an English gentleman."

Caitlin considered her father's words carefully that night. And in the winter, when her father died and when she turned seventeen, she went to Lord Armfield's bed.

But she didn't go to him because of his money, or his power, or his ability to shield her from the harsh realities of life. She went because Mason Armfield wanted her. Because the man she truly loved no longer seemed to want her.

And above all else that winter, Caitlin O'Leary had needed to be wanted.

Three dark forms glided silently across the moonlit pasture and climbed the hill to the ringed fairy fort, a black circle of pines, surrounded by a deep trench. The men moved swiftly over the silver landscape, their bodies taut with tension, their ears tuned to any unusual sound, their eyes searching the near horizon for the other four members of their party.

Their companions joined them at the ancient fort at exactly midnight. Each wore a black hood over his head, the symbol of the secret brotherhood. The Black Oaks, like the White Boys and the Moonlighters, was an agrarian sect formed in an attempt to even the balance of power between the English aristocracy and the Irish peasantry by midnight acts of terrorism. The Black Oaks had risen out of grinding subjugation and heartless tyranny, a group founded with a moral purpose which had somehow become clouded with time.

The black hoods did little to hide their identities in a community where a man was known by his one coat or shirt. Michael was the most easily recognized, standing nearly a head taller than the next tallest of them, who was Kevin. No other two men in Kerry equalled their height or the breadth of their shoulders.

"I see you've decided to join us this fine evening," said the smallest of the hooded figures in a voice as tightly strung as a fiddler's bow at a crossroads dance. "I had my doubts that you'd be among us," Rory continued, "after that affray we nearly had in the pub tonight."

"I came along to see that no harm comes to my friends," Michael replied, "not to fight your battles, Rory Doona. You're a quarrelsome dog with a dirty coat. If a man were to fight alongside you, he'd sure come away with fleas."

Rory shifted the torch that blazed in his hand, sending a shower of fine sparks downward to sizzle in the wet grass. "Watch who you're callin' a dog, McKevett, or ye might get bit," he growled.

"Come along now, the two of you," Sean interjected. "The good landlord will have no one to hang for our crime if we murder each other before we've done the deed."

"Aye, let's get on with it," Seamus Quirke said in his raspy seaman's voice. "Morning will be breaking over our heads before we know it."

Rory raised his torch, and together they trooped down

76

the gentle slope of the hill to where the black ribbon of the River Laune looped through the valley and flowed west toward the bridge and the town. Their heavy brogues made wet squishing sounds as they trudged through the mud along the river bank. In the distance a dog howled its loneliness to the full moon, and frogs croaked in rhythm to the river's burbling. The knot of men hurried toward the concealing shadows of the woods.

Michael's heart pounded in his chest and his breath came in heavy gasps that had nothing to do with their hike. The rough fabric of the black mask scratched against his cheeks as the moisture of his breath collected around his mouth and nose. He could smell the fear in his own sweat and that of his companions, bitter and rank.

As he carefully picked his way among the gnarled tree roots and dark ferns, Michael asked himself for the tenth time why he had joined this silent, hooded gang tonight. And for the tenth time, he didn't like the answer his conscience supplied.

He had raided with the Black Oaks before, several times in fact, but never without good reason. Last summer they had burned Travis Larcher's wheat field after he had evicted a young widow with seven children because she had refused to visit his bed.

Two months ago they had beaten some sense into a Kilorglin agent when the scoundrel had shot and killed a lad of only twelve for stealing a loaf of bread. Old, moldy bread at that.

But tonight was different. Michael held a deep, if grudging, respect for Mason Armfield. Armfield was a fair-minded, unobtrusive landlord who seldom wielded his unconditional power over the peasantry. Michael was jealous of Armfield, but not so jealous that he was blinded to the dishonesty of what they were about to do.

They reached the bridge and passed through a round, muddy viaduct beneath it. When they emerged from the rancid tunnel, the town lay to their right: the church, the postmaster, a small general store, O'Brien's forge and the three pubs. To their left was the back road leading to Armfield House, a Georgian mansion with extensive outbuildings and four fine barns.

As they crept silently along the narrow dirt road, the spitting torch in Rory's hand lit their way beneath the arched avenue of trees. The kerosene-soaked brick of turf blazed on the end of the pike; its smoke drifted through the clean night air and fouled its sweetness, even as their stealthy pilgrimage disturbed the natural tranquility of the forest.

They exited the shelter of the trees and hurried across the open pasture to the largest of the four barns. An owl soared noiselessly over their heads, dived and ensnared a hare with its talons. The hare shrieked. The sound rippled along the men's tight nerves.

Michael gritted his teeth and tried to dispel the feeling that this blessed night had been cursed forever by the horror of the Big Wind. Could anything good ever happen again on the night of January sixth?

William, the piper, quickly crossed himself, pulled a bottle of whiskey from his pocket, and took a long swig to dull the sharp edge of his anxiety. "May God fasten the life strong in all of us tonight," he breathed and passed the bottle to Kevin.

The owl and its victim had temporarily unnerved Cornelius, the little tailor, as well. His teeth chattered loudly in his head and his knees were fighting with each other as he shook with fear. "There's evil out tonight," he whispered, casting a nervous glance into the silent shadows around the barn. "There's evil for sure. 'Tis so thick I could stitch a button onto it."

"Oh, hold your tongue, Con, before I pull it out and poke it in your ear," Rory said as he led them into the shadow of the barn on the opposite side from the house. "We're here to teach Armfield that he's playing cut, shuffle and deal with the wrong deck of cards when he messes with the Black Oaks. The loss of his fine barn will bring that scoundrel to heel for sure." He stood on tiptoe and lifted the torch to the rafters of the barn.

"Wait a minute." Michael stepped up to Rory and stayed his hand and the torch. "How do you know there aren't animals in that barn?" he asked. "We'll check inside before you put fire to it."

"You've taken leave of your senses entirely, man." Rory brushed Michael's hand aside. "I hope there are animals in there. At least a horse or two to make up for my mare and foal."

"You'll not kill innocent animals while I have my breath and body together," Michael assured him with a deep ring of authority in his voice. "It's one thing to burn a man's barn, but it's another to burn a living creature. You'll not do it, I tell you."

"O murder," Seamus exclaimed impatiently. "I told you it was a mistake to bring him along, knowin' how daft he is about horses."

"Come on, Michael . . ." Kevin grasped his forearm tightly and pulled him away from Rory. "You'll have us all in a whirlwind of trouble if you don't let Rory get on with lighting that fire."

"We'll not burn the horses." Michael crossed his arms over his broad chest, his face as hard as Connemara marble. As Michael stood against them all, including Kevin, he knew why he had come on this raid. He was there to protect Armfield and his property, to make

79

certain that Rory didn't take his petty meanness too far. The realization shocked Michael, but somehow set his conscience at ease. "The barn will be enough, Rory," he said in a tone that was not to be denied.

"So, get the bloody animals out if it's out you want them," Rory snapped. "But as soon as you've done the job we're going to fire this damned barn, and we're going to run for the bare life, neither stopping nor staying till we reach home."

Michael needed no further urging. As he hurried around the side of the barn, he flattened his body against the wall and tried to stay in the shadow whenever possible. He lifted the bar and slid the heavy door open with a loud creak.

Inside the moonlit barn Michael saw five horses: four mares, and penned into the back stall was Armfield's prize, his white stallion. The mares whinnied nervously at the intrusion, and the stallion rumbled inside his cubicle, snorting his disapproval.

One by one Michael untied the mares and led them to the door. With an encouraging prod to their rears, he sent them thundering across the pasture into the night.

It was while he was untying the last mare that he smelled the fire. At first he thought it was only the smoke from Rory's torch, drifting in through the open window. Then he saw a pile of straw beneath the window burst into a mountain of flame.

"You bastard, Rory Doona!" he hissed. "You couldn't wait, could you?"

Michael hesitated, weighing his chances of rescuing the stallion without being caught and hanged. The fire would bring the landlord and his men running in a matter of minutes, maybe seconds. They could save the stallion.

He turned to run out the barn door. But the horse in the rear stall screamed in fear and kicked wildly at the pen that held him. His giant hooves splintered the boards.

The fire roared even higher as it spread along the straw-covered floor and climbed up the boards of the stalls. Michael knew that Armfield would be too late for the stallion. Head down, he plunged through the flames and stumbled toward the back of the barn. The smoke rolled around him so thick that he could hardly see. It filled his lungs, seared his throat and burned his eyes.

Michael grabbed the horse's mane, but the animal reared and struck his thigh with its hoof. Pain exploded up and down his leg, but he grabbed at the mane again, using all of his considerable strength to hang on.

"Come along, lad!" he shouted. "Come on now or we'll both be roasted sure." He pulled the stallion toward the door, but it bucked, refusing to go through the wall of flames. Michael tore the black hood off his head and threw it across the horse's eyes. With all his might he slapped the horse on its rump and it leaped blindly through the fire and out the door.

Michael followed, fighting his way through the flames and smoke. He smelled the stench of his scorched hair and coat, and his hands stung as if a thousand tailor's needles were pricking him.

Memories flooded over him, overwhelming him with their intensity. He had saved the horse, but this time it was he who would die, burning alive in this hell.

Suddenly he was through the fire and out the other side. The lurid red glow was behind him, and the barn was empty. He could hear the horses in the pasture whinnying their fear. There were other voices too. Angry, excited voices. Coming closer by the moment.

Michael ran out of the barn and fled across the pasture, running as hard as he could for the safety of the trees. He tried to ignore the shooting pains in his thigh and the fiery agony in his hands.

He heard the shouts and the pounding footsteps at his heels. Michael knew who followed him, just as he knew that he would lose his pursuer once he reached the trees. An Irishman knew the forest of his childhood better than any English landlord knew his own estate.

Michael also knew that he was badly hurt. He had been beaten and burned before, and he recognized a serious injury when he felt it.

He needed help.

Michael darted and weaved a hare's zagged path through the thick woods until he no longer heard the footsteps behind.

The he turned and ran toward the west end of town and the bridge.

He ran in the direction of the O'Leary's pub.

He ran to Caitlin.

Chapter Four

"Oh, Michael, whatever have you done to your hands? You've roasted them sure." Caitlin stood shivering in the doorway of the empty pub, wearing only her chemise and petticoat. "Come inside and I'll see to them right away."

Michael hesitated and looked back over his shoulder into the dark forest behind the pub, but only the black trees moved in the night breeze. "I don't know if you should open your door to me, Caitlin," he said. "There may be someone on my heels, and him not very happy at all. I'd hate to bring misfortune on you in return for your kindness."

She pulled him inside, closed the door, and shot the heavy bolt home. "Hush and sit down over there next to the fire," she said. " 'Tis a sorry night when an O'Leary turns away a Mac or an O' from her doorway and him in trouble."

She hurried to the bar and grabbed a bottle of clear liquid from beneath the counter. "Here, this will cut your pain in half while I mix up a plaster for those hands of yours."

When she handed him the bottle of poteen, she saw

his green eyes trail slowly over her scant clothing. His urgent knocking had sent her running to the door without first slipping into her dress. Her copper curls floated in glorious disarray around her head and shoulders, and her pretty face had the softness of sleep. And even though Michael was badly hurt, she could feel his awareness of her bed-warmed body.

He grimaced from the pain in his hands as he took the bottle from her and drank deeply of the liquid fire.

Caitlin hurried to the table in the corner where she began to mix a salve of mutton fat and beeswax in a small bowl. When she had the plaster thoroughly blended, she walked over to him and set the bowl on a stool beside the hearth. "We'd better take off your coat," she said as she tugged it off his shoulders and gently down his arms. "Be careful. We don't want to be removing any more of your hide than you've already burned away."

She dropped the coat onto the hearth, picked up the bowl and sat down beside him. He obediently held his hands out to her. The boyish vulnerability in the gesture went straight to her heart. She hated to see this strong man reduced to a helpless child. But she was thankful for the opportunity to help him.

She turned his palms toward the light of the fire and gasped when she saw the terrible wounds. His flesh was raw, scorched, with open blisters that wept into deep fissures where blood pooled and crusted. "Ah ... Michael," she whispered, her heart sinking, "they're bad burns. Bad, indeed."

"I'm sorry, love, but I didn't know where else to go," he said. "There was no one else I could turn to and—"

"Sh-h-h. 'Tis all right. It's glad I am you came to me." She leaned forward and placed her hand on his broad shoulder. "You mustn't worry. I'll tend to your poor hands."

With infinite care she smoothed the salve over the red and blistering flesh. Her gentle hands caressed his with a healing touch that was more intimate than a lover's.

But no matter how tender her touch, she knew that she was causing Michael terrible pain. His face was gray, and his square jaw tightened as he clenched his teeth. But he didn't withdraw his hand. He watched her without saying a word as she wound a long white bandage around the worst burn on his right hand. His eyes were like those of a wounded animal, trusting and grateful for her ministrations.

"How did you do this, Michael?" she asked cautiously, not sure that she wanted to know the answer.

He stared at her for a long moment before answering. Pain and poteen had fogged his brain. "It was the horse," he said. "He was Princess Niav's enchanted stallion. He died in the fire ... five years ago. But tonight I got him out in time."

"What are you talking about?" she asked. "What horse?"

He didn't answer, but closed his eyes and swayed toward her. His face had paled to a deadly white. The shock of his injuries had finally hit him.

Quickly sliding off her stool, Caitlin knelt before him on the floor, slipping easily into the vee between his spread knees. As she moved her palms slowly up his hard thighs, she discovered yet another injury, a swelling just above his left knee. He shuddered at her touch, and she thought she had hurt him. But when he opened his eyes she saw a different pain in those emerald depths, the ache of unfulfilled desire, a desperate need

85

that mirrored her own. Dear God, how she wanted this man.

She reached up and gently caressed his cheek. The stubble of his heavy beard rasped against her palm. Turning his head, he pressed his warm lips into her palm, and she felt the kiss in the most intimate parts of her body.

They would be lovers again someday; she knew it. Every time she touched him, she felt it . . . the inevitability. Despite Michael's stony fortress, despite Mason Armfield, it would happen. It was only a matter of time. But this wasn't the time. Michael's greatest hurt was yet to come, and her bandages couldn't shield him from that.

"Ah, Michael," she said, her eyes glittering with tears of pity. "You may have saved a stallion tonight, but look at what you did to your hands. You may never carve another of your lovely horses."

Startled, Michael looked down at his hands, swathed in white strips. "Never carve? You mustn't say such a thing, love. They can't be that bad, surely." His eyes searched hers for reassurance, but she had none to offer. She had seen enough wounds to know that his hands would never be the same again.

A loud knocking at the door sent them both to their feet, their hearts pounding in their chests.

" 'Tis Armfield," Michael whispered. "He's followed me here after all. I'm sorry, Caitlin. I never should have brought my own troubles to your doorstep."

"Sh-h-h," she said, pressing her finger to her lips. "Just keep a shut mouth and I'll take care of His Honor."

She hurried to answer the urgent summons that grew more insistent by the moment. When she opened the door, Mason Armfield swept inside, his full gray cloak billowing around him. For once, the landlord was without his freshly starched cravat, and the top half of his linen shirt was unbuttoned.

Caitlin was relieved to see him alive and whole. But her mind was churning. What had happened tonight? Michael had said something about saving Princess Niav's stallion. What had the Black Oaks done to Lord Armfield, and why had he followed Michael here?

Mason said nothing to Caitlin, but his eyes flicked coldly over her, taking in her state of undress. He crossed the room and stood before Michael, whose feet were planted widely apart in a defiant stance. The landlord looked down at the bandages on his hands and the scorched coat lying on the hearth. Caitlin was suddenly conscious of the stench of smoke that wafted from Michael's clothes.

"I expected better of you, McKevett," Armfield said. "For some reason I thought that you were different from the rest of these barbarians. I considered you a gentleman, even though you *are* Irish."

Michael stared back into Armfield's gray eyes, his gaze steady and unwavering despite the quantity of Caitlin's powerful poteen in his bloodstream. "If you were intendin' to compliment my character, Your Honor, I must say you missed by a mile."

"What did I ever do to you or yours, that you would set fire to my barn?" Armfield asked.

Michael glanced over at Caitlin, and she caught her breath. *Burned his barn?* She couldn't imagine that Michael would have done such a thing. "I didn't set your barn afire," he said with conviction.

"But you were with those who did," Armfield insisted. "I saw you running away into the woods. I chased you myself. There are only two men as large as you in the county. Are you trying to tell me that it was Kevin O'Brien and not you I chased?''

Caitlin's heart leaped to her throat, and she felt a terrible hopelessness closing around them. Armfield's meaning was clear. He would have his pound of flesh for the loss of his barn—either Michael's or Kevin's. And Caitlin knew that Michael would never betray Kevin.

"Kevin O'Brien didn't burn your barn," he said. "I was—"

"It wasn't Michael," Caitlin said, stepping between them and cutting off his confession. "He was here with me all evening. He couldn't have been the one to set fire to your barn." She released the breath she had been holding with a sigh of resignation. She had made her decision in an instant and there was no turning back now.

Armfield's eyes narrowed over his aristocratic nose as he looked down at her. "It seems that I'm to be disappointed twice in one evening, Caitlin," he said softly.

Caitlin heard the hurt in his voice, but she tried not to think about it. There were lives at stake, hers and Michael's.

Armfield reached out and took her bare arm in a tight grip. She saw Michael move toward her, jealous fury on his face, but she shot him a warning look. If he came to her defense, it would only make matters worse. Carefully, she pulled her arm out of Armfield's grasp. Her amber eyes pleaded with the landlord, but he was looking at Michael, his eyes dark and threatening.

"What is this Irishman to you, Caitlin," Armfield demanded, "that you would lie to me to protect him?"

"I'm not lying," she said evenly.

"And I suppose that he burned himself here, helping you tend your turf fire?"

"He did," she replied.

"And do you really expect me to believe you, Caitlin?"

Armfield knew she was lying. All three of them knew that. But as long as she stood by her lie, the landlord couldn't hang Michael for barn burning without prosecuting her as well for conspiracy. And Caitlin was willing to gamble her life for her friend's. "Tell me, Your Honor," she said, "was that fine white stallion of yours lost in the fire?"

Armfield's scarred face showed no emotion, but his eyes glittered in the firelight. "No. The horses were led out of the barn."

"Ah, thanks be to the saints for that blessing." She smiled up at him slyly. "Or is it someone here on earth that you owe your thanks to? 'Twas a brave soul indeed who went into a burning barn to save that fine horse of yours. I know how much the animal means to you. I'd think you'd be terribly grateful to that man . . . if you only knew who he was."

Armfield said nothing as his eyes cut back and forth between Michael and Caitlin. His breath came hard as he fought an internal battle that registered only in his haunted eyes. Finally he turned on the heel of his finely tooled riding boot and strode toward the door, where he whirled around to face them. "I don't owe that man a thing." His tone was heavy with unspoken meaning. "One stallion in exchange for his life and those of his friends. I'd say he got the better of the deal . . . this time." He opened the door and said over his shoulder, "If there are any debts owed, I'd say that this unnamed fellow owes his life to you, Caitlin. I would never let him forget that, if I were you."

He slammed the door behind him, leaving them in a heavy, awkward silence. When she turned to face Michael, she saw the wonder, the gratitude on his face, and, for the first time in five years, she didn't feel the stone wall between them.

"Armfield is right, lass," he said. "I owe you my life. I thank you."

"You musn't thank me." She shuddered as the realization swept over her; trying to save her friend, she had surely damned him. "I've made you a terrible enemy, Michael," she said with a sigh. "Lord Armfield won't forget what happened tonight. And he'll not rest until he's destroyed you."

In the village of Lios na Capaill there were three places where a lonely man could go and be sure of finding a crowd: Caitlin's pub on Saturday night, the chapel on the hill during Sunday morning Mass, and Kevin's forge on a rainy day. When gentle sprinkles became drenching downpours, even the hardiest farmers, turfcutters, and thatchers left their work and headed down the muddied road toward the village with broken or dull tools on their shoulders.

A noisy, boisterous lot, restless from inactivity, they converged on Kevin's forge. As they awaited their turn with the busy smith, they tossed horseshoes—ever in ready supply—exchanged gossip, and collected small bottles of "magic water" from the banding wheel that their wives would use to banish the warts.

They read the notices that were nailed to the horseshoe-shaped door, bits of fluttering yellowed paper that announced the coming markets, hiring fairs and auctions. And when Kevin and his assistants were distracted, the lads stole the second anvil and dragged it away to the barn where they engaged in contests of manly strength, seeing who could "toss" it over a stick held higher and higher about three feet in front of them.

Kevin reveled in these busy times. He took great pride in the fact that he made, repaired, and sharpened every tool used in the village by every tradesman and housewife. From O'Brien's forge came a steady stream of iron wares: thatchers' knives, coopers' bands, carpenters' saws, anchors, griddles, slanes, pitchforks, needles and nails, not to mention his own smithing tools. O'Brien was a master craftsman with two excellent journeymen, Michael McKevett and Sean Sullivan, working for him. Together they supplied the village with the best ironware in County Kerry.

"Kevin, what can you do about this?" asked Pete Mahoney, a grizzled octogenarian. His gnarled forefinger pointed at one of the two remaining teeth in his head. "It's hurtin' so bad I can't eat nor sleep. 'Tis complaining more than me old wife used to, and ye know how that woman could scold ... may she rest in the arms of the angels," he added, reverently crossing himself.

Kevin guided Mahoney toward Sean, who was putting the final edge to a new slane blade. "Sean, here, will take care of you," Kevin said. "He's a good lad and he'll have that tooth out before any grass grows on you, sure."

"But I want Michael to do the deed," the old man complained with a wistful look toward Michael, who was trying to blow the bellows, using his wrists and forearms instead of his bandaged hands. Rivulets of perspiration streamed down his naked chest and back, sweat wrung from pain as much as from exertion.

Kevin cleared his throat uneasily and avoided the

hostile look that shot from Michael's green eyes as he stopped to wipe the perspiration from his brow with a rag that had been stuffed into the waist of his leather apron. "Michael burned himself here in the forge a week ago," Kevin said, keeping his voice low so that only the old fellow could hear. "He can't use his hands just yet. You'll have to let Sean pull that tooth, if it's out you want it."

Mahoney cupped his hand behind his right ear. "What's that you say? Burned his hands, did he?"

Kevin chanced another look at Michael and shivered at the anger he saw on the young man's face. Black, ugly anger. Kevin had never seen that deep, seething hate on any man's face, let alone Michael's. In one week the soft-spoken, peaceful Michael had disappeared as though snatched away by the fairies. This changeling they had left in his stead radiated a dark bitterness that both frightened and saddened O'Brien. He would have to talk to Michael about it soon, even if it was a sorrow to them both. This boil festering between them had to be opened before it could heal.

With a gentle but insistent hand, Kevin guided Mahoney toward Sean, who seated the old fellow on the anvil and carefully tied a string around the snag of a tooth.

Out of the corner of his eye Kevin watched Michael, who had left the bellows and was conversing with young Father Brolin by the window. The priest had brought in a brazier two weeks before and had asked that its chain be welded as soon as possible. Michael had repaired it that very day as requested, but the father hadn't bothered to pick it up until now.

With a critical eye the priest turned the brazier this way and that, examining the weld in every angle of the feeble light. As Kevin watched Michael bite his lip in irritation, he silently prayed that the lad would control his temper and wouldn't ask to be paid for the job. It was bad luck to charge a man of the cloth, not to mention bad manners. And sometimes Kevin worried about Michael's lack of respect for the matters of God.

Not that Kevin himself liked the young father; if he were honest, he would have to admit that he didn't. Father Brolin, a newcomer to Lios na Capaill, lacked the quiet humility of Father Murphy, the elderly priest who had served the parish for the past forty years. Father Murphy had petitioned the bishop for another priest to assist him now that he was getting too old to roam the dark countryside at midnight, baptizing those who had just arrived on earth and administering last rites to those who were departing.

Young Father Brolin had yet to find his place in the hearts of his parishioners. It was whispered that he was more interested in their pocketbooks than their souls, though Kevin wouldn't listen to such mutterings and shamed his neighbors for even thinking such blasphemies.

"So, what will be the charge for that tiny mend?" the priest asked. His golden hair glimmered like a halo around his fine head, but the proud tilt to his chin wasn't quite as humble as became a saint.

Kevin caught Michael's eye and shot him a warning glance. "No charge, Father," Michael replied, his face rigid with dislike.

The priest seemed pleased and favored Michael with his most benevolent smile. "Bless you, my son," he said, "and bless those hands which do the Lord's work. May they soon be completely healed."

He clutched the brazier to his chest and left Michael standing there, skeptically examining his newly blessed hands. Kevin watched Michael flex his bandaged fingers and grimace at the pain. Kevin winced along with him.

"Ow-w-w!" Mahoney howled and jumped up from the anvil. He clapped his hand across his mouth.

"There ye go, Mahoney. That bloody bugger will never give ye another day's trouble," Sean said as he proudly held up the tooth which dangled from a string. The procedure was tried and true: a stout thread around the offending tooth, the other end tied to the anvil peak, and a red-hot iron thrust into the patient's face. It never failed.

Sean sighed, relieved to have the job done. He brushed the thatch of blond bangs off his forehead with the back of his hand. "That'll be two pence," he said, holding out his open palm to the old man.

"Aye ... well, ye've caught me a bit short today," he said, spitting blood onto the floor. "Can I bring you some fresh eggs the next time I'm through town?"

Sean looked over at Kevin, who nodded his approval. "That'll be fine, sir," Sean said with a bright smile as he patted the back of Mahoney's tattered jacket, raising a small cloud of dust.

Kevin knew there would be no eggs, fresh or otherwise. Mahoney's chickens had died the same winter as his scolding wife about thirty years before. But Pete Mahoney wasn't trying to cheat anyone, he just didn't always keep account of such things. As Kevin watched the old man shuffle away, he felt the pride swell in his heart. This was one of those days when he knew how important he and his forge were to his community.

But as Kevin watched Michael try to pick up a hammer, his stiff, bandaged fingers unable to curl around the handle, the sweat popping out of his forehead, and his face white with pain, Kevin didn't feel all that proud.

Their eyes met, and Kevin saw something worse than

anger in those green depths. He saw his own fear mirrored in Michael's eyes. Both men were terrified of what they would find when those bandages came off.

Michael fought back the rising panic as he trudged down the narrow road, his brogues splashing wetly in the puddles left by the day's rain. A fine, cold drizzle fell on his face and bare head, but he didn't notice. He didn't notice the rose and mauve sunset or the cap of gray haze that covered the majestic, hooked top of Carrantuohill, the highest peak of the Macgillycuddy's Reeks, the highest peak in all of Ireland.

Michael's mind was further down the road in a pub with a pretty, red-haired barkeeper and the ordeal that was ahead.

"Come see me in about a week, Michael," she had said, "and we'll take those bandages off. Then we'll know what we've got. Don't try to pull them away yourself or you'll do more damage. I'll soak them in salt water first and take them off slow-like."

A week had passed. In fact it had been nine days, and he couldn't put it off any longer. Half of Michael's heart waited anxiously, desperate to see what was left of his hands, of his world. But the other half was afraid to know.

A sickening rage swept through him as he thought back on that night. Rory Doona had nearly burned him alive, and he wasn't likely to forget it. He looked up to the western slope of Carrantuohill where Rory lived on a small tenant farm. Rory had wisely not shown his face this past week, and if he knew what was best for him, he would keep it well hidden for a bit longer.

As Michael approached the pub his apprehension grew. In only a few moments he would know whether his dreams were dead or if Caitlin's nursing had saved him.

Caitlin. The very thought of her filled him with a sweet ache that both hurt and thrilled him. He was glad that she would be the one to take off the bandages, the one to share whatever he found. If it proved to be the worst, at least he would be with the one person who would understand his loss.

In the distance the pub's mullioned windows glowed, warm and inviting. But the warmth quickly faded as Michael saw a tall, cloaked figure mounted on a white stallion coming down the road from the opposite direction. Michael knew who the rider was and where he was going. To the pub, of course. To Caitlin.

The anger that Michael had been harboring toward Rory Doona quickly shifted to Mason Armfield. Jealousy seared him as he stopped in the middle of the road and considered what to do. He wasn't going into that pub with Armfield. He had wanted this difficult time to be a private moment between himself and Caitlin, and he wasn't interested in sharing his pain with an Englishman.

When the horse and rider passed the pub and proceeded toward him, Michael considered that maybe he had been wrong, after all. Apparently Armfield was headed elsewhere.

"Good evening." The landlord dipped his silver head in a cursory nod.

"Evening, Your Honor," Michael returned without enthusiasm.

Armfield's pale eyes swept him from head to toe, evaluating, as a man does his competition. Michael watched carefully to see if the Englishman would dismiss him as a less than worthy opponent. But he didn't. It almost seemed to Michael that he saw a flicker of respect cross those scored features, but perhaps it had only been his fancy.

Armfield sat quietly on his horse for a long while, looking down his fine, aristocratic nose at Michael. Then, as though making a decision, he gracefully dismounted. As the two men faced each other, Michael towering over the Englishman, Michael realized what the gesture had cost Armfield. And he wondered, as he had the night of the raid, at this strange bond between himself and a man who was, by all rights, his enemy.

"I hear that your burns are quite bad," Armfield said, staring down at Michael's bandages. "I hear that you may not be able to smith again."

" 'Tis early yet," Michael replied curtly. "They're not finished healing."

"I hope you recover," Armfield said with a degree of sincerity that surprised and touched Michael. "You're a fine blacksmith and you have a special way with horses. You're one of the few men in Kerry who really knows how to handle a fine animal."

"Thank you, sir." Michael accepted the compliment, but something told him that the landlord had more on his mind.

"I've heard other things as well," Armfield said evenly, "rumors about what happened the night my barn burned."

"Ah, rumors fly like chaff in the wind. I wouldn't pay them any mind."

Armfield's gray eyes held Michael's without wavering. "I heard that Rory Doona set that fire while you were inside, trying to rescue the horses."

"That's a fine story, Your Honor," Michael said with a hollow chuckle. "The lad who told you that tale had a bard among his grandfars, sure."

Again those cold eyes raked him, appraising. "If I

were Rory Doona," he said slowly, "and if I were going to burn a barn over someone's head, it wouldn't be you, McKevett. I think Doona is a fool."

"Not many would argue with you, sir, and certainly not meself."

"I haven't seen Doona since that day. It wouldn't surprise me to hear that he's lying in a ditch somewhere with his neck broken."

Michael held up his bandaged hands for inspection and shrugged. "I couldn't wring even a wee chicken's neck with these hands. So I guess Sweet Justice will have to wait to have her day with old Rory."

Armfield smiled, but there was no warmth in it. "If you'll swear to me here and now that Rory Doona was the one who set my barn afire, there will be a rope around his neck this very night and Justice won't have to wait. She's an impatient lady, I've heard."

Michael laughed and shook his head. "Thank you for your kind offer, Your Honor. But I'll make no such confession against a fellow Irishman. If there's anything worse than a barn burner, it's an informer. Besides, 'twould be a shame to waste that neck on a poor dumb rope that would get no pleasure from the stranglin'."

"As you wish." With a regal tip of his head, the landlord mounted the stallion, wheeled him around and headed back to the pub.

Michael watched as Armfield dismounted and went inside without a backward glance. Michael couldn't walk into that pub now, not with Armfield there. He couldn't bear to see the light in Caitlin's amber eyes when she served Armfield his customary glass of brandy.

Michael turned and headed home, the rain falling hard and cold on his face. He'd rip away those bandages himself. And if he found the worst, he'd handle it alone.

"I met Michael Mckevett on the road a few minutes ago," Mason Armfield told Caitlin when she placed his glass of brandy on the table. With one swift movement, he caught her hand and pulled her onto the chair across from him.

She cast a quick look around the pub, but it was late and the only remaining customer was Pete Mahoney. The old man sat at the bar, holding his hand to his jaw and spitting the occasional glob of blood onto the rush-covered floor.

"I think Michael was on his way here," Armfield continued, "but he seemed to change his mind when he saw that I was stopping in."

Caitlin thought immediately of Michael's bandages. She had been expecting him to come by the past two days and had wondered why he hadn't. She felt a sinking sense of loss at the thought of Michael turning away because of Mason Armfield.

But the landlord was watching her closely, and she couldn't allow her disappointment to show on her face. "Perhaps he just decided that he didn't need a pint after all," she offered lamely.

"Why did you lie for him, Caitlin?" His hand closed over hers so tightly that her fingers hurt.

She shrugged. "Michael's an Irishman. And we Irish protect our own."

"There's more to it. Tell me, now." His grip squeezed until her fingertips went numb.

"Michael McKevett didn't burn your barn," she said, leaning across the table and keeping her voice low. "He ruined his hands savin' the horse's life. I'd think you'd be grateful for that."

He studied her for a long time, then slowly released her hand. "I suppose I am grateful," he admitted as he took a sip of the brandy. His gray eyes watched her carefully over the rim of the glass. "Was McKevett ever your lover, Caitlin?"

Her heart leaped into her throat, and she felt the blood rush to her face. Was Michael ever her lover?

She thought of the tender kisses, the stolen caresses, the whispered vows of eternal love exchanged between two young people under the light of Erin's full moon. How could they have known that night what the future would hold?

Caitlin looked across the table at the Englishman who had taken her virginity, but had never once said that he loved her. Because of this man, she was soiled, unworthy of the man she truly loved.

Caitlin's memories of Michael and their summer were precious, untarnished remnants of her innocence. She decided not to share her memories with Armfield. She had given this man enough already.

"I was a virgin when I first came to you, and you had the stained sheets to prove it," she said with a note of bitterness in her voice. Her amber eyes bored into his until he finally looked away. "I'd think that would be enough for any man—even an English landlord."

"Oh, Jay-sus . . ." Michael gritted his teeth and bit back the rest of the curse as he plunged his hands into the bucket of warm salt water. Tears flooded his eyes and for a moment he was back in that burning woodshop, back in the barn, in the midst of those searing flames.

A guttural moan rolled out of him and filled the barn.

In her stall the old cow lowed her sympathy. Her calf's eyes widened with fear at the recognition of pain in another living being.

Michael fought the urge to take his hands out of the water and left them there for what seemed like an eternity in hell. Finally the fiery stinging began to ease a bit and a welcome numbness took its place.

He lifted his hands from the bucket and sat, looking at the soggy bandages, working up his courage. If there was anything worse than not knowing, it might be knowing. But the time had come, and he couldn't put it off any longer. With his teeth he loosed the knots Caitlin had tied at his wrists, and he unwound the strips until both hands were bare.

At first he wasn't sure what he was seeing in the dim light of the candle lantern that hung on a nail above his head. But gradually his mind comprehended the sight before his eyes. Red, mottled skin. Angry purple welts crisscrossing both palms and the back of his right hand. Blisters, broken and flat. Scabrous patches of blood covering what had been open wounds. The fetid stench nauseated him, and he gagged several times. But there was no putrification. Caitlin had done her job well.

He steeled himself, lowered his hands into the bucket, and gently rubbed them together to remove the dead tissue and the remainder of Caitlin's plaster. It hurt like the very devil, but he sucked in his breath and finished the job. Then he patted them dry with one of Judy's old dish towels.

It was when his hands were completely dry and he tried to open them and spread his fingers that he felt the tightness. The skin was drawn and tough, not supple as it had been before. He tried to open his hand all

101

the way, but he couldn't. Fear washed icy cold over him, making him temporarily forget the pain.

It doesn't matter, he told himself. *I don't need to open my hand all the way to carve. If I can just hold a chisel.*

His pulse pounded in his ears as he reached into his coat pocket and pulled out a chisel and the tiny mare that he had been carving the night before the raid. His fingers closed stiffly around the chisel, the end of its handle against his palm. It was too early to try. He should wait a few weeks, at least a few days, but he had to know tonight.

Placing the point against the wood, he pushed. The pain shot up his arm and into his shoulders, tying his muscles into spasmic knots. With a groan he swallowed the pain and tried again, guiding the chisel along the leg of the horse, defining the indentation of the hock. Sweat streamed down his face and his entire body shook with the exertion. The handle of the chisel dug into his palm. What had once been the welcome, loving press of the tool against his flesh now hurt more than he had thought possible.

But the pain didn't matter, if only his hands would do what he willed them to. They had to carve again. How else could that enchanted herd of stallions that raced the verdant landscape of his imagination come into the world—except through his hands?

Slowly the point of the chisel rounded the hock and started up the flank. But his fingers were stiff, clumsy, disobedient. The control was gone. The chisel slipped and in an instant the razor-sharp point had gouged a ragged rip through the mare's side. Michael shook his head, denying what he saw. It wasn't his hand that had done this. It was a stranger's hand, a scarred imitation of his own that no longer knew how to carve. It was all gone.

Princess Niav's enchanted herd of horses thundered across his soul, stampeding, frantic to escape, but finding the way out barred.

"No!" The cry rumbled through the barn, shattering the night silence. But the voice wasn't Michael's. It was the roar of the beast deep inside him. "I'll kill you bloody bastards. I'll kill you all."

Michael hurled the chisel across the barn. The point stuck, quivering, in the door frame—a scant thumb's breadth from Kevin O'Brien's head.

Chapter Five

For a moment Kevin thought he was seeing the ghost of Patrick McKevett risen from the grave and sitting in his barn. But the hatred that Kevin saw burning in Michael's eyes was more powerful than any drunken meanness in his father.

Kevin wasn't sure whether or not the chisel that had just missed his right temple had been deliberately thrown. He couldn't believe that Michael had tried to kill him. But as he stared into those blazing green eyes, he couldn't be sure.

"You'd best leave me alone just now, Kevin." Michael's voice was hoarse, dry as kiln ash. The sound of it frightened Kevin more than the deadly chisel.

The smith pulled the sharp point out of the wood and walked over to Michael, who sat in a pile of hay with a bucket between his knees. In a gesture of trust Kevin held the chisel out to Michael, handle first. "How many's the time I've told ye, lad, don't leave your tools lyin' about? Someone could be hurt by one of them."

"Someone might be hurt, indeed, if he doesn't know when to make himself scarce." As Michael reached out and took the chisel, Kevin noticed that the bandages were gone, but in the dim light he couldn't see the extent of the damage.

Kevin sank down into the straw beside Michael. He tried to hide his trembling and to keep his voice even. It wouldn't do to show fear to the lad now. "You'll not be hurtin' me, Michael," he said gently.

"Are ye sure?" Michael's hand tightened around the handle and Kevin cringed inwardly.

"I'm sure. Put that thing down, now, and show me your hands."

Kevin watched the struggle on the young man's face, rage wrestling with affection and respect. Slowly Michael laid the chisel in the hay and held out his hands, palms up.

"Mother of Mercy." Kevin shuddered at the sight of the crusting blood, the festering lesions. A wave of nausea surged through his guts. "Ah, lad. Do they hurt so bad?"

Michael drew his hands back to himself and lifted his chin, his eyes still cold and guarded. "They hurt."

Kevin couldn't wait. He had to ask the question that had tormented him for the past nine days. "Do you think ... do you think you'll be able to smith again, Michael?"

It was the wrong time to ask; he should have waited. He sensed the explosion of grief, hate and fear inside the young man.

In an instant Michael was on his feet, his giant body trembling under the onslaught of his emotions. "Yes, Kevin," he muttered through tight jaws, "I'll be able to smith. Isn't that what ye've been waiting to hear? I'll be your bloody smith till my dyin' day. But I'll tell you what I can't do ..." He bent down and scooped up the little wooden mare with the gouge in her side. "I can't carve. Does that make you happy, Kevin

O'Brien, that I'll never carve again? Does it rejoice your soul?"

He threw the horse at Kevin, ran out of the barn and kicked the door closed behind him.

Kevin sat quietly for a long time, turning the mare over and over in his palm. He touched the delicate carving with his fingertip and traced the deep rip down her side. Then his hand closed around it and he squeezed, squeezed until tears streamed down his cheeks and into his red beard. Tears of joy.

Kevin O'Brien's soul rejoiced. God had returned his son to him—a woodcarver no longer, a blacksmith forever.

Caitlin turned herself before the full-length, beveled mirror and tugged at the lace front of the night gown that wouldn't cover her ample breasts. The gown had obviously been made for a smaller woman, the hem not reaching the floor by several inches. Around her slender neck hung an emerald and diamond necklace, the necklace of a fine lady, not a simple barmaid.

"Do I look like her when I wear her clothes?" she asked softly, studying the pretty woman in the mirror whose red hair glistened in the candlelight.

"No," came the reply from the bed. Armfield pulled the linen sheet up to his waist and crossed his arms over his bare chest. "Why do you ask?"

She shrugged and turned to face him. "I just wonder sometimes why you ask me to wear her things. I wonder if I remind you of her in any way."

"No. Not at all." Through narrowed eyes he watched as she walked across the carpeted floor on bare feet to the draped canopy bed. He reached down and pulled back the sheet for her.

With a little sigh she crawled in beside him. "I suppose your wife was a great lady ... "

"Yes." He leaned over her and trailed his fingertips lightly down her throat to the swell of her breasts that spilled over the lace bodice.

Caitlin watched his hand, but made no move to touch him. "And did you love her very much?" she ventured.

"Enough."

"How did she die?"

Caitlin knew that she shouldn't have asked. But it was too late to take back the question once it was spoken. She hated the look of pain that crossed his face and wished that she could wipe away the hurt and those terrible scars.

"They killed her," he said quietly as he withdrew his hand and leaned back on the down pillows. His pale gray eyes scanned the linen sheet, not meeting hers. "The Carders killed her the night they did this—" He pointed to the ragged white lines on his cheeks.

Caitlin caught her breath as a sharp fragment of his pain stabbed her. So, that was what had happened to him. She had heard of the Carders, an agrarian sect who terrorized landlords by tearing their faces with wool-carding combs. There had been much speculation in the village about how Armfield had acquired his scars, but no one had dared to ask.

"Why?" she said. "Why would they do something like that? Why did they kill your young wife?"

"Because I killed their families," he said simply, his voice curiously void of emotion.

Caitlin turned toward him, raising herself onto one elbow. "I don't believe that. You're not a cruel man."

"Not cruel, but foolish. My father left his property to me when he died, but not his wisdom. I exploited my tenants and treated them worse than my animals.

107

Some of them died because of my neglect. But they punished me for it. I'm reminded of my sins every day when I look into a mirror ... or a pane of glass ... or a still pond."

Caitlin listened silently, knowing that this was a rare moment for Mason Armfield. There was no one else in the world to whom he would have confided his pain, his guilt, and she was honored and touched.

That was why Caitlin was there, in a landlord's bed. Because Armfield needed her, whether he knew it or not. And, although being needed wasn't as satisfying as being loved, it was better than nothing.

Caitlin allowed Armfield to think that she came to him because he summoned her, because he was the lord of the manor and not to be denied. And, certainly, that was true. No Irishwoman could say "no" to an English landowner. If he wished to lie with her, he had only to say the word, and she was his. But she didn't have to hold him the way she did now, cradled against her full breasts. She didn't have to stroke his scarred cheek and murmur soothing words to him, the words of a mother to a wounded child.

All he could demand was her body in his bed. Of her own volition she gave him a companion to whom he could confide his deepest thoughts and feelings.

Caitlin sighed and closed her eyes as she felt his hands moving under the silk of his wife's nightgown, seeking the warm solace that her body offered.

Even an English landlord needed a friend from time to time.

"Are ye never going to speak to me again, Michael? Is that how you're intendin' to punish me?"

Michael laid the board that he had just drilled on

108

the forge workbench and looked out the window. Though it was midmorning, the night's frost still glittered on the bare limbs of trees that slept, cold and dead. Michael felt like those trees. But their sleep was only for a season, and Michael couldn't forsee a spring in his future.

He drew a deep breath and turned to Kevin. "I've nothing to say to you. At least nothing you'd want to hear. I just want to be left alone."

Kevin wiped his hands on his black apron and bit the corner of his red mustache. "So, it's alone you want to be? Ye might as well be a hermit on Carrantuohill for all the conversation we've heard from you these past two weeks. You haven't said enough words to Sean and me to fill a widow's pipe."

Michael picked up a length of rope and threaded it through the hole he had drilled in the end of the short board. "Sometimes 'tis best not to say what's on your mind if it would burn a man's ears to hear it." Even after two weeks Michael felt the hatred inside him, burning hot as the forge oven. The intensity of his own anger frightened Michael; he knew what could happen if the beast broke loose. He hoped that Kevin would let the subject rest awhile longer.

Kevin watched him, his feet apart and knees locked, his arms crossed over his broad chest. "You've got somethin' stuck up your arse, lad, and it's time you and I had it out."

'I'll not talk to you about this, Kevin, not now." Michael tucked the board under his arm and headed for the door, but O'Brien stepped in front of him and cut off his path.

"We didn't mean for you to burn your hands, Michael," he said, "and we're all sorry as the devil that it happened."

109

Michael's fingers tightened around the board. His face went as white as the trees outside, his eyes just as frosty. "Rory set fire to that barn and me inside. Then the bloody lot of you ran away and left me to roast like a pig. I'll not forgive you for that, Kevin. And I'll tell you now, I'm intending' to kill Rory Doona the very next time I set eyes on him."

Kevin laid his hand on Michael's forearm, but Michael shook it away. "We heard the landlord's lads a comin' and there was just enough time to set the fire and run. We called to you to come out, Michael, truly we did. Ye must not have heard us."

Michael considered Kevin's words but only briefly before rejecting them. "No. I don't want to hear it. I don't believe you."

"Damn it, lad. You don't want to believe me because then you'll have nobody to blame for what happened to your hands. You want someone to hate. And most of all, you want a reason to murder Rory Doona."

"And what if I do? Why should you care what happens to Rory?"

Kevin stepped closer and Michael could feel his hot breath on his face. "I don't give a tinker's damn what happens to Rory. He can bake in hell with never a drop to quench his eternal thirst for all I care. But I do care about you, son." Kevin put his hand on Michael's arm again, and this time he didn't throw it off. "You don't know how it's pained me all these years to see you walkin' around with the burden of one murder on your shoulders. And as strong as those fine shoulders of yours may be, Michael, I don't think they can carry the weight of another corpse."

* * *

Why couldn't you have left me alone with my anger, Kevin? Why did you have to take that away too? Michael stood in the forge yard beside his wheel, looking up at the perpetual black smoke that puffed from the stone chimney. He had tried all day to hang onto his anger, but it was gradually slipping away to be replaced by bitterness. He preferred the rage because it made him feel alive; the bitterness only left him empty.

The bristly hemp rope chafed his sensitive palms as he tied it to a spoke of the wheel over his head and adjusted the swing so that it hung straight.

Michael stood back and surveyed his work with pride. Now Danny wouldn't fall off the wheel when he was spinning with the other children. He could sit in the swing instead and ride as long as he liked.

Thinking of this swing had been the only joy in Michael's life since the night of the raid. He had tried to carve several times with the same result. The chisel handle hurt his palm so badly that he couldn't guide the tool. So, he had decided not to try again for a while. The pain in his hand was bad enough, but the agony of not being able to carve was unbearable.

Spinning the wheel, he watched as it carried the swing around and around. Danny would like that. Michael sighed a white puff of resignation into the frosty evening air. If he couldn't find joy in carving, at least he could give the children of the village a bit of pleasure by thinking of new ways to entertain them.

"What is it you have there, Michael, a new invention?"

Michael turned around and squinted as the last rays of the evening sun caught his eyes. Silhouetted against the amber sunset was the rotund figure of Cornelius Gabbitt.

Before this morning's talk with Kevin, Michael might

111

have cursed the little tailor or at least turned his back on him. But Michael's hate seemed too far away for him to summon it.

"It's a toy for the garsoons," Michael replied. "They've taken a fancy to whirling around on this wheel."

Cornelius walked over and gave the wheel a spin. Michael had balanced the mechanism perfectly, and the wheel turned a long time before stopping. Neither man spoke as they watched it.

Finally Cornelius coughed as though clearing the way for his next words. "I hear that you're not able to carve now since the ... ah ... fire."

"That's right." Michael could see the misery in the tailor's watery eyes. Before he might have enjoyed it, but now it seemed a waste. Wasn't it bad enough that he, himself, had to suffer? Why should Cornelius be weighed down with guilt? The entire world could grieve with him and he still wouldn't be able to carve.

"I heard that your hands hurt when you try to carve. I've been thinking about that day and night since I heard it." Cornelius adjusted his lacy cravat and fingered the brass buttons on the gentleman's coat he wore, one of his finest creations.

Michael decided to be kind. "Ye shouldn't trouble yourself about it, Con," he said gently. "What's done is done. Maybe it's my lot to make wheels for the children to play on. Maybe I wasn't meant to carve at all."

"You must never say that. The good God put the magic in your hands, the magic to bring lovely things into the world. That's a wondrous gift, and He wouldn't give you such a gift only to snatch it back like a Saxon."

Michael held out his palms for the tailor's inspection. "I'd like to believe you, but it appears you're wrong this time."

Cornelius winced at the terrible scars and looked away, blinking his eyes rapidly. "They look pretty bad, surely, but I was thinking maybe these would help." He stuck his hand into his coat pocket and pulled out a pair of gloves, sewn of the softest kid leather with stitches so tiny that the eye could scarcely see them. The palms and the thumbs were specially padded with several layers of leather.

"I've watched you carve there by the fire in the pub," he said, "and I thought a lot about what kind of glove might spare you the pain and help you grip your chisel. I hope they'll fit. I measured them by eye . . ." His voice trailed away as he held out his peace offering to Michael. The little man's heart shone in his moist eyes.

Michael couldn't trust himself to speak, so he simply took the gloves and carefully slipped the supple leather over his hands. They fit perfectly; Cornelius Gabbitt was a master craftsman.

The tailor eyed his workmanship critically, then nodded in quiet satisfaction. "When I heard that you couldn't carve because of what we did to you . . . I couldn't bear it," he said. "I tried to think what it would be like if it was me own hands. I tried to think of how it would be to know that I'd never be able to sew again. I know what it's like to feel the magic flowing through your hands. But to feel it gone . . . would be worse than dying, I'd think."

"It is," Michael whispered. " 'Tis worse."

"I couldn't sleep for thinkin' about it. So I went to the chapel one night and I asked the good God to help me think of a way. And He did. I thought of the gloves while I was prayin' there on my knees and I know 'twas Him who told me. He wants ye to carve your lovely

113

.horses again, Michael, surely, or He'd never told me about the gloves."

"I have Lord Armfield's mares shoed, and I'm done for the day," Sean told Kevin. The young man's voice sounded tired but held an underlying tone of excitement and apprehension. "I'd like to have a word with you, Kevin, if you aren't in too big a hurry to get to the pub and your evening pint."

Kevin stood at the forge window, watching Michael and the half-dozen children who scampered around him, eager to try out Michael's new swing.

"What is it you want, Sean?" Kevin asked absentmindedly. He hated it when he and Michael quarreled, especially when he knew that Michael had every right to be furious. If someone had lit a fire over *his* head, he'd have murdered them first and asked "why" later.

Sean took off his leather apron and leggings and hung them on an iron hook on the wall. He cleared his throat several times and cracked his blackened knuckles one by one. "There's something I've been wanting to ask you for some time now, Kevin," he said. "I was just waiting for the right moment and—"

"Yes ... yes ... what is it, lad?" Kevin wasn't in the mood for a serious conversation with Sean right now when there was bad blood between him and Michael. Tenderness mixed with jealousy flowed through him as he watched Michael lift Danny and gently place him in the swing. Michael and Daniel shared a bond, a warm closeness, that Kevin envied.

"I want to ask you for Judy's hand," Sean said, his usually deep voice high and squeaky. "She's eighteen now and that's plenty old enough to be married. I've

114

spoken to her and she's consented to be my wife, if we have your blessing, that is."

"That's fine, lad," Kevin murmured. "Do whatever you think is best." He wasn't listening to Sean. He was watching the look of pure joy on his son's face as Michael turned the wheel and sent him spinning through the air.

The color flooded back into Sean's blanched cheeks and he ran a shaking hand through his haystack of hair. "Really? Oh, thank you, Kevin. You won't be sorry, surely. I'll be good to her, you'll see. Judy won't know a day's misery with me as her husband."

"What!" Kevin whirled on his heel. "What did you say?"

"I ... I said I'll be a good husband to Judy and—"

"Husband? To my Judy? You?"

"Well, yes. You just said—"

'Never mind what I just said. You know I never listen to you, lad. What's this about you wanting to marry my Judy, and you as poor as a beggar who's just been robbed of his rags? You don't even have the price of a matchmaker in your pocket, or you wouldn't be asking yourself."

Sean pulled himself up with a semblance of pride. "No one is ever truly poor who has the sight of his eyes and the use of his feet," he said, quoting one of Kevin's favorite proverbs. "Besides, I have two cows now and twelve hens and—"

"And the cows tied in one end of that hovel of yours. My Judy won't be living in no byre cottage with two cows for company."

"But I've built them a pen and a lean-to and moved them outside. I've been workin' day and night, I have. I would have built a barn too, but if I did Old Larcher would raise me rents to the sky and me barely able to

115

pay them now. I wouldn't ask Judy to live with cows, Kevin," he pleaded. "I love her dearly, don't ye know?"

Kevin shoved his hands deep into his pockets. "Aye, I know it, lad. I've seen it coming' a long way off. You two have been looking at each other like love-sick cats lately." He turned back to the window with a sigh of resignation. "If she'll have you, I'll not stand in your way."

"Oh, thank you, sir. Thank you."

Sean danced out of the forge, tripping over his own feet. Kevin watched from the window as he skipped over to Michael and told him the happy news. Michael nodded his enthusiastic approval and embraced his friend.

Kevin blinked away a cloud of mist that obscured his vision. So, Judy would be leaving. Pretty little Judy whose sparkling eyes had brightened his darkest days. She would belong to another man now, his little girl no longer.

Sean Sullivan was a good man, one of the best Kevin had ever known. Kevin remembered the day three years before when he had first laid eyes on Sean. The lad had swaggered into Kevin's forge and announced that he was the finest journeyman smith in five counties and he was looking for a forge that was worthy of him. Sean had sworn that he could weld six rods together in one firing, and Kevin had promptly tossed him out on his arse, thinking him an empty-headed braggart.

Then Kevin had gone down to O'Leary's pub for a pint and, when he had returned, he had found three pairs of his best pliers welded into a solid lump. Furious, O'Brien had gone after the lad with every intention of thrashing him soundly. But by the time he had caught up to him three miles west of Kilorglin, his anger had subsided and a grudging respect had set in. So, instead of beating the young man, Kevin had hired him. Now it seemed that Sean Sullivan was to be his son-in-law.

Kevin sighed as he watched Sean and Michael spin the children on the wheel. He had always hoped that one of his daughters would marry Michael. Then Michael would be his son truly and for all time.

Ah, well. There was always Annie.

"So, what have we here?" Sir Larcher asked his agent as they reined in their matching bays beside Sean's humble cottage. "Since when has Sullivan moved up in the world? That's a fine pen he has there. Though it's not much of a barn. It's a pity to keep animals in such a place."

Morton Collier sucked air through the gap in his front teeth as he surveyed Sean's handiwork. "I heard at the pub that he's trading the company of the beasts for that of a woman, Kevin O'Brien's daughter. I'd have thought that a friendly cow would be more to his liking." He snickered unpleasantly.

Larcher reached into his breast pocket of his riding jacket and produced a tiny gold box. He opened it, took out a pinch of snuff and snorted it up his bulbous nose. Replacing the box in his pocket, he pulled out a lace-edged handkerchief and mopped the sweat from his bald head. "An Irish cow, and Irish female ... it's a delicate wager which would be more likely to give a man lice," he said.

"I don't recall you worrying about lice when you were trying to bed that young widow tenant of yours," Collier said recklessly. He regretted his words the instant he had uttered them.

Sir Larcher glared at him through bloodshot eyes, his nostrils twitching from indignation and snuff. "If I ever hear another word about that from you, you'll be back digging turf again, Collier," he said. "And you'll be lucky to have a roof over your head at all, even one shared with a cow. Do you understand?"

"Yes, Your Honor." Morton's Adam's apple bobbed as he swallowed, and his scrawny neck strained above the velvet collar of his faded maroon jacket. The garment was a pathetic statement of Morton's social status, neither peasant nor aristocrat.

Sir Larcher's mood was ruined for the day, and someone was going to pay. "I heard a rumor in town today that Sean Sullivan may have been one of the scoundrels who burned Armfield's barn last month. What do you think of that?"

Anxious to shift Larcher's anger to anyone else, Morton quickly agreed. "I believe it's true, Your Honor. I never have trusted that Sullivan. He's a clever one, he is. Too clever, if you ask me, sir."

"Than let's drive him out of here. We don't need the likes of him stirring up the peasantry. They're like a flock of sheep who will follow any goat that comes along. Raise his rent. And make sure it's high enough that he can't pay."

Daniel O'Brien pulled his quilt higher around his shoulders and burrowed into the snug warmth like a chick seeking refuge beneath the hen's fluffed feathers. In his right hand he clutched the tiny stallion Michael had carved for him. In his left he held the tiny mare he himself had carved. She was stubby and fat, not sleek and delicately proportioned like the stallion, but the stallion liked her anyway and so did Daniel. Each night when he closed his eyes, he held them both tightly in his hands. They gave him comfort, and tonight Danny needed all the comfort the horses and his quilt could provide.

Something was terribly wrong in Daniel's world, but he didn't know what it was. No one would tell him. They all thought that he was a baby, and big people didn't tell babies what was wrong. They just left them to worry in their beds.

Everything had been fine during tea, but then Sean had come by, raving and cursing about his landlord raising his rent. Danny didn't know much about landlords, but he knew that rents were something that all big people worried about and a rent increase was enough to destroy a man entirely.

Sean, Kevin and Michael had gone outside to talk, away from the women, but in a few minutes they were shouting and swearing at each other. Danny couldn't remember ever hearing Sean and Michael disagree.

Then Kevin and Sean had left, taking Kevin's hunting knife with them.

When Annie and Judy had asked Michael where they were off to, he wouldn't tell them. And that was bad news, no matter how it was told.

Danny could hear Judy upstairs in the loft bedroom she shared with Annie, crying her eyes out. And Annie was praying, hard and fast. Some calamity was going to befall them all, surely.

Michael was lying across his bed in the corner, but Danny could tell that he wasn't asleep. He hadn't even taken his clothes off yet. Danny was glad that Michael hadn't gone away with his father and Sean. As long as Michael was there in the house with them, Danny felt safe.

The boy was about to drift off into a restless sleep when he heard Michael stirring. He opened his eyes and saw, by the feeble light of the banked fire, that Michael was pulling on his wooden-soled brogues.

"Michael, where are ye going?" the boy whispered, his voice choked with fear.

"I'm going' for a walk. Shut your eyes and go back to sleep, lad."

"But I'm not sleepy at all. Can I come with you on your walk?"

Michael stood and looked at him for what seemed to Daniel a terribly long time. Then he said, "It's a briar on the seat of me breeches you are, Danny. Wherever I go, it's you behind me. Come along."

In seconds Daniel had slipped on his shirt, pants, coat and shoes. "I'm ready," he said breathlessly, a bubble of excitement growing inside him. He loved going out with Michael at night. Sometimes they went on wonderful journeys far and wide across the moonlit countryside.

The boy hobbled to the doorway and lifted the heavy bar. Michael followed him, pulling on his great coat.

Once outside Michael lifted the child and set him on his broad shoulders. Danny twined his fingers in his friend's thick dark waves and held on as they started down the road and out of town.

"What were you and Sean and Da fighting about after tea?" Danny asked from his perch on top of the world.

"Ah, Sean was in a thick stew, he was, because old Larcher's gone and raised his rent again, just because Sean built a pen for his two cows. Now Sean can't support a wife, so he and Judy will have to wait to get married."

Danny was sorry to hear such bad news, but he beamed with pleasure anyway. He loved it when Michael talked this way to him, man to man. The others thought he couldn't understand, but he did. He knew that Sean and Judy liked each other and wanted to get

120

married. He had seen them kissing behind the barn when they thought no one was around. He knew a lot about Sean and Judy.

"But why were you yelling at Sean and him at you when you two are best friends?" he asked, determined to have his question answered directly.

"We weren't yelling. We were disagreeing."

"Sounded like yelling to me."

Michael chuckled and Daniel bobbed up and down on his shoulders. "Sean and I were of two minds about how to handle the problem."

"I'll bet that you were right and Sean was wrong," Daniel said with staunch loyalty.

"I don't think either of us was right or wrong, Danny," Michael said as he turned west at the crossroads. "We're just different, that's all."

When they reached the edge of the fog-shrouded woods, Danny felt a shiver of anticipation. Normally he would be afraid to go into the forest at night, but when he sat on Michael's shoulders, nothing could harm him.

The branches of the trees snatched at Danny's curls and he had to hang on tightly when Michael ducked beneath the low limbs.

"Where are we going?" the boy asked as they neared the edge of the forest and a pasture that glowed silver in the moonlight as wisps of ghost-white fog drifted toward them over the dark grass.

"To see a horse," Michael replied.

"What horse?"

"Princess Niav's enchanted horse."

Danny couldn't believe his ears. "Really?"

Michael didn't reply, but pulled him down off his shoulders and set him on the high stone wall that surrounded the pasture.

Michael gave a long, low whistle and in a moment a

white stallion came galloping out of the fog, his long mane flying, his ivory coat glowing in the moonlight.

The horse trotted up to them, but stopped several paces away, his fine ears pricked, his nostrils flared and twitching.

"Would you ever hope to see anything more lovely in this world or the next?" Michael breathed as their eyes devoured every graceful curve, every fluid movement.

"He's a beauty for sure," Danny agreed. "But he's not Niav's enchanted horse. He's Lord Armfield's white stallion."

"He's anything you want him to be, Danny. He's anything your heart can dream."

"I like to dream." Danny sighed deeply and held out his hand to the animal, who stood his ground, silently judging the situation and his nocturnal visitors. "I like to dream that I'm big and strong like you, and then I don't have to be small and afraid."

Michael's giant hand reached out for the boy's shoulder, and Danny reveled in the touch. "That's why we all dream, Danny," he said gently. "Everyone feels small and afraid sometimes—"

"Even you?"

Michael smiled and ruffled Danny's copper curls affectionately. "Even me. But in our dreams we're bigger than ourselves and happier. Dreams take the wasp's sting out of life. When life gets too painful, we can slip away to that enchanted land inside our heads and live there for a while."

"Do you do that too?" Danny asked, amazed at this revelation of his friend.

"Too often," Michael replied. "That's the problem with dreams. Sometimes you get so far out there in the Land of the Ever Young that you can't find the road back home. Or, like Oisin, when you do find your way home, everything and everyone has changed while you were away and things are even worse than you remember."

Danny didn't understand a word of what Michael was saying, but he was thrilled that Michael was saying it to him. He loved the soothing drone of his friend's deep voice and the way Michael treated him like a man instead of a helpless lame boy.

But sometimes, like now, Michael got a distant look in his eyes, and Danny suddenly felt alone as though Michael had left him behind and gone somewhere else. Maybe to the Land of the Ever Young.

Danny watched breathlessly as Michael held out his hand to the horse. The stallion walked toward them.

"That's right, old lad," Michael whispered. "Come along and say hello."

The horse shook its full mane, sending the silver strands flying in the moonlight. Then he walked up to Michael and nuzzled his hand with his nose.

"That's it," Michael said as he stroked the velvet muzzle with his scarred palm. "You remember me, don't you? We're old friends now, you and I."

Danny reached toward the horse, but he snorted, tossed his head and galloped away, scattering the fog as he ran.

Michael watched the stallion go with that faraway look in his eyes. Then he said something else that Danny didn't understand. "He was worth it." Michael looked down at his hands and flexed them. "Indeed, he was."

Mort Collier staggered to the front door of his cabin and threw open the top half. He held his forearm over his eyes to protect them from the rays of the morning sun that pierced his poteen-soaked skull.

"Oh, murder, what a night," he groaned, wishing he could remember the fine evening he had spent playing cards and drinking with His Honor and that gentleman from Dublin who had walked away with all their money.

He stumbled out the door to the watering trough and plunged his head into the cold water. Shaking his hair like a dog, he sent droplets flying onto the chickens at his feet. He kicked at them, and the flock scattered, cackling their disapproval.

He was awake now. Wet and cold, but awake.

It was when he turned toward the barn that he first realized something was wrong. The place was quiet. Too quiet.

Fear pumped through his bloodstream and erased every trace of his hangover.

Smeared on the barn door was a red-black ugliness in the shape of a tree. An oak tree. Painted in blood.

"Those damned—"

He ran around the side of the barn to the pen where the landlord kept his prize pigs. Three fine boars all fattened and ready for slaughter.

And slaughtered they were.

The corpses lay in pools of coagulating gore, their throats cut and gaping, black and ragged, from ear to ear. They looked as though they were all having a good laugh at some hideous joke.

The seven brood sows, the foundation of Larcher's stock, lay lifeless in their pens, having suffered the same fate. The sick, sweet smell of blood filled the morning air along with the drone of a thousand green flies.

Morton covered his mouth with his hand and raced for the big house. But the blood, the stench, the flies, were too much for him. The bile welled up from his

124

stomach and gagged him. He fell to his hands and knees in the middle of the dirt road and lost the water he had just drunk, along with any remnants of loyalty that he had harbored toward his fellow Irishmen.

Chapter Six

" 'Tis a joy to me eyes to see you back at the anvil again, lad." Kevin's broad smile split his red beard as he watched Michael cut a thick iron rod with a hammer and two clefts. "Though it's a puzzle who would have asked for a wheel so large as that one."

Michael's naked torso gleamed with a fine sheen of sweat in the amber glow of the forge fire as he laid down his hammer, pulled a rag off a nail on the wall and mopped his brow with it. For the first time in weeks Michael smiled, a tired, satisfied smile. "No one asked for it. It's for meself, for the wee ones. They all want swings like Danny's to sit in, and that smaller wheel won't hold them all at once."

The starlight went out of Kevin's blue eyes. "Ah ... I see."

The disappointment in Kevin's voice angered Michael. Why was it that every time he did something to please himself, he displeased Kevin? "I gave you a full day's work before I started this wheel," he said. "Surely you don't believe I owe you my every waking minute."

"No, of course you don't. I just thought you were doing something useful."

126

"And what about that fancy iron cross you're making for your grave? What use is that? And what about those fancy roses you're hammerin' out there to put on it? I don't suppose you'll be rising up out of your grave every dawn to sniff the morning dew on them."

Kevin brought his hammer down and with four blows he had flattened and curled a bit of iron into a delicate rose petal. "This is a gravemarker worthy of a fine smith," he said with wounded pride. "Long after I'm dead and cold this cross will show the world that I was a master of my craft." Kevin held up the petal with tongs, eyed it critically and plunged it, sizzling, into the dark water. "I'm going to leave something of beauty behind that will remind everyone who sees it that Kevin O'Brien lived and breathed and was a master of his trade."

"And that's why I carved wood," Michael said, hoping that maybe this time Kevin might understand. "I wanted to bring something wonderful into the world, something that would remain after I'm gone."

"I don't understand why you're still grievin' the loss of your carving, Michael. I've taught you the fine craft of smithing. And you're good at it, lad. You've learned more in these past five years than most men do in a lifetime. Ye've a gift for it." Kevin's thick biceps rippled as he hammered a dainty leaf from another glowing lump.

Michael shook his head and didn't answer. There was no point. How could he explain to Kevin the difference in cold iron and living wood?

When he had carved he had felt the life of the tree flowing through him. A living bit of Erin herself there in his hand, a spirit that joined his in creating something that was of the tree and yet of himself. If he were

127

to try to tell Kevin that, he would surely accuse him of hanging out in fairy forts after dark.

So, he didn't even try to explain. "The life of a smith is a noble one, indeed, Kevin. And 'tis grateful I am that you taught me." Michael laid the rods for his new wheel aside, pulled a length of heated iron from the fire and beat out a perfect horseshoe in one heating, an accomplishment which Kevin valued above all others, a skill which Michael took for granted. "Why wasn't Sean to work today?" Michael asked cautiously.

Kevin missed one lick with his hammer. "I told him not to come into town this morning. We two had a grand time raisin' the devil last night. I figured he needed a bit of rest today, what with him bein' so stirred up over his rent. That Larcher's a cold-hearted bastard. May the curse of the raven be on him and may his trouble be in his throat."

"Aye," Michael agreed. "Put Larcher on a spit and a dozen Irishmen will wait their chance to turn him. But I'd say that the hand of justice might have knocked upon his door last night...." Michael studied Kevin carefully, trying to read his face.

Kevin said nothing, but his ruddy cheeks flushed the same shade of red as his beard. "Aye. I just hope His Honor's prize hogs went to confession and had their souls cleansed of any little piggy sins, or else they're roastin' this very morning in hell's ovens."

Michael turned his back to Kevin and blew the bellows while he waited for the sick feeling in his guts to abate, but it didn't. "I'm glad I wasn't along," he said finally. "You lads will come to grief in the end if you keep taking your vengeance on innocent animals."

" 'Tis a good thing you weren't along, Michael, you and your daft ideas about talking and reasoning with

128

landlords. When did you ever see a landlord who had a bit of compassion in his Saxon heart?''

Before Michael could answer, the horseshoe-shaped door flew open and Annie and Sorcha hurried inside, their woolen cloaks limp with rain. The pungent smell of wet wool mixed with the smoke and metallic scents of the forge. Annie's long blond hair hung in damp strings around her face and shoulders, and the creases in Sorcha's face were pinched even deeper than usual.

"What's wrong, love?" Kevin asked his daughter. "The both of you look as if you've laid eyes on the ghost of Cromwell himself."

Annie's dimpled chin quivered, and she bit her lip. "It's almost as bad as that, Da," she said. "It's all over town. The Black Oaks killed Lord Larcher's prize pigs last evening."

Sorcha stepped closer to Michael and peered up at him, her faded brown eyes narrowed with suspicion. "Larcher's agent, that awful Collier man, came to the rectory this morning while I was making breakfast for the good fathers and he was asking about you, Michael. I told him that you were a good lad and would never do anything so evil. Did I speak the truth, Michael, or not? Tell me now, and don't be lying to the mother that bore ye.''

Michael threw another rod into the fire and avoided her gaze. "I had nothing at all to do with His Honor's pigs meetin' their maker. I was home in bed. Isn't that so, Annie?'' He looked to Annie for confirmation, but she blinked her blue eyes and shrugged her narrow shoulders.

"Well . . . I did hear you and Danny go out, and you were gone a long time.''

"Don't be daft, girl." Kevin pumped away on the giant bellows. A cloud of fine gray dust rose from the

129

fire as the air puffed through the glowing embers. "If Michael had gone out butcherin' hogs, he wouldn't have taken little Daniel along, now would he?"

"Well, I—" Annie swallowed her words as the forge door opened again.

Michael's heart leaped when he saw that it was Caitlin, seeking shelter from the rain. Her bright red cloak filled the dark forge with warm color just as the sight of her pretty face warmed Michael's eyes.

She glanced around the forge quickly, noting its occupants. Michael could sense Annie and Sorcha pulling inside themselves as they squared their shoulders and lifted their chins.

Their reactions were typical of the women of Lios na Capaill. Caitlin was different in a village where differences were not tolerated. She didn't need a husband to keep her, because of the popularity of her pub. And that set her apart from the widows and young single women who prayed daily for God's blessing of a fine, strong husband.

The women didn't condemn Caitlin for owning a pub; it was respectable work for a woman alone. But she would have been held in higher esteem had she not been quite so successful.

Another serious mark against Caitlin was that she never attended mass. She seldom went to confession, and Father Murphy alone knew what terrible sins she committed. The villagers could only guess at her transgressions, but they had fertile imaginations.

And there was something too bold about those whiskey-colored eyes. Something too wild about the red hair that billowed around her shoulders, a mass of waves and curls, which she didn't even try to tie back.

Sorcha's gnarled hand closed over Annie's forearm and the older woman led her toward the door. Annie hung back, watching Michael's eyes, which followed Caitlin's every movement.

"Come along, child," Sorcha said. "It's time for respectable women to be at home, fixing tea for their families."

Caitlin ignored Sorcha and pulled her wet cloak from her shoulders. Her copper hair glistened with the droplets of rain, and Michael longed to feel those curls, damp and soft, around his fingers.

When her amber eyes met his, Michael wondered if she could see inside him, his thoughts, his secret dreams of touching her. Sometimes, a certain light glimmered in her eyes, suggesting that perhaps she had dreams of her own.

"Don't tell me ye've a horse that needs shoeing or a plow that's dull, Miss O'Leary," Kevin said as Annie and Sorcha walked out the door. His tone was sharp and impersonal, not at all like the familiar way he addressed her in the pub, when the women weren't around. That was how most men in the village addressed Caitlin, formally in front of their women, intimately when they were in her pub.

"No, Mr. O'Brien. I've no dull plow," she said. "But I've something important to tell you . . . and Michael. Sir Larcher and his agent came to my pub this afternoon. They were looking for Rory and his friends. His Honor's hogs were butchered last evening while he and his agent were gambling in Kilorglin with an English gentleman."

"Were they now?" Kevin pulled his pipe from his pocket and lit it with a coal from his fire, drawing a long puff. "I can't imagine why the good landlord would think that Rory had anything to do with it."

"Ye mustn't tell me lies, Mr. O'Brien," she said. Her body was taut with tension, and there was a sense of urgency about her. "I know about the Black Oaks. I know who they are, all of them. I'm not deaf or blind, and I know what's said and done in my pub. I want to help you, but you must be telling me the truth, and all of it."

Michael laid his hammer on the work bench and walked over to her. "What are you talking about, Caitlin? How can you help the Black Oaks?"

"I told Larcher that Rory and his friends were in my pub last night, drinking until just before dawn. I told him that Rory, William, Seamus, Cornelius and Sean were there. He didn't ask about the two of you. If he asks again, should I tell him that you were both there as well?"

Her eyes burned in her broad face. Michael could feel her searching his soul again, reaching inside, trying to see and to understand. He also saw her concern, more than the concern of a close friend. "No, Caitlin. You don't have to say that I was there." He saw the relief wash over her, and he was deeply touched. Tearing his eyes away from her, he turned to O'Brien. "Well, Kevin, should she say that you were there in her pub last night?"

Kevin's face twisted with indecision as he fingered the bowl of his pipe. Finally he cleared his throat and said, "If you would be so kind, Caitlin. But only if His Honor asks again. Just be careful what you say. A person often ties a knot with his tongue that can't be loosed by his teeth."

"I'll be careful, Mr. O'Brien. I've no reason to make things harder for you lads. I'm only after helping."

As she turned toward the door, Michael took the red cloak from her hands and spread it over her shoulders. His knuckles brushed her hair, and he was thankful that his scarred hands could still feel that wonderful softness. He turned his back to Kevin, who had taken up his hammer again and was pounding out rose petals. "You're a good lass, Caitlin O'Leary," Michael whispered. "A credit to old Erin, you are, and a fine friend in trouble."

"I'm an Irishwoman," she said simply, as though that explained everything.

But Michael knew why she had lied for the Black Oaks, or at least he believed he knew. Caitlin had thought that he had been on that raid. Michael wanted to think that he was the one she was protecting, just as she had put herself between him and harm the night he had burned himself. A murderer, such as himself, wasn't worthy of such loyalty, but he blessed her anyway.

He walked with her out the door and into the misting rain. Across the road the fields rippled in verdant waves as the evening breeze swept the thick grass. Wisps of fog floated down the village street, sifting between the shops, muting the shuffle of the villagers on the road, enfolding them in the hushed gray haze.

Moved by affection and gratitude, Michael placed his hand on Caitlin's shoulder. He could feel her vibrancy radiating through the wool as he fought the urge to take her in his arms.

"Thank you, Caitlin, for caring," he said, his face close to hers, so close that he could have kissed that red mouth. But he couldn't allow himself that liberty. Instead he lightly traced the outline of her lower lip with his fingertip. She caught his hand between her own, turned it palm up and ran her fingers over the deep scars.

"Michael," she said, her voice tremulous, "why didn't you come to the pub and let me take off the bandages for you?"

133

A dozen excuses, all lies, ran through his mind, but he couldn't bring himself to utter even one. "I didn't come because Armfield was in your pub that night."

She bowed her head and stared at the ground for a long time. When she finally looked up at him, he was surprised and dismayed to see her amber eyes bright with tears. "I understand." Then she turned and walked down the village street toward the pub. Michael watched until her red cloak disappeared in the fog.

The sound of the fiddle and the pipe drifted through the village and across the moonlit countryside, calling Kevin's friends and neighbors to his ceili for a bit of dancing and a drop o' the pure. The broad door of the livery had been taken off its hinges and laid on the floor inside the barn. On its worn surface three nimble-footed dancers jigged to a lively tune.

The musicians stood on an elevated platform near the back wall. William O'Shea and his son, Billy, piped away, their fingers flying over the tin whistles in harmonies that had been perfected on long winter evenings beside their turf fire. The deep thud of Padraic Donahue's bodhran filled the straw-scented air and set the rhythm for the breathless couples that twirled across the dirt floor of the old barn.

"Are ye happy tonight, love?" Sean asked Judy as he whirled her expertly through the intricate turns of the Kerry reel, the full skirt of her new dress flying, her dark hair gleaming in the light of the lantern.

"I am, indeed." Her black eyes shimmered as she clung tightly to him to keep her balance through the lively steps. "I can hardly wait for Da to announce our banns. I want to see Sally O'Shea and Mary McCloskey turn green with envy."

"Naw, 'tis I will be the envy of every man here to be marryin' the fair Judy O'Brien. Many's the bachelor that set his hat for you, lass. But I'm the one who caught you in the heel of the hunt."

Judy giggled and ducked her head, but not before she saw her sister's scowl from the other side of the room. At Annie's side stood young Father Brolin, wearing the same frown, the same disapproving quirk to his delicate eyebrows. Judy squirmed inside her new blue dress. "You mustn't hold me so tight, Sean," she said with gentle reproval. "Annie's watching, and so is Father Brolin. My, but he can make you feel guilty with just the look of his eye."

Sean laughed and tightened his grip around her slender waist. "Don't worry about the good father. 'Tis his calling to make sure that no one has any fun at the ceili. If he makes you feel guilty enough, you might come to confession tomorrow morning and drop a coin or two in the coffers."

"Hush, Sean Sullivan. He'll hear you, sure. And if Annie were to hear such blasphemy from your lips, she'd never let me marry you."

"Ah, you worry too much," he said as he led her from the dancers toward the happy circle of drinkers in the corner. They stopped midway to speak with Annie. "Annie loves me dearly," he said, favoring her with one of his broad, easy smiles. "And it's happy she is that I'm to be her brother soon. Isn't that so, Annie?"

"Aye, it's happy I am that you're marryin' me sister," Annie admitted reluctantly. "But it's happier I'd be if you'd save all that cuddlin' and snugglin' till after you've made her your wife. Even with Da raising your pay, 'twill be months before you'll stand before the priest."

"I do believe you're bitter with jealousy, Annie,

dear." Sean's grin was mischievous, but a glimmer of compassion shone in his pale blue eyes. "It's a big hug you need to sweeten you up a bit." Before she could complain he had enfolded her in a hearty, but fraternal embrace and placed a resounding kiss on her cheek. "There. See how nice that was? Why should you begrudge your baby sister such innocent pleasure?"

"That's not the way you were hugging Judy, Sean Sullivan, and you know it, sure."

Sean shrugged and lifted one golden eyebrow. " 'Tis true. I'm sorry, Annie, love, but if I were to give you the same kind of squeeze as I was givin' your sister, she'd have me hide drying on the barn door come morning." He tweaked her nose playfully. "Why don't you get out there and find a lad who'll give you the kind of lovin' you're in need of? I know at least a dozen who would be glad to oblige. Then you wouldn't have time to stand around frettin' about who's being squeezed."

Annie lifted her dimpled chin and glided away to join Father Brolin and Father Murphy beside the casks of ale.

"Now she'll be worrying about who's drinking too much," Judy said with a sigh. "Annie spends all her time worrying that someone somewhere is having a bit of fun."

Sean shook his head and cast a sad look toward his best friend, who sat on a bale of hay, hoisting an ale and tapping his feet to the music. " 'Tis a shame and a pity that Michael doesn't give her what she's needing, and himself in need of some good loving."

His hand slipped discreetly from her waist to pat her bottom. She jumped and grabbed his hand, forcing it back up to her waist. "You'll not be taking liberties with me, Sean Sullivan," she said. But his bright smile melted her anger. "At least, not here where me sister and the priests can see."

"Michael, the others want to ride on our wheel." Danny's voice sparkled with excitement and pride. From his seat on the hay Michael studied the eager, golden-speckled face over the rim of his pint. "Even the mothers and fathers want to ride. Can they, Michael? Can they?"

"I think it's a generous man who shares with his neighbors," Michael replied after a long swig of ale.

"But can the wheel hold them all without cracking?"

"Aye, it's strong enough to hold the tallest and broadest of them all." Michael rose from his bale and led the boy from the crowded barn into the yard separating the forge from the house. Five children sat in the swings and squealed with glee as their parents and older siblings took turns spinning the giant wheel.

"Michael says you can all take rides, big and small alike," Daniel announced with aplomb.

In a twinkling the swings were emptied of children and the adults had taken over with no one to turn the wheel. Michael stepped up to the bar that was suspended from one of the spokes and leaned his considerable weight against it. With a hearty push from Michael the well-balanced wheel began to turn faster and faster, to the delight of the adults. The hardworking Irish reveled in the childish play and responded, as their children had, with shrieks of laughter.

Their joy was contagious, and a crowd quickly gathered to wait their turn at the wheel.

"This is a wonder you've made here, Michael," Will O'Shea exclaimed as he climbed down from the swing to make room for his daughter, Katrin. "What do you call this thing, anyway?"

"I don't have a name for it yet," Michael replied, wiping his brow with his sleeve. The effort of turning the heavy adults had brought out the sweat in spite of the cool night. "I guess I'll have to think of something."

"Haven't had this much fun since I was a wee lass," old Bridget, the village midwife, said as she climbed into the seat and clung to the ropes, her tattered frieze skirt tucked around her knees, her brown face wrinkled into a toothless smile. "It's a fine thing ye've put together here, Michael McKevett. It makes garsoons of us all," she said with a cackle.

For the next two hours Michael spun his neighbors, and they forgot about fields that needed to be plowed and planted, wool that needed to be spun, rents that should, but probably couldn't, be paid on time.

Finally Michael was winded and his hands ached. He stopped and accepted the pints that were passed his way. The larger men of the village took over the pushing, though none could push it as fast or as long. Michael watched them, his heart soaring, and it had nothing to do with the free ale that was flowing through his blood. It was his pride in the wheel that gave his spirit wings. He had created it, had dreamed it and brought it into being with his hands, scarred though they were. The wheel was his gift to the village, a gift of joy, and the people had embraced his offering.

For the first time since the Night of the Big Wind Michael felt a part of his village, an outsider no longer.

"They love your invention, Michael," Caitlin said as she walked up to him and laid her hand on his sleeve.

He covered her hand and squeezed it companionably. "Aye, they've taken a fancy to it right off. They're as bad as the children, even worse, the way they fight for a go at it."

They stood in the shadow of an old oak, out of the silver moonlight. She was so close that Michael could feel the warmth of her body. Her nearness, the flush of his recent success, and the ale made him forget that he shouldn't hold her, that he wasn't worthy of her company. But perhaps even a murderer deserved a bit of happiness. He slipped his arm around her waist and lowered his head to hers. Her hair tickled his nose and smelled sweet, like flowers.

"Would you go for a walk with me, Caitlin? 'Tis a shame to waste this lovely moonlight."

"A shame, indeed."

He could hear the smile in her voice, though it was too dark beneath the tree for him to see her pretty face. His heart pounded as his arm tightened possessively around her waist and he drew her closer.

This was a strange night, a strange, but glorious night when the world seemed to be spinning in his direction and his dreams were within his grasp. Especially one soft, warm, feminine dream that was his for the taking.

He turned his back on the wheel and the merrymakers and led her down the hill toward the River Laune.

"You did it. You murdered his honor's pigs. And I don't care how long it takes, I'm going to prove it." The agent's eyes popped, if possible, even farther out of his head, and his Adam's apple bobbed above the tight collar of his frayed velvet jacket as he looked into the faces that surrounded him. They were the Black Oaks; he knew it. He just couldn't prove it yet. "I know it's you, Rory Doona, and your band of ruffians who've been terrorizing the good citizens of this county for the past three years. I'll see you hang yet."

Rory stood, feet apart, arms akimbo. A sarcastic smile creased his swarthy face and his dark eyes bored into the agent's until Collier finally looked away. "You'll not be stretchin' our necks without some evidence in your hand. It's been two months since his honor's pigs became ghosts. I'd thought that you'd be givin' it up by now. Where would a fool like yourself be getting such evidence in a village full of folk who stand by their own, folk who hate the likes of you?"

Collier's eyes narrowed and he glanced around the barnyard where his enemies danced, drank, and enjoyed each other's company. No one had said a word to him all evening. Not a kind word, anyway. He was an outsider, like the aristocracy he served. Collier was no longer a true Irishman, but he wasn't English, either. His chosen occupation had cost him the fellowship of his own, yet he would never be accepted into the landlords' world. He was a man in-between. A man alone.

"We'll see how loyal your friends are when I start passing some coins under their noses. An Irishman will sell a friend for considerably less than thirty pieces of silver."

Satisfied with his rebuttal, Collier turned and marched down the dirt road toward the river and Larcher's estate. Rory started after him, fists clenched, but Sean grabbed him by his coattail. "Let him go, Rory. It's no use breaking your shin on a stool that's not in your way. Just leave him be. If he hasn't found any proof against us in two months, he's not likely to now. It'll all blow over like a bad wind."

Rory watched the retreat of the lone figure down the dark road and shook his head. "No. That one won't quit till he sees us all jigging at the end of a rope. It's us or him, lads."

Rory turned to Seamus, Cornelius, and William, who were standing silently in the background. "What do you say, boys? Should it be us or Collier who's the first to meet his maker?"

Seamus stroked his ginger beard and spat. "Well, I ain't ready to meet the saints just yet. But it wouldn't bother me none to send old Collier on to them."

"You're crazy, the lot of you," Sean said. "You've no need to murder the man, except to satisfy the meanness in you."

Rory stepped up to Sean, bristling with indignation. "It was for you we did the deed, Sean Sullivan. Or have you forgotten so soon? And it's for all of us and our families that we'll do this one. Would you see your brothers swinging from a tree because they helped you in your time of need?"

Sean wrestled with his common sense and his loyalty to the Oaks.

"So, which side are you on?" Rory asked. "Are you with us or against us, Sean? There's no place to stand in between."

They sat at the edge of the forest, side by side on a pallet of his great coat and her red cloak. The night breeze bore the distant sounds of the ceili' down to the river; the merry sound of the fiddle, the low thud of the bodhran, the raucous singing. But Michael and Caitlin had left that world behind and had found their own shadowed hideaway among the trees, watching the river flow past, a liquid ribbon of moon silver.

"Do you remember the first time we sat here together?" he asked, his voice deep and hushed, although there was no one to hear but the frogs at the river's edge, a hare rustling the brush behind them, and a raven nesting in the arbutus tree above their heads.

She turned her head and looked into his eyes that shone with affection. Her old friend had returned to her, and tonight there was no wall between them. "Of course I remember. 'Twas a lovely spring night like this one. That was the first time you ever held my hand."

He reached over and took her hand, folding it between his own. "So I did," he replied. "Took me hours to work up the courage. I thought sure you'd snatch it back, but you let me hold it all afternoon."

"And all evening."

He sighed and nodded. "Aye, all evening. And a fine, long evening it was."

Slowly, sensuously, he stroked the back of her hand with his fingertips. Shivers of pleasure traveled up her arm and into her body. But, as he continued to gaze thoughtfully at her hand, Caitlin wondered if he was comparing it to Annie's or Judy's. Her hands were larger than most women's and they were chapped from the long hours in soap and water, washing mugs and glasses. She had never thought about her hands before, but tonight she wished that they were smooth and dainty like Annie's.

"What are you thinking, Michael?"

He looked up at her, his eyes soft, a smile on his lips. "I was thinkin' about the night when you tended my burns. Your hands were gentle and loving. No one ever touched me with so much kindness before, Caitlin. You've been a good friend to me." His hand tightened around hers, and a sadness took the place of his smile. "I'm sorry I've treated you badly, lass. I never meant to hurt you. Truly I didn't."

It was a long time before she could trust herself to

142

speak past the knot that was swelling in her throat. Finally, she said, "Why did you shut me out, Michael? I've wondered all these years what I did wrong."

Moving closer to her on the pallet, he pulled her into the circle of his arms. "Ah, love. Ye did nothin', nothin' at all. 'Twas I who did wrong, and a terrible evil it was. I'm a sinner who doesn't deserve to be loved by someone so fine as you."

The tenderness of his touch brought tears to her eyes, tears of guilt, as she thought of Armfield. Would Michael think her such a fine person if he knew?

"We've all committed our share of sins," she said. "But we must learn to forgive ourselves."

His hand cupped her chin, forcing her to look up at him. "Can you forgive me for ruining what was between us?"

She nodded. "I do, indeed." Laying her hand against the side of his face, she felt the rough stubble of his beard on her palm. The last time they had sat together beneath these trees, his whiskers had been nothing more than youthful down.

As he folded her more tightly against him, she became acutely aware of the changes in them both. Her body was a woman's now, soft and lush. His was hard and lean with the well-rounded muscles of manhood. They both reveled in their differences.

" 'Twas in this very spot I first kissed you," he said, his voice husky. "Do you remember our first kiss, love?"

"I remember."

His fingers glided through her silky tresses. "You were such a pretty girl, Caitlin. I'll never forget the way you looked, lyin' there in the grass with daisies in your hair and your lips still red from my kisses. I've thought of that over and over again. It gives me such pleasure to remember it."

He shifted his weight, and before Caitlin realized what was happening, she was lying back on the pallet. He lay beside her, resting on one elbow.

As he smiled down at her, his fingertip traced her lipline. "I've watched you grow more lovely every year. And I've dreamed of kissing you again. Of making you my own." He closed his eyes and sighed deeply. "Dear God, sometimes it's all I can think of. Sometimes I've thought I'd go mad from thinking about it."

"I know. 'Tis the same for me, Michael. Every time I see you, every time I hear your name, I think of us together. 'Tis a lovely dream, indeed." She turned her body toward his, pressing the fullness of her breast against his ribs. "But I've dreamed it so many times that it's as threadbare as last summer's clothes."

He lowered his face to hers and his breath fanned her cheek. The warmth, the power, that radiated from him made her want to be closer, much closer.

"Caitlin, a body needs more than a dream to keep it warm on a cold, lonely night." His voice smooth, with golden undertones, poured over her like honey.

Tangling her hands in his thick, dark waves, she whispered his name. He needed no further encouragement; his mouth covered hers, and when he kissed her all thoughts left her head like doves released from a dove cote. Only the purest, simplest impressions remained. The subtle, sweet taste of him. The hard length of his body pressed against hers. The soft touch of his lips on hers as he kissed her gently, lovingly, as he had five years ago.

But Michael was no longer a lad and tender kisses weren't enough. This time his mouth took hers completely; his tongue probed, mated as primitive desires borne on the fertile night wind swept over them both, encouraging them in the ancient ways of a man and a maiden.

And it still wasn't enough.

"Caitlin, I want . . ." His breath came fast and ragged as his hand moved restlessly down her throat and over the bodice of her dress. The caress made her breasts ache with the need to feel his touch on her bare skin.

"I know," she said, her lips against his. "Me too."

Slowly, giving her plenty of time to object, he unlaced the front of her dress. Her eyes granted him permission and his fingertips lightly brushed the linen aside.

The round fullness of her breast glowed milky-white in the moonlight, crested with a delicate circle of pink. "Jaysus," he whispered, "what a lovely sight you are, lass. 'Tis like seein' the bosom of sweet Erin herself."

He moved to touch that creamy beauty, but stopped, his hand poised above her. In the moonlight they both saw the contrast, his scarred, mottled flesh against the glorious perfection of her breast. He shuddered, and with a moan that sounded like an animal's, he pulled his hand away.

She could feel his pain, sharper and hotter than their desire had been only moments before. She knew that the scars on his hands represented the wounds of his heart. He didn't feel worthy to touch her, and Caitlin knew the pain of feeling unworthy. Tears of compassion glittered on her lashes. "Ah, Michael, I've waited so long for you to touch me. Surely you'll not disappoint me now."

She lifted his hand and pressed his scarred palm to her lips. Carefully, she covered each finger with kisses, loving kisses that healed all they touched. Then she pressed his hand over her breast.

"Ah, lass ..." he whispered, cradling the exquisite softness in his rough palm. "No one's ever given me such a precious gift as this. I love you dearly. I always have. I'm only sorry that we've wasted so much time."

The night breeze stirred the leaves over their head, a spring breeze full of the promise of birth, of growing things, of life renewing itself in the neverending spirals. Erin whispered on the wind, and they heard the ancient druidic poem of fertility. They heard it in the deepest recesses of their bodies and hearts.

Chapter Seven

They sensed it before they heard it—a vibration that hummed through the stillness of the forest, disrupting the tranquility. An evil had invaded their paradise.

"Michael, what is it?" Caitlin asked. The fear in her voice stirred his protective male instinct.

"Sh-h-h, someone's coming," he whispered as he tugged the bodice of her dress into place across her breasts. He raised her to sit beside him, wrapped his arms around her and held her close.

"Here be as good a spot as any." The high, tightly-strung voice reached them through the trees as they pulled back into the shadows.

A scuffling. Some muffled curses. A knot of men in black hoods burst from the woods into the moonlit meadow, half-carrying, half-dragging a figure that struggled vainly against them. Their prisoner's hands were bound behind his back with a length of white cloth. A gag of the same material covered the lower half of his face.

But even from their hiding place twenty paces away, Michael and Caitlin recognized the hapless fellow by his shabby velvet coat.

"It's Morton Collier," she whispered, her lips close to Michael's ear. "Who are they? What are they going to do to him?"

Michael shouldn't have been surprised, but he was. Burning a barn was one thing. Even the butchering of some hogs could be condoned. After all, pigs were slaughtered every day. But murder. Murder couldn't be tolerated by any civilized man.

"Stay here," Michael said. "You mustn't move or make any sound, no matter what your eyes see or your ears hear."

She nodded. Quickly he rose, slipped through the dark trees, and followed them down to the river's edge. He knew them all by their clothes, in spite of the hoods. The tallest was Sean, the smallest Rory, and the others: Seamus, William and Cornelius.

"Who's there?" Seamus called in his raspy sailor's voice. "Oh, it's only Michael, lads. Carry on."

"Wait! What is it you're doin' there?" Michael ran up to Rory and William who held the trussed Collier by his collar and trouser band. The gag had slipped down around his scrawny neck.

"They're after murderin' me sure," Collier said in a thick Kerry accent void of its usual aristocratic affectation. "Ye've got to stop them, Michael. You're a good and fair lad. Ye mustn't let them drown me in the river like a cur dog."

"Stay out of this, Michael," Rory hissed. "It's no business of your own. Go away and forget what you saw."

Michael looked down at the quivering bundle of hate that was Rory Doona, all wrapped up in a tattered greatcoat and covered with a black hood. He had vowed to kill this man the next time he saw him, had dreamed it and savored every gruesome detail of the dream. But as he looked down at Rory he saw just how small the man was, not just in stature, but in every way that made a man. Rory Doona simply wasn't worth killing.

"You've no reason to murder Collier," Michael said, "limb of the Devil that he is—"

"No reason have we?" Rory's voice rose another octave. "Are you forgettin' that this man is an agent and a cruel one at that? What about him raisin' Sean's rent for no reason? The good God knows how many innocent people he's ruined by throwin' them off their land. And many more's the crimes he's committed against the sons of Erin."

"Not to mention his crimes against her daughters, me own daughter even," William interjected. "Little Katrin said that tonight at the ceili he tried to put his hand under her skirt. What kind of a man does a thing like that to a wee lass only eleven years old?"

"Go along, Michael," Sean said from behind his black mask. "This has gone too far already. We can't turn him loose now. If we did, we'd all be hangin' from the trees come daybreak."

Michael shook his head in disbelief and sadness. Sean was right, of course. If they set Collier free, he'd run straight to the constable and every one of the Black Oaks would die. But Sean wasn't a killer. Michael could see pain in the eyes that stared out at him from the ragged holes in the hood.

He couldn't save Collier, but he could save Sean.

He grabbed Sean's arm in a blacksmith's grip that cut off the blood flow. "You'll come with me now," he said, "and leave these lads to do their dirty work alone."

"I'll do no such thing. I'm in it with them all the way."

Michael saw that Sean meant what he said. Whether

his heart was in it or not, he was going to go through with it. Michael pulled back his fist and let it fly. The punch caught Sean's chin and snapped his head backward. He dropped to the ground.

"I hope you're not figurin' on doing that to all of us," Rory said. A knife suddenly appeared in his hand. The blade flashed in the moonlight as he waved it under Michael's nose.

Michael studied him coldly for a moment. Then his hand shot out again. He grabbed the little man's wrist and squeezed until Rory cried out and dropped the knife into the grass. As Michael's fingers bit into his flesh, it occurred to him that he could ruin Rory's arm. One twist and those bones would splinter. One good jerk and Rory would suffer the pain of mutilation as he had.

He wanted to do it. The beast inside demanded that he do it. But he couldn't. Rory deserved the worst that could happen to him, but Michael wouldn't be the one to give it to him. Not this time.

Michael saw the fear in the black eyes glittering behind the mask. He could smell the rank terror in Rory's sweat, and he was satisfied. Slowly he released his arm. "If you ever take a weapon against me again, Rory Doona," he said, "me hands will be around your neck instead. And sure you'll find it a tight fit."

Without another word Michael scooped up the unconscious Sean and slung him over his shoulder. Then he turned and headed toward the forest.

He had to get Sean and Caitlin away from here. Away from the wickedness that was about to happen.

Michael pulled the worn leather gloves from his hands and tucked them into his shirt pocket along with the chisel. It was finished. It had taken him two months, but he had done it.

He stood, brushed the bits of straw from his breeches, and lifted Caitlin's pub sign from the barn floor. Despite the pain and stiffness in his hands, the magic had flowed through his fingers again, a slow trickle at first, then a flood. And this sign was the most beautiful thing he had ever carved.

His finger lovingly traced the deep lines of the stallion who reared on his hind legs, his thick mane caught in the wind, his muscle and sinew intricately detailed.

Caitlin would be pleased, and he could hardly wait to present it to her. She had given him so much, had healed not only his hands but his heart as well. It seemed only right that her sign had been the first thing his hands had carved after the fire.

"Annie said that you were after seeing me," Michael said an hour later as he stood with Caitlin's sign tucked under his arm, watching his mother stir a pot of rabbit and cabbage stew over Father Murphy's fire. The pungent aroma of the stew filled the rectory, which was quiet except for the steady tick of the mantel clock. Michael had chosen a time when he knew that the priests would be in the chapel next door, listening to afternoon confessions. The only thing worse than Father Brolin's self-righteous pomposity was Father Murphy's sad eyes that looked into Michael's and made his burden of guilt almost unbearable. He hadn't been to confession in five years, and he couldn't imagine himself going anytime in the future. Some sins were too deep, too painful to be admitted with the heart, let alone spoken with the lips.

"Yes, there's a deep sorrow on my soul, and I must

151

have a word with you, son." Sorcha tucked the fringed edges of her black shawl into the waistband of her apron and lifted the kettle from the crane. Michael quickly laid the sign on a rush-bottomed chair and took the pot from her, conveying it to the falling table that she had unfolded from the wall.

He turned around to see her studying the sign with disapproval.

"Well, I don't have to ask who you carved that for," she said with a disgusted shake of her head.

"No, I don't suppose you'd be long wondering, since it says, 'C. O'Leary, Publican' right across the bottom. I was on my way to the pub with it when I met Annie on the road. I hope Caitlin likes it," he said wistfully, then he bit his tongue. He had heard the longing in his own voice and hoped that his mother hadn't noticed.

He glanced over at her and saw a look as dark as bog oak. "I'm sure she'll like it fine," Sorcha replied, her words served with a generous measure of sarcasm. Turning her back to him she took a flat iron from its alcove beside the fireplace and set it on a rack to heat over some turf embers. She clucked her tongue and put on her saddest expression, the one that crinkled her parchment skin and made Michael cringe. "I'd tell you what a fool you are," she said, "to be chasin' after that red skirt of hers, but it would do no good sure. To address a head without knowledge is like the barking of a dog in a green valley," she finished with a self-righteous tilt to her chin and a smug lift of her eyebrow.

Michael thought of the night Caitlin had bandaged his hands, and an anger swept through him. "Caitlin is a good woman, and—"

"And when did you decide that? Before you took her down to the river that night, or after?"

Michael felt the blood rush to his face, staining it

152

crimson as an arbutus berry. Picking up the sign from the chair, he pretended to brush the dust from the crevices. "I don't know what you're speaking of."

Sorcha crossed her flat bosom and cast sullen eyes heavenward. "Have mercy on him, Holy Mother. He's but a lad, a boy led astray by the wiles of a wicked woman."

Michael strode across the flagstoned floor to the door. "I'll not listen to such talk. You should be ashamed, judging a fine woman like Caitlin O'Leary so harshly." He yanked the door open. Suddenly he found himself face to face with Annie, who wore the mortified expression of an eavesdropper caught in the act.

"Next time, Annie," Michael said, "just ask us to speak up a bit. Then you won't have to stretch your ears to hear what's no concern of your own."

As he stomped down the road toward the pub, he cursed Annie for telling his mother about his walk with Caitlin down by the river. In a village as small as Lios na Capaill, there were always eyes to see and ears to hear what you were doing, and many a tongue to wag about it. But Michael knew that it was Annie who had informed on him. Everyone at the ceili had been having too much pleasure of their own to worry about anyone else having theirs. And he recalled seeing Annie and young Father Brolin casting disapproving glances his way just before he and Caitlin had taken their moonlight stroll.

Annie had tattled on him more times than he could remember. *Someday she'll reap the consequences of all her spying,* he thought, *and it'll be a bumper crop sure.*

Usually, Caitlin's customers were contented and relaxed, lazily sipping their ales as they exchanged idle gossip. The only excitement was the occasional affray, but today the pub hummed with the energy of a crowd with news.

Caitlin looked up from the bar as Michael walked through her door, and she knew by the pleasant smile on his face that he hadn't yet received the word.

"Michael, did you hear?" Kevin shouted across the room.

With a wistful glance in Caitlin's direction, Michael set a large piece of wood against the wall and lowered himself onto the bench beside Kevin. "No, I guess I haven't. Old Daniel O'Connell hasn't gotten himself arrested again, has he?"

"No, nothing so far away as that," Kevin assured him. "It's murder . . . right here on our own doorstep."

The entire pub hushed to watch Michael's reaction. Caitlin walked over to his table and quietly served him a pint, not trusting herself to look him in the eye.

"Murder you say?" Michael glanced over at Sean, who seemed to find something fascinating about the toe of his boot. "And who's turned up a corpse?"

"It's old Collier," Kevin replied. "Many's the day he'll rest in the clay, and there'll be many a dry eye at his wake, sure."

"Kilt he was? How can you be certain?" he asked.

Caitlin winced inwardly. She was sure that Michael didn't really want to hear the details, but it would seem strange if he didn't ask.

"They found him in the river this morning down by the bridge in Kilorglin," one of the farmers offered, "floatin' face down, he was, that ugly velvet jacket of his caught on a log."

"Maybe he decided to take his own life," Michael suggested half-heartedly. "After all, Collier was a dark and dour fellow without a friend in the world. I'd have put an end to me own misery long ago if I was him."

"Well, if he kilt himself, 'twas a fine job he did of it," Kevin said with a bitter grin. "Seems he took the trouble to beat himself soundly from head to toe and then he fell on a knife four times before he threw himself into the water."

Stabbed four times? Caitlin shuddered. Heaven knows, she had no great love for any agent, and especially Collier. But beaten, stabbed and drowned? It was a sorry death for even the worst man, to be sure.

"Aye, the constable came by my place, looking for old Rory and his buddies," said Jimmy Foley, the village butcher and Rory's neighbor. He pulled his seat closer to the fire and lit his pipe, swelling with importance at being on the receiving end of everyone's attention. "Seems some low-down informer told him they saw the deed done."

An angry murmur went through the crowd. "Ireland would have been free long ago had it not been for informers," Sean muttered with a dark sidelong glance at Michael.

Caitlin sent Sean a questioning look. Surely he didn't think that Michael would inform . . .

"I told the constable that I haven't seen a hair on Rory's hide since the ceili last Saturday night," the butcher continued. "Though, I did see him early Sunday morning with Seamus, Will and Cornelius. They were heading up the road toward Carrantuohill."

"Now would be a good time for those lads to stay up on the mountain like monks and consider the worth of their immortal souls," replied Paul Gannon, the village gravedigger, stroking the length of his long nose thoughtfully. "If they come down any time soon, I'll be havin' employment."

155

The laughter was mirthless and sour around the pub as they silently lifted their mugs in unison and drank an unspoken toast to Rory Doona. No one in Lios na Capaill wanted to see him or his friends hang.

But even more, they didn't want Rory to have reason to visit their homes at midnight wearing a black hood and carrying a bloodstained knife.

"So, is this what you had in mind?" Michael held the sign up for Caitlin's inspection. He had waited until the last customer had left before presenting it to her.

"Oh, Michael, 'tis a lovely sign. I had no idea you were going to do anything so—so—" Her eyes sparkled with delight as she reached out and touched the rope scrollwork around the edge. " 'Tis happy I am that you're back to carvin' again and that the first thing you carved was my very own sign."

He grinned broadly, pleased with her praise, and she was reminded of the shy lad she had loved so long ago. A boy much different from the man who had kissed her so fervently beside the river.

She took the sign from him and laid it carefully on the nearest table. "I'll cherish this forever, Michael," she said. "I only wish my father had lived to see it. He would have been bustin' with pride."

"He would have been proud of you, Caitlin." Michael stepped behind her and placed his hands on her shoulders. "You've honored his memory by the fine way you run this pub."

She was silent for a long moment; then she sighed. "Da wanted a son, you know, not a daughter to run the place. He told me that from the day I was born. He only taught me to be a man, Michael. I had no one to teach me how to be a woman. The fever took my mother when I was a babe. I can't even remember her . . ."

Caitlin's own confession surprised her. She had never put her self-doubt into words, let alone voiced them to another person. But Michael was listening intently, a quiet look of understanding on his face. So she continued. "Do you think I'm unwomanly, Michael? Do you think me rough or crude because I've no husband and because I run a pub?"

His full lips curved with a sad, sympathetic half-smile, and his hands moved up from her shoulders to twine in the auburn silk of her hair. "Ah, Caitlin," he whispered, "what man alive wouldn't know that you're a woman? Only a man with no eyes, and one who hadn't touched you, sure."

He lowered his head and pressed his lips to hers. Holding his passion in check, he kissed her with the gentleness and respect due a lady-in-waiting in Queen Victoria's court. "You're a good woman, Caitlin O'Leary," he murmured into her hair.

She slipped her hands inside his coat and her arms encircled his waist. The warm scent of him filled her with the painful longing that occupied her thoughts by day and tormented her with forbidden dreams at night. She lifted her face to his, eager for another kiss.

But he gently put her away from him and walked to the door. "You're a fine lady to be sure," he said, his face registering his internal battle. "A lady who deserves much better than meself. And I'd better leave now, before I forget that."

Ordinarily Michael would have savored the peaceful green of the trees that rustled with the early evening breeze. Ravens cawed from the limbs overhead and

157

scolded him for venturing into their domain. A tiny brown hare with a dandelion puff-ball tail scooted across the path in front of him, then stopped in the middle of the dirt road to look back at him.

But Michael didn't notice the trees, the ravens, the hare, or the bluebells on the side of the road. His spirit was in turmoil, his thoughts whirling.

He was on the main road to Armfield House, answering a summons delivered by old Carmody, Armfield's ancient caretaker.

"His Honor will see you in the big house at half-five this evening." Carmody had announced at the forge that morning. "Don't keep him waitin' if you know what's best for ye." His message delivered, the old fellow had tugged his green felt cap into place on his bald head, turned and walked away, leaving Michael to wonder why the landlord wanted to see him.

It had to be about the Black Oaks. Armfield wanted to question him about Collier's murder, and what would he say? The only alibi he had was Caitlin, and Michael wasn't about to sully her reputation by admitting that she had been down by the river with him. Besides, it was best if no one knew that he had been anywhere near the river.

He came to the fork in the road and took the curve to the left, a walk he had seldom taken, to the front door of the mansion.

Wisteria crept up the front wall of the Georgian mansion, softening the gray stone walls with its lavender lace. A hound bounded around the corner of the house to meet him, tail waving, tongue lolling stupidly from the corner of his red mouth.

"Hello, lad," Michael muttered, stroking the silky black ears. Somehow Michael knew that the hound's master wouldn't be as happy to see him. He rapped on the door, using his knuckles instead of the heavy brass knocker. If knuckles were good enough for the peasantry, they were good enough for the aristocracy.

A moment later the door was opened by Sally Goodman, Cornelius' widowed sister. Like her younger brother, Sally was short, stocky and well-fed. Her snowy white apron and the frilly cap she wore on her silver head bespoke cleanliness and no nonsense.

"His Honor is expecting you, Michael." She ushered him into the spacious foyer. "If you will please wait in the library."

She led him into a room that was as large as Kevin O'Brien's entire cottage and left him alone to marvel at the splendor of a way of life that was beyond his experience or comprehension.

From the baroque ceiling with its elaborate plaster scrolling to the polished wooden floors covered with plush, hand-hooked rugs, Michael's dazzled eyes drank in every detail.

It wasn't the room's opulence that fascinated him but the craftsmanship: the heavy French tapestries that draped the walls, the chandelier in the center of the ceiling that dripped with crystal splendor, the armory of muskets and pistols locked behind the leaded glass doors of carved gun cabinets. So much workmanship, so many master craftsmen.

Only one piece stood out from the others, a misfit in a room filled with only the finest. A small desk crouched in the corner, its curved legs almost graceful, but not quite, the carving on the drawer fronts adequate, but hardly exceptional.

"So, tell me, is that a well-built piece of furniture or not?"

Michael spun around and saw Mason Armfield standing in the doorway, an ivory pipe in his hand, the other hand thrust into the pocket of a silver, evening coat with satin lapels.

He stepped into the room and slid the mahogany doors closed behind him. The evening sun streamed through the lace curtains and lit his prematurely white hair.

Michael glanced away uneasily. It was difficult to look at Armfield's face, to see those horrible scars that disfigured an otherwise handsome face. Michael knew what it was to wear the scars of the past. He flexed his fingers with their permanently tightened skin and felt a strange kinship with the Englishman.

" 'Tis a goodly bit of carving," he said, as he slowly ran his fingertips over the engraving on the desk drawer. The landlord seemed to want a truthful answer, so he decided to be completely honest. "I wouldn't recommend the fellow who stuck it together, though. He was a fair carver, but not much of a carpenter. Wasn't from around here, I'd say. Kerry's full of lads who do better work than this."

Armfield's thin lips curved up at one corner. "The gentleman was from Sligo, I believe," he said wryly. "And carpentry wasn't his trade, only a pleasant pastime."

As Michael studied the man's scored features, it suddenly became clear to him that Armfield had built the desk himself. Michael was embarrassed to see this side of a man who showed very little of himself to the world. It made Armfield vulnerable in some way, and Michael didn't want to think of him as vulnerable. It made it too difficult to hate him.

Armfield walked to a sideboard and poured a bit of sherry into a small crystal glass. He didn't offer his visitor a drink, but then, Michael wasn't really expecting one.

"I was at Caitlin O'Leary's pub last night," Armfield said evenly as he stared into the russet liquid. "Late last night, after everyone else had gone."

A rage kindled inside Michael. But he knew that Armfield was goading him and he was determined not to show his jealousy. "Yes, and . . . ?"

"And I saw the sign you carved for her. It was a fine piece of work."

From the tightening in the man's scarred jaw, Michael could tell that the compliment had cost Armfield a great deal. "Thank you," he said without warmth.

"I am beginning a major restoration of Armfield House," he said, spinning the sherry in its glass. "My father did very little repair on it, as did my grandfather, and the old place needs some work. I want you to do the necessary carpentry. I will expect your best workmanship, and for that I will pay you well."

Michael's dignity rose along with his ire. "I *always* do my best work, whether I am paid well or not at all."

"Did Caitlin pay you well for the sign?" Armfield asked bitterly.

So, Armfield was jealous, too. The thought satisfied Michael deeply.

"Caitlin and I are friends," he replied. "And payment between friends isn't necessary."

Armfield glanced over at the clock on the mantel. Michael's eyes followed his and he noted that it was five minutes before six.

The landlord walked over to the window, slid the lace curtains aside and looked out onto the back half of his property. "Do you like art, Michael?" Somehow Michael got the idea that Armfield didn't give a damn whether he liked art or not. He seemed to be stalling, marking time.

"Some I do, some I don't," Michael replied. "Can't

161

say as I've laid me eyes on all that much of it." He glanced around the room at the portraits of generations of Armfields. They all looked overfed and underworked. Their sallow complexions could have benefited from a day in the sunshine, cutting turf.

"I like the picture of the hunt," he said, pointing to a large painting over the fireplace. "I like the way the fellow painted the horses, so strong and proud."

"You like horses, don't you, McKevett?" Armfield cast another look at the clock over his shoulder, then continued to stare out the window. Michael wondered if Armfield was expecting an important visitor.

"I love horses," Michael replied. "The good God must have made them on the seventh day of Creation, after he'd had lots of practice."

Armfield turned and gave him a look that puzzled him. It was as though in that moment he and the landlord had met on common ground. Two men from different worlds with nothing in common except their scars and a love of horses.

"Let me show you something." Armfield left the window and placed his glass on the desk.

He reached into the bottom drawer and pulled out a rolled piece of parchment. Lovingly he spread the paper across the desk, weighing down the corners with books.

"There," he said proudly. "Isn't that the finest display of horse flesh you've ever seen?"

Michael bent over the desk and caught his breath. "What is it?"

"It's a pen and ink sketch of an event called a carousel. Louis XIV staged it to impress his teenaged mistress. Do you suppose she was duly impressed?"

Michael stared down at the drawing, which captured the pageantry, the fanfare of the occasion. Hundreds of riders rode in a giant circle around a courtyard, dressed in the gaudy attire of the period, sporting plumes and jewels on ornately embroidered costumes. But Michael had no eye for the riders or their courtyard. All he saw was the ring of horses, majestic steeds, decked out in jeweled bridles, their regal necks wreathed in garlands, their trappings elegant beyond his most fanciful dreams.

"Princess Niav's stallions," he whispered. "Hundreds of them riding four abreast in a circle . . ."

"What did you say?" Armfield asked. "Who is Princess Niav?"

Michael shook his head as though coming out of a fairy's trance. "What? Oh . . . it doesn't matter. What did you say they called this—this—"

"Carousel. It's derived from the Spanish word *carosella* which means 'little war.' In the twelfth century the Arabs rode around in circles and threw clay balls at one another. The balls were filled with scented water, and if the warrior didn't catch the ball correctly, it broke all over him. Then he would have to bear his disgrace until the scent wore off. It was training for warfare."

"But these dandies aren't away to the wars in those ribbons and sashes, surely," Michael commented, his nose wrinkled in distaste.

Armfield chuckled. "Hardly. By the time the tradition was handed down to old Louis, it had changed flavor considerably. Their only sport was to ride in circles and spear a brass ring with their swords. The display was more to impress the ladies than to prepare for battle."

"It must have been a wonder to behold," Michael said. "All those fine horses prancing in a circle. Nothing could be more beautiful."

Armfield glanced again at the clock on the mantel and walked to the window. He looked out and smiled. But it wasn't a happy smile, Michael noticed. He looked like the cat who had just chewed the lark and spit out the feathers.

"That will be all today, McKevett," Armfield said curtly. "I'll summon you when I'm ready for you to begin. Goodbye."

The dismissal was so abrupt that Michael was taken aback. He glanced down once more at the drawing, trying to carve it into his memory for all time, then he headed for the door.

"One more thing," Armfield called after him. "You'll come and go from the back door from now on with the rest of the servants. Don't forget."

Michael fixed him with a baleful glare as the insult cut a deep slash through his pride. "Oh, don't worry, Your Honor. We Irish know our place. I'm not likely to forget."

He left by the back way, as instructed, through the courtyard where the workmen had already stowed the plows and wagons. In the stables the horses and cattle were settling down to their evening feast of oats and straw.

The repairs on the barn were nearly completed and, except for the discoloration of the smoke on the slate roof, it appeared almost as good as new.

Michael chose the narrow, wooded path to town, the one he and the Black Oaks had walked the night they had raided Armfield House.

He had gone only a few yards when he saw her, a glowing spot of scarlet among the dark trees.

Suddenly it was all clear, too clear. This was why Armfield had been watching the clock, watching out the window, waiting to dismiss him at exactly the right moment.

Mason Armfield had wanted Michael to see her on the back road to the house.

Michael stepped off the path and behind a tree, his soul churning inside him. Caitlin was coming to see Armfield, to be with him. There was no other reason for her to be here, alone, at this hour, and Armfield had made damned sure that Michael knew it.

He watched from behind the tree as she strolled past him, her hood thrown back onto her shoulders, her copper hair blowing in the evening breeze.

A bitter jealousy welled up from Michael's stomach as he watched her. The beast roared, and this time the fury raged, not in his chest, but in his loins.

He thought of their precious summer so long ago, of their stolen caresses beside the moonlit river, and he was suddenly sick with disgust. For her. For Mason Armfield. For himself.

Caitlin was a whore. No, she was worse than a whore. She was a landlord's tallywoman.

Chapter Eight

"I sincerely hope that you aren't involved with those Black Oaks, Caitlin." Armfield watched her closely over the rim of his brandy glass. "If you are, even I won't be able to save you."

"I've nothin' to do with the Black Oaks. I can't imagine why you'd think I'm involved with them," she said as she left the sofa where she had been sitting beside him and walked over to the library window. Looking down on the sleeping village below, her eyes sought out the O'Briens' barn. A light glowed softly in the byre window.

Caitlin wondered, not for the first time, what she was doing here in an Englishman's mansion. She was Irish, and she belonged with her own kind. She should be with an Irishman tonight, not here with this Saxon whose gray eyes studied her like a hawk watching his prey.

Armfield stood, set his drink on his desk, and followed her to the window. Standing behind her, he placed his hands lightly on her shoulders, "I suspect you because I know that you're involved with Michael McKevett, and he's one of the Black Oaks."

Caitlin turned from the window to face him, her amber eyes glittering with unspoken challenge. Armfield wasn't sure of his facts; she knew that much for certain. He was casting his net to see what he could catch, and Caitlin didn't intend to be snared like a hapless salmon.

He reached up and twisted one of her curls around his forefinger. Then he tugged ... too hard. But she was determined not to wince. "We landlords have our informants," he reminded her. "And I pay mine handsomely."

She reached up and carefully unwound her hair from his finger. With a defiant lift to her chin, she said, "Too handsomely, it seems. Whoever sold you that news is as great a liar as the clock of Strabane. Michael had nothin' to do with those murderers. And I've had nothin' to do with Michael except to serve him a pint from time to time there in me pub."

Her face registered none of her internal misery when she uttered the lies. Caitlin hated to be dishonest, especially with someone she cared for, and she was fond of Mason Armfield. Though he frightened her sometimes, like now, when his eyes turned to ice.

Armfield would be a formidable opponent if crossed, one whose wrath Caitlin didn't want to incur. He had shown her a glimpse of his heart; he had trusted her. And if she betrayed that trust, he would hate her more than his worst enemy, because she had been his friend.

His hands closed around her forearms, his fingertips biting into her flesh. "Don't lie, Caitlin." His voice was low and menacing. "You lied to me once to save that Irishman, and I'll not be made a fool of twice."

She nodded. "I understand."

"Be sure that you do." He pulled her into his arms, crushing her breasts against his chest. "I have a certain

167

... affection ... for you. But even that has its limits. You mustn't push me too far.''

He bent his head and pressed his mouth to hers. His lips were hard, punishing and rough, and the change in him startled her. Once, she had welcomed his touch. Though he was aloof and distant during their lovemaking, he had always been gentle with her. But tonight his kisses were possessive and greedy.

Thoughts of Michael rushed, unbidden, to her mind, but she quickly pushed them away. If she thought of him now, she wouldn't be able to bear having Armfield's hands on her.

She closed her eyes and submitted to his touch. For tonight, it was all she could do. Long ago Caitlin had chosen this path and, having chosen it, there was no turning back.

Michael rolled over on his back and stared up at the rafters, barely visible by the feeble glow of the banked embers on the hearth. He tried to unwind himself from the quilt that twisted around his bare limbs. No matter how he lay, he couldn't get comfortable. The quilt that had always been so soft before chafed his skin tonight. His entire body tingled, overly-sensitized to every touch.

He could hear Danny's soft breathing from the outshot bed and Kevin's raucous snoring, which drifted in from the bedroom. Annie and Judy had long since gone up the ladder to their loft bedroom.

But Michael couldn't sleep. Every time he closed his eyes he saw Caitlin. He saw her eyes sparkling with moonlight just before he had kissed her. He tasted her lips, warm and moist against his. And her breasts ... he could still feel that lovely softness at his fingertips.

But it was another man's hands that touched her tonight. Long, slender, aristocratic hands.

Did she moan softly when Armfield kissed her? Did she encourage his hands to roam over her breasts—and further?

The pictures flooded Michael's mind, pricking at him like a thousand tiny devil's darts.

The thought of her and Armfield together repulsed him. And yet, he had never wanted her more than he did tonight, his loins burning and tight with burgeoning desire.

Finally he threw back the quilt, dressed and slipped out of the house into the night.

He ran aimlessly across dark fields, down narrow paths and through the woods. He ran until his heart pounded and his breath came in ragged gasps that had nothing to do with lust.

At last, he stopped and bent over double, trying to ease the pain in his side. Sweat poured down his face and his body steamed with exertion. When he stood upright and looked around, he saw the ruins of Kenmare Abbey, a gray specter, gleaming under the full moon. He had run ten miles, nearly to Kilgobnet, without stopping.

Inside the ruined walls of the abbey Michael sank onto a tumbled gravestone. As he rested, the cold of the night seeped through his sweat-soaked clothes and chilled his flesh. He looked around and reminded himself that a wise man wouldn't be here. The abbey had a bloody history and such places were best avoided after sundown.

Two hundred women and children had been murdered here by Cromwell's men. The soldiers had herded their victims inside those walls, barred the doors, and set fire to the place.

Sometimes, the locals claimed, when the sea wind blew from the south, they could hear the women's screams and the cries of the babies.

But tonight there was no wind, and Michael was thankful. He had enough trouble right now dealing with flesh and blood mortals. He didn't need to be tormented by those who hadn't the decency to lie still in their graves.

The eery solitude of the place stole over him, replacing his anger and frustration with an uneasiness that made him wish he had thought to bring along his blackthorn stick to ward off ghosts and goblins.

Michael quickly supped his fill of the abbey and its sepulchral silence. He rose from his resting place and left the tumbled sanctuary.

When he was nearing the edge of the cemetery, he heard it, and his heart nearly stopped. A hiss that sounded like a black cat or some malignant spirit with evil on his mind.

"Who's there?" he asked, his blood thundering in his ears.

A dark figure stepped out from behind the stone wall and blocked his path.

"Put your fists down, Michael McKevett," came the whispered reply. "It's only me, Rory."

The black silhouette against the moonlight brought a coldness to Michael's soul, and for a moment he wished that he had met up with a ghost or banshee instead.

"Rory Doona," he said. "You've done it now, murderin' old Collier like that. The constable is turning the county inside out looking for your worthless hide."

Rory laughed, his cackle, as sharp as the teeth of a hound, cut through the night air. "It's a poor Irish soldier who can't stay three steps ahead of an Englishman," he said, then turned and spoke to the thick brush behind him. "Come on out, lads. It's Michael McKevett himself, come calling on old friends."

Seamus, William, and Cornelius crawled out of the bushes. Even by the pale light of the moon Michael could see how ragged and dirty they were. Men on the run. Hunted and harried. He didn't mind seeing Rory in that state, but he hated to see the others so miserable. Michael remembered when they had been carefree, hardworking citizens, their chief worry being how to pay the rent and keep their families in praties.

He couldn't help wondering how different the last few years of their lives would have been, had they not joined the Black Oaks.

"We heard that you went to Armfield House this evening," Rory said. "We want to know what you had to say to His Honor."

Michael's temper flared. Couldn't he relieve himself in the woods without the entire county knowing where and for how long?

"It's no business of your own," he replied. "It had nothing to do with the murder or the Oaks, if that's what you're worried about."

Rory scowled, his face as black as Toal's cloak. "He didn't even ask after us?"

"Not a word, Rory. Believe it if you will, some people have other things on their minds besides your whereabouts."

"Did he take you into the library, Michael?" Seamus asked, shifting his wad of tobacco from one cheek to the other. "Did you see where he keeps his guns?"

"I saw, " Michael replied carefully. "Why?"

William shifted his feet and cast a quick sideways glance at Rory. "Because we want you to help us steal

171

some of them. We're hard put to defend ourselves without guns."

Michael cringed at the thought of this motley gang storming Armfield House. "The Devil himself couldn't do it unless he was drunk, and him not foolish enough to try. Armfield would shoot you all dead before you got past that thick front door of his."

"The door's not been made that can stand up to the boot of Rory Doona," the little man boasted.

"You're a worthless braggart, Rory," Michael said, "with two heads on all our sheep. Haven't you stretched the rope around your own neck tight enough?"

"Have you no compassion for your comrades?" Cornelius pleaded, wedging his portly body between Michael and the bristling Rory. "Won't you tell us the lay of the house, Michael, and help us out a bit?"

Michael's heart twisted for his old friends, but he was determined not to assist them in making their situation even worse. "You can't keep making trouble, Con. Don't you see that the more you trample dung the more it spreads? You're making things worse for yourself, not better."

Rory sniffed and pushed Cornelius aside. "Don't waste your breath, Con. His mind's made up. He chose the landlord's side long ago. For all we know, he's the one who informed against us."

"That's a lie and you know it," Michael protested, but Rory and the others had already turned their backs to him and were headed into the woods.

"If I ever find out 'twas you who informed on us, I'll murder you, sure, Michael McKevett," Rory shouted over his shoulder as he disappeared into the darkness. "And 'twill be a bad death with dishonor before it."

* * *

"Michael, where have you been? It's worried to death I've been these long hours waitin' for you."

The diminutive form in a billowing white nightgown hurried toward him across the dark field. They met in the middle of the pasture beneath a maple tree.

"Annie, what are you doing out here in the dead of the night and you in your nightgown?"

He caught her by the waist as she threw her arms around his neck and stood on tiptoe to kiss his cheek.

"I heard you leave hours ago and I've been wonderin' where you were and what you were about. You were so quare at supper and hardly ate a bite. I knew something was wrong with you."

He disengaged her arms from his neck and patted her hair that flowed over her slight shoulders and down her back to her hips. "I've been for a walk—"

"A walk? All the way to Tipperary and back it must have been."

"Just about." The concern in her eyes was a balm to his wounded pride. "You shouldn't have worried, Annie. But it's a kind heart you have, and I love you for it."

"Do you, Michael?" she asked, her eyes searching his with an intensity that made him glance away. She reached up and her hands cupped his chin, forcing him to look down at her. "Do you love me truly, Michael? For it's truly I love you."

"Annie, I—" His speech about brotherly love knotted in his throat and nearly choked him. There was a light in her blue eyes that he recognized, having seen it recently in a pair of amber ones. The night breeze gently fanned the silken hair away from her slender neck, and for the first time, Michael noticed that beneath the thin fabric of her nightgown, little Annie had become a woman.

173

Confusion swept over him, along with the heat from a fire that had been banked, but not extinguished by the long walk and the encounter with Rory. Michael was appalled at his body's reaction to her. How could he be feeling this way about Annie?

She stepped closer to him, and he could smell the sweet fragrance of spring in her hair. "I've loved you forever and ever, Michael McKevett," she said. "I've just been waiting for you to notice. But you haven't given me the twinkle of your eye in all this time. Tell me, do you love me at last?"

"Ah, Annie . . ." He bent his head and buried his face in her hair. She was so innocent that it broke his heart. What did she know about what went on between a man and a woman? Between a landlord and a red-haired barkeeper?

Anger welled up in him, adding to the inferno that blazed in his loins.

"You can kiss me if you want, Michael," Annie was saying. He heard her through a fog of desire that had little to do with the young woman in his arms. "If you love me truly, I'll let you kiss me."

Before he knew it, she had pressed her lips to his. At first he was surprised, surprised that she tasted so good, that her body felt so womanly pressed against the hardness of his. Of their own volition his hands went around her tiny waist and pulled her even closer as he whispered, "Stop it, Annie. We shouldn't—"

"We can, if you love me, Michael," she replied as, once again, she covered his mouth with hers.

His hand glided around the curve of her waist, marvelling in the warm softness just below the thin material. Then his fingers moved upward, closed over the roundness of her small breasts and gently squeezed, feeling them mold to his palm.

She caught her breath and pulled her mouth away from his. "Michael! What are you doin'?" she gasped. "Ye've no right to touch me there!"

He pushed away from her and held her at arm's length. "I'm sorry, Annie. I just got carried away by your charms and I—"

"I understand, Michael." Her face brightened and the shock quickly faded into delight. "But you mustn't take such liberties with me . . . until after we've wed."

She turned, lifted the hem of her white nightgown and fled across the wet grass toward the house.

"Until after we've wed?" Michael stared after her open-mouthed. "Oh, Mother of Mercy what have I done?"

Michael woke to the a glorious spring dawn that crept over the tops of the MacGillycuddy's Reeks. The deep blues of night faded into gold as the sun woke Erin and set her birds to singing.

For a moment Michael didn't know where he was. The ground beneath him was damp and strewn with pine needles, cones and bluebells. Then he remembered. He had slept in the fairy fort.

He had been so overwhelmed with shame and confusion about what had passed between him and Annie that he hadn't been able to go back to Kevin's cottage. He had taken advantage of the daughter of a man who had been a father to him. With one careless, selfish act he had brought disgrace on their household. Kevin would never forgive him. Michael would never forgive himself.

But this morning he felt wonderful, refreshed, because he had slept in the fort. Few men would even venture near a fairy fort after sundown for fear of the

Good People. But Michael wasn't afraid. There were places, like the abbey, that felt evil whether it was daylight or dark. But Michael had always felt at ease in this sacred ring of trees. More than at ease, he felt at home. He looked up into the branches of the pines and sighed, deeply satisfied. Here he felt as though Erin herself cradled him close to her bosom. There was nothing here to hurt him. Whatever or whoever resided in this place understood him in a way that the villagers never would. The kinship that he felt with the fort and its ancient presence fed and strengthened his spirit.

He stretched and yawned, trying to imagine why he felt so happy. Heaven knows, he should feel dreadful after yesterday.

Then he remembered. The dream that had wakened him just before dawn. A sparkling, glorious dream of horses. Fantasy horses, spinning around and around, four abreast, with garlands of flowers around their graceful necks. Their bridles were spangled with jewels, their saddle blankets embroidered with gold and silver.

And on their backs rode the people of the village: his mother, looking young and carefree again, her wavy brown hair streaming down her back as she rode a white Arabian. He saw old Bridget, the midwife, on a glossy black mare, laughing like a girl as she reached out with a silver sword to pierce the center of a glittering brass ring.

But his favorite vision was that of little Daniel, riding a mighty stallion draped in full battle armor. The lad's back was straight, his head held high, his mouth open in a mighty battle cry as he rode his steed against the dreaded Saxons.

Michael shivered with delight as the details of the dream flooded back into his mind. It was an enchanted dream and Michael didn't have to ask where it had come from.

He bowed his head and whispered his first prayer of thanksgiving in a long time. But he didn't pray to Mary or any of the saints. He gave thanks to a much older deity—the spirit of the fort that had cradled him through the night, and shown him a glimpse of a wondrous future.

The early morning sunlight shone warmly on Caitlin's face as she walked along the river, taking the back road from Armfield House to her pub. But the sun's warmth didn't cheer her as it usually did. It was going to take a lot more than a sunny morning to set her life right, and she was beginning to doubt that her life would ever be right again.

Caitlin was a strong-willed woman who usually got what she wanted, one way or the other, by employing her sharp wit and determination. But there appeared to be no solution to her problem of Michael and Lord Armfield. She was caught in a snare that she alone had set.

If she had never given her virginity to Mason Armfield, she would be free to offer herself to Michael fully, knowing that he would find her virtue intact. But there was no point in longing for that which was gone forever. What was done, was done, and until she had the courage to tell Michael about the landlord, her secret would remain between them.

As Caitlin approached the ringed fort she thought of the Good People who inhabited that mystic circle of trees. The village had been named for its fairy fort, Lios na Capaill, the ancient Gaelic words meaning, Ringed Fort of the Horses. If she could only communicate with those timeless spirits who lived within those sacred pines, would they have any answers for her?

Caitlin shook her head. No. The answer lay within herself. She knew what she had to do; she had to tell Michael about Armfield.

Then and there she decided that she would tell him the next time she saw him. She would risk his anger and contempt. If his love for her was strong enough, perhaps he could accept the truth with time.

Abruptly she stopped and stood still, her heart in her throat. It was Michael, coming out of the fort. She was close enough to see that his hair and clothes were mussed, as though he had slept among the ancient pines.

Now, she told herself. *I'll tell him now. There could be no better time.*

He didn't see her, but turned away and began walking up the hill toward the village. She hurried after him but she stopped long before she reached him. Paralyzed with fear, she could go no farther.

I'll tell him the next time, she promised herself. *The very next time I see him, I'll tell him all about Mason. And surely he'll find it in his heart to forgive me.*

Chapter Nine

"What's the matter with ye, Michael? We missed your face at the table this morning, and Annie was frettin' something awful." Daniel hitched the strap of the heavy seed bag higher on his thin shoulder, propped his hands on his hips and assumed a demanding stance that reminded Michael of Annie.

Michael avoided the boy's question as he carried a makeshift workbench from the forge and across the yard, through the flapping flock of chickens, ducks, turkeys and guinea hens, who were Annie's and Judy's treasure. The chickens and ducks provided fresh eggs and an occasional Sunday stew. The turkeys brought a pretty price at the Christmas market, and no self-respecting Irishwoman would be without a guinea hen or two in her fowl run because their cries were said to frighten away the rats.

Michael ignored the birds and Danny's question as he left the bench beneath a small birch that provided a circle of shade in the center of the yard. With a wave of his arm he shooed a hen and her chicks from a freshly-cut log that lay at the base of the tree. As he lifted the wood onto the bench, he could feel Danny watching him in silent disapproval. He couldn't bring himself to look into those wide brown eyes, so he stared down at the log and tried to imagine it with a neck and head.

Finally he turned to the boy and placed his hand on his shoulder. "I took meself on a long hike last night, and I didn't get back till awhile ago."

Daniel instantly dropped the authoritative posture and stuck out his lower lip in a pout. "Ye should have taken me along on your hike."

Studying the sullen little face, Michael thought over the events of evening last, then nodded in agreement. "Right you are, Danny. You should have been along to keep me from mischief."

Daniel's eyes sparkled with keen interest. "And what mischief was that?"

"Nothin', lad," he replied quickly as he saw Annie coming toward them from the house. He turned the boy in the direction of the fowl run and gave him a swat on the bum. "You'd better get along and feed the chickens before Annie gives you the lash of her tongue."

"Daniel O'Brien, have you fed those chickens yet?" Annie's voice cracked across the yard like a jarvey's whip, startling the nervous turkeys into a flapping frenzy. Their fluttering wings filled the air with the dusty smell of fowl. "Mind you, you'll not have another bite to eat yourself until those hens have had their fill."

Danny sighed and hobbled away, dragging the heavy feed sack behind. Michael's heart went out to the lad. Feeding the fowl wasn't hard work, but it was woman's work in a village where duties were clearly defined and divided. Women tended the yard and house, men the fields. Daniel wasn't strong enough to do the manly jobs of smithing or farming, though lads his age were already apprentices. So Daniel O'Connell O'Brien was left with females' chores, and Michael hated seeing the harm it did to the boy's spirit, a spirit that had already suffered more than its share of affliction.

Michael watched the lad scatter the seed for the hungry fowl. If Danny were his son, he would find some manly occupation for him. Maybe something to do with wood. The boy seemed to have a gift for carving.

But Michael had to put the thought aside. As Annie approached, his concerns became more immediate. "Good day to ye, Michael," Annie said. "We missed you this morning." She wore the grin of a cat who had just lapped a bowl of warm buttermilk. He could almost see the bubbles of cream foaming in the upturned corners of her mouth. Where was the blushing, shamefaced maiden of last night? Her blue eyes searched his, and he felt like the Devil himself being scrutinized by the Blessed Virgin.

"I wasn't hungry." He turned his back to her, picked up a large awl and bored a hole in one end of the log.

"I hope you weren't upset by anything we said or did last evening. You still love me truly, and you want to marry me, don't you?"

"Well, I—"

"That is what you said last night, isn't it?" Her big blue eyes filled with tears and her rosebud mouth trembled. "You did say you loved me. I heard you say it with your own lips just before we—"

"Sh-h-h . . ." He cast a quick glance around the yard and laid the awl on the bench. With a firm hand on her forearm he pulled her down to sit beside him in the lush spring grass dotted with dandelions and daisies. "Annie, I do love you. I've always loved you dearly, as me own little sister."

"Little sister?" Tears rolled down her cheeks and dripped off her quivering, dimpled chin. "Since when do you kiss yer little sister like that—and her in her nightgown and the two of you alone in the night?"

"Come on, Annie. Be fair. You're the one who kissed me."

"But you're the one who touched me on my—"

"For heaven's sake, Annie, don't say it!" He clamped his hand over her mouth and glanced furtively about the yard. But their only eavesdroppers were the mother hen and her chicks, who wallowed happily in their dust baths. "Somebody might hear you," he whispered, "and what would they think of us both?"

She shook her head and pushed his hand away. " 'Tis ashamed you are . . . of me . . . of what we did together." A sob caught her last words.

Michael groaned and hung his head. What a terrible mess this was, and him in the thick of it. "No, Annie, I'm not ashamed of you. It's just that—"

" 'Twas a sin, what we did." Annie pulled a handkerchief from her pocket and blew loudly into it. " 'Twas a black and evil sin of the flesh, and I'll have to be confessin' it before the day's over."

"No, Annie. 'Twasn't a sin, surely." He plucked a daisy from the grass and pulled the lavender petals off one by one while his brain sought the right words. "It was just a . . . a sign of affection between two people who—"

"Who love each other and want to be married?" she asked hopefully.

"Who love each other, yes, but—"

"Oh, Michael." She covered her face with the kerchief and her sobs started anew. "You don't want to marry me. You just want to use me and throw me out on the dung heap."

He tossed the defrocked daisy aside and took her hands in his. "Annie, that's not true. I'd never throw you on the—I'd never hurt you, you know that."

She sniffed and looked down at his scarred hands

that held hers. He saw the disgust on her face. His touch repulsed her. The realization would have wounded him, except for the thought of Caitlin kissing those scars, pressing his palm to her breast. What did it matter if Annie didn't welcome his touch?

He released her hand, and she dried her eyes on her apron. Then she fixed him with a piercing look that made him feel more lowly than an eel on the bottom of Killarney Lough. "I know why you don't want to marry me, Michael," she said glumly.

"You do?"

"Yes. Everyone in town knows that ye've got your eye peeled on that Caitlin O'Leary, and her a woman with a tainted reputation."

"Don't say that about Caitlin." *Even if it's true, I don't want to hear it,* he thought bitterly.

"Oh, and now ye've taken her side against me." Annie's voice was cold and cutting, and it occurred to Michael that when she was angry like this, she wasn't particularly fair to look upon. In fact, all she needed was a pair of horns to look like the Devil himself with long, yellow hair. "And just what were you and she doin' the night of the ceili when you went wandering down to the river in the dark by yourselves?"

Her words sliced into him like a Dane's battle axe, and he crossed his arms over his chest defensively. "Annie, hush. I don't want you to say things that—"

"Don't you tell me to hush, Michael McKevett," she snapped. "I know where you learned the wickedness that you did to me last night. You learned it from that awful Caitlin O'Leary."

"Exactly where did he touch you, child? You must tell me."

183

Annie squirmed miserably, wishing the good God would just strike her dead then and there so that she wouldn't have to endure this mortification. "On ... on my ah ... my bosom."

There was a long silence on the other side of the confessional curtain, and Annie could feel Father Brolin's disapproval radiating through the thin cloth. "Did he touch both of your breasts or only one?"

"I'm afraid 'twas both, Father," she replied, dying a little, but not enough to be out of her misery.

"And did he touch your breasts over your dress or beneath it, Annie?" The priest's voice sounded queer, deep and hoarse as though he were having trouble breathing. Annie decided that he must be terribly disgusted and angry with her. She felt dreadful for having to put him through this ordeal.

"Over my nightgown, Father."

"And did he touch you anywhere else?"

"Aye, he patted me head and put his big hands around me waist."

"No, that's not what I meant. Did he touch you farther down?" He drew a long, shaking breath. "Did you let him fondle your womanhood?"

Annie blushed scarlet as his meaning became clear to her. "No, of course not, Father!" The air in the cramped, dark confessional was suddenly stale and thin, and Annie could hear her own labored breathing.

"I thought I knew you before, Annie O'Brien." The priest sounded deeply wounded. She heard him shifting his body in the tiny cubicle. "I always thought you were a fine, godly woman. But I must tell you that I'm very disappointed in you. This was a grave sin against purity, meeting a man in a lonely place at night, wearing only your bedclothes. You were inviting the Devil's mischief."

"I know. But I love Michael so, and I thought he loved me. I thought he wanted to marry me."

"He must marry you, Annie. No decent man will have you now that you've been soiled by the hands of another. You must make sure that Michael understands this."

Annie lifted her small, dimpled chin and set her jaw with O'Brien determination. "Oh, I'll make sure he understands, Father. And if I can't show him the error of his ways, his sainted mother will, sure."

"Just go away and leave me to my grief. I can't bear to lay me eyes on you after what you've done." Sorcha refused to look up at her son as she carefully plucked at the weeds that infested her husband's grave.

Michael stood over her with his hands thrust deep in his pockets, looking down at his father's chipped gravestone. He wondered how she had discovered that it was he who had done the damage. "How ... how did you find out?" He felt like a lad of five caught with his breeches around his ankles.

"Annie told me herself, the poor child. She's torn apart with grief and remorse at what you did to her, and you not willing to make an honest woman of her."

Michael's anger flared, the chipped tombstone and his humiliation quickly forgotten. "Damn Annie's tattling," he swore. "What happened was between the two of us and she might have kept it to herself. But I suppose that was asking too much. Annie's never been one to keep a secret, especially when it's to her advantage to tell it."

Sorcha's face twisted into a martyred grimace that reminded Michael of the tortured Christ on the crucifix that hung over the altar in the chapel. "Just listen to you cursin' like a heathen. I raised you to be a decent

185

Christian man, but ye've disappointed me again. 'Tis a heavy burden for a woman of God to bear."

Michael looked up at the ancient round tower silhouetted against a clear blue sky that held only white, rainless clouds. He no longer felt the warmth of the sun on his face or smelled the sweet clover, humming with honey bees. The perfect spring day had suddenly changed to the dead of winter, and Michael could feel the bite of frost in his bones.

"You know, Mama," he said wearily. "I've tried my whole life to make you happy, to give you reason to think well of me. But no matter what I do, you find fault with it. Is there anything in this world I could do that would please you?"

Sorcha looked up at him, her mournful eyes slanting slyly at the corners. "Of course there is, Michael. Marry Annie and give me a houseful of grandbabes to carry on your darlin' father's name. Nothing would make me happier."

"Climb up there and see if it works," Michael told Danny, pointing to the crude log apparatus he had suspended on chains from the wheel.

"What's it supposed to be?" Daniel eyed Michael's latest invention suspiciously.

"What do you mean, what's it supposed to be? It's blind ye are, lad, with stones for eyes. 'Tis a horse as sure as you live and breathe. A fine, prancing stallion ready to whisk you away with Princess Niav to the Land of the Ever Young."

Danny walked around the wheel and took a long, critical, second look. "Aye, it is, indeed. I see it now. There's his neck and head sticking out there in front." He nodded slowly, his freckled face widening with a

186

grin of discovery. "A fine horse he is, if you but look at him the right way."

Michael laughed as he lifted the boy onto his new mount. "Don't you know, Danny, to never count the teeth of a gift horse. If this one works, I'll carve you another that might look like a horse no matter which way yer lookin' at him. Hold on now for the bare life and away with ye."

Michael gave the wheel a push and Daniel was off, spinning into a joyful oblivion. "How's that, Danny, my lad?" Michael shouted, but he knew from the look of rapture on the tiny face that his log pony, crude as it was, had passed the test.

"I'm on the hunt," Danny yelled back in his best aristocratic English tone. "We'll have the hide of that bloody fox stretched before sundown."

Michael gave the wheel another push and turned to walk back to the forge when he saw Kevin striding across the grassy field from the house. It was the middle of the afternoon, and Kevin never left the forge this time of day without good reason. From the long measure of the smith's step, Michael had the sinking feeling that they were about to have the encounter he had been dreading. Kevin's face was dark as a November sky, and it occurred to Michael, not for the first time, that Kevin O'Brien might murder any man who trifled with one of his precious daughters.

"I need a word with you, Michael," the man called, beckoning to him.

For a moment Michael entertained the thought of turning around, running all the way to Cobh Harbor and boarding an emigrant ship for America. But he had a feeling that if Annie wanted him for her husband and Kevin wanted him for a son-in-law, America wouldn't be far enough away.

187

They met near the gate of the stall where Sir Larcher's racehorse pranced and danced, impatient to be shod.

Michael leaned back against the wooden railing and assumed what he hoped was a casual pose with his right hand in his breeches pocket and his left arm propped on the upper rail.

"Yes, sir, what's the problem?" he hoped to heaven that he had forgotten some task at the forge.

Kevin's eyes flashed blue fire. And with his bristling red beard he looked for all the world like Len, the mythical blacksmith whose hammer sparks and fiery dews had fallen to the ground, creating the glittering lakes and streams of Killarney.

"I want to know what your intentions are toward my Annie," Kevin announced without preamble.

"My intentions? Oh, aye, well—"

"She says that you've given her certain assurances of your affection for her. She wasn't sayin' exactly what those assurances were ..." When Michael didn't fill the silence, Kevin continued. "She was as happy and bright as a May morning yesterday, and today she can't stop crying. She told me that she had to go to confession. Now what would a sweet child like herself have to confess? I'd like to know."

No, you wouldn't, Kevin, Michael thought, staring at the horse that galloped around the pen, head and tail held high. *You wouldn't want to know. And since I'd like to see myself combing my gray hair someday, I'll not be so foolish as to tell you.*

"I'll speak to her, Kevin. I promise," he said, trying to close the conversation before a trip of his tongue got him into an even worse mess.

Kevin hitched his thumbs through his galluses and chewed the end of his mustache. His pale eyes glimmered with a strange mixture of pleasure and suspicion. "See that ye do, lad," he said. " 'Tis a hard thing for a man to see a woman cry. And especially if it's his own darlin' daughter who owns those tears."

The sun was beginning to slip behind the purple tops of MacGillycuddy's Reeks when Michael led the newly-shod mare from the forge and into the holding pen. "There you go, lass," he murmured lovingly to the animal. "You'll win another purse for His Honor at the races wearin' those shoes, sure."

Michael glided his palm over the horse's withers, savoring each graceful curve and tucking it away in his memory for future reference.

The bay snorted, lifted her tail in the air and pranced to the other side of the pen where she eyed Michael coquettishly, as though expecting him to follow.

"Women!" He shook his head in mock disgust. "They're forever making eyes at us bachelors and wantin' us to run after them. But if we do, we're damned forever. 'Tis as hard to fight with a woman as with the wide ocean."

He turned away from the horse and walked back to the forge. Surely he could find a few more jobs to do before going home for evening tea. He was in no hurry to look into Annie's sorrowful eyes or to face Kevin's suspicions.

With his hand on the door handle he cast a long, wistful look down the street toward Caitlin's pub. Caitlin. Landlord's tallywoman. All these years he had denied himself the pleasure of her company because he had considered himself unworthy of her, only to discover that she was a whore.

Michael closed his eyes for a moment and thought

of her loveliness, the gentleness of her touch. The word "whore" was so harsh, so ugly. He couldn't bear to think of Caitlin that way, no matter what she had done. Surely she didn't touch the Englishman the way she had touched him that night by the river.

Michael opened the horseshoe-shaped door and stepped inside. He jumped when he saw Annie standing beside the giant leather bellows. As always, her piercing blue eyes bored into him, making him feel guilty for what he had been thinking.

She was wearing her Sunday dress, a blue calico, and her special lacy shawl. Ordinarily he wouldn't notice how Annie was dressed, but it occurred to him that she was wearing her best for him. The knowledge made him feel more uneasy than flattered.

"A fine pattern of an evening isn't it, Annie?" he said, not meeting her eyes. "Handsome weather we're having, don't you agree?"

"'Tisn't the weather I've come to talk about, Michael McKevett." Her voice held that bossy tone that she used with Daniel and Judy, and Michael's ire rose.

He walked past her to the bellows and pumped it viciously. The smoldering coals came alive in a shimmering red glow, and fine ash dust scented the air. "I'd have a word with you as well, Annie O'Brien," he said gruffly. "I'm wondering why you had to go wag your tongue to my mother and worry her about what's between you and me."

Annie's eyes widened and her dimpled chin quivered with indignation. "Waggin' me tongue, was I? That's the most unkind thing ye've ever said to me, Michael. I was crying my eyes out and wringing my hands when I walked out of the confessional. And Sorcha, loving me as she does, wanted to know what was wrong. I couldn't

190

lie to her with my soul just newly cleansed, now could I?''

"No. I suppose that would have been too much to ask,'' Michael muttered as he yanked a heated rod from the fire and threw it down on the anvil.

She breathed a sigh of relief. "I'm glad you understand. Your mother's a fine woman, and I'm looking forward to being her daughter-in-law.''

Michael held the rod over the cleft and brought the hammer down with all his might. He cut the rod with one blow, scattering a shower of sparks onto the floor. The sound echoed off the stone walls, making his ears ring with the metallic reverberations. He saw Annie cringe and it gave him a feeling of satisfaction, but even that was tinged with shame.

After all, he had touched her in a way that was totally forbidden, even if it was done more frequently among unmarried people than most folks were willing to admit.

She had every right to assume that he loved her and wanted to marry her. Everyone in the village assumed that Michael and Annie would wed. He had lived with the O'Briens all these years, and it was a natural conclusion, considering his relationship with Kevin.

Michael had never courted another, and the only woman anyone had ever seen him give the twinkle of his eye to was Caitlin. And everyone in Lios na Capaill knew that Caitlin wasn't the kind of woman a man married.

"Annie . . .'' Michael set the iron bar and his hammer aside and wiped his hands on his leather apron. "We aren't ready to be married and—''

"I'm ready. I'm ready this very day.''

"But are you sure that I'm the one you want? You've said yourself that I'm a strange one, always dreamin'

191

of things to carve and with my head in the clouds. Is that the kind of husband you're after?"

She stepped up to him and reached out to take his work-blackened hands in hers. But she hesitated and clasped his wrists instead. He tried to pull away, but she held on tightly and he would have had to hurt her hands to be free of her.

"You're the one I want, Michael McKevett," she said without hesitation. "I've never loved another ... even if you have," she added, her lower lip protruding in one of Danny's pouts. "I know that I won't be your first."

"I've never loved another." *At least, not as completely as I wanted,* he silently qualified, thinking of how he and Caitlin had been interrupted by the Black Oaks that night by the riverside.

She beamed and threw her arms around his neck in a strangling grasp. "I knew it. I knew that you've loved only me. When shall we do it, Michael?"

"Do ... do what?"

"Get married, of course. Father Brolin said that we should be wed as soon as possible, before our fleshly lust leads us into more sin."

"Oh, he did, eh?" Michael silently cursed the young father. What did a priest know about lust, fleshly or otherwise?

"Can we do it right away, Michael? Let's don't wait. There's no reason to wait, is there?"

Michael walked over to the window. Looking up to the crooked peak of Carrantuohill, he wished himself there, wished himself anywhere on God's green earth but here. This dainty girl, with all of her feminine ways, had her fist around his throat and was dragging him to the altar—whether he wanted to go or not.

Michael knew how to fight against another man, no matter what his size or his temper. But what chance did a man have if he tried to fight against a woman, a golden-haired, blue-eyed lass who had decided that, because you were foolish enough to let your hand stray a bit, she would be your wife?

And even if he put the thought of Annie aside, he still owed Kevin. What kind of man took advantage of a friend's daughter and then avoided his responsibility to her? Not an honorable man, to be sure. And Michael carried enough sins from the past. He didn't want to add to his burden by violating his conscience today.

From the window he watched a horse galloping down the village street, a white stallion carrying a tall, dignified rider wrapped in a gray cloak. The rider pulled up his horse in front of O'Leary's pub, dismounted and swept inside, the cape billowing around him. An arrow of jealousy found its mark in Michael's chest, and he winced from the pain. He turned to Annie who waited, her blue eyes wide and expectant.

"No, Annie, there's no reason to wait," he said. "Let's do it right away and have it done. But I'll tell you this much. In the years to come, I don't want to hear you crowing about how you forced me to marry you." Her face fell again, and he could see her preparing to cry. "I'm marrying you because it's the decent thing to do under the circumstances, and because I want to have a family." He paused, then decided to tell her the rest. "And I think I should warn you that I'm not in love with you. I'm sorry if that hurts, Annie, but you should know before you marry me."

To his surprise, her face registered only mild disappointment. "Ah, Michael, you love me. You just don't know it yet." She reached up and cupped his chin in her palms. "And I don't care why you're marryin' me, as long as we're wed."

Caitlin bade the Gannon brothers a good night and sighed tiredly as she glanced around the nearly-empty pub. Only Mason remained. He sat at his corner table, wearing the self-satisfied smile that had made Caitlin uneasy all evening. He had been watching her, even more than usual, as she had moved among her customers. His gray eyes had a bitter gleam that made her wonder what secret he was harboring.

"I'll have another brandy, Miss O'Leary." He lifted his empty glass. "And a pint of your best ale while you're at it."

Ale? Mason never drank ale. He was behaving strangely tonight, indeed, she thought as she drew the pint.

"Brandy and ale is a quare mix," she said, setting the glass and mug on his table. "Ye'll have a bellyache sure if ye go puttin' both in your stomach at once."

He reached out and grasped her wrist. "The brandy is mine. The ale is for you. You've had a busy evening, and you deserve a pint of your own fine brew." Pulling her down into the chair across the table from him, he added. "Besides, I'm celebrating tonight, and I'd like you to join me in a toast."

"And what are we toasting?" she asked warily, pulling her arm out of his grasp.

"I have some good news about a friend of ours." He ran his long fingers around the edge of his glass and watched her carefully. "One of my informants earned himself a pretty pence for this tidbit."

Her fingers tightened around the handle of the mug. "Whose good fortune are we toasting, Your Honor?"

she asked. But somehow she knew the answer before he uttered the words.

"To Michael McKevett ..." He lifted his glass and touched its rim to her mug. "... and to his bride-to-be."

Caitlin felt her heart stop, and time slowed to a crawl. As though from far away she heard herself ask, "His bride? Michael is gettin' married?"

"Yes, indeed. The fair Annie O'Brien has consented to be his wife."

Caitlin couldn't speak. She couldn't even move. Michael and Annie? When had this happened? Only this morning she had vowed to tell Michael about Armfield. If she had summoned the courage, would it have made any difference?

"Well?" Armfield was watching her closely, a wry smile on his face. "Aren't you going to drink to your friends' health and happiness?"

Without a word she lifted the mug and swallowed a long draught. And for the first time since Caitlin could remember, the famous O'Leary ale tasted bitter on her tongue.

Chapter Ten

Judy put the last stitch into the hem of Annie's new nightgown, bit off the thread with her teeth, and carefully wrapped the needle in its paper before presenting the gown for Annie's inspection.

"There. It's a fine job I did, and on such short notice," she said, fingering the lace collar and the delicately embroidered pink roses on the bodice.

Annie groaned as she rose from her prayer stool beside the fire. She had knelt there for over an hour, paying the penance for her transgression with Michael by saying her rosary. Taking the nightgown from her sister, she held it up to her chin. "Only two more days," she said. "I can hardly wait to be Annie McKevett. Isn't that a grand name, Judy? Annie Mc-Kev-ett." She rolled the word off her tongue, as though savoring the taste of each syllable.

Judy sighed and put the needle, thread and her mother's bone thimble back into the sewing box that Michael had made for her. She had sewn day and night on that gown, and a simple "I thank you" from Annie would have been nice to hear. But that wasn't Annie's way.

She slid the box into her keeping hole, a small recess in the side of the hearth. Each member of the family had their own alcove where they kept their most personal belongings. Kevin's held his pipe and tobacco, Annie's her prayer book, Michael's his carving chisels, and Daniel's housed the menagerie that Michael had carved for him.

" 'Tis a fine name and a fine husband you'll be getting," Judy said. "Michael's a treasure, to be sure, and it's lucky you are to have him. So big and strong and handsome. You're the envy of every girl in Kerry."

"Do you think so, really?" Annie sat down on a stool beside Judy, carelessly crumpling the gown in her lap.

"If I weren't mad in love with Sean, you'd see my brown eyes turn Erin green." Judy glanced around and leaned toward her sister, her glossy locks falling in a black curtain across her cheeks. She lowered her voice to a whisper. "Are you looking forward to it ... the wedding night, that is?"

Annie's mouth dropped open and she blushed violently. "Why, Judy O'Brien! What sort of thing is that for one sister to ask another? 'Tis ashamed I am of you."

"Oh, Annie, you're always ashamed about something you needn't be. You and Michael will be husband and wife, one flesh, as Father Murphy says. There's no shame in your comin' together as man and woman."

Annie put both hands over her ears and shook her head. "Hush. I won't listen to such talk from you. Those things aren't to be spoken of. 'Tis bad enough they must be done to bring children into the world."

In exasperation Judy reached over and pulled Annie's hands away from her ears. "They aren't bad things. They're nice things, and I can hardly wait until

Sean and I can be wed. It's happy I'll be to finally lie beside him."

Judy O'Brien, if I didn't know better I'd think that you two have already ... fornicated."

"We have not. At least, not all of it. But we did do just some little things, and they were lovely to do."

Annie rose, snatched her dress from the chair and stomped across the floor to the ladder. "I never thought I'd hear anything so disgusting in all me days. And I'm not looking forward to any of it. Father Brolin told me to just lie still, close my eyes and think of the Blessed Virgin. And that's what I intend to do."

Judy watched as Annie and her nightgown disappeared into the loft bedroom. The look on her face was one of amazement, tinged with pity. *Lie still, close your eyes and think of the Virgin?* she thought. *My, that doesn't sound like much fun at all, at all.*

Glimmering shafts of sunlight filtered through the leaves of the trees, sprinkling the dense woods with golden patches of fairies' dust. As Michael carefully picked his way through lacy ferns and around bramble bushes, he could sense the Wee People watching him. Forest sprites, leprechauns and all manner of fairies, good and mischievous, had lived in these woods long before Saint Patrick had set foot on the emerald isle. Of course, the priests denounced the belief of such spirits as foolish pishogue, the tales of old widows.

But Michael didn't have to see the Good People to know they were there, crouching behind the moss-covered rocks, sitting on the limbs above his head, watching his every move.

Ahead to the left of the path he saw what he had been searching for all morning. A fallen tree, broken by last night's storm. It was an arbutus, a strawberry tree, named for the tiny red berries that were so fair to the eye and so bitter to the tongue. *Not unlike women,* Michael thought ruefully.

He walked up to the splintered tree and laid his hand on the flaky bark of its gnarled trunk. Closing his eyes, he took a deep breath and gathered an unseen force deep inside himself. He sent it out through his palms to the spirit of the tree ... a message of comfort, conveying his understanding of its misfortune. After several moments he felt that his message had been received and a bond had been established between the carpenter and the living wood. He pulled his axe from its sheath on his back, swung and buried the blade in the tree's flesh, knowing that the arbutus understood its sacrifice was not in vain.

Michael went through this ritual every time he cut into a tree. No one had taught him to revere the life and soul of the wood; he simply knew.

He supposed that if his fellow villagers saw him trying to communicate with a tree, they would consider him daft entirely. But it didn't matter. He only did this when he was alone in the forest with no one to see, no one to judge, no one to ridicule. Or, at least, Michael thought he was alone.

Caitlin stood behind a tree to his left, watching his solemn rite. She had been walking through the forest, trying to escape the terrible sadness that overwhelmed her every time she thought of Michael's coming marriage. She had come upon him suddenly, and she was fascinated by his ritual that she had never seen before, but somehow recognized deep in her spirit.

"What were you doing just now?" she asked.

"What?" He nearly sliced off his foot with the axe. He whirled around and saw her standing there among the trees, looking like the incarnation of Erin herself, her copper hair glowing in a shaft of sunlight that spilled down on her from a break in the branches overhead. For a moment he seemed happy to see her. Then the old, guarded look came into his eyes, and he turned his back to her.

"You shouldn't sneak up behind a man when he's choppin' wood," he said irritably, as he brought the axe down and buried it deep in the wood. "I thought you were one of the Good People come to visit me. 'Tis a wonder I didn't lame meself."

"I'm sorry. Why are you so angry with me, Michael?" Her amber eyes were soft with pleading. "What have I done to you?"

"I just told you. You nearly caused me to cut off me—"

"No, not that," she interrupted. "I'm wondering why it is that you've not been by the pub in so long, and why you wouldn't even look at me when we met on the road the other day. The last time we talked was when you gave me the sign you carved, and I thought we parted friends—good friends."

"I'm gettin' married, Caitlin," he said simply as though that explained everything.

"I know, I heard." She remembered the night when Armfield had told her and the knife of her pain cut deeper. Why hadn't Michael told her himself? What had she said or done that would make him so furious with her? "Good fortune to you and Annie. May you live long together and die in Ireland." Her tone was less congratulatory than her words. She walked around the fallen tree so that she could see his face. "But does that mean you and I can't be friends anymore? Can't you still come into my pub for a pint and some conversation?"

200

"I'd think you'd have plenty of conversation with His Honor," he said bitterly. "Or have the two of you no time for talking when you visit his house at sunset?"

He knew. The realization sliced through her as keenly as his axe cut the tree. He knew after all—and he hated her. Hot tears flooded her eyes as her ruddy complexion turned dark red. She hung her head and bit her lip.

"Ah, Caitlin, you mustn't cry." He took a step toward her and held out his hand, palm upward. "I'm sorry. I shouldn't have said that. What you do is none of my concern. Lord knows, I've no right to cast stones in your direction."

She shook her head and refused to take his hand. She heard the conciliatory tone in his voice, but her shame wouldn't allow her to touch him. "When did you find out?"

"A few weeks ago His Honor asked me up to the house to talk about doing some carpentry for him. When I left I saw you arriving by the back road." He lowered his voice and added, "I didn't think you were delivering poteen."

She thought of the long nights when she had tossed and turned, wondering how to tell him, trying to summon her courage. But he had known all along. "Is that why you've been avoiding me?" she asked in a small, shaking voice. "Do you despise me now that you know?"

To her surprise and relief, he put his hands on her shoulders and pulled her against his chest. "No, of course not." His big hand smoothed her hair as though he were comforting a child, and her tears flowed even faster.

As she slipped her arms around his waist and hugged him to her, it occurred to her that she would never be able to hold him this way again. A harsh, dry ache squeezed her throat. "I love you, Michael," she sobbed. "Please, don't hate me."

"I don't hate you, Caitlin," he whispered, his lips against her cheek. "I just hate the thought of you being with another man. Any other man . . . except me."

His words surprised them both. She pulled back and looked up at him. For a long time they stood, staring into each other's eyes, searching for the words that shouldn't—couldn't—be spoken.

Finally, she closed her eyes, leaned forward and rested her forehead on his broad shoulder. "Ah, Michael . . . if you feel that way about me, what are you doin' marryin' another?"

"I, Michael McKevett, take you, Annie O'Brien, to be my lawfully wedded wife . . ."

The words of the solemn vow he had uttered echoed over and over in Michael's mind as he watched his friends and family lift their glasses for the tenth toast of the evening proposed by Michael's new father-in-law.

Kevin was definitely on the sunny side of the world, as he hoisted his poteen and wished the newlyweds health, happiness, prosperity, and many children. The celebration would be long remembered as having more than enough food, drink and music to keep the guests, who filled the house and spilled out into the yard, deliriously happy.

Michael looked down at Annie who hadn't left his side for a moment since the ceremony at the church. Her blue eyes glittered with triumph as she clung possessively to his arm.

Again he thought of the sacred vows he had made only an hour ago. When he had spoken those words he had meant them sincerely. But as he had stood before the priest and his friends and repeated that promise of undying love, he had seen another face before him, a face with golden freckles, wreathed in copper curls. He had spoken those vows to the woman who was in his heart, not the one he had held by the hand.

Did that make him somehow less married to Annie? Was it the secret intentions that bound the heart, or was it the spoken word alone that married a man to a woman?

Michael didn't have time to decide before his friends lifted him with many a grunt and groan onto their shoulders and carried him and his bride out into the yard where the fiddlers were tuning and the pipers, eager to play, ran nimble fingers over their tin whistles. The deep thud of the bodhran vibrated through the night, and the dancing began.

Michael took Annie's hand and led her to the center of the circle of dancers. He could feel her excitement, her joy, and it was contagious. Before he had finished whirling her through the eight-hand reel, he was caught up in the celebration of their union.

Kevin, Judy, and Sean moved among the guests, plying them with drink, making sure that they had fresh-baked cakes with sweet butter for their knives and tobacco for their pipes. It would never be said in Kerry that Kevin O'Brien hadn't given his daughter a decent wedding. Kevin had kept two distillers from the Gap of Dunloe busy for a fortnight, producing enough poteen to lay an army low. And low his guests were laid. One by one as the night went on they found a place to quietly, and some not so quietly, pass out, until the place looked like a battle field littered with corpses. But these soldiers suffered no pain from their afflictions.

Only the hardiest souls survived, those who had drunk less or could hold their liquor better. In the late hours of the night the musicians succumbed to the excesses of drink and song, and the dancers sought other entertainment on Michael's wheel.

"What's these things ye've put on here now, Michael?" asked old Bridget, the midwife, as she hoisted her skirts, crawled onto one of the log horses and sat facing the wrong way. The quality and quantity of the poteen that Bridget had consumed that night would have made a rabbit spit at a dog.

"They're horses. Can't you tell?" Danny piped as he climbed aboard the animal in front of hers. "And yer lookin' at his arse," the boy added, collapsing in a fit of giggles. He was still full of vinegar despite the late hour.

"I knew that," Bridget said as she turned around to face forward. Her speech was slurred and her movements none to graceful, but she accomplished the feat without mishap.

Paul Gannon, the gravedigger from Carrantouhill, mounted the third horse, and even Father Murphy lifted the long skirt of his black cossack and climbed onto the fourth horse.

Michael braced his shoulder against the suspended bar and pushed. The wheel gathered momentum with every circuit until the riders whirled through the air, screaming in childish delight. For the next hour or so Michael pushed while they took turns riding ... everyone, that is, except Annie. And Michael reveled in their joy, temporarily forgetting his wedding and the reason for the celebration.

It was well after midnight when Michael left the wheel for the others to turn and joined Annie, Sean and Judy by the front door of the cottage.

"You'd better save your strength, Michael," Sean

advised him, puffing on his pipe. "You'll be too spent to do your duty to your new bride."

Judy giggled and blushed. Annie raised her nose two inches in the air and looked sorely offended.

Michael didn't answer. He should be looking forward to "doing his duty" to his new wife, but for some reason, he wasn't. In fact, it was a thought that he was putting out of his mind for as long as he could.

"That's a wonderful invention you've got there, my son," Father Murphy said as he walked over to join them. He carefully straightened his cossack skirt and combed through his few remaining strands of silver hair with his fingers. "Such a machine is a boon for mankind. 'Tis good for the soul to be a child again, even for a few moments."

"I think it's a frivolous toy that does nothing to glorify God," said Father Brolin, who had joined the group in time to hear the older priest's benediction.

Father Brolin's criticism was answered with stony silence from Michael, who objected to having his marvelous wheel called frivolous. Father Murphy was equally resentful; he didn't like being contradicted, especially before the members of his flock.

"I don't see why everyone's making such a fuss over it," Annie said. Michael looked down at her and saw the bitterness on her pretty face that had shone with happiness only an hour before. "It's just an old wheel with some silly looking log horses on it."

Michael wasn't surprised at Annie's reaction. Her nose was always out of joint when she wasn't the center of attention, but he was surprised at his own reaction to her jealousy. He was furious with her, far more angry than he would have been had she attacked him personally. Everyone thought the wheel and horses were wonderful—everyone except Father Brolin, who didn't count, and Michael's new wife. What did it matter if the whole county praised his invention if his own family didn't take pride in his accomplishment?

" 'Tis a fine wheel, Michael," Judy said gently, laying her hand on his shoulder. "Annie's just jealous because your wheel is getting more attention than her, and her the bride."

"Maybe you should take Sweet Annie upstairs now and give her a bit of attention yourself, so that she won't feel neglected," Sean suggested with a knowing smirk and a nod toward the cottage door.

Michael looked down at Annie's hostile face, and he felt a healthy resentment toward her. The joy of the evening was gone for him anyway. Her insult to his invention had thrown a bucket of water on his mood, and all he wanted was to be away from her. Alone he could recapture some of the joy he had felt watching his friends and neighbors enjoy his wheel. For those brief moments he had felt a part of the community, accepted, respected, even embraced. But he couldn't afford the luxury of a long walk tonight. He was a husband, and husbands had certain duties to their wives. Besides, no one present, including his wife, would understand his reluctance to climb that ladder with his bride and take what was his manly right to take.

"Come along, Annie," he said gruffly as he led her into the house with many encouraging hoots and cheers from the guests. "I wouldn't want you to feel neglected on your wedding night."

Even the cemetery at the edge of town wasn't far enough away. As Caitlin knelt at the foot of her father's grave, she could still hear the merrymaking at Michael's and Annie's ceili. Every Irish man, woman, and child in Lios na Capaill was celebrating their marriage—except Caitlin. Once again John O'Leary's daughter found herself on the outside looking in.

Of course, she had been invited with the rest of the villagers, but she had decided to spare herself the ordeal. She couldn't bear to see Annie's radiant, triumphant face. It would be even more painful to see Michael. If he was smiling, happy to be married to another woman, Caitlin would be heartbroken. If he looked frustrated and trapped, she would feel just as bad. Caitlin tried to hope that he would be content with Annie. There was no point in them both being miserable.

"Annie and Kevin got him at last, Da, just as you said they would," she whispered, carefully laying half of her freshly-picked flowers on his grave and half on her mother's. She sat down in the wet grass and pulled her cloak around her shoulders, fighting back the tide of emotions that threatened to overwhelm her.

Until today, when she had stood in her empty pub and listened to the church bells toll Michael's wedding bans, Caitlin had never realized how badly she had wanted to be married to Michael McKevett.

The women of the village often said, "It's a lonely wash that hasn't a man's shirt in it." But Caitlin had never thought her wash lonely until today. She, Caitlin O'Leary, needed a man after all. She needed Michael. But today he had married another woman.

Could it be that Michael was truly in love with Annie? Had she been deluding herself that she was the one he loved?

She remembered his lips on hers that night by the river, the fire in his eyes when he had touched her. No, Michael loved her. So, how had this happened? Why wasn't she the one lying beside him tonight?

Was he holding Annie the way he had held her? Caitlin tried not to think about it. If she thought about them now, she would cry, and she was determined not to shed any tears over Michael McKevett. From the merry sounds that drifted down the street toward her, she guessed that he wasn't shedding any over her tonight.

Looking up at the waning moon that dangled in the dark sky just above the pointed top of the ancient round tower, Caitlin shook her head sadly. Michael's marriage was cursed from the very start. Everyone knew that happy marriages were made when the moon was growing and the tide flowing.

"Let him be happy," she told the moon. "Let them live together in peace and grow old together with grace." But she didn't believe that the moon heard her. Because in the deepest part of her heart, Caitlin knew that she didn't really want Michael to be happy with any woman other than herself.

"Can't I open my eyes yet, Annie?"

"Not yet."

He peeped with one eye and caught a glimpse of her thin body wriggling into a long white nightgown.

"I saw you peeking, Michael McKevett. I hid my eyes while you undressed. You could be a gentleman and do the same for me."

"But I didn't mind if you looked," he said irritably as he burrowed deeper beneath the new quilt that had been a wedding gift from Judy. "And I don't know why you won't let me open my eyes. I've seen you in your nightgown a hundred times or more."

"Not in this nightgown. All right, you can look now."

Michael opened his eyes, and the sight that greeted

his eyes melted his anger. Annie looked like an angel. Her long golden hair flowed onto a snowy linen nightgown that was decorated with more ribbons and fancy embroidering than he had ever seen. He recognized the lace collar as the one that Judy usually wore on her blue Sunday mass dress.

" 'Tis a vision of loveliness, Annie," he said, trying to express enough appreciation to please her. "Is that what you and Judy have been sewing all those times when you wouldn't let me see what it was?"

"Indeed. Do you like it?" she asked shyly.

"I do."

Michael spoke the truth. He liked the gown and even more, the thought that she cared enough to do all that sewing just to please him on their wedding night. But he wished she didn't look so holy in it, so like the Blessed Virgin herself, innocent and untouchable. He was already wondering how he would bring himself to lie with her. When he had kissed her and touched her breasts, it had felt so wrong, as though he were violating a child, a member of his own family. In this nightgown she looked more like his sister, Annie, not his new bride.

This wasn't the way Michael had planned his wedding night, not at all as he had imagined it over and over again on long winter nights, when loneliness had overwhelmed him. But then, he had never imagined spending this night with Annie. His dreams had always been of a red-haired lass and in his fantasies she hadn't been wearing a white nightgown that covered her from neck to wrists to toes.

"What are ye thinking of this minute, Michael?" Annie asked suspiciously as she stood, looking down at him from the side of the bed.

Michael felt the flush of guilt and anger heat his

face. He had no right to be thinking of another woman on his wedding night. Yet, it seemed now that even his thoughts were not his own. Did marriage mean that a woman owned every secret of your soul? Was nothing his own anymore?

"Come to bed, Annie," he said with a gruffness that surprised and pleased him. There. That was how a husband kept his wife in line. If she began prying into that which didn't concern her, he would simply be stern with her and avoid the issue.

She gingerly lifted the quilt and sheet with thumb and forefinger and slid in beside him. Her mood had changed abruptly from shyness to simmering hostility, as though she had read his thoughts of Caitlin after all. She sat with her arms crossed protectively across her tiny breasts, her bottom lip protruding absurdly.

"You've been so cross with me, Michael, ever since you asked me to marry you." She flounced around beneath the quilt like a setting hen rearranging her nest.

"And just when was that, Annie?" he asked, unable to control the bitterness in his voice. "When did I ever ask you to marry me? You were the one who wanted to be wed so badly if I remember."

Tears filled her blue eyes. "I thought you wanted to marry me, too. You said that you loved me. And you touched me the way a man touches a woman when—"

"Annie, hush." He leaned over her and pushed her back against the pillow. The quilt fell low around his hips, revealing his nakedness. He saw her quickly avert her eyes in embarrassment. "I'll not quarrel with you on our wedding night. It's not right. If you're still upset with me come morning, we can fight then. Does that suit you?"

She nodded.

"Are you easy then?" He stroked her forehead with his fingertips.

She bit her lower lip and nodded again, but she didn't feel at ease. Her body was hard and tense beneath his, and her hands were clenched into fists at her sides.

He bent his head to kiss her, but she turned her face away. So, he placed the kiss on her cheek instead. He tasted the salt of a tear and his conscience smote him again. Was it so obvious that he wasn't in love with her?

His hands moved slowly over her arms, trying to soothe her wounded feelings. "Ah, Annie," he murmured. "We've been such good friends for so long. Can't we still be friends even though we're wed? I'd hate for marriage to change what's between us."

"I just don't want you to be sorry that you married me," she said tearfully, sniffing in his ear.

He cupped her chin with his hand and held her face still while he brought his lips down on hers. There was nothing to say. He didn't trust himself to look into her eyes, afraid that she would see his heart wasn't hers.

His lips moved over hers and found them less soft and pliable then they had been that night in the meadow. She accepted the kiss, but gave nothing in return.

Closing off all feelings and thoughts, Michael moved his hand from her chin, down her slender neck and over the embroidered bodice of the nightgown. He could feel her heart pounding against his palm, and he wondered if it were from fear, or anger, or both.

"Could we put out the light?" she asked in a small, trembling voice.

"Surely." Michael licked his thumb and forefinger,

reached over to the nightstand beside the bed and squeezed the wick of the candle between his fingers.

The darkness helped. He couldn't see the wounded look in her eyes and he didn't have to worry about her seeing his guilt.

His hand moved back to her chest and with infinite care he stroked her small breast through the nightgown. When his fingertips eased the linen aside and slipped inside the gown, a liquid heat surged through his loins. Michael felt betrayed by his body's response. This was wrong somehow. He and Annie might be married, but it was still wrong.

The moment he touched the silken tip of her bare breast with his thumb, he remembered a moonlit night and another breast, but he cast the thought from his mind. It was surely adultery for a man to think of another woman while loving his wife.

"What's wrong, Michael?" came the small voice in the dark. "Don't you find me as womanly as Caitlin?"

He caught his breath and pulled away from her. How had she known? Had she the fairies' gift of reading minds?

"What are you talking about?"

"Don't pretend that you don't know," she said. "I followed the two of you the night of the ceili. I saw what you did together there under the trees. I saw how you touched her and did those dreadful things to her."

"You watched us?" Michael felt a rage greater than his shame swell inside him, nearly to bursting. "You—you spied on us?"

"I saw you walk away with her, holding her hand and whispering in her ear. I needed to know what my husband-to-be was doing."

Michael leaped out of the bed, eager to get away from

her as quickly as possible. "I wasn't your husband-to-be then. You had no right. No right at all!"

He found his breeches and shirt in the darkness and pulled them on. At that moment he hated her, hated her through and through. How could she have watched them? Had she no shame at all?

"Michael, what are you doing? Where are you going?" she cried.

"I'm going to get away from you before I say or do something to you that a man mustn't do to his wife."

"But Michael, you can't go away and leave me alone on our first night together. We didn't . . . you know."

"I'll not make you mine tonight, Annie." He went to the bedroom door and opened it. "I'm afraid that if I lay me hands on you now, it'll surely be to wring your neck."

Michael tiptoed down the ladder and through the house. The guests who could stand and walk had gone. The others lay strewn across the kitchen floor, wrapped in their heavy woolen cloaks. Old Bridget was sprawled across the kitchen table, her toothless mouth gaping. Beneath the table lay Paul Gannon and his brother, Eoin.

Michael could hear Kevin's raucous snoring through the closed door of the downstairs bedroom. Watching his step, Michael left the cottage and closed the door quietly behind him. It wouldn't do for his friends and neighbors to see him deserting his marriage bed.

Once outside, Michael put as much distance behind him as quickly as possible. He made his way through the sleeping village, across the meadow and past the fairy fort toward the river. The half moon in the sky gave enough light for him to pick a path along the river's slippery bank. Then he crossed the stone bridge and climbed a small hill that overlooked the town.

When he finally reached the crest of the hill, he stopped,

213

his energy spent but not his anger. The very thought of Annie watching him and Caitlin in the forest made him sick with fury. That evening by the river with Caitlin had been the loveliest night of Michael's life, and Annie had turned it into something shameful and sinful. He would never forgive her for that. Though she wasn't likely to ask for forgiveness. In her mind she had done nothing wrong.

He sat on a large boulder, wet with heavy dew, and looked down from the mountain slope on the moonlit landscape below. It was a clear, crisp night with no fog or rain. From his vantage point he saw Lios na Capaill, two neat rows of cottages and shops lining the one main road, their thatched roofs gleaming gold and silver in the moonlight. At the end of the road stood the church with its surrounding cemetery and the ancient round tower.

His eyes carefully avoided O'Leary's pub and Kevin O'Brien's cottage. He had come up here to temporarily escape his problems, and from this high point he could almost believe that he had left those troubles below in the valley. The scene was always the same; Lios na Capaill didn't change without warning, like the people he loved.

Michael saw the meadow that stretched down to the bog and the river. In the center of that field was the dark circle of pines, the fairy fort. He thought of the enchanted dream the fort had given him, but no joy came from the memory. The dream was too far away tonight, too far even to touch, let alone grasp.

To Michael's left lay Armfield House, gray, somber, solitary, like its master. As always, the cobbled courtyard was empty, save for the shadowy shapes of wagons and farm implements. As Michael watched he thought that perhaps one of the shadows moved, then another, but he couldn't be sure.

Slowly he became aware that something in the village

was different tonight, after all. When Michael had come up to this lonely place before, he had found peace and solitude. But tonight there was danger in the darkness; he sensed it vibrating through the still, moist air, prickling along the back of his neck, raising his hackles. Something was wrong.

A blast shattered the silence. A gunshot. Followed by three more. Michael sprang to his feet as the sound echoed through the sleepy glen. He knew instinctively who was shooting and what had happened. The Black Oaks had tried to rob Mason Armfield of his fine guns.

Michael watched breathlessly as a dozen men bearing torches poured into the courtyard of the great house, then mounted horses and fanned out to search the countryside. He heard the baying of the hounds as they were set on the trail.

So at least some of the Oaks had escaped, Michael reasoned. But who? And who, if anyone, had been shot? He thought of Cornelius and his gift of the gloves. *God, don't let it be Cornelius,* he prayed. He thought of William's merry piping, and Quirke's bawdy, seaman's humor. *Don't let it be them either.* He thought of Rory Doona lying dead, a bullet parting his black hair. The thought of Rory dead didn't sadden Michael at all. Any man who lived by the code of violence, was bound to die by the hand of violence.

Then a chillingly vivid picture flooded Michael's mind— Mason Armfield robbed and killed. For some reason the image of Armfield murdered disturbed Michael deeply. He didn't want the man dead, and he didn't know why.

Perhaps it was because Armfield loved horses, or because he loved Caitlin O'Leary. And any man who loved beauty deserved better than to be murdered in his own home.

Chapter Eleven

"Bless me, Father, for I have sinned..." Annie felt as though she had transgressed more in the past month than in the whole of her twenty years combined. "God is punishing me for the sins I committed with my husband before we were married, the ones I told you about at my last confession."

"And did you do your penance as I instructed you, child?" Father Brolin's voice warmed her all over as it reached out to console her through the thin curtain that separated them.

"I did, but it wasn't enough. God is punishing me by taking the love of my husband and giving it to another woman."

"God would never deny a woman the love of her husband. Only the man himself would do that. How do you know that he loves another, Annie?"

"Last night ... last night after the wedding, when we should have ... come together ..."

"Yes?"

"We didn't."

"Then the marriage wasn't consummated?"

"Ah, no. I don't think so." She hoped that the priest

wouldn't require details as he had before. It had embarrassed her terribly to talk about distasteful matters of the flesh with such a holy man.

"Did he cleave unto you, Annie? Did you become one flesh?"

"No. We argued and he left without ... doing it to me."

"And what did you argue about?"

"Caitlin O'Leary."

There was a long silence on the other side of the curtain. Annie wondered if Father Brolin had heard her. Then he said, "Is Caitlin O'Leary the woman who you fear has stolen the love of your husband?"

"Most surely, Father. I know it. I saw them not long ago in the woods at night. They were kissing and—and he was touching her the way he touched me that time."

"And you still chose to marry this man, knowing what a sinner he was? I'm surprised and ashamed of you, Annie. You've always been such a good, decent woman."

Annie couldn't bear the reproach. From old Father Murphy perhaps, but not from Father Brolin. He seldom had anything but praise for her piety. "I'm sorry, Father," she said, choking back a sob. "I tried not to love Michael. I know that he doesn't come to Mass, and it breaks me heart. And the things he did with that woman, it makes me feel strange and sick inside just to think of it. But what can I do?"

"You must encourage him to come to Mass, Annie. He'll never be able to love you the way he should if he isn't walking close to God and in favor with the Church."

She shuddered to think of how Michael would react if she asked him one more time to go to Mass. She had prodded him as often as she dared over the years, until he had finally told her not to say another word to him.

"But Father, many's the time his precious mother and meself has begged him with tears in our eyes and on bended knee to come to church, and he won't. I think he's done somethin' so terrible that he can't confess it . . . probably with that awful O'Leary woman."

"But you're his wife now, Annie," the priest reminded her. "A wife has great power over her husband, even as Eve had over Adam when she caused him to fall. But a godly woman can lead her husband back to the Church as quickly as to the Devil. What kind of wife do you want to be, Annie McKevett?"

"A godly wife, Father," she sniffed without conviction.

"You must lead him back into the fold. As long as he walks the paths of sin, your Michael is fair game for the evil women of this world, like Caitlin O'Leary."

"Michael, would you put that paper down and pay me some mind? What I'm after tellin' you is more important than those chicken scratches you're making there."

Michael laid his sketching aside on the kitchen table and folded his hands before him. He tried to don his "patient" face, a mask he had been wearing a lot lately. "I heard what you said, Annie, and you heard my answer. I appreciate your concern for my immortal soul, truly I do. But I wish you wouldn't fret so about it. Have ye nothing else in the wide world to occupy your mind?"

She sighed and sat down on a rope-seated chair beside him. "Your saintly mother is right, Michael. You do treat the matters of God lightly. We'll be years prayin' your soul out of purgatory, if you even make it there."

Michael looked down into her sorrowful eyes, which, except for their pale blue color, resembled his mother's. At trying times such as these Michael wondered why God had ever invented a place such as purgatory. Surely a man served his penance here on earth long before his death. Every man Michael knew had gone through hell and back several times while still walking the green earth. But he decided not to share this bit of home-spun theology with his distraught wife.

"What has you so worried about my soul all of a sudden, Annie? I thought you'd given me over to the Devil long ago."

"Well . . . I was talking to Father Brolin this morning and—"

"Ah, yes, the good father." Michael nodded knowingly. "I should have recognized his hand in this. And did he convince you that it's your wifely duty to save your heathen husband?"

Annie ducked her head, and the look on her face made Michael wonder what, indeed, she had told the priest.

"Father Brolin said you'll never be able to love me properly as a husband should when you're so far from the Church and the love of the good God."

So, she had told him everything. Was nothing private, not even the most personal things between a man and wife? The thought of the pious young priest judging Michael's treatment of his wife on their wedding night galled Michael and made him wish that it were at least permissible to give a priest a bit of your mind, if not a taste of your knuckles.

"I'll thank you not to discuss me with your priest again, Annie," he said, gathering up his paper and rolling it tightly. "If it's your own sins you're after confessin' that's fine with me, but I'll confess me own, if you please."

"But Michael, you *don't* confess them. That's what worries me so."

"Worry about yourself, Annie," he said, his hand on the door handle. "Worry about your own sins of self-righteousness and jealousy."

"Self-righteousness? Jealousy? And who would I be jealous of?"

His green eyes pierced hers with an intensity that made her look away uncomfortably. "We both know the answer to that one. Don't we, Annie?"

As Annie watched him leave she seethed inside. How could he accuse her of the sin of jealousy? If he hadn't fornicated with that terrible woman, she'd have no reason to be jealous.

For all she knew, he had gone to Caitlin's bed last night after he'd left hers. The more she thought about it the more certain she was that he had done just that. Where else would he have gone so late at night, except a pub? He was probably going there right now to see that woman.

Annie wasn't one to sit and wonder. She had to know for sure. Taking her blue woolen cloak from a peg on the wall behind the door, she slipped it over her shoulders and followed him.

Several times as Michael hiked through the woods toward town, he thought he heard someone behind him, a dry twig snapping, a rustling in the bushes. When he turned, he saw no one, but he could feel eyes on him, human eyes, not those of the forest spirits.

As he approached the end of the stone bridge that

220

spanned the river, he heard it again, louder this time. There was no mistaking the sound of a shoe scraping on rock. He wheeled around, but the rays of the setting sun caught his eyes. "Who's there? What is it ye want?" he demanded.

A figure stepped out of the dark tunnel beneath the bridge. Michael instantly recognized the dirty face and the black mat of uncombed hair. "Rory! What the devil are ye doing this close to town? You'll be shot on sight if the constable or landlords catch the wind off you."

Michael cast a quick look down the road, but he saw no one. He made his way down the slippery bank toward the water's edge. With an unceremonious shove he pushed Rory back into the tunnel. Inside the viaduct it was musty and dark and smelled of decay and Rory's stale sweat.

"I didn't come in for me pleasure, you can be sure." Rory bristled and brushed his coat with his fingers as though to remove the contamination of Michael's touch. "I've come because of Cornelius."

"Con?" Michael's heart lurched into this throat. "What's wrong with him?"

"He's dying. Could be gone already for all I know. Last night we took some guns from Armfield House, but His Honor's lads caught us as we were leaving and ol' Cornelius took a shot in the chest. He's beggin' for a priest, and I've come to fetch him one."

Michael couldn't bear the thought of Cornelius receiving last rites. Surely there was a way to save him. "How about a doctor? If you could get him to a doctor maybe—"

"And where would we be findin' a doctor that would tend his wounds and not deliver us into the hands of the constabulary? They're Englishmen first and healers second. A poor Irishman's doctor is the Grim Reaper himself." Rory shook his head and picked his jagged front teeth with a dirty fingernail. "A priest is all that Con requires now, thanks to you, Michael McKevett. If you'd been a true friend and helped us, Cornelius would never have been shot."

Michael's temper exploded. He reached for the front of Rory's coat and lifted him onto his toes. "If anyone's to blame for Con's misfortune, 'tis you," he said, his deep voice trembling with anger. "You murdered old Morton Collier, and the others are paying the price for it. You'll not stop until every one of you are dead. That's what it'll take to satisfy the hate in you, Rory Doona. You're a weak man, weak, foolish and cruel. And I despise you for it."

Rory said nothing, but his black eyes burned with fury as he glared up at the man who held him off the ground like a helpless child, the man whose blacksmith hands, scarred as they were, could still straighten horseshoes or break his neck.

Finally Michael released him, and his thoughts turned to Cornelius. "I'll get the priest for Con. I'll find Father Murphy and send him along to you. If you come into town you'll be spotted and hanged, sure, and that won't help poor Cornelius any."

Rory eyed him suspiciously, deciding whether or not to trust him. "You don't know where the lads are holed up, and I'm not after tellin' you."

Michael shrugged. "So, don't tell me. Go along into town yourself if it pleases you. I'm sure I don't care if they stretch your neck from here to Kilorglin. I was only thinkin' of poor Con and him needing a priest."

When Michael turned to walk out of the tunnel, Rory grabbed at his coattail. "So be it—I'll tell ye. But I swear upon me dear mother's grave, Michael McKevett, if you tell a soul I'll see you dead if I have to come back from hell to murder you."

Michael shot him a look of contempt that told the little man he didn't fear him on either side of the grave. "I'd not inform on a fellow Irishman. Not even you, Rory. When I decide it's time to even the score between the two of us, I'll gladly do the deed meself."

Glancing nervously over his shoulder, Rory lowered his voice to a whisper. "They're up on Carrantuohill. There's a sheep shelter on the northern slope that's not been used for years. That's where we hid last night after they set the dogs on us. There's lots of hare in the woods below, and the dogs were too busy sniffing them out to bother with us."

Michael nodded and walked out of the tunnel into the fresh evening air. "I know the spot," he said. "I'll go into the village and tell the good father straight away. Tell Cornelius to hang on, that a priest is coming."

Constable Sheldon stroked the end of his neatly clipped, black moustache thoughtfully as he surveyed the young woman who stood beside his desk. Moments before she had walked into the police barracks—actually, she had sneaked in—and had volunteered the information that he hadn't been able to buy, beg or beat out of the villagers in the past two weeks.

"I must thank you for bringing this matter to my attention, Miss O'Brien."

"I'm Mrs. McKevett now," she corrected him, "I was wed to Michael McKevett last evening."

"Yes ... I had to help several of your guests find their way home last evening. A couple of the more rowdy of them kept me company last night behind bars. Tell

223

me, Mrs. McKevett why you were so kind as to share this bit of news with me?"

"That isn't difficult to figure out," Travis Larcher said. The landlord left the barred window where he had been standing, silently listening to the exchange. He reached into his brocade jacket, pulled out a small leather purse and jingled it before her face. "She heard that I'd offered a handsome reward for the capture of those ruffians who murdered my good steward. Every Irishman has his price, and, apparently, the same holds true for their women."

Constable Sheldon watched with interest and grudging respect as the new Mrs. McKevett lifted her dainty nose in the air and fixed his honor, Travis Larcher, with a baleful glare.

"I'll have none of your blood money, sir. There's many an Irishman and Irishwoman whose honor can't be bought. And among the sorry lot who can be bribed, I'd bet there's a drop or two of Saxon blood flowing through their veins."

The constable almost laughed aloud at the highly offended quirk of his lordship's scraggily brows, but he had too much respect for the lady to make matters worse for her.

"Mrs. McKevett," he said, "how are we to know that what you've told us here is the truth?"

"Why would I lie, sir?"

He studied her thoughtfully, remembering the righteously indignant tilt to her chin when she had announced her information, the way her small chest had swelled with self-importance and her eyes had sparkled with the excitement of one who loves bearing tales. Constable Sheldon knew her type, and he would have hated her, except that people like her made his life so much simpler.

You would lie for the same reason that you would tell the truth, he thought. *To build yourself up at the expense and suffering of others.* But he didn't say these things. There was no point in alienating a useful informant, especially one who informed for free.

"Of course you wouldn't lie, Mrs. McKevett," he said, ignoring Larcher's contemptuous sneer. "You've shown what an honest citizen you are by handing these desperate criminals into the hands of the law. I am deeply in your debt, madam."

She smiled brightly, and Constable Sheldon knew that Annie McKevett had received exactly the compensation she wanted. "You just find that Rory Doona," she said. "Hang that worthless rogue and this village will be a safer place for us all."

"Aye, there's the bridegroom himself. And he doesn't look the worse for wear, lads."

The raucous jibes greeted Michael the moment he stepped into the smoky, ale-scented atmosphere of O'Leary's pub. Those who had celebrated with him until the wee hours of the morning had congregated here in the pub at sundown to wet their already dry gullets and exchange memories of the fine time they had spent at the wedding.

"He looks a mite peaked around the gills to me," observed Paul Gannon from his place beside the fire.

"Probably had a rough night. Must have been all the dancin', or was it climbin' that ladder afterwards with his new missus that wore him out?" Paul's younger brother, Eoin asked. "I believe he's walkin' a bit stiff. What do you say, Sean?"

Sean grinned broadly over the rim of his mug. "Aye, a bit bowed-legged he is, indeed."

The farmers in the corner collapsed, helpless with giggles. Michael tried to ignore the good-natured teasing, but it wasn't easy, considering what had—or hadn't—happened on his wedding night. What would his friends think if they knew that he had spent the better part of the night roaming the countryside instead of bedding his new bride?

Caitlin was busy behind the bar. When he caught her attention, their gaze held for a second or two, long enough for him to see the hurt in her eyes. Her pain confused and angered him. If she felt so bad about him being with another woman, why did she spend her nights in the arms of another man?

He tore his eyes away from hers and walked over to the table against the wall where Kevin sat, drinking and sharing a pipe with Sean. He slid onto the bench next to his father-in-law.

"Where have you been, lad?" Kevin asked, his ruddy face creased with concern. "We were expecting you to join us long ago."

Where, indeed? Michael could hardly tell them about Rory, or how he had searched all over town before finding Father Murphy at the Shaws', praying for their five children who were all stricken with fever.

"I had things to do." Michael said carefully.

"Nothing to do at the forge," Kevin replied with a hint of reproach in his voice.

"You don't need me at the forge now that you have old Sean here and him almost your son-in-law."

"He doesn't need you, 'tis sure," Sean agreed, draining his ale. "But we both like to see your face once in a while. Lately you've been spending all your time messing with that wheel of yours."

"I have plans for it, wonderful plans," Michael said

as he reached into his pocket and pulled out the rolled paper. "Would you like to see?"

Before they could answer, Caitlin leaned over his shoulder, and he felt the warmth of her body as she set a glass of ale on the table before him. Disappointed, he noticed that she didn't place it in his hand as she usually did, nor did she give him the benefit of her smile as she quietly turned and walked away.

Kevin reached out and stayed Michael's hand as he began to unroll the paper. "I'll look at it later, lad. We've news to tell you."

Michael's heart jumped against his ribs. He knew by the excited tenor of Kevin's voice that it was bad news. Every eye in the pub turned toward him. If there was anything better than hearing bad news yourself, it was watching someone else hear it for the first time.

"And what news is that?" he asked reluctantly.

"The Black Oaks struck again last night," Sean said, his words heavy in the smoky air. "It seems they tried to rob Mason Armfield of some of those fine guns of his. But all they got was a bullet. The landlord caught up with them as they were leaving and he thinks he shot one of them. His men brought out the horses and dogs, but by then the lads were well up into the mountains."

Paul Gannon drew on his pipe and puffed a circle of smoke into the air. "That Rory Doona's a fine mountain man. Knows his way all over those slopes, and it'd take a better man than Mason Armfield to find him if he didn't want to be found."

They all nodded in agreement.

"Just think," Sean said, leaning over and clapping a hand on Michael's broad shoulder. "While we were all celebrating the union of Michael and Annie, Rory and his friends were running for the bare life of it. And one of them may be dead this very minute of his wounds.''

Michael stared down at the rolled paper on the table and thought of his wheel, and the beautiful horses that might never have been carved had it not been for Cornelius and his gift of the gloves. Michael thought of the little tailor up on that mountain, in pain, maybe dying without benefit of a priest. If Con died before Father Murphy found him and gave him last rites, would Cornelius go to heaven, purgatory or hell?

Closing his eyes, Michael tried to imagine an eternal resting place for a generous soul such as Cornelius. If there wasn't a place for Con in one of those celestial palaces, perhaps Princess Niav would whisk him away on her enchanted stallion to the Land of the Ever Young. Surely there was a need for a gifted tailor in that bright land, and Cornelius would be happy as long as he could sew.

''Michael, I'm surprised 'tis you who's last to leave tonight,'' Caitlin said as she filled his mug for the final pint of the evening. ''I'd have thought that you'd be eager to be home with your new bride.''

She tried to keep the bitterness out of her voice. Her pride wouldn't allow her to let him see her hurt and disappointment. As she briskly applied a damp cloth to the tabletops, she felt him watching her every move, his eyes caressing her. Anger swelled in her throat until she could hardly breathe. A married man had no right to look at another woman that way. But most of her anger was directed at herself for feeling so much joy just to be alone in the same room with him.

''I waited until the others had gone because I have something to show you, Caitlin,'' he said, taking a roll of paper from inside his shirt. "I didn't think the others would appreciate it the way you would."

She moved around to his side of the table and sat on the bench, taking care not to sit too close to him. But when he pushed his sleeves up to his elbows, the sight of his muscular forearms quickened her pulse and weakened her resolve to keep him at a distance.

Carefully, he unrolled the paper and spread it before them on the table. Caitlin leaned over the drawing, her long copper waves spilling over her shoulders and onto the paper.

"Oh, Michael, what lovely horses!" she exclaimed. "I didn't know you could draw such things."

"Neither did I, until I did it," he said with quiet pride. "No man knows what he can do until he tries."

"But they're so beautiful with the flowers around their necks and those fancy bridles and saddles. Whatever made you think of something so pretty?"

"I saw a picture like this at Armfield House," he said with a hint of jealousy in his voice. "It's called a carousel, a parade of horses decked out in their finest, prancing around in a circle for the lords and ladies to admire."

"But what's this?" Her fingertip traced the giant wheel above the horses' heads. "It looks like the wheel you hung your swings on."

"That's right. I'm going to carve those horses, Caitlin. A feverish light glimmered in his green eyes, a gleam much like the fire she had seen and felt when he had held her beside the river.

"I'm going to carve big horses, like the little toys I carve for Danny and the children. And I'm going to mount them on the wheel so people can ride them. Not just lords and ladies, but common people like you and me, and old Bridget."

As she listened, Caitlin saw his vision clearly and the beauty of it thrilled her. "You could do that, Michael. I know you could. It would be such a fine thing, a wondrous thing to see and to ride. However did you think of it?"

He grinned shyly. "I spent a night in the fairy fort, and it came to me in a grand dream."

She nodded. " 'Twas the fairies brought you the dream. I've always known they favored you, Michael. How else could you carve those horses of yours and draw something out of your head, like this?" She pointed to the paper stretched before them. "How could you have thought of something so wonderful except the Good People sent it to you in a dream?"

He reached out and covered her hand with his. The simple gesture caused her desires to come flooding back. Even though he had married another, she couldn't help loving this man whose touch set her afire. A man who could dream glorious dreams and make his visions realities.

"I thank you, Caitlin, for liking my carousel, for tellin' me that I can make it and that it will be wonderful. I feel it in my heart, but 'tis a joy to hear the words spoken aloud."

She shrugged, but didn't remove her hand from his. "It's the truth. And the truth costs nothing to tell."

"Caitlin, there's somethin' I must say to you ..." The silence grew heavy as he struggled for the right words. Finally, he turned on the bench to face her, and his haunted eyes held hers. "I didn't take Annie last night. I want you to know that. I couldn't touch her and hold her ... the way I did you."

She pulled her hand away and tucked it into her pocket. "Hush, Michael. You mustn't tell me these things. Tomorrow you'll hate yourself for telling me, and me for hearing it."

"I'd never hate you, Caitlin," he said, unable to stop the words from spilling out. "I love you. I always have and I—"

"Michael, no. I don't want to hear you say that." She shook her head and covered her ears with her palms. "If you say it, I'll always remember it and the remembering will only bring more pain. It's too late now."

Circling her waist with his hand, he pulled her toward him on the bench. She shoved her hands against his chest, but they both froze.

From the street outside came a low rumble, an ominous sound that became louder by the moment, the angry, churning roar of a mob spilling into the village.

"Holy Jaysus," he said as they both jumped to their feet and flew to the window.

"What is it, Michael?" she asked, her hands tightly clasping his arm. "What's happening?"

The constable and his men rode down the narrow road. The light from their staves cast eery, dancing shadows on the shops and houses along the street. Villagers poured out of the cottages, men and women in their nightshirts, children by the score, clutching blankets around their bare bodies.

The constabulary led three horses by the reins. Two horses carried riders with bound hands and feet, barely clinging to their mounts. The third horse carried a body draped over its saddle.

"Who are they?" Caitlin asked, her voice a harsh whisper.

When they saw the prisoners' frightened faces,

231

stained red by the light of the torches, Michael's broad shoulders sagged, and he released a long, defeated sigh. "They're me brothers. They're what's left of the Black Oaks."

Chapter Twelve

Michael and Caitlin ran out of the pub into the street and were caught up in the confused swirl of villagers, constabulary, horses and prisoners. They were swept with the throng down the road toward the barracks, the constable leading the macabre parade.

When they reached the barracks, the officers dismounted and pulled their two prisoners from the horses' backs, but they left the corpse draped across the saddle, his hands and feet tied together beneath the horse's belly.

"Leave him there," the constable said, nodding toward the body as he unlocked the door of the barracks. "That one isn't going anywhere."

Caitlin clung to Michael's hand as he fought his way through the crowd, until they stood beside the horse that carried the body. Although Caitlin tried to steel herself against the sight, she still gasped when she saw Cornelius's face. The little tailor had always been so gay in life, but in death his face was grotesque with swollen white skin hanging limply from his jowls, mouth gaping open and dripping blood, sightless eyes staring into eternity.

Horror and fury coursed through her. What a terrible loss this was . . . the waste of a good man in a world where truly good men were hard to find.

She looked up at Michael, and she shuddered to see the rage and grief on his face.

"God damn Rory Doona," he said as he reached down and gently closed the corpse's eyes. "It should have been him, not Con."

"Looks like they've got them sure," said a voice over Caitlin's shoulder. She turned to see Sean and Kevin standing behind her. They, too, were looking down at Cornelius with sorrow on their faces.

"Aye, it's the hanging tree for them this time," Kevin said. "No one can save them now."

The crowd was pushing in on them from all sides. There were cries of shock and grief as friends and relatives of the prisoners realized what had happened.

With an officer on either side, the captives were led to the door of the barracks. But before they could be taken inside, another group of riders charged through the crowd. The leader cracked his heavy whip, lashing anyone who stood in his path. Men, women and even children howled in pain, as the villagers scattered and cleared the way for the landlord and his men.

"So, Constable Sheldon, you've finally caught the bloody bastards," Travis Larcher said when he reached the door of the barracks. "Good job you've done, sir. Now hand the scoundrels over, and I'll take care of them from here."

The constable stared silently up at the landlord whose bay pranced about, as impatient and irritable as its owner. Other than the slight twitch of the constable's thin black moustache, he showed no reaction to the landlord's demand. He turned to his men. "Take the prisoners inside and lock them up, boys."

No sooner had he uttered the words than Larcher nudged his horse into the tight space between the officers and the door. "I'll take them from here," he repeated. "There's no reason for you to bother locking them away. My men have nooses all prepared."

Constable Sheldon stepped up to the bay and caught its bridle in a tight fist. "There will be no lynchings in my village tonight, Your Honor," he said with quiet authority. "These men will remain behind my bars until the magistrate comes through next week. Then they'll have their trial. You're welcome to attend the execution, if you're eager to see a hanging."

Larcher stared down at the constable for a long, silent moment. The only sound was the sizzling and spitting of the turf pike torches. Larcher silently counted the constable's four officers and his own dozen men. Then he smiled unpleasantly at the constable. "I have more troops than you, Sheldon. I'll take these prisoners by force, if I must."

Caitlin couldn't help but admire the constable's courage, though his stand was foolhardy. It was clear that Larcher intended to see the Black Oaks hanging from the trees come morning.

"Well, what will it be, Sheldon?" Larcher asked.

The constable released the horse's bridle. He drew his gun and pointed it directly at Larcher's face. A collective gasp rippled through the crowd. "If you try, Your Honor, you'll pay the price," Sheldon said. "I've never shot an English gentleman. I don't want to do so now, but my duty is clear in this case, and I'll kill you if you force my hand."

From the look on Larcher's face, it was evident that he didn't believe Sheldon. No constable was going to kill a landlord for the sake of two Irish criminals. Sheldon was bluffing, and everyone in the village knew it.

Caitlin saw the terror and the bewilderment in William O'Shea's eyes as he looked up at the landlord who wanted to lynch him. What had Will done to Larcher that he would demand his death? She heard the cries of Margaret O'Shea, William's wife, and his children's sobs. Caitlin's heart broke for her fellow Irishmen. Someone had to do something—but what?

Michael answered her question when he stepped forward to stand beside the constable, placing his formidable bulk between Larcher and the prisoners. Caitlin was terrified for him, but she had never been more proud. She quickly followed his lead, and after a long moment of heavy silence, so did Kevin and Sean. One by one the more courageous of the villagers did the same until the landlord's horse was pushed backward by the sheer force of their numbers.

"You can't take us all, Your Honor," Michael said quietly. "Why don't you just wait for the trial and spare everyone the grief of the fight?"

There was a commotion in the back of the crowd and, once again, the villagers parted to let another rider through. Wrapped in a gray cloak, the man rode a white stallion. His sharp eyes swept the scene, noting every detail, but he said nothing as he brought the horse to a halt beside Larcher's bay.

Without so much as a glance in Armfield's direction, Michael continued his gentle persuasion. "If you lynch them tonight," he told Larcher, "they'll be heroes, and we Irish will be singing their praises for the next ten generations. Is that what you want, sir?"

"These men are coldblooded murderers." Larcher surveyed the crowd that had gathered around the constable with an uneasy eye. "I want to see them hang for killing my agent."

"Then let them have their day in court," Armfield

said, his aristocratic voice resonant in the night air. "It won't make any difference in the end. McKevett is right. If you lynch these criminals, you'll make patriots of them. And, God knows, the Irish have more than enough dead heroes to incite their passions. Give these men a trial, and they'll hang like the common murderers they are."

As the crowd waited tensely for Larcher's decision, Caitlin watched Michael and Armfield. They were staring at each other, looks of mutual respect on their faces. They were very much alike, these two men she loved. It didn't seem strange at all that they would be fighting on the same side. Caitlin thought sadly that if it hadn't been for her, Michael and Armfield might have been friends.

Finally, Larcher reached his decision. He pulled his horse up and rode away from the barracks door, motioning for his men to follow. "They'll have their trial," he shouted over his shoulder. "But I'll not be satisfied until I see them dead and hanging from a tree with the crows picking their corpses. And that goes for Rory Doona, too."

They watched Larcher ride away, followed by his men and Mason Armfield. With a sigh of relief Caitlin turned to Michael. "It seems old Rory was the only one who escaped," she said. "Too bad that if one was to be spared 'twas himself."

"How do you suppose they were captured?" Kevin asked.

"Someone must have informed on them," Sean speculated, "but I can't imagine who would have turned the lads in."

"It doesn't matter who did it," Michael said grimly. "I know who Rory Doona will blame."

Somehow Caitlin knew that Michael was speaking of

himself, and his words sent a shiver through her, a chill of premonition. She looked up at Michael, who towered over her, strong, intelligent, and capable. Rory was a small man whose words were sharper than his teeth, and he was no match for Michael. So why did she have this heavy feeling in the pit of her stomach? She tried to console herself with the thought that Rory was a fool and a coward. But Caitlin knew in her heart, there was no creature on God's green earth who was more dangerous than a foolish coward.

A cold drizzle of rain fell from the gray sky onto the silent throng gathered around the old oak behind the barracks. The black, gnarled limbs of the hanging tree creaked in the wind, sending shudders down the spines of those gathered to witness the executions.

The deep, steady boom of the bodhran filled the wet air, echoing the heartbeat of Erin and her children. Throughout Ireland's troubled history the beat of the bodhran had stirred many a brave heart to rebel and had uplifted those souls going into battle, filling them with courage.

But there was no fight left in the crowd assembled in Lios na Capaill that morning. They were a band of weary soldiers, whose heroes were about to pay the supreme penalty for their rebellion. And the predominant feeling in the crowd assembled beneath the hanging tree was quiet gratitude: thankfulness that they weren't the ones being led from the barracks.

Clearly defined clusters of people represented the different social groups of the village. Larcher and his men stood at the foot of the tree—the spot that afforded the best view. Mason Armfield watched from his horse, alone as usual. Paul Gannon, the gravedigger from Carrantuohill, and his younger brother, Eoin, stood beside the families of the condemned. Paul had already done his work the night before, and two fresh graves waited to receive the mortal remains of Seamus Quirke and William O'Shea.

The O'Brien clan—Kevin, Annie, Daniel, Sean and Judy—stood in a tight knot beside the priests. Michael stood apart, alone, as did Caitlin, who watched from the back of the crowd. Silent tears mixed with the raindrops on her ruddy cheeks.

Shivering, Michael raised the collar of his great coat around his neck and ears. He didn't want to be there. He didn't want to see this. But he had to. These men were his friends, his companions. They would be here if he were the one being hanged.

Seamus Quirke was the first to be led out of the barracks. Michael had never seen the man without his black, wool, seaman's cap pulled down over his head. Now he seemed naked and vulnerable without it, his ginger hair blowing in the cold, damp wind.

With his hands tied behind his back and a stern-faced officer on either side, the old sailor took his place beneath the oak. Quirke stood tall and straight as a mast. His face showed no fear, only hate and contempt for his executioners. Above his beard, his cheeks bore the purple and red tracings of a face that had been "slammed by the door of the Atlantic." Michael wondered how many storms Quirke had weathered only to meet his death at the end of a rope. It only proved the old proverb, "If a man's born to hang, he need not fear water."

The crowd broke into fresh sobs as William O'Shea was led out of the barracks. Will was a great favorite of the village, a kind, joyful man whose music had lifted many spirits.

As William was led to the tree, the sweet clear notes of a pipe floated down from the hillside above them. Faces in the crowd turned toward the grassy knoll. William's oldest son, Billy, a small, plaintive figure stood alone on the rock-strewn hill. The song he played was an ancient ballad, a lament for the passing of a hero. The haunting notes stirred even the heartstrings of the constable and his men, who paused solemnly before proceeding.

As Billy played, Michael watched the boy's father. The smile of radiant pride on Will's thin face twisted Michael's heart. He couldn't imagine the pain of a man hearing his son play for the last time. Tears flooded Michael's eyes, blurring the image of William's face.

The officers slipped a noose over Will's neck, and the sound of the pipe ceased. The villagers watched as the boy ran down the hillside to his mother's side. Tiny Margaret O'Shea put her arms around her five children and wept silently as they buried their faces in her skirts and bosom.

Father Murphy and Father Brolin stood on either side of the condemned man, reading from their prayerbooks. William's lips moved in silent prayer.

Michael watched Will's face just before they slid the black hood over it, and he knew that the last thing William looked upon in this life was his wife's tears. For a moment Michael thought of Annie and tried to put himself in Will's place. If he were dying it wouldn't be Annie's face that he would want to see last. It would be Caitlin's. The realization cut deep into Michael's heart. In moments such as this, with death so near, the heart spoke truthfully.

The constable himself looped the noose around Quirke's neck, being careful to tuck it beneath his full red beard. But as Sheldon moved to place the hood over the sailor's face, Quirke said, "Wait. Can't a dyin' man say a last word before he goes to meet his maker?"

The constable nodded.

"I must say it to Sir Larcher," Quirke said with a nearly apologetic tone. "I must say it to his face."

Larcher stepped out of the crowd and walked up to the condemned man. "Yes? What is it?" he asked, his bulbous nose held high as he scowled down at the old sailor.

"I just wanted to tell ye ..." He took a deep breath and a sly smile played across his leathery features. "That it's me dyin' wish that you die with the Devil's pike through your black heart. May the Old Horned One himself roast your arse for his breakfast, and may he swallow ye sideways."

The crowd gasped at the vehemence of the curse. Everyone knew that a dying man's curse, along with that of a widow's, was the worst a soul could have put upon him.

"You take that back, you bloody bastard!" Larcher shouted, his face livid with rage. "Take it back now or I'll—"

"And what will ye do?" Quirke asked with a bitter grin. "Ye can't hang a man twice, now can you?" Having spoken his piece, Quirke spat a long brown stream of tobacco juice full into the aristocrat's face.

Larcher backed away, wiping at the stain with his lacy handkerchief. "Hang him! Hang that bloody heathen now!" he shouted.

The constable nodded. Two of the officers grasped the other end of the sailor's rope, which was looped over a limb of the oak, and they pulled. Two others did the same to William O'Shea's rope.

Will's children began to cry hysterically, and his wife swooned into the arms of her friends.

Michael turned his face away. He couldn't watch. He had seen men hang before, and he had never forgotten the sickening stretch of their necks, the grotesque dance they did as they struggled against the rope that robbed them of breath, the pungent stench of their urine and the evacuation of their bowels.

Michael pushed his way through the crowd. He couldn't watch them hang, not these men.

But he didn't get away fast enough. Though he didn't see the executions, he heard the horrible death gargles mixed with Larcher's laughter. And Michael knew the sound would haunt him for the rest of his life.

The peals of childish laughter reached Michael before he rounded the corner of the forge and entered the O'Briens' yard. It was a merry, delightful thing to hear after such a grim morning, Michael thought. No matter how low a man's heart had sunk, it could always be uplifted by the laughter of children.

Daniel and a bevy of his friends were crowded around the wheel. When Michael approached, Daniel hobbled over to him, a look of mischievous glee on his freckled face.

"What are ye doin' now, lad?" Michael asked. "Sounds like you're havin' too much fun entirely. Ye must be doin' something ye shouldn't."

Danny took Michael's hand and dragged him over to the wheel. "Look." He pointed to the log horses that were carrying strange new riders on their backs. "We're having a hanging ourselves. Just watch."

The bigger boys sent the wheel spinning, and two scarecrow figures with black hoods over their heads and nooses around their necks whirled through the air, scattering straw from their dangling limbs.

The children cackled with glee, only this time their merriment sounded evil and bitter, like Larcher's laughter.

"Stop it!" Michael roared as he reached out and grabbed the wheel with both hands. He ripped the straw men from their nooses and threw them into the children's startled faces. "Have ye no respect for the dead?"

"But Michael—" Danny pleaded tearfully as he clutched at the hem of his friend's coat. "We didn't mean to do anything wrong."

But Michael didn't hear the child's plea. A fury had been building inside him since the night the Oaks had been captured. It had festered during the mock trial, in which an "impartial jury" of twelve Englishmen had declared them guilty of murder.

The rage ripped loose inside him until Michael couldn't control it. With arms and hands that could toss an anvil the length of the forge, he gripped the giant wheel and yanked it off the pole. He tore the log horses from their chains and hurled them across the yard, into the briars.

The children watched, stricken dumb with fear at his reaction to their play. The only sound was a dry sob from Danny.

Having destroyed his creation with his own hands, Michael's anger was spent. Through glazed eyes he saw the broken wheel and the scattered horses. But when he looked down at the children and the shattered expressions on their white faces, he realized what he had done. He had destroyed their dreams. The carousel had been their path to the Land of the Ever Young.

But Michael was too numb to care. He turned and walked away, away from his dream, away from the children with their fearful, round eyes that stared at him.

It didn't matter, not in a world where men hanged other men from trees until their faces turned black and their tongues swelled out of their mouths. There was no place in such a brutal world for enchanted horses.

Michael knew the boy wasn't sleeping, though his eyes were closed tightly. Too tightly. His freckled nose crinkled and his golden eyelashes batted against his cheeks as he peeped from one eye. "If yer going to fool me truly ..." Michael said as he sat on the bed and tweaked a lock of the child's curly red hair, "... ye'll have to learn to snore when you're awake, as well as when you're sleeping."

The brown eyes snapped open. "I don't snore when I'm asleep."

"You blow the thatch right off the roof and the chickens with it, you do. And I should know, havin' slept in the same room with you all these years."

"I miss you sorely, Michael," the boy whispered so as not to wake his sister who was sleeping in Michael's bed and had since the wedding. "Judy doesn't tell me stories at night, and she doesn't go out for walks in the moonlight."

Michael sighed and nodded his head. "I miss those walks too, Danny. You were good company, indeed. We'll have to go on another adventure one of these nights soon."

The child's eyes glittered at the thought. "That would be grand, Michael. Could we go see that horse again, the landlord's—I mean, Princess Niav's horse?"

"We'll do it soon, lad. We don't want the old boy to forget us." Touched by the love shining in the child's eyes, Michael sifted his fingers through Danny's hair. He felt a stab of guilt for his behavior that morning.

244

Children were innocent beings who only mimicked their elders.

"I'm sorry I destroyed the wheel, Danny." His deep voice was heavy with regret. "I was feeling terrible about the hanging and I let loose my anger on you little ones. 'Twas a bad thing to do, and it's truly sorry I am."

Tears filled the boy's eyes. "I understand."

"You do?"

He nodded. "It's an awful thing to be hanged. A painful thing—for the person who's hanged and for the ones who love him. And it was a sorry thing for us to make fun of another person's misery."

Michael was struck silent, amazed at the boy's perception. "How do you know all of that?"

"I thought about it a long time ... all day. I knew we must have done something dreadful, or you wouldn't have yelled at us and tore your wheel apart. You never yelled at me before, so I knew it was a real bad thing we done."

Michael gathered the boy to his chest and squeezed him long and hard. "I love you, Danny. You're a fine lad, and it's a good man you'll be when you grow older, a man I'll be proud to call my friend."

The small arms stole around Michael's neck, and he had never worn a warmer scarf. "Will you put your wheel back together again, Michael? All the lads were asking me if you would."

"No, I don't think so." Seeing the disappointment on the boy's face, he quickly added, "I'm going to build another wheel that's even bigger and better. And I want you to help me. The carvin' is hard for me now with me hands scarred and all. I'll need some help with the fine details. Would you be my apprentice, Danny?"

The child answered with a big hug that told Michael

clearly Daniel O'Connell O'Brien would do anything in the world for his friend, anything at all.

As Michael kissed the lad goodnight and climbed the ladder to his and Annie's bedroom, he wished that he had sons and daughters like Danny, at least three or four of each. Michael sighed as he contemplated the fact that until he and Annie began to live together truly as husband and wife, there could be no children.

Michael lay in bed beside his wife and stared at the dark window, waiting for the first ray of dawn to signal the close of this endless, sleepless night. Everything in the room reminded him of the dead men; his clothes which hung limply on a peg in the wall, Annie's statue of the Virgin which sat on the windowsill. Where had the Virgin been today with her tender mercies? Michael could imagine her letting Seamus Quirke die. The old sailor was as hard and scaly as the barnacles that had crusted his ship's hull, and heaven alone knew how many men he had killed or maimed in his day.

But what sins had William O'Shea committed against the good God that he deserved to be hanged like a goat before the eyes of his wife and children? And what of Cornelius Gabbit, a man whose tender conscience had sent him to the chapel to pray for another man's burned hands? Michael knew that neither Cornelius nor William had killed Morton Collier. Rory had done the murder, and the others had simply watched.

Shutting his eyes, Michael tried not to think. He tried to escape to the Land of the Ever Young. But it was too far away tonight; his mind couldn't summon a single enchanted stallion to whisk him away.

Behind his closed lids he saw the faces of the condemned; Con's dead eyes, Will's peaceful smile as he listened to his son's piping, and Quirke's hate-twisted face. Michael knew that those images would haunt him for many nights to come, but he couldn't bear to think of that right now. If he could only keep their ghosts away until morning.

He knew that Annie wasn't asleep, either. She had dozed earlier, when they had first gone to bed. But now, he could tell by her restless stirrings that she too was awake.

Michael would have liked to turn to his wife, take her in his arms, and share this difficult night with her. If she were Caitlin, he would have poured out his heart to her hours ago, holding her warm body against his, drawing strength from her closeness. But he couldn't imagine doing such a thing with Annie. Annie wasn't one to give, to comfort and nurture. It simply wasn't her way.

He heard her pull in a deep breath and hold it. The bed shook ever so slightly, as though she were crying. In the dim light, he saw her wipe her hand across her face. Raising himself onto one elbow, he peered down at her in the darkness. "Annie, what is it? Ye aren't cryin', are ye?"

She answered with a long sniff, followed by a racking sob. Reluctantly he laid his hand on her shoulder and shook her. "What is it, darlin'? Tell me why you're crying."

She hiccupped loudly as she tried to swallow her sobs. "It's the hanging. 'Twas a terrible sight to behold. I'd never seen a hangin' before and I didn't know it would be so awful."

Michael felt a tug of pity, along with a surprising sense of companionship. The deaths had affected her, too. For once, Annie was thinking of someone other than herself. Tenderly he brushed the hair away from her face and dried her tears with his fingertips. "I know,
247

'twas a horrible thing, and those responsible should be hanged as well.''

Fresh sobs tore through her, and Michael was alarmed at this sudden change in her. Since when did Annie feel the pain of others so acutely?

"Michael ..." She reached up and clutched his shoulder in a grip that caused him to wince. "... do you think I'm a wicked person? Do you hate me?"

He pulled her hand away from his shoulder and held it tightly in his own. "No, surely not. I get angry with you sometimes, but I don't hate you and I don't think you're wicked, just a nuisance from time to time. Why would you ask such a thing?"

She didn't reply but cried harder. He pressed his lips to her forehead. "Don't cry, Annie," he murmured as he wrapped his arms around her slender body and held her close. "I don't hate you. I'm just not a very good husband. I'm sorry. Come to meself, now, and hush your crying."

Settling his head on the pillow, he cuddled her against his chest. Her small hands sought his waist, and she clung to him. Her touch on his bare skin stirred a response in his body that surprised him. Bending his head to kiss her cheek, he found her lips instead.

Her kiss was shy and tentative, but he didn't sense the hostility that had been there on their wedding night. Her lower lip trembled as he kissed it, and Michael felt his pity for her grow along with a sense of protectiveness, the need of a husband to shield his wife from the harsh realities of life. It was the first husbandly emotion he had felt for her, and it stirred other feelings as well, more primitive, distinctly male emotions.

His hand moved over the crisp linen of her nightgown and down her back to cup her hip. With his fingers splayed, his big hand covered her small buttock, and he felt her shudder. He sensed that her trembling was from fear, and the realization made him even more protective.

"Be easy, Annie," he said as his hand moved up the bodice of her gown, loosening the tiny buttons. "I'll try not to hurt you."

His fingertips slid inside the gown and found the small mound of her breast and the nub of her nipple. She gasped softly, and he didn't know if it was from shock or pleasure. Carefully he allowed his hand to roam, to discover the soft plane of her belly, the tiny indentation of her navel.

When she didn't object, he moved his hand even lower, to uncover and explore the mystery of her womanhood. But the moment he touched her in that secret place, she shivered again and said in a tearful voice, "Michael, please. Your hands . . . the scars . . . they're so rough. Do you have to touch me there?"

Instantly the magic spell was broken, and an icy anger washed over him. He thought of how Caitlin had begged for the touch of his scarred hands. His caress had been a gift of affection to Annie. By rejecting his lovemaking, she had rejected the deepest part of himself. He felt open, vulnerable, and wounded.

"No, Annie, I don't have to do any of that. There's only one thing a man must do to give his wife a baby." He lifted her gown and positioned himself over her. "Don't fret. I won't take long."

Without skill or even gentleness he plunged into her, tearing through the fragile barrier. She whimpered only once, then lay perfectly still, neither denying nor encouraging him until he had finished.

Michael rolled off her onto his side and stared out the window. The first rays of dawn filtered through the lace curtains, and the holy Virgin looked down at him, an expression of disapproval and sorrow on her face.

The long night had finally ended. Michael had never felt so empty inside, and his emptiness had nothing to do with the seed he had deposited at the gate of his wife's womb.

He had just made love to a woman for the first time in his life, to the woman who bore his name and would someday bear his children. But Michael felt soiled and sinful in a way that he had never felt when he had touched Caitlin. Michael felt as though he had just committed adultery.

Quietly he rose from his marriage bed and dressed. Then, as he had on their wedding night, he left his wife alone.

But tonight he took Danny with him. They went on a long walk to see an enchanted stallion, and for a stolen hour they escaped to the Land of the Ever Young.

Gingerly Annie reached beneath the quilt and touched the stickiness on the inside of her thighs. She wasn't sure if it was her own blood or the stuff that men put into you to give you babies. Either way, she knew that she was married now; Michael had done that disgusting, hurtful thing to her, and she had let him. That made him hers forever. And, if she were honest, she had to admit that it hadn't been all that hurtful or all that disgusting.

After the initial pain, she'd felt a warm pleasure stir inside her, a feeling that had shocked her. What kind of woman was she, taking pleasure in such degradation? She had felt a strange sensation deep in the pit of her stomach, the same feeling she had experienced when she told Father Brolin about her sins with Michael. Only

250

these sensations were much stronger. They made her want something, though she couldn't imagine what it might be. If Michael had only taken a little longer, something wonderful—or terrible—might have happened.

Maybe he would do it to her again, tomorrow night. At least now she knew how to get her husband to take her in his arms. All she had to do was cry.

Chapter Thirteen

"Annie, my child, you have certainly outdone yourself this time." Father Brolin beamed a benevolent smile down on Annie as he held up the elaborately embroidered prayer stole. "May God bless those precious hands that did such lovely work."

Annie's broad grin melted slightly at his last words. She would have preferred that he had blessed her more directly. "The precious hands" that had done such lovely work were mostly Judy's, and Annie didn't want to share the father's enthusiastic blessing with her sister. After all, the stole had been her own idea, even if the actual work had been Judy's.

"Would you like a cup of tea before you leave?" Father Brolin asked as he wrapped the stole around his neck and affectionately fingered the embroidering.

"That would be lovely, Father," she replied, thrilled with the invitation. "But let me fetch it for you."

She turned and hurried toward the hearth, but he quickly intercepted her with a gentle hand on her arm. "You'll do no such thing," he said, guiding her toward a chair and seating her with great aplomb. "A lady in your delicate condition must be careful not to exert herself."

Annie blushed, and as the priest poured the tea, she arranged her skirts as best she could to hide her thickening midriff. She was embarrassed to have the good father see her in this state. Now he knew for certain that she was no longer pure and undefiled. She had allowed Michael to do those distasteful things to her body, and the baby growing inside her was proof. She could feel Father Brolin's disgust radiating through the thin facade of courtesy. He was disappointed in her, nearly as disappointed as she was in herself. What would he think if he knew that sometimes she almost enjoyed the act?

"Here you are. I'm sorry I don't have any cakes to offer you, but ...." His voice trailed away as he gave a sweeping gesture to indicate the untidy room. "Sorcha's ailment has been flaring up even worse than usual lately, and she hasn't been able to do her duties here at the rectory."

Annie looked around the room at the layer of gray-white dust covering the holy statues and the clock on the mantel. The table linen was stained and wrinkled. Piles of fine turf ash spilled from the hearth onto the floor that had once been finely polished maple, but was now scuffed and dull.

Annie could hear Sorcha snoring in the bedroom off the sitting room. Each time Annie had been to the rectory in the past few months, Sorcha had been asleep. "Dear Sorcha," she said with a well-placed sigh. "She means well, she does, but her poor hands just pain her so. And she's no lass anymore, you know." She took a sip of the weak tea. Father Brolin was a fine man, but he made dreadful tea. Somehow the fault endeared him to her. How could a holy man like himself be expected to perform such mundane duties? "I'll come by tomorrow and clean up a bit," she offered. "I'll have the place shining and the smell of bread and soup in the air before sundown."

"Ah, you needn't do that, child," he said, though he looked pleased at her offer. She was glad she had made it, especially if she wouldn't have to carry it through. "I'm sure you have plenty to do there at home, caring for your husband and getting ready for the little one."

Annie's face crumpled into a pout. "My husband's hardly ever at home these days. He's doing some work for Lord Armfield there in the great house. Michael stays there, he does, all the time. We never see his face anymore, and when he is at home, he's in a quarrelsome mood, dark and dour."

"That's bad news indeed, Annie." The priest's finely arched golden eyebrow lifted. "You mustn't quarrel with the husband the good God gave you. You're the woman, and the woman must be the peacemaker."

Annie squirmed under the father's critical eye. She hadn't intended to tell him about her latest argument with Michael, but she needed to let him know just how heavy her burden was. "I try to keep the peace, truly. But the man's impossible. Only this morning he scolded me for bringing this stole to you, said I had more important things to do, like cleanin' me own house. Imagine that ... more important things to do than serving the Lord. I believe he's jealous, Father, jealous of my love and devotion to the church."

"That's certainly possible, the infidel that he is."

Annie's heart rejoiced to see that the good father understood her tribulation. "And to think that *he* would be jealous of a poor stole for a holy man, when he's still lusting after that harlot, Caitlin O'Leary. I met her just the other day on the road, and you should have

seen the look on her face when she saw that I was ...
you know, with child. She looked at me as though I'd
stolen something that was her own."

Annie rose from her chair and placed her cup on the
table. Then she walked to the window and looked out,
her back to the priest. She could feel his eyes on her,
his heart extended toward her in sympathy. What a
kind and loving man he was. Why couldn't Michael be
good and holy like the father?

"It like to broke my heart, Father," she said, hanging her head. " 'Tis a terrible cross to bear, an unfaith-
ful husband."

To her delight, he left his chair and joined her at the
window. She felt so much stronger when he was near.
He put his hands on her shoulders and turned her to
face him. "You must have faith, child, and bear whatever the Lord puts in your path. Trials come to purify
our souls."

His closeness nearly took her breath away and made
her dizzy. She put her hands on the front of his cossack
to steady herself. "I know, Father. I try to be strong. I
pray all the time and ..."

Suddenly all thoughts of prayer and Michael and
soul-enriching trials left her mind. In that instant, something had changed between them. She could have sworn
that the light of gentle sympathy in the priest's blue
eyes had flared into something far more intense. She
could feel his warm breath on her face as his hands
tightened on her upper arms. The feelings that rushed
through her confused her, frightened and excited her.
Annie was no longer a virgin, and she recognized the
magnetism drawing them together, an attraction that
had nothing to do with the concern of a priest for a
troubled parishioner.

She knew that she should pull away from him. He

knew it too; she could see the conflict on his handsome face. But she couldn't, and she didn't think he could, either.

"What in heaven's name is going on here?" The deep voice, like the voice of God himself, shattered the quiet of the room, and they jumped apart like guilty children.

Annie whirled around and saw Father Murphy standing in the doorway, his face flushing purple all the way up to his bald pate. "Annie McKevett," he said, his voice shaking with barely controlled rage, "go home to your family this instant, and I'll see you in confession before the day's over!"

Annie turned and fled the cottage, the wrath of God, and feelings that had come, surely not from herself, but from the depths of hell to ensnare her soul.

The mantel clock struck four, the sound reverberating through the silent room as the old father glared at the younger priest.

"Isn't it enough that the Church of England denied us the right to practice our faith all those years? What good did it serve for the Great Liberator, Daniel O'Connell himself, to set us free to serve God if the likes of you blaspheme his holy name, seducing one of the flock He has put in your care?"

Father Brolin refused to meet the priest's angry eyes as his own gaze darted furtively around the room, to the door that hung open from Annie's hasty retreat, to the pot of tea water that bubbled over the fire, to the empty cups on the table.

The older priest saw the cups too, and the lines across his forehead deepened. "What devilment happened here?" he demanded. "You'll tell me, and you'll tell me now."

Father Brolin snapped to attention, his posture as

defensive as the lift of his stout jaw. "Nothing unseemly happened here. The young lady was merely confiding in me and—"

"Let me guess, the silly lass was telling you what a dreadful man she's married herself to, and what a terrible trial it is to live with such a man."

"Well, yes . . . she said something like that. How did you know?"

"Because I know Annie O'Brien McKevett for the foolish, self-righteous, lying little beggar that she is."

"You mustn't say such things about—"

"Hold your tongue, lad. I'll say whatever I damn well please, and you'll listen. There are two things that can't be cured—death and the want of sense. That girl has never had a bit of sense, and I've always had my doubts about you."

Brolin could no longer contain his indignation. He stepped closer to the old priest, his blue eyes blazing. "Just what do you think happened here? What sins of the flesh do you think I'm capable of committing?"

"I don't know. And neither do you. You have your head stuck so far up your . . . up in the clouds that you think you're the Christ himself, above all sin. But, you're a man, John Brolin. A man made of flesh and blood. And if you don't watch yourself that empty-headed wench will lead you down a path straight to hell. And while you might just deserve that end, I'll not allow you to blaspheme the name of God and the Holy Catholic Church. Do you understand me?"

Father John Brolin bit back the harsh words that rushed to his lips. No. He didn't understand. He was only concerned for that poor girl's soul and had only been trying to help her through her vale of tears. "Annie McKevett is a married woman," he said, "a woman with child, for God's sake. And I am a priest, a servant of the Church. She would never be a temptation to me. And I must say, I resent your accusations."

Father Murphy shook his head as the anger slowly left his eyes to be replaced by sadness and shades of pity. "To deny a temptation is to give it great power, lad. If someday you find yourself bound hand and foot by your own sin, you know where my confessional is, and it's there I'll meet you."

"Rory's back in Kerry. I heard the news today at O'Leary's pub." Sean brushed a strand of straight blond hair off his forehead as he settled down on a bale of straw in the corner of the barn and took out his pipe.

Michael glanced up from his carving and shook his head in disapproval. "Put that pipe away," he said, his hammer and chisel suspended over a giant wooden horse. "A closed candle lantern is the only fire His Honor will allow here in the barn with his precious stallion." Michael looked lovingly at Armfield's pride and joy, who pranced at the end of a rope anchored to the wall.

He set the hammer and chisel aside and walked over to the animal. Carefully he laid his palm on its flank and smoothed the glossy white coat, memorizing the graceful indentation along the withers. Then he returned to his wooden replica and with infinite care carved the same groove in its flank.

"Did ye hear me? I said Rory's back in Kerry. What do you think of that?"

"I think the lad who told you that must have been short of good news to be relating a tale such as that." Michael continued to carve, but a knot was starting to form in his gut and he had to concentrate to hold the chisel steady.

" 'Twasn't a lad that told me. 'Twas a lass, Caitlin O'Leary herself. She said he came into her pub last night late. He was talking about how he was going to get even with you for informing on the Black Oaks and gettin' them hanged."

"Those lads were caught and kilt through no fault of mine. Rory can think different if he likes, it's no concern of mine."

" 'Twill be your concern if he comes after you with that big knife of his." Sean's fear for his friend was evident in his voice.

Michael stopped carving long enough to reassure him. "Rory Doona is a coward and as dull as ditchwater. I'll not lose any sleep on account of him or his knife."

Sean's blue eyes narrowed. "Aye, but a coward's more dangerous than a brave man. He'll not think twice about comin' up behind you and murderin' you without ever looking in your eye. Ye mustn't think yourself safe, Michael. If ye do, we'll be layin' you beneath the sod, with Annie a widow and her child fatherless."

Michael turned his back to his friend and ran his hands over the horse he had nearly finished. He had saved this horse, the armored stallion, for last. Five dainty mares adorned with bells and flowers were standing in Armfield's woodshop next door, waiting to be placed on the giant wheel and whirled into the Land of the Ever Young. This stallion was the sixth and final horse he would carve for his magical wheel.

But Michael wasn't thinking about the stallion with intricate fishscale armor draping its strong back and protecting its noble head. He wasn't thinking about the painful hours he had spent carving with hands that would never be as nimble as before. He wasn't thinking that the completion of his dream was here, literally within his grasp.

He was thinking of the child, his child, growing inside Annie. Last night as she had slept, he had laid his hand on her belly and felt his baby move against his palm. It was a girl. Michael didn't know how he knew, but he knew it was a strong, healthy daughter who had sensed her father's presence and kicked against the confines of the womb, communicating with him in that silent, secret way that animals and trees communicated.

Michael loved his little girl fiercely, sight unseen. Even if his marriage to Annie wasn't all it might have been, the baby girl was perfect, and she was his.

The thought of Rory Doona brought a deep fear to his heart. A fear that he had never known before, the desperate need for self-preservation. He couldn't afford to die, not now. He had a daughter of his own to live for.

"Rory and I will have it out someday," he said, more to himself than to Sean. "And 'twill be a fight to the death. I've always known that, felt it in my bones. I'll just have to make sure it's he who winds up the corpse and not meself."

Caitlin had stood, studying him for a long time. She'd watched as, unconscious of her presence, he rubbed the wooden horse's foreleg with sanded paper, rubbed and polished until the wood was as velvety smooth as the horse it had been carved after.

She'd watched the play of his muscles as he sanded, biceps knotting and stretching with every stroke, his bare chest, arms and back glistening with the fine sheen of sweat. His handsome face was crinkled into a grimace of concentration.

The sun was just beginning to set, but the woodshop was still warm with the lazy sultry heat of late summer.

The evening rays streamed through the mullioned windows of the shop, and motes of sawdust danced in the air, miniature constellations swirling on golden shafts of sunlight.

He stopped sanding, and she knew, even before he turned to face her, that he was aware of her. "Caitlin." She saw the joy in his eyes as he spoke her name, the hunger as his gaze swept over her. Then she felt the old wall come up between them, and he looked down at the floor, his thick lashes shielding his green eyes and their secrets. "I suppose ye've come to see His Honor," he said, his voice guarded and cold.

The contempt in his tone cut her deeply, but she swallowed the pain, determined to hide it. "No," she said quietly as she stepped into the shop, "I came to Armfield House to see you."

Once again there was a flicker of joy in his eyes, then he turned away from her and went back to his sanding. "What has brought you all this way to see me?" She heard the hope in his voice, and it cheered and saddened her. So, he still loved her. What good did it do either of them?

"I came to warn you that Rory is back in Kerry. He came to my pub last night, and he's spouting mischief about the harm he'll do you."

He paused only a moment, then went on sanding. "I've been warned already. But I thank you no less."

Caitlin moved around to the opposite side of the horse. She wanted to see his face, his eyes, when she talked to him. They spoke so seldom these days. " 'Tis a lovely horse you've done here." She laid her hand on the animal's back. Touching Michael's carving was almost like touching him. She could feel his power, his compassion in the wood, but if she were ever to tell him such a thing, he would think her daft.

"He's the last one, and he's nearly finished. All I have to do is paint him and hang him on the wheel, along with the others." He waved his arm toward the far wall where five ponies stood side by side: a roan with a necklace of pink roses circling her neck, a bay with her right leg lifted in a flirting pose, a dappled gray whose full mane and tail were caught in a silent wind, and a gentle black pony with garlands of lilies and daisies cascading over her shoulders.

" 'Twill be the glory of Erin, your wheel, when it's finished," she said, feeling a pride in his work that ran as deep as though she herself had accomplished this miracle. "The like has never been seen in this world or the next. 'Tis a wonder. What is this on the stallion's back?" she asked, tracing the ornate fishscale texture of the drapings.

"He's an armored horse, like the kings and knights rode long ago. I saw a picture of such a horse in a book in His Honor's library. Armfield lets me look through his books when I'm finished with me work in the evenings."

"I saw the new bannister you made for him" she said. "It's a fine bit of work, and he's most pleased with it."

"Told you that himself, did he?"

She couldn't miss the sarcasm in his voice. She also couldn't help feeling angry with him. After all, he had someone else too. "I met your Annie on the road the other day," she said carefully. "It appears you're to be a father one day soon."

"Yes, isn't it grand?" His green eyes sparkled and a battle of mixed feelings raged inside her; joy for him, jealousy toward Annie, pain that he was lost to her forever.

Her joy for him won over jealousy. " 'Tis grand indeed, Michael. I know how you love children, and no one would be a better father than yourself." She took a deep breath and walked around the horse to stand beside him. Her eyes searched his, and she saw that a storm of emotion raged inside him as well, joy against pain. "Are ye happy now, Michael?"

He nodded, but the pain lingered in his eyes. "I am."

"With your lovely wheel almost finished and a babe on the way, I guess you must have everything you ever wanted now."

His hand lay on the horse's back, and she gently covered it with her own. She had meant the gesture to be friendly, one friend sharing a moment of pleasure with another. But the instant she touched him, the air between them vibrated with an intensity that had little to do with the friendship between two people and more to do with the deep needs between a man and a woman.

His eyes burned with an emerald flame that threatened to scorch her if she got any closer. There was a darkness, a depth of passion in Michael that she had never felt in any other man, not even Armfield.

His other hand came up and burrowed through the hair along the back of her head. In one movement he pulled her toward him and she thought he was going to kiss her, hoped he was going to kiss her as he had that night beside the river. But he didn't. He only looked down at her, his eyes caressing every line of her face.

"No, Caitlin," he whispered, his voice deep and husky. "I don't have everything I ever wanted. Not everything."

She could have him. His heart was open to her, and she knew that his body ached for her as much as hers did for him. All she would have to do was reach out

263

and lay her hand on his bare chest. One touch and he would take her then and there.

But by taking her he would violate his marriage vows and that code of honor which he embraced, not because of a structured catechism, but because of a tender conscience, the rare sensitivity that made him the man she loved and respected.

Besides, even though she could see the painful need in his eyes and sense the loneliness of his heart, Michael had said that he was happy now, and who was she to disbelieve him? Wasn't a man only as happy as he thought himself to be?

While Caitlin still had the strength, she turned her back to him, and, by walking away, she gave him back his wife, his unborn child, and that fragile happiness that he had been so long denied.

She was beautiful, there was no denying. From beneath lowered lids Armfield studied the young woman who sat on the other end of his diamond-tucked velvet settee. She didn't sit on the edge, back straight, prim and posed as the many great ladies who had sat on this sofa before her. Caitlin reclined like a sleepy, languorous cat, graceful, but totally at ease with herself.

She was a peasant. One could tell by the way she held the dainty crystal snifter in a firm grasp and by the way she drank the expensive brandy in draughts as though it were ale. She was common, without a drop of aristocratic blood in her veins. Armfield's gaze traveled down the translucent ivory skin of her throat to her full breasts that spilled over the top of his wife's satin and lace gown. Caitlin O'Leary was a peasant, to be sure; but she was an exquisite peasant.

"I haven't seen you as often lately," he said, trying

to sound casual. His pride wouldn't allow him to admit, even to himself, that he had missed her company.

"If ye wanted me here, ye had only to send for me," she replied, her eyes tilted at the corners as she smiled at him, a smile that quickened his pulse and sent his blood flowing into the nether regions of his body.

"I like it better when you come without being summoned."

He reached over and twisted one of her red locks around his forefinger. The strand glimmered like polished amber in the light of the silver candelabra on the tea table. Armfield tried to imagine her hair piled on top of her head, the way his lady had always worn hers, but he couldn't picture that riotous mass of curls submitting to combs. And he wasn't sure he would want it contained, anyway.

At his touch she glanced away and shifted her body ever so slightly in a way that told him his caress was unwelcome. She had been doing that a lot lately, though he wasn't sure what had caused the change in her. He didn't want to think *who* might have caused the lapse in her affections.

"I've been busy at the pub," she said. "What with the harvest and all, the lads have a terrible thirst. 'Twas a great harvest this summer with all the barley and oats ..."

He knew that she was trying to keep the conversation from becoming personal, and she was forestalling the time when he would lead her to his bedchamber. "I'm leaving for England soon," he said, searching her face for even a fleeting sign of disappointment, but found none.

"How long will ye be away?"

"A month or so. What present would you have me bring you?" He knew there was no point in asking; she

265

always said, "nothing." It was a sore spot with him, her refusal to accept gifts from him. Heaven knows, she needed many things, and he could make her life far more pleasant and comfortable if she would accept his generosity. But she didn't, and he knew why. As long as she took nothing from him, she stayed independent of him, and their relationship remained an open ledger upon which the debts recorded were his. He didn't like the feeling that it was he who owed her. He was the landlord; she was the peasant. Caitlin O'Leary kept forgetting that fact, and he was running out of ways to remind her.

"You needn't bring me anything," she replied, draining her brandy glass. "Just return safe and sound."

His eyes searched hers and read a degree of friendly concern in those russet depths. But the lust was gone, and he missed it sorely.

She set her glass on the table and walked over to stand before a beveled mirror that hung on the wall above a sideboard. At first he thought she was enjoying her reflection, then he saw her examining the heavy gilded frame. "How did they do this?" she asked.

Walking up behind her, he placed one hand on her waist. "How did they do what?" His other hand swept the red curtain of hair away from her nape, and his fingertips stroked the delicate skin he had bared.

"How did they paint this gold stuff on here? Is there such a thing as gold paint?"

"It's a process called gold-leafing." He carefully eased the satin off her shoulder and dipped his head to nibble at the white skin. "Why do you ask?"

"Ah . . . it's just curious I am." She turned to face him, and he was delighted to see that familiar gleam of interest in her eyes. "Mason,"—she laid her hands on the front of his linen shirt—"there's somethin' you can bring back to me from England, if it's not too much bother."

His heart leaped, and he fought to keep the eagerness out of his voice. "Certainly. What will it be?"

"Would you bring me some of that lovely gold paint?"

He smiled and pulled her closer until her full breasts were against his chest. "Gold leaf it is. And what will you cover with gold, my little Midas?"

He saw the confusion in her eyes. She often failed to understand his references. Then he was surprised to see a flicker of shame cross her face just before she dropped her gaze to stare at the floor. " 'Tisn't for me, " she admitted reluctantly. " 'Tis for another."

Armfield didn't have to ask. He had seen her go into the woodshop that afternoon. He had gone down afterwards and seen the armored stallion himself. Jealousy spilled through his veins, hot and potent. One arm went around her waist and crushed her to him. The other hand tangled itself in her hair and held her fast as he kissed her with lips that were brutal and bruising.

Then he pulled her down onto the hand-hooked rug and peeled away the satin. He was the landlord, by God, and he would take her there on the rug like the peasant that she was.

Chapter Fourteen

"I'm surprised, wanted man that ye are, that you'd show your face in this village." Caitlin set a glass of whiskey on the table and gave it a shove in Rory's direction.

"I just had to come back and catch a glimpse of your darlin' face," he jibed, hoisting the mug in an exaggerated salute to her.

Caitlin collected a coin from him and slipped it into her pocket. The apron was full. It had been a busy night, but the crowd had thinned down to Paul Gannon, his brother, Eoin, and Rory, who had just arrived. The others had already left for McElroy's harvest ceili.

"That'll be all for you tonight, Rory," she said when he held the empty glass out to her. "Your mood's foul enough without the fire of whiskey poured on it."

Despite his protests, she returned to the bar and gave it the nightly closing polish. As she rubbed the wood to a bright shine, she listened to the dark mutterings from Rory's table with growing apprehension. Apparently he had sampled a drop or two before coming to her pub; he was even more rude and raucous than usual.

"That damned Michael McKevett," he cursed, "I've

thought of little else than the pleasure I'll have stickin' him like a sow with my knife. He'll squeal sure, you'll see.''

Caitlin was accustomed to hearing idle threats. The lads were forever and a day proclaiming their evil intentions toward their fellow villagers. And the next night the "murdered" neighbor would be sitting at the bar, raising a toast with his would-be murderer, plotting the destruction of yet a third party. But something told Caitlin that these were no ordinary threats. Rory, coward that he was, had whiskey courage in him, along with a nursed grudge that he had carried for months.

She thought of Michael and his newfound happiness, of his wonderful carousel nearly completed, and the baby on the way. Her apprehension grew by the minute.

"I'll have another," Rory shouted, banging his glass on the table. "What does a man have to do in this place to get his gullet wetted?"

Caitlin dried her hands on a towel, folded it neatly, and laid it on the bar. Then she walked over to his table and stood, hands on hips in a defiant stance. "The bar's closed for tonight, lads," she said. "You'd best be movin' along now."

"I'll gladly move along," Rory said, "right into that bedroom of yours."

Paul and Eoin caught their breaths, waiting tensely for Caitlin's reply. It was common knowledge among the lads that Caitlin was not a female whose temper a man wanted to rile. They had all tried their luck with her at one time or the other, only to feel the lash of her tongue.

She fixed Rory with a look that would melt the Stone of Tara. "The day you visit my bed is the day jackasses sprout wings. And you, Rory Doona, will soar with the eagles over Carrantuohill."

Paul and Eoin collapsed in a fit of laughter, but Rory failed to appreciate her humor. He had been ridiculed all his life; it was the one thing he couldn't bear.

Moving with great agility for a man who had just drunk enough to fill Lough Sweelin, he reached out and grabbed Caitlin's arm. In a heartbeat she found herself in his lap, his arms tight around her and his whiskey-sour mouth clamped over hers. The stale, sweaty stench of him nauseated her, filling her with loathing. With a strength born of fury and years of hefting ale kegs, she twisted away from him, stood and slapped him hard across the face.

For several seconds the only sound was that of Rory's ragged breathing as he clutched his hand to his cheek. Slowly he rose to his feet and with great deliberation placed his hand in his coat pocket where everyone knew he kept his prized possession, his knife.

Paul and Eoin leaped to their feet, ready to fight if they must to protect their favorite barkeeper from their most quarrelsome neighbor. But Rory knew the rules: you didn't murder a woman—at least not in front of witnesses.

"If you were a man, Caitlin O'Leary," he hissed, "you'd have your throat cut right now."

Her anger dissipated her fear as she glared down at him, aware that, although she was a woman, she towered over him. He was drunk and soft from laziness. She was healthy and strong from hard work. Without the knife she would take him on any day. And win.

"Don't be so sure," she said, her voice even and steady. "That's a fault that may kill you someday, Rory. You underestimate your enemies. And I'll tell you another thing. If any harm comes to Michael McKevett or his family, you'd best keep your eyes open for the rest of your days. Because sure as you close them to sleep, you're a dead man."

Rory saw the fear in Annie McKevett's blue eyes as she backed away from him, her arms wrapped protectively around her distended belly. He had crashed through the door of the cottage moments before only to find her alone and Michael gone. He was disappointed . . . and relieved. His courage had sagged a bit during the walk from the pub, but the terror in her eyes made him bold.

"Where's Michael?" he demanded, backing her against the wall. On the hearth a pot boiled over, sending pungent plumes of smoke and steam into the tense atmosphere.

Annie looked at the overflowing pot, but made no move toward it. She simply plastered herself against the wall and stared up at Rory, her face as pale as the whitewash behind her. "I don't know. Truly I don't. Da and Judy and Daniel are gone to McElroy's harvest ceili, and Michael was to come here and collect me after his work at Armfield House." She chattered on, her voice high and squeaky. "He should have been here long ago. I can't imagine what's keepin' him. Can I get ye some tea?"

"This isn't a social call, and I'm sure that you know that well." He glanced around the room, and his fear grew as he saw the signs of Michael McKevett, the man he intended to murder. Michael's carving tools lay in his keeping hole in the hearth, his smith's apron hung on a peg on the wall and one of his shirts lay on the table. A big shirt it was, and Rory felt a shiver of fear run through him. Michael McKevett wouldn't be an easy kill like Morton Collier.

Rory knew that he should never have come to Michael's home like this. He should have ambushed him on a lonely road. But the whiskey coursing through his veins had numbed his brain, and he couldn't think clearly. Besides, he was tired, a man on the run without enough food or sleep, and it was Michael McKevett's fault.

"What—what do you want with Michael?" Annie asked. But Rory could see in her eyes that she knew.

"I'm going to kill him," he replied matter-of-factly. "He's a dirty, low-down informer, and he caused the death of me friends."

"Michael didn't inform on you lads. He was a Black Oak himself once and he'd never betray his own." A note of conviction in her voice set Rory back for a moment. Even though she was terrified, her words had the ring of truth.

"But Michael was the only one who knew where we were hiding, except for the good Father, and he would never have told."

"But ye can't know that for sure. Someone else might have known about the sheep shed. Maybe 'twas one of your neighbors there on Carrantuohill. Maybe 'twas Paul Gannon or his brother or—"

"How do you know about the sheep shed?" He stepped closer to her.

Her face crumpled and a wild look came into her eyes, the look of a rabbit with its hind leg caught in a trap. "I—I heard you were captured there in that sheep shed there on the north slope—"

"But that's not where we were when the constable and his boys caught up with us. After the good Father came and heard Con's confession, we moved on up the mountain. 'Twas there they caught them, all but me, and I slipped away." He moved closer to her and put his hands on her shoulders. His fingers bit into her

272

flesh, and she turned her face away from his hot, whis-key breath, looking as though she were about to vomit. "How did you know about the sheep shed, Annie McKevett? I'll not ask you again."

He knew that she understood his threat. He didn't care that she was a woman with child. If she was the one who had informed on the Oaks, he would kill her as easily as look at her.

"Uh ... Michael must have told me," she stam-mered. "Yes, that's it. Michael told me about the sheep shed later. After the hanging."

Rory was a liar himself. He had lied since the day he was born, and he recognized another liar when he saw one. " 'Twas you," he said, nodding knowingly. "I thought I saw a bit of blue skirt in the woods after I left Michael that day at the bridge. 'Twas your blue skirt, Annie McKevett, and 'twas you who turned in the lads. Yer the reason they got hanged."

"No! It wasn't me, surely. It was Michael. He did it. He told me so himself, he did."

For the first time since Rory could remember, he was looking into the face of someone who was a bigger cow-ard than himself. And he hated the sight of her. He hated her weakness. Her fear. Her lies.

He struck her hard across the face with the back of his hand, and she howled at the pain. It felt good. So he hit her again ... and again ... and again.

Michael looked down at his mother's prostrate figure and shook his head in resignation and despair. He could almost see his father's skeletal hands and arms as they reached up through the sod and clasped her to the damp earth, slowly pulling her down into the grave. No matter how hard Michael pulled from this side, Patrick

McKevett, dead and buried though he was, pulled harder. This was a battle he was bound to lose, and Michael wondered why he bothered to fight at all.

"Come with me to the ceilí now, Mama. Annie's waiting for me to collect her. If you don't come along, she'll think I've forgotten her, sure."

"You go on without me," she said, her voice cracked and dry on the summer night air. "I've a few more prayers to say before I leave."

"And I suppose your prayers will take most of the night?"

Her wizened face screwed up tightly at the sarcasm in his voice. "They'll take as long as they take. 'Tis no concern of yours. Leave me now and go on to your wife. I'm only your mother. I know that I'm not the most important woman in your life anymore."

Michael silently cursed his father's bony hands. It was either curse the dead or curse the living, and as much as she pained his heart, he wasn't ready to curse his mother yet. He peeled off his coat and spread it over her shoulders, tucking it around her chin. "I'm going now, Mama. I'll leave the ceilí early and come back for you then."

Behind them came the sound of hurried footsteps and the creaking of the gate as someone entered the cemetery. Even in the subdued light of the half moon Michael recognized the scarlet cloak.

"Caitlin . . . what are you doing here?"

"I've been looking high and low for you. Michael, you must go home straight away!"

She ran to him, and he caught her hands in his to steady her as she tried to get her breath. "What's happened?" he asked. A bolt of fear shot through him, along with the strange feeling that he had lived this

274

moment before. Somehow he knew what she was going to say next.

"It's Rory. He was in the pub tonight, threatening you and your family. Michael, you must go home to Annie right away. I'm afraid that he's going there to kill you, and if he finds her alone . . . I don't know what he might do to her."

As Michael raced down the dark road through the village his mind ran ahead to the cottage, to what he would find when he arrived there. As he ran he screamed a silent prayer to the heavens. *God, have mercy and keep her safe until I get there! Rory, if you hurt her, yer dead sure . . . Holy Mary, Mother of God . . . don't let her die!*

In the distance he could hear his neighbors singing and dancing in McElroy's barn, but as he neared O'Brien's cottage, his ears strained for another sound, the sounds of violence, the sounds of screams.

He burst through the door and stood for what seemed like an eternity, listening to the heavy silence that told him nothing. His eyes scanned the kitchen, and he noted in the recesses of his fear-frozen mind that the chair was overturned, smoke filled the room from the pot that boiled over into the fire, a bowl of bread dough lay on the floor.

"Annie!" He stumbled into the room and whirled around, looking in every corner. "Annie, where are you, girl?"

He spied the door to Kevin's bedroom ajar and a shock went through him. He walked across the floor toward the door, knowing in his heart what he would see on the other side. With a feeling of inevitability he pushed it open.

Annie lay on the floor at the foot of Kevin's bed, her golden hair a tangled mess around her shoulders. Her pretty face, swollen and bruised, was almost unrecognizable; her eyes were closed. Her right arm was twisted at an angle that meant it was broken.

Michael dropped to his knees beside her, stunned and shattered. "Annie, darlin' girl," he whispered as he gently touched her battered face, her broken arm. He bent down and laid his head on her small chest. He heard it . . . the strong beat of her heart, and he whispered a quick prayer of thanksgiving.

It wasn't until he lifted her in his arms that he saw the blood streaming down her legs.

When he laid her on the bed and raised her skirt, Michael knew God hadn't answered his prayers after all. The Holy Virgin hadn't protected the babe he loved more than any other in the world. His fervent prayers had been in vain. He was going to lose his tiny daughter after all.

"Michael, come and sit down. You're wearing out Kevin's good floor and your own legs besides." Caitlin pulled a straight-backed chair from the table over to the fire and poured a cup of tea from the kettle she had put on to boil. She took a bottle of whiskey from Kevin's keeping hole and poured a healthy measure into the cup of strong tea. "Here," she said, pulling him down onto the chair, "drink this and it will steady your nerves a bit."

"I don't want it." His green eyes were haunted and so full of pain that she could hardly bear to look into them.

"I'm not carin' whether you want it or not. Just drink

it as I said," she admonished him in a tone usually reserved for rebellious youngsters.

He took the cup from her and held it between shaking hands. "Annie's losing the baby, sure," he said with a desperate look at the bedroom door. "Even old Bridget won't be able to save a child that comes so early."

Caitlin placed her hands over his to steady the cup and brought it to his lips. "There'll be other babies."

He wrenched the cup out of her hand and hurled it across the room. It hit the wall and shattered across the flagstone floor. "Damn it, I don't want other babies!" he shouted, his voice harsh with grief. "I want this baby. I want Annie to live and carry my little girl until she's big enough and strong enough to—Oh, God—" His words died, and he covered his face with his hands.

The emotions that had been building inside Caitlin all evening overflowed, feelings of love and sorrow born of empathy. She dropped to her knees beside his chair and put her arms around his neck. In an instant he clutched her to him. With his face buried in her hair he wept, silent, bitter tears that spilled down her cheeks and neck.

"Michael, I'm so sorry," she whispered as she cradled his head between her palms and kissed his forehead. "I wish there was something I could say to—"

The door to Kevin's bedroom opened, and Caitlin turned her head to see Father Brolin looking down his fine, thin nose at her. His blues eyes were narrowed with disapproval, and his chin had a haughty lift to it.

"I should think that you'd have the decency to control your fleshly lusts with your wife suffering the pains of childbirth in the next room."

For a long moment Michael stared at the priest uncomprehending. Then, as the rebuke hit its mark, he slowly, deliberately pushed Caitlin away from him.

"This isn't what you think," she said, her temper rising to Michael's defense. "I was only comforting him."

"It doesn't matter," Michael replied, cutting her off. His eyes were empty as he stared up at the priest. "How is Annie?" he said, his tone void of all emotion.

"She'll live," Bridget answered as she came out of the bedroom. Lifting her apron, she wiped the blood from her hands and arms and dabbed at the sweat on her face. "But the babe came and she was dead, of course. Annie just didn't carry her long enough. Ye mustn't have any others, Michael, mustn't at all. If Annie goes through that again, I couldn't be sure I'd save her."

No more children? Caitlin couldn't bear to look upon Michael's agonized expression. If any man in the world deserved to be a father, surely it was Michael McKevett. How could something like this happen to him of all people?

"Are ye certain?" he asked quietly.

"Aye, it's sure I am," Bridget replied a bit irritably. She was old and tired, and she wasn't accustomed to having her judgment questioned. "I've seen it time and time again. Annie's a wee one herself, not built for having babies. After that beating and that birthing, she'll never be right inside. You'd best see to it that she never gets with child again."

Having handed down her judgment, Bridget went back into the bedroom and closed the door, leaving a terrible silence behind.

But Father Brolin wasted no time disturbing the quiet. "I hope you heed her warning, McKevett. I know what a foolish man you are when it comes to matters

278

of the flesh. I just hope you don't take her in a moment of weakness and cause her death."

Caitlin could hold her tongue no longer. "What kind of a priest are you?" she shouted in his surprised face. "Have you not a kernel of compassion or the good sense of a guinea rooster? This man's just been told that his child is dead and he'll not be able to have another and—"

Michael laid a restraining hand on her shoulder and slowly rose to his feet. "Don't, Caitlin. You've a kind heart, but I don't need you to fight my battles. Besides, my quarrel with the good father has gone beyond harsh words. Hasn't it, Father?"

He walked over to the priest and stood, looking down at him, his silence more menacing than words. Caitlin could feel the tension building in him, and from the frightened look on Father Brolin's face, she knew that he could feel it too.

"I—I don't know what you mean," the priest stammered.

"Ah, surely you do." Michael pulled back one big fist, he swung and a half-second later the priest lay on the floor, holding his jaw and moaning.

"In the future I'll thank you to stay out of me path and away from me family, such as it is," Michael said before he started toward the door.

"You'll burn in hell for this, McKevett!" the priest shouted. "I damn you to hell for all eternity for striking a man of the cloth!"

"You can't damn me, man," Michael said as he opened the door. He sounded tired, empty. "My own father damned my soul long before you ever set eyes on me."

* * *

279

Caitlin followed him several yards down the road before he heard her and turned. She rushed into his arms, and they held each other tightly. There was no passion or desire in the embrace, only healing comfort.

Finally, she pulled away from him and, looking up into his eyes, she read his intentions. "I know what you're going to do," she said.

"Rory murdered my baby girl, and he's going to pay the price just as soon as I put me hands on him."

"I know." She bit her lower lip and closed her eyes for a moment. Then she opened them, having made her decision. "Rory's down by the bog. I saw him heading that way when I ran for the priest and Bridget." There. She had told him, and that made her a part of whatever was going to happen. But she was willing to take that responsibility. This was something Michael had to do. There was too much pain inside him for one man to bear. He had to let it out, and if Rory Doona was the worthy recipient, so be it.

As she looked up at Michael she saw a side of him that frightened her. His eyes were like those of an animal, a wounded, but ferocious animal. But this beast was the predator, not the prey.

"I hope you find Rory," she said. "And I hope that when you do ... you kill him."

"Oh, I will," he said. "I most surely will."

The Druids' human sacrifice stone stood, as it had for over two thousand years, in the center of a great field overlooking Laune River. The rock was the focal point of a natural amphitheater about twenty paces wide, its northern boundary touching the ringed fairy fort.

Michael stood beside the stone, which came nearly to his waist and was so wide that even he couldn't put his arms around it. The top of the rock had two scoops, carved out centuries ago by a mystic hand. One of the bowls was large and shallow; the perfect shape and size to cradle the chest of the condemned. The other concave was smaller and deeper, designed to catch the blood that poured from the slit throat of the sacrifice.

Rain had collected in both indentations and, looking down, Michael saw his own image in the still water. But it wasn't a follower of Saint Patrick he saw reflected there. It was a son of ancient Erin, the face of a Druid.

Michael closed his eyes and carefully laid his hands on the rock as he had many times before and, as always, he felt the power of the stone emanating into his palms. He remembered the first time he had ever touched the stone. Old Bridget had found him there, studying the rock, and she had told him what it was and how it had been used. She had encouraged him to lay his hands on it and allow it to tell him its own story. Young Michael had gingerly touched the stone, expecting to feel the horror and pain of its victims. But then, as now, he had felt only a great wisdom borne of age and vast experience.

But tonight, standing there in the moonlight, the stone was different, even as Michael himself was different. There was a power in him that matched the power in the rock. The energy that flowed from him through his hands wakened something in the stone, and Michael felt the vibrations throughout his soul. His hands tingled and his arms went numb.

Behind closed lids, he saw them clearly in his mind's eye, the Druids, the high priests who had stood in a sacred circle around this stone and prayed all night for the soul of the one to be sacrificed.

He saw the people arriving at the break of dawn, standing in a much wider circle on the raised earthen amphitheater to witness the execution. He heard their chants uttered on behalf of the condemned; they prayed that he had learned a lesson from his mistakes in this life and that his soul, quickened with wisdom, would do better in the next life.

Michael opened his eyes and leaned over the rock. He dipped his hand into the dark water and brought a handful to his lips. He sipped the water, the tears of the stone, making it a part of his body forever. Then he plunged his hands into the water, cupped his palms full and, as the high priest had done with the spilled blood of the sacrifice, Michael flung the water into the air. A thousand glittering droplets flew through the moonlight and fell, shimmering wetly on the dark grass.

"What are ye going to do with me, Michael? Why are ye bringin' me out here? If you're going to kill me, kill me now and get it done with."

Michael tightened his grip on Rory's collar as he pulled him across the dark field toward the stone. "Don't tempt me. You'd best be using what time ye have left to say your prayers."

"Then you *are* going to murder me?"

"I'm going to execute you."

" 'Tis the same thing," Rory whimpered, pulling against the strong hands that held him tightly.

"Not exactly the same."

Capturing Rory had been easy, too easy. The fool had been down in the bogs, exactly as Caitlin had said, and he had even dared to build a fire to warm himself. The beast inside Michael would have savored the hunt, the stalking, the eventual attack. But Rory was hardly a challenge when he wasn't on his mountain. Michael had found him, disarmed him of his precious knife and bound his hands behind him before the small man had even gotten a glimpse of his captor. It had been much too simple.

"Do you know what this is?" Michael said as he pulled Rory up to the stone and shoved him against it.

"Yes . . ." Rory's voice quivered, and there wasn't a trace of his usual bravado or boasting. " 'Tis the witches' rock."

"The Druids' stone. Do you know what they used it for?"

Rory's eyes grew wide in his dark face as he stared up at his tormentor. But Michael was too deep in his own pain and shock to appreciate his victim's fear.

"Aye, they kilt virgins here, young, innocent lasses. They'd slit their throats and—" His words trailed away, and Michael watched as realization dawned on his swarthy little face.

"You're wrong. 'Twasn't virgins or innocents they killed here. That's a tale told by the priests to discredit the Druids. 'Twas criminals who were executed here, criminals convicted of certain terrible crimes. Do you know what those crimes were, Rory?"

He shook his head, his teeth chattering despite the warm night.

"If a man committed high treason, his life was taken here on this stone. Or if he murdered a member of his own family." Michael's breath came faster and his voice deepened. "Or if he murdered a child."

"But—but I didn't do any of those things. I didn't betray or murder anybody. Surely you'll not kill me just because I thumped on your wife a bit. If ye knew what she did, you'd understand."

"Shut your mouth!" Michael's hands tightened on Rory's coat collar. "You don't even know what you did, but you're going to know before you die. Annie was carrying my babe, a little girl. You knew she was with child. One look would have told you that. But you beat her, and the babe was born, and she died." Michael paused to draw a shaking breath. "Because of you, she'll never see the sunshine or feel the soft rain on her face. Because you're a worthless coward with no more honor than to strike a woman."

"But it wasn't a babe," he pleaded, shrinking back against the stone. " 'Twasn't born yet."

Michael backhanded him hard across his right cheek; the sound crackled in the still night air. "She was my child. I felt her moving in my wife's womb. Don't you tell me that she wasn't a babe yet. She was my daughter, and you murdered her. Now I'm going to kill you. I'm going to slit your throat and throw your blood into the wind just like—"

"No! You can't kill me, Michael. Yer not a murderer."

"Ah, but I am. Five years ago I killed a man just like you . . . a man who needed killin'."

"But yer a decent man, I know that now. Annie told me herself that she's the one who informed on the lads and got them hanged. She deserved the beating she got, Michael. She deserves to get sacrificed here on this rock for the traitor that she is. At first she swore 'twas you who informed, but later she admitted that it was herself did it."

One by one Rory's words found their way into Michael's grief-stunned mind. Half of his brain screamed, "No!" while the other half knew that Rory spoke the truth.

Annie. Forever the informer, forever telling tales that destroyed others. Michael thought of Will O'Shea and his son piping from the hillside. He thought of Cornelius Gabbitt and the gloves. Annie. God damn her into hell itself!

"That doesn't change anything between you and me," Michael said. "You still killed my little girl, and nothing can change that."

Gathering all the grief inside him, Michael pulled back his fist and smashed it into Rory's jaw. There was no time for an orderly, ritualistic killing. The beast inside demanded a more primitive response. He would strangle him with his bare hands, the hands that Rory had scarred.

Rory recoiled from the blow. His head snapped back and hit the stone with a dull thud. He crumpled onto the grass in a heap. Michael dragged him to his feet and threw him backwards across the stone. He leaned over him, circled the thin neck with his fingers, and squeezed.

But as he dug his fingertips into the soft flesh, Michael realized that, once again, he would be denied satisfaction. Rory Doona was already dead.

The stone had killed him. He had died too easily. Without suffering.

As Michael allowed the body to slide off the rock to the ground, he wished that just this once the Druids were wrong and the priests right. He didn't want Rory to come back in another life and try to better himself.

He wanted Rory Doona to burn in the eternal fires of hell.

Chapter Fifteen

The white stallion galloped over the dark field, his full mane tossed by the wind, his feet pounding in rhythm with his rider's pulse. Mason Armfield's cape billowed out behind him, glowing silver in the moonlight. He rode as though pursued by Satan himself.

But the devil he was fleeing had soft red hair and skin as white as December snow on the hooked peak of Carrantuohill. And even as his horse thundered over the land, Mason knew that he couldn't escape those whiskey-colored eyes. No matter how far or hard he rode he would still want her, and he would hurt, knowing that she didn't want him, not anymore. Caitlin wanted another man. And Mason hated him for it.

At the same time, Mason wished to God that it was anyone other than Michael McKevett. Had it not been for Caitlin, the two men might have been friends. And if Michael had been English aristocracy and not peasant Irish, and . . .

Mason's stallion leaped the stone wall and galloped across the open field toward the ringed fairy fort. Mason smiled wryly as he spotted two men in the center of the field about two hundred paces ahead of him. One of the figures was easily recognized because of his enormous size. It was Mason's nemesis, Michael McKevett. As the landlord slowly neared the two men and the large stone, he realized that the second man was Rory Doona, and that Rory was dead.

When Mason was about thirty feet from them, Michael turned his head and their eyes met. In the moonlight Michael's face was as white as the ancient stone and as ghastly as that of the dead man whose body was draped limply across the rock.

"Good evening, Your Honor," Michael said smoothly, covering his shock at being discovered. "Fancy meeting you in this lonely place."

"Yes, apparently the wheel of fortune is turning in my direction for a change." Mason nodded toward the corpse. "I see that Sweet Justice has finally had her day with our friend there."

"Aye, it appears that old Rory's time had come."

Mason studied the dark rivulets of blood that streamed down onto the dead man's face from a wound on his head. "It also appears that someone helped him along on his journey into eternity. And I was just fortunate enough to come upon the murderer himself— in the act." Mason reached into his coat pocket, pulled out his dainty, but deadly, silver pistol, and pointed it at Michael. "It's not every day a man finds his rival with blood on his hands."

Silently Michael stared at the pistol. Then he lifted his gaze and his green eyes bored into the landlord's with an intensity that Mason felt to the toes of his doeskin boots. "I could kill you this minute," Mason said. "I could shoot you and save the constable the trouble of hanging you."

Michael's green eyes didn't waver. "Ye could, but I

287

don't believe ye will. I think you'd find it as hard to murder me as I would to murder you."

Mason's hand began to tremble, and the gun wavered ever so slightly. He wanted to kill him. It would be so simple. This was the perfect opportunity, and somehow, Mason knew that if he didn't kill Michael McKevett now, he would never again have the chance. But McKevett was right. He couldn't do it.

Reluctantly the landlord put the gun back into his pocket. "Did you kill him for some particular reason?" he asked, waving vaguely toward the body. "Or did you have nothing better to do this evening?"

"He beat me wife, Annie," Michael replied stoically. "And she lost the baby we were to have."

Mason nodded his understanding. "That's as good a reason as any, I'd say, for killing someone. You must never let a man rob you of someone you love without making him pay a price."

His words were weighted, and he saw by the look on Michael's face that his meaning wasn't lost. The landlord reached into his coat pocket again, only this time he withdrew a document. "This is a ticket for first-class passage aboard a ship bound for England. I had purchased it for myself, but I've decided to postpone my trip several months. I want you to have the ticket." He held the paper out to Michael.

"But I have no reason to go to England," Michael replied.

Mason hesitated, choosing his words carefully. "With this ticket you could take along a wagon and a horse and—"

"I have no wagon or horse."

"You have now. You can collect them tomorrow morning at Armfield House. And with this wagon and horse you can tour the English fairs with your carousel. Just think what a great success you'll be."

Mason watched the lines harden in McKevett's face.

"But I'm a blacksmith and a woodcarver, not a busker doing tricks at fairs."

"Better a live busker than a hanged smith, I'd think."

Michael shrugged and looked down at the limp figure lying across the stone. "There's no reason for my neck to be stretched. No one knows I did the deed except—"

"Except an English landlord whose testimony would be accepted without question."

Michael's eyes narrowed and his jaw tensed. "What jury would condemn a man for killin' a man who beat his wife and murdered his child?"

"A jury of my choosing," Mason replied, hiding the emotions that raced through him behind a mask of indifference. "Don't misunderstand me, McKevett. If I want you hanged, you'll be dead before this time tomorrow night."

"And is that what you want? Do you want me dead?" Again those green eyes pierced his, seeing things that Mason allowed no one to see.

"I want you out of my sight," he said.

"Out of Caitlin's sight, you mean."

"Whatever." He tossed the ticket onto the ground at Michael's feet. "The ship leaves the day after tomorrow. That should be just enough time for you to dispose of that body and say goodbye to your family. Make certain they understand one thing clearly: you won't be returning to Ireland."

* * *

"Michael, I can't believe yer leaving me, and me lying here, bruised and battered. 'Tis cruel you are, cruel and heartless." Annie watched her husband through eyelids that were swollen nearly closed from the abuse of Rory Doona's knuckles and the tears she had shed.

He looked down at her without a trace of his usual compassion. "If there's a soul in this room who's cruel, I'd say it's the one who delivered three innocent men into the hands of the law to be killed."

Annie's heart sank. Michael knew it all now, and he would never forgive her.

"It's because I'm sick and can't have any more babies. That's why you're leaving me, I know it," she whined.

"That has nothing to do with it, Annie," he said, his voice too tired for exasperation. "I'm leaving because I must, not because I want to."

"But I don't understand."

"Ye don't have to understand. Just kiss me goodbye and I'll be on my way."

He leaned over her bed, but she turned her face away and closed her eyes. "I'll not send you away with a blessing, Michael," she said bitterly. "If yer leaving me in my hour of need, 'twill be without a God Be With You."

She waited for him to press the point, but he didn't, and by the time she opened her eyes he was gone.

On his way out, Michael met Judy at the door of the cottage. She had a basket full of eggs in one hand and a milk pail in the other. He took the heavy can from her and set it near the churn. She placed the basket on the table and, wiping a stray tear from her cheek with the corner of her apron, she turned to face him. "Michael, I can't believe it's true. Tell me you're not leaving us, for I couldn't bear to see you go."

He held out his arms to her and in an instant she

was hugging him tightly around the waist and sobbing, her face buried against the front of his shirt. He stroked her glossy dark hair with his palm. "Hush now, Judy. You mustn't cry. It's your bright smile I want to remember, not your tears."

She pulled back and looked up at him, her black eyes streaming. "Michael, don't go. I know that Annie's been unkind to ye, and she hasn't been a good wife, but if you'll stay I promise I'll have a talk with her and—"

"It isn't because of Annie I'm leaving," he said. " 'Tis another reason entirely ... one I can't tell ye. I'd never leave the ones I love without a good reason."

"Can't you tell me what it is?" she asked. "I'll tell no one, I swear, and maybe we can think of a way for you to stay."

"I know you'd never tell, Judy. But I can't tell you for your own sake. It's best you never know."

Bending down, he kissed her forehead. She returned the kiss sweetly to his cheek, and he felt an ache in his chest.

"I love you, Michael. Till I see you again, may God keep you in the palm of his hand, and may He never close his fist too tight on you."

He smiled and dabbed away her tears with her apron. "I love you, too, Judy. You've been a fine sister to me. May you and Sean live well together as man and wife, and may you both die in Ireland."

Her lower lip began to quiver again and a sob caught in her throat. "And where will you die, Michael?"

"I don't know. But I can feel in my bones that it won't be here in the arms of old Erin."

Michael stood silently, watching Kevin pound the hatchet blade into a sharp edge. He had seen Kevin do

291

better work, but that had been when the smith's mind had been on the task at hand. At that moment neither man cared whether the hatchet blade was sharp and well-balanced.

"It's nearly sundown," Kevin said, looking out the forge's one window at the darkening summer sky. "You'd best be on you way." Without a glance at Michael, he went back to his work.

Michael stepped up and put his hand on the smith's burly forearm, halting the hammer. "I don't want to leave without your blessing. Kevin, please . . ."

When Kevin finally looked up at him, his eyes glowed with anger and the red fire of the oven. "You want to be blessed for leaving my daughter on her sick bed, for leaving me to work here alone in this forge without—"

"You have Sean. He's to be your son-in-law soon. Surely you can take him to your heart and love him as a son."

Kevin's ruddy face flushed darkly. "I took you to my heart and look what you're doin' to me, lad. You marry my daughter and now you destroy her by deserting her. No, I'll never take another to me heart again. Never again."

"I must go, Kevin." Swallowing hard, Michael spoke the words of confession that had to be said to his father-in-law, if to no one else. "I murdered Rory Doona last night and Lord Armfield saw me. If I don't leave, he'll see me hang."

Kevin threw the hot blade into the bath. "I figured 'twas something like that."

"And still, you'd condemn me for leaving when my life depends on it?"

"I don't condemn you for killing Rory. If you hadn't, I would have done the deed meself, after what he did to my Annie. But—'' Kevin's voice broke and he turned his back to Michael. His broad shoulders shook with emotion. "I don't want you to leave, Michael," he said hoarsely, "for I'm afraid that if I let you leave, I'll never see your face again."

Michael choked back his own tears as he tried to think of some word of comfort for this man who had been his father. How could he promise Kevin that they would see each other again, when he himself knew it was impossible?

"Kevin, I must go now," he said softly, laying his hand on the man's shoulder. "Bless me . . ."

Without turning around Kevin said, "May the strength of three be with you on your journey, Michael, my son. And may we see each other in heaven if never again on this earth."

Michael reached out and touched his shoulder lightly, then withdrew his hand. "I thank you, Kevin. God be with you till then."

From his perch atop Michael's shoulders, Danny sensed that something was terribly wrong. Michael was too quiet, and the bounce was missing from his step. He trudged along the narrow road without his usual comments about the birds and roadside flowers. And although they had been walking for half an hour, Michael hadn't told him a single story yet. When they passed a ring of golden-topped mushrooms that sprang up through the short grass in front of the McGillycuddy's gate, and Michael didn't tell him the story of the fairies' dance, Danny knew that it was bad news indeed.

"Where are we goin'?" It was Danny's standard question, but this time there was a small quiver in his voice.

"To Armfield House," came the clipped reply.

"To see the white stallion, Niav's enchanted stallion?"

"No, to see a mare and a wagon."

A mare and wagon weren't as exciting as an enchanted stallion, but Danny didn't care. As long as he was with Michael, all was right in his narrow world. Almost all.

"What's the matter with ye?" His small fingers tugged at his friend's dark curls. "I think the old witch's black cat has your tongue entirely."

The strong hands tightened around Danny's shins. "I've a mouth of ivy and a heart of holly today, lad," Michael replied. "Since this time yesterday I've had to do some of the hardest things a man can have forced upon him. And the hardest is yet to come."

"And what is it ye must do, Michael? Is it such a hard thing to look at a mare and a wagon? Is it because I'm too heavy for yer shoulders now that I've grown bigger?"

Michael was quiet for a long time, long enough that Danny wondered if he had heard. Finally he said, "You've grown a lot in the past few months, it's true. But I wish I could carry you forever."

Danny pondered that statement as they turned down the road that led to the barns where Armfield's mares were stalled. As far as he was concerned, Michael was welcome to carry him forever, or at least until he got to be a man, which was the same as forever from Danny's point of view.

Michael poked his head into three of the barns before he located the mare of his choice, a sturdy draft horse, wide of back, and heavy of muscle. Michael bridled her, then led her out into the courtyard, where he knelt on the cobblestone and allowed Danny to slip down from his back.

"Are you going to shoe her for His Honor?" Danny asked, surprised at the way Michael was handling the horse, almost as though she were his own.

"No," Michael said as he lifted and examined each foot and shoe. "His Honor has made a present of her to me, kindly gentleman that he is."

A certain note of bitterness in Michael's voice made Danny wonder if this were one of those times when big people said one thing but meant another. "Is it a present, truly? Ye don't have to pay for her at all?"

Michael laughed, but it wasn't a happy sound. "Aye, I'm paying a dear price for her, surely. Not with coin. Only with pieces of me heart." He reached down and smoothed Danny's curls, and the boy thought that he had never seen Michael looking so sad. "The dearest pieces," he added. "Come along, lad. I've something to show you, something that I need help with, and 'tis only yourself can do the deed."

Daniel followed him to the woodshop, swelling with pride. It seemed that he was forever needing Michael; it felt good to have Michael need him for a change. He wondered what task it was that only he could do.

Inside the shop Danny smiled at the five horses standing in a row against the wall. The young boy had spent many hours here in the past few months. He had sat in the corner on a low stool and whittled figures that were getting more lifelike and detailed all the time. He had watched carefully as Michael carved, sanded and painted. At times, Michael had even allowed him to carve a saddle buckle, or a rose, or a sweep in the mane and tail.

But today there was a new horse in their midst, a

horse that was pieced together and roughed out, with none of the details defined.

"I thought you were done with your horses," Danny said, running his hand lovingly over the block of wood that promised to be an animal someday. "I thought you had enough for your wheel."

"I do, for now," Michael replied, watching the small hand. "But someday I want to make an even bigger wheel with more animals. And I want this to be the grandest horse on my new, big wheel."

Danny's eyes glowed at the very thought. "Can I help you with him? You said yourself I'm getting good at carving ... damned good, you said, though I can't say that 'cause Annie would switch me if I did. Can I help you with him?"

"That's what I want to talk to you about. Come to meself, Danny lad."

Michael sat on the earthen floor in a pile of wood shavings and held out his arms to the boy. Danny needed no encouragement. Inside the circle of Michael's arms was the safest, happiest place on earth, and he savored every minute there.

But today something was different. Michael held him tighter against his chest. So tightly that Danny knew for sure that something was terribly wrong.

"Ah, Danny," Michael whispered, kissing the top of the boy's curly head. "I'm going to have to go away for a while ... for a long while."

Danny's throat squeezed shut. This was worse than he could have ever imagined. "Where is it you're going? To Killarney? Maybe all the way to Cork?"

"To England."

England was on the other side of the world, by America and China. It was across the sea, and Danny couldn't bear the thought of the wide ocean separating him and his friend. His small arms tightened around Michael's neck. "No. Ye mustn't go ... unless ye take me with you. Take me on your journey with you, Michael. I'll walk, I will. Ye won't have to carry me the whole way."

Danny put his hand up to Michael's face and felt a dampness on his cheek. Michael was crying. This was the end of the world, surely, because Michael never cried.

"I can't take ye with me, Danny, though I want to, desperately bad. I've thought about it to be sure, but I can't."

"Why not?"

"Because I may not be back for a very, very long time. And, as much as I love you, you aren't me own son. You're Kevin's son and—"

"But he doesn't want me. He doesn't love me the way you do."

Michael frowned and shook his head. "You must never say that. Your father loves you dearly, he just doesn't know how to say it and show it. 'Twould break his heart if I were to take you with me. And what of Annie and Judy? They would cry day and night if you were to leave them, they love you so."

"But what about you? Won't you be sad if you go away? You'll be all alone, Michael. Won't you be sad to leave me, just a little bit?"

Michael said nothing, but looked down into Danny's eyes. Danny saw the tears and knew that they were for him. Michael took the boy's hand and held it against his broad chest. "You don't need to ask if I love you, Danny. You know how much I do. And you don't have to ask if I'm sad to be leavin' you behind. Just be quiet for a bit. Close your eyes and feel what's in my heart."

The boy did as he was told. He closed his eyes and was quiet. He could feel Michael's heart beating against the palm of his hand, hard and strong. But he felt more than the pounding. He felt a terrible pain in his own chest, as though the very core of him was being torn out by a cruel hand. Gasping from the pain, Danny opened his eyes.

"There'll surely be times when you'll wonder how I could leave you if I truly loved you. You'll wonder if I really cared about you. That's when I want you to remember what you felt just now. Remember what was in my heart the day I left you. Promise me you'll do that."

Unable to speak around the aching knot in his throat, Danny nodded.

"And there's one more thing that I want you to do for me while I'm gone."

Michael eased the boy off his lap, walked over to the workbench, and lifted the box that contained his chisels and gouges. Reverently he placed the box in Daniel's hands. Then he led the boy over to the new horse.

"I want you to finish this horse for me while I'm gone. The bridle, the saddle, the mane and tail. Even the face. I want you to do it all yourself. Sean agreed to come get the horse tonight and take it to your father's barn where you can work on him anytime you like."

Though this was the darkest day in Daniel O'Connell O'Brien's short life, he felt as though the sun itself was beaming down on his head, warm and life-giving. "You . . . you want me to . . ."

"That's right. You've been a good apprentice, working by my side all this time, and you've learned a lot. You've a natural gift for the wood, lad. The carving is inside you as surely as it's inside me. I wouldn't ask you to do it if I wasn't sure ye could."

"But, what if I make a bungle of it?"

"You'll do what I do when I make a mistake. I think of a way to fix it, and I try again. He's your horse, lad.

Your very own. Carve him into anything you like. There's no one to say you've done him right or wrong."

Danny looked down at the gift in his hand, the box that could not be more precious to him if it contained Queen Victoria's rubies and emeralds. "But your tools—"

"They're your tools now. I know I couldn't leave them in better hands than Daniel O'Brien's."

Danny put his arms around the horse's neck ... his horse. "I'll make him a beauty, I will. You'll see."

Michael nodded approvingly. "I'm sure you will."

"But when will ye come back, Michael? When will you come back to Ireland?"

Michael turned away so that Danny couldn't see his eyes. "When you finish the horse, lad. When you've done everything that you can possibly think of to make him a wonder to behold, that's when I'll come back to Ireland."

Daniel watched silently from the door of the woodshop as Michael drove away in the wagon, the stout mare pulling the load of horses and the giant wheel. At the bend in the road, Michael stopped and turned back to wave one last time. But Danny couldn't wave, couldn't bring himself to say goodbye.

He couldn't help thinking that his friend would never return. Michael was like Oisin, going away with the enchanted horses to the Land of the Ever Young. And like Oisin, if he stayed away too long, by the time he returned everything would be changed, everyone would be gone.

Lifting his chin, the boy hobbled back into the woodshop where his horse stood, as alone now as Daniel O'Brien himself. Without hesitation he picked up the chisel and started to carve. He carved and carved until the sun went down and he could no longer see.

He had to carve as quickly as he could. Michael couldn't come back until the horse was finished and a wonder to behold. And somehow Danny knew in his heart that if Michael, like Oisin, waited too long to return, they would all be dead.

The moment Michael walked into the pub, Caitlin knew that he had changed. "Michael, what's wrong? What happened to you?" She slid the heavy bar across the door and pulled the curtains over the windows, signaling to any prospective customers that O'Leary's pub was closed for the night, and she was not to be disturbed.

Michael sank onto his usual stool by the hearth, but tonight he didn't carve. His scarred hands clutched each other restlessly between his open knees as he leaned forward on his elbows and stared into the fire.

She sat at his feet and looked up at him, trying to read the changes in his face. Where was the gentle light that had shone in those green eyes, eyes that softened with empathy at another's grief and registered the guilt of a sensitive heart? A light still burned in those emerald depths, but it was a glimmer of angry coals, smoldering and hot. The change frightened Caitlin, and at the same time, she was drawn to him as a weary traveler is lured to a roaring fire on a cold winter night.

"I've just said farewell to my family," he said. "I kissed me mother goodbye in that cursed graveyard. I'll never see her alive again—I know it. And now I've come to bid you goodbye, Caitlin." There was a new tone in his voice, as well, a deep, husky quality used by those men who had been through the forge's hottest fire and had come out fine tempered steel.

She slowly shook her head, rejecting his words, denying the horrible, sinking feeling in the pit of her stomach. "Goodbye? But you've only just arrived. I haven't even served you a pint—" She jumped up from the hearth to fetch him a drink, but he reached for her and grasped her firmly by the wrist.

"I didn't come here for an ale," he said as he pulled her back to the floor. "I don't have time for such things tonight."

Something in his words, something in his eyes made her breathing tighten. His hand, still clutching her wrist, sent a shiver through her.

"I'm leaving Ireland in three days, sailing from Cork to England at the request of His Honor Lord Mason Armfield." He spat the words out as though they were sour on his tongue, and Caitlin felt a stab of guilt. Somehow this was her fault, though she wasn't sure how.

"But how can he force you to go, Michael, if ye don't want to be going?"

One corner of his full lips curled into a rueful smile. "He's the landlord, and he can do what he wishes with the likes of us, Caitlin. Surely ye know that better than most."

Her cheeks grew hot beneath his scrutiny. She felt ill at ease with this new Michael, like the shy lass she had once been instead of the confident woman she had become. It was a feeling that Caitlin hadn't experienced in many a year, and she didn't care for it much.

"But how?" she asked. "What happened?"

He released her wrist and she felt a sense of loss. Instantly she missed the strength that his touch imparted.

"I murdered Rory Doona last night." His eyes searched her face as though looking for condemnation, but he found none.

301

"I'm relieved to hear that he's dead," she said simply. "And I'm glad 'twas you who killed him. One of you was bound to die sooner or later. I'm just happy 'twas Rory and not you."

"So am I. Tonight I realized that some men deserve to die. And I believe I'll sleep soundly now for the first time in five years." He sat quietly for a long moment with a faraway look in his eyes. Then he blinked as though remembering Caitlin's presence. "But His Honor saw me do the deed, love, and if I don't leave Ireland tonight, he'll have me hanged by morning."

Caitlin winced. " 'Tis my fault after all," she said, nodding sadly. "If it weren't for me, he wouldn't care a whittle what happened between you and Rory. He wants you out of Ireland because he thinks that if you were gone, I would love him better."

Michael leaned forward on the stool until his face was only a hand's width from hers. She could feel his soft breath on her cheek and smell the warm, masculine scent of his body. "And is that what will happen, Caitlin? With me gone will you love His Honor better?"

" 'Twill make no difference," she replied. "If you stay or if you go, I'll not be able to love him the way he wants. Never again."

Not since I gave my heart to you, Michael, she thought. *I gave you my love years ago when we were only children.* But Caitlin kept her thoughts to herself.

Shortly after that night, Michael had found out about her relationship with Mason Armfield. If his love had been as strong as hers, he would have searched his heart for a kernel of forgiveness, of understanding. But he hadn't. Instead, he had married another.

She couldn't profess her love for him now, even though she sensed that he wanted to hear it. This feeling she harbored for him was a priceless treasure, and she had to guard it even from him.

"Why did you come here tonight, Michael?" Her eyes locked with his, searching and finding only a darkness that frightened and excited her.

He reached for her and, circling her waist with his big hands, he drew her between his spread thighs. "I think you know why I'm here." His fingertips stroked her cheek and trailed down her throat and across the swell of her breast. The intimacy of the simple touch washed through her like a liquid heat, leaving her weak with desire. She closed her eyes and swayed toward him.

He caught her to him, burying his hands in her hair. "We both knew this was going to happen. We've known from the first. 'Twas as sure to happen in the end as the sun setting on Inishnabro."

She nodded slowly, watching his lips, so full and sensual and so close to hers. "I knew that we'd have more than that night by the river," she whispered. "There had to be more."

He moaned softly and covered her lips with his. His mouth took hers with a fierce possessiveness that robbed her of breath. Her hands found his shoulders, and she clung to him for support as he pressed her closer into him, into the hardness of his body that told her how much he wanted her.

"Ah, yes, we'll have more than that, lass," he said as he stood and pulled her to her feet. "The spirits intend for you and me to have great deal more."

His hands went to her bodice and began to loosen the lacings. "I can't go through the rest of my life wondering," he said as he pushed the thin, linen chemise aside. "I'm tired of dreaming of how it would be to hold you, tired of imagining the softness of your skin
303

and the curves of your body. I want to know how it feels to be inside you, loving you, making you my own. I have to know."

The touch of his palms on her bare breasts made it difficult for her to think, to speak. "But—but what if wondering is better than remembering? What if we do this and then the remembering drives us mad with wanting each other again and you so far away?"

He scooped her into his arms and carried her to the door of her bedroom. "Then it's mad we'll be. But anything would be better than having nothing to remember."

If there was ever a spot that could be called lonely in Ireland, it was surely The Pass of the Deer, a deep cleft that ran about two miles through the mountains on the north road between Killarney and Macroom.

With his new mare and his wagonload of dreams, Michael trudged along the narrow road, the sweltering rays of the midday sun beating down on his bare head.

Overhead enormous masses of rock seemed poised in the air, almost perpendicular on either side of the road. The ragged cliffs were covered with stunted arbutus, rowan tree, yew and holly. Not a single song of a bird or the hum of a bee interrupted the heavy silence. Not a hint of breeze stirred the oppressive heat.

Rivulets of sweat trickled down his forehead and neck as he walked beside the wagon to give the mare a rest and his legs a stretch.

The horse was a sturdy, lively beast, and Michael was pleased with their progress. They would reach Macroom by sundown and that was over halfway to Cork. He should have no trouble meeting his ship.

As tired as he was, he dreaded nightfall, dreaded the

time when he would lie down to sleep ... alone. Strange, he'd slept alone all his life, and until now he hadn't minded. But that was before last night. Before Caitlin.

Every time he thought of her, a sweet longing coursed through him. It was an ache that hurt worse than the heartbreak of leaving Lios na Capaill, of leaving Kevin, Sorcha, or even Danny. He had left a part of himself, the best part, in her keeping.

He had risen early and kissed her cheek once as she slept before he slipped away. He should have awakened her and bade her a proper goodbye. But he couldn't. If he had, she might have begged him to stay, and after last night, he could never have refused her anything.

Closing his eyes against the bright noonday sun, he remembered the candlelit coolness of the night, remembered the silken caresses and the kisses that seared and intoxicated him like the purest poteen. He remembered her limbs, long, shapely and wonderfully bare as she lay across her bed, her arms held out to him in total surrender. He had never seen a woman's body before, and he drank in the sight, reveling in her beauty and her willingness to let him see and touch her. With no hint of embarrassment, only desire, she had pulled him to her, welcoming him as a friend and lover.

Michael had abandoned himself to the joy of loving her, claiming the happiness that he had always denied himself. There was no longer any reason to hold back.

That night beside the Druid stone, he had forgiven himself for both murders. The waters of the stone had cleansed his blood-stained hands, and he had no longer felt unworthy to touch her.

His hands had moved over her, caressing, exploring, passionately expressing his feelings for her with fingertips that were forever scarred, but had never been so sensitive. And when he had finally entered her, making her his own, he had felt as though he were coming home to a beloved familiar place that he had always known, the one place in the world where he truly belonged.

As his body had found its release, his soul had exploded outward, searching for another to bond with. In that moment he had found her spirit open, waiting to receive him. Now he truly knew what the priests meant when they said, "Two shall be one."

He had never felt that with Annie. When his heart had reached out to her, he had found her closed and guarded. What should have been a bonding act between a husband and wife had left him feeling empty and more lonely than before. He had known in his heart that love-making wasn't supposed to leave you empty and aching. But until last night, he had never realized what it was to love completely, to have his love accepted and returned.

Undoubtedly the priests would say that what he had done had been a sin, that his marriage to Annie was sacred and his love for Caitlin was profane. But as Michael walked that long road to Cork, he felt no pain at leaving Annie. He hardly even felt the heartache of leaving Kevin, his mother, or Danny. He knew that when he boarded that ship in Cork Harbor and sailed away to England, the tears he would shed would be for dear old Erin, and for her lovely, red-haired daughter who had shown him the joy of being a man.

Caitlin stood at the edge of the ringed fairy fort, her face to the night wind. She pulled the scarf from her head so that the breeze could blow through her hair, making her one with the night.

"Michael," she whispered, and the wind carried the word away to the east, toward Cork.

Closing her eyes, she placed her hand on her breast, where his hand had rested last night as he had slept beside her. She had lain awake most of the night, cherishing every minute with him, and had finally drifted off to sleep just before dawn. She had woken to find him gone.

Her palm glided down the front of her dress and stopped on her belly, which was taut and flat. A shiver went through her as she remembered the moment when he had plunged into her and planted his seed deep in her womb. She had received him as completely as a woman could receive a man, and he had been hers. Nothing could break the bond that had been forged, even if they were separated by the Irish Sea and all of Queen Victoria's armies. Nothing could take from her the part of himself that he had left behind.

Caitlin opened her eyes and held her left hand up to the moon. It hung so low in the dark Kerry sky, she could almost touch it. "Bring him back," she whispered to the silver orb, feeling the force of its feminine, mystic power. "Every night you bring the tides back to the shore. Surely you can bring Michael back to me."

Chapter Sixteen

" 'Tis the smoke and steam from those new loco-motives that's blighted the praties sure," Paul Gannon said, shaking his head sadly as he hoisted his one mug of the evening and sipped gingerly. Most of the men with families were rationing their intake of ale, holding on to what few coins they had. With the first diggings of potatoes turning to a putrid mush in their bins, a man had to conserve his resources. The potatoes had failed before, but never so badly as this.

"Naw, 'tis that new manure we used this spring. We all should have known that no good would come of using bird shit. Whatever lad thought of that fine idea should have his neck stretched."

Caitlin listened quietly as she moved from table to table. A few weeks ago she would have tried to lift the mood of the pub, encouraging them to sing or even dance a step or two to the sound of the pipe. But it seemed pointless now. With more and more diggings turning bad, there was a sense of impending doom hanging over the village, and there was no tune so merry as to dispel that cloud.

She filled Eoin Gannon's mug to the brim. If a man could only afford one drink, it should be a hearty one.

"Well," Eoin said, "I had a talk with this lad who has a cousin twice removed who knew a professor at the university there in Dublin." Eoin leaned back in his chair and pulled deeply on his pipe, a philosophical lift to his right eyebrow. He had not a single hair on his bald and shining pate, having lost it early in life. But he sported the finest pair of bushy black eyebrows west of the Irish Sea, and they lent him an air of distinction. "And after discussin' the matter at some length, we decided that the blight comes from mortiferous vapors rising from blind volcanoes deep inside the earth itself."

"Aw ..." Paul dismissed his younger brother with a wave of his hand. "The only mortiferous vapors rising around here are from the seat of your breeches."

"No one knows the true source of the potato blight," came a quiet voice from the corner. Caitlin and her customers turned in unison toward the lone figure who sat quietly sipping his brandy. "If I might give you gentlemen a word of advice," Mason Armfield said, his deep voice more grave than usual, "I would suggest that instead of wasting your time arguing about the cause of the blight, you spend your energies in pursuit of an answer to the dilemma that you and your families will soon be facing."

The Gannon brothers looked at each other in surprise, and Eoin's eyebrows shot up in indignation. "And just what remedies might you suggest, Your Honor?" he asked with thinly veiled sarcasm.

Sean Sullivan joined the conversation from his seat at the bar. "Maybe the first step would be to hold on to those vegetables and grains we've been raising in our poor gardens instead of handing them over to the landlords to pay the rent. My Judy has raised enough fine cabbages and carrots to keep us eatin' all winter, but old Larcher will have his share. Isn't that so, Your Honor?"

Caitlin held her breath and waited for Armfield's reply to Sean's insult. Hunger brought out the rebellious streak even in those who had always played the peacemaker.

Armfield stared down into the brandy in his glass. "I've already waived all payments of food from my tenants," he said quietly. "And I've offered them work on my estate to pay their rents during this difficult time."

"That's decent of you, Your Honor, truly it is," Sean said. "But what of the rest of us who aren't so lucky as to have you for a landlord? Larcher is coming by day after tomorrow to collect his wagonload, and if we don't hand it over, we'll be living in a ditch come nightfall. 'Tis little comfort to have food in your belly if ye've no roof over your head."

The men in the room waited, but Armfield sipped his brandy in silence. Finally the conversation at the tables returned to speculations about the causes of the blight.

One by one they finished their solitary pints and trailed away much earlier than usual for a Saturday night. Finally, only Armfield remained.

When Caitlin offered to refill his glass, he dismissed her with a wave of his hand. She sat down in the chair opposite him and drummed her fingertips on the table until he looked up at her, his gray eyes guarded as always these days.

"Do you have something to say, Caitlin?"

"I was just thinking."

"Yes?"

She took a deep breath and watched his eyes trail

310

down her throat to her bodice. "You might help them. You could speak to Larcher," she said. "He might listen to you, you being English and all."

"I might," he said simply. "And he might."

He rose, lifted his cloak from the peg on the wall and swirled it around his shoulders. She walked him to the door and watched as he mounted the white stallion and rode away into the darkness.

Caitlin sniffed the night air and wrinkled her nose. The evening breeze carried the pungent stench of rotting potatoes, a smell so foul that it could never be forgotten. It was the stench of death.

There were bad times coming. She could smell it on the wind and see it in the frightened, drawn faces of her neighbors. Terrible times. Coming soon.

Caitlin placed her palm over her abdomen and shuddered. Could there be a worse time to be bringing a child into the world?

"I swear to God, Larcher, you make me ashamed to be English. Where is your decency, your sense of compassion? How can you call yourself a gentleman?"

Larcher lifted his multi-layered chin several notches and looked down the bulbous length of his whiskey-reddened nose at Armfield. "I *am* an English gentlemen, sir," he replied haughtily, "and I'll thank you to remember that this is *my* home and that is *my* sherry you're drinking. As long as you partake of my hospitality, I'll ask you not to insult me simply because we disagree on politics."

Mason looked into Larcher's watery-blue eyes and hated the man through and through. He hated the coldness, the ignorance, the bigotry. Most of all, he hated Travis Larcher for being what he himself had been

311

years before. "We aren't talking politics here. We're talking about the survival of human beings, living, breathing men and women who shoe your horses, bake your bread and sew your clothes. Don't you have any sense of obligation toward your tenants?"

"Obligation? Toward those heathens? Those Catholic barbarians are the blight on this land, not the rotten potatoes. They have been breeding like rats, until the land is overrun with them. Don't you recognize the hand of God here, man? It's the divine will of Providence. This is what we've been praying for all these years."

Mason shook his head. Suddenly he felt sick inside. "I would never pray for a catastrophe like this, and don't be so quick to lay the responsibility on God. If this horror has been handed down from the heavens, then you can be sure that it's a test. A test to see how well you and I and the other landowners provide for those whom He has put into our keeping." Mason's hand went involuntarily to his scarred cheek and his eyes had a faraway look as he remembered. "God exacts harsh penalties from those who fail his tests. Remember, Larcher, He expects a great deal from those to whom He has given a great deal. A wise man would not disappoint Him. At least, not more than once."

The blank look in his fellow Englishman's eyes told Mason that his words were wasted. So, he placed the glass of sherry in the man's hand, turned around and walked to the door.

"And as far as your hospitality is concerned," he said as he paused in the doorway, "a true English gentleman would never offer his guest such an inferior sherry . . . and even an Irish heathen would know better than to water it down. Good evening, Travis. Sleep well."

312

So, this is what it's like in the Land of the Ever Young,
Michael thought as he stood in the middle of the village
common of Stow-on-the-Wold in Glouchester. From
every direction he was greeted by the sights, sounds,
and smells of the fair: the aroma of fresh-baked breads
and cakes, and strips of meat that smoked over pedlar's
fires; the gayly decorated stalls with brilliant tatters of
cloth that flapped in the crisp autumn breeze; the low-
ing cattle and bleeting sheep. Pungent animal odors
filled the air as the stock was led into makeshift pens
where they would be auctioned off to anxious farmers
who had waited all year for this event.

But the children ... the children were Michael's
delight. They scampered around him, dozens of them,
hanging from his arms and trying to jump on his back.
"Off with ye," he cried, shooing them away in mock
desperation. "Yer like a pack of wild billygoats, climbin' all over me. Do I look like a mountain to you?"

"Yeah, you do a bit," one little boy replied. "You're
the biggest man we ever saw. Are you going to let us
ride your wheel again tonight? Are you?"

Michael shook his head wearily. "No more tonight,
lad. The flying horses and the magic wheel have all
been packed away for their trip tomorrow morning."

"Trip? Are you going on a journey?" A score of
excited faces lost their glow, and Michael felt a sweet
sadness along with his fatigue.

"Aye, I'm sorry, but I must be off first thing in the
morning. In three days they're havin' a fair in Chipping
Campden, and there's many a lad and lass there who
haven't had a chance to ride the magic wheel yet. We
must give them a turn at it, don't you think?"

The children looked at each other to see if any among
313

them cared enough about the children of Chipping Campden to sacrifice the wonderful wheel. One little girl with bouncing brown curls and a generous nature shrugged. "I suppose they should have a chance to ride it."

The others shook their heads sadly and one by one they left Michael to seek other entertainment.

He strolled among the stalls, pausing to watch a pair of acrobats, a father who lay on his back and whirled his young daughter on his feet. Michael tossed one of the coins he had collected that day into the man's ragged hat, and both father and child gave him a grateful smile.

At one of the bread stalls he purchased a strange pull of bread, twisted around a stick and baked to a golden crispness over the open fire. It was hard, but tasty, and the girl who served him was a comely lass. Her complexion was pale, not ruddy like a healthy Irish girl, and her hair was a dull brown, but her smile was saucy as her eyes swept over him. Her gaze lingered briefly, questioningly, on his scarred hands, then traveled on, appraising his body in much the same way as the farmers had evaluated the cattle at the auction. Michael remembered that she had ridden his wheel three times that day.

"I had a fine time on those flying horses of yours," she said, her voice warm with invitation. "I heard it said that you made that wheel and the horses yourself."

"That's true enough," Michael replied, trying not to sound too terribly proud of himself. After weeks of hearing nothing but compliments about his fine invention, it was getting difficult to be humble.

"And you're so strong," she cooed, "pushing that big wheel all day and not even getting tired."

Michael laughed wryly and bit off a hunk of the

bread. "That's not so true," he said, rubbing his sore back. "Every inch of me body feels as though Cromwell's army had tramped over it. It's done for, I am."

"What a shame," she said, her eyes sweeping him again. "I have some liniment that might help those aches and pains. If you want to come by after I've finished tonight, I could loan you a tin of it. Better yet, I could rub it in for you myself."

Michael grinned and looked down at the ground, avoiding the lascivious glimmer in her eye. He wasn't accustomed to such boldness in females as he had found here among these Protestant English lasses. "I think I'd better not," he said. "But I thank you kindly for the best offer I've had in a while."

She smiled, disappointed, but appeased. "You're Irish, aren't you?"

He nodded.

"I thought so. I could tell by your brogue."

"Is it so strong then?"

"Yes, but I think it's very nice. Gentle and sweet sounding, like water running through a brook. I saw you with all the children around you. Aren't they a bloody nuisance?"

Michael cringed. That was another thing he was finding difficult to adjust to ... women using profanity. A good Catholic girl would never say, "bloody."

"No. Wee ones are never a nuisance. They're the best folk on God's green earth. The world hasn't spoilt them yet."

He pulled off the last bit of bread and handed her the stick. She promptly twisted another braid of dough around it and propped it over the fire. "Do you have children of your own waiting for you back in Ireland?" she asked coyly, brushing the flour from her hands onto her apron that had once been white, but was now

315

smudged a dingy gray from the smoke and ash of the fire.

Michael swallowed that last bite as though it were lead. "No. I've no little ones of me own."

She clucked her tongue sadly, but her eyes held no regret. "Then you have no wife either, waiting for you back in Ireland?"

Michael's eyes softened and he smiled, a gentle, dreamy smile. "Oh, aye. I have a lovely wife in Ireland. She's strong and kind and a beauty besides. Nearly broke me heart, it did, to leave her behind."

"Do you miss her badly?" the girl asked, her own ambitions put aside as she shared his bittersweet longing.

"Aye, desperately bad. Sometimes I think I'll die from missin' her."

"Ah ... that's so romantic," the girl said, leaning one elbow on the stall counter and resting her chin in her hand. "That's what I like about you Irishmen, you're so romantic. What's her name, this lovely lady of yours who's waiting back in Ireland?"

"Her name?" Michael blinked as the image faded and again he was aware of the English face before him. "Me wife's name is Caitlin. Caitlin O'Leary."

He walked away, leaving the girl alone with her fantasies. "Caitlin O'Leary," she sighed. "What a romantic name."

Caitlin polished the spotless bar for the tenth time that evening, hung the cloth on a hook and put her hand into her apron pocket. Jingling the two coins there, she wondered how she and the rest of Ireland were going to survive the winter. She had almost no customers now, nor did the other two pubs in the village. With people roaming the streets, begging for work or a scrap of bread, few had the money for a companionable drink, even if there had been a companion to share it with.

Then there was the other reason why no one was coming into the pub. Even if the potato crop had flourished, there would have been a large percentage of people who would have avoided Caitlin's pub.

Everything the villagers had suspected about Caitlin O'Leary had finally been proven true. She was a bad woman, through and through. The proof was there ... an evergrowing bulge beneath her skirt.

For as long as she could Caitlin had worn loose clothing and stayed behind the bar whenever possible. But yesterday the Gannon brothers had eyed her suspiciously and now word was quickly spreading all over town.

Only this morning old Bridget, who had always given Caitlin a curt nod of her head when meeting her in the village, had crossed the street to avoid her.

It was only a matter of time until everyone knew ... until *he* knew.

She walked over to the fireplace and groaned wearily as she sank onto a stool. What would Mason do when he found out? Not knowing about Michael's last night with her, the landlord would assume that her baby was his. Although he hadn't summoned her to the mansion for a long time, and she hadn't gone voluntarily, she was sure that he still considered her his property.

Even if she couldn't prove it, Caitlin knew instinctively that this child inside her was Michael's. She couldn't allow Mason to think that he had fathered a child, but she wasn't looking forward to telling him about Michael.

Slowly she stirred the pot of soup on the stove that was getting thinner every night. A week ago she had gathered every scrap of vegetable she could find and

317

had tossed it into the iron kettle along with a bucket of water and a handful of maize. Each night she had added a bowl of water to replace the meager portion she had eaten, and tonight's fare boasted not a tidbit of carrot, onion, or cabbage. She was only fooling herself and her stomach that it was anything other than water. This had to stop. It was bad enough to suffer the weakness and pangs of hunger, but when Caitlin realized that she was starving a baby that had not yet even entered the world, her pain became unbearable.

Leaning forward, she rested her arms and head on her knees. Dear God, what an awful time this was. She wanted so much to be happy, happy for the baby, Michael's baby. Any other time she would have been joyful, married or not, to be carrying a child of his. But she didn't know how she was going to keep herself alive long enough to bear the baby, let alone feed it once it was born.

Oh, Michael, she thought, *if you knew, would you be happy? Or would it only make your burden heavier?* She ached to tell him, to share that special, bonding joy that was meant to be shared between a man and woman, a father and mother.

Tears, the first she had shed in a long time, burned her eyes and rolled down her cheeks. She had never felt so alone or so frightened in her life, but she couldn't let Michael's child die. The baby had to live, even if Michael never knew of its birth. This child was all she had left of the man she loved, of their one night together.

Caitlin lifted her chin and ignored the pain in her empty stomach. She would find a way. She always did. But how?

* * *

"I knew that you would come to me for help, Caitlin. It was only a matter of time."

Caitlin searched those cold, gray eyes for any light of affection, even the familiar spark of passion, but she saw only bitter triumph.

Armfield rose from his diamond-tucked leather desk chair and walked across the library floor toward her, the heels of his doe-skin boots clicking on the polished wooden floor. Passing her, he walked over to the fireplace where he stood with his hands stretched out to the rolling flames.

The big house was chilly and full of drafts, not snug and cozy like the cottages in the village. A gust of frigid wind rattled the stained glass window, and Caitlin shivered to think that all that stood between her fellow Irishmen and this vicious winter was English goodwill—a rare commodity, it seemed, even in Armfield House tonight.

Armfield was angry; she knew him well enough to know that. His back was straight, too straight, and he moved carefully as though he were wound so tightly that any sudden movement might cause him to shatter.

"Mason, I wouldn't have come if wasn't to keep body and soul together—"

"Don't you think I know that?" He whirled around and she saw his scarred jaw tighten. "God knows, you haven't come for your own pleasure in months."

She felt a sharp pain slice through her—his pain. She knew that he would never be this furious with her unless she had hurt him badly.

"I'm so sorry," she said, walking up to him and laying her hand on his arm. "That's not what I meant to say. I only want ye to know that I wouldn't be after bothering you unless it was terribly important."

"Bothering me?" His eyes searched her face, then he shook his head slowly and turned away from her. "Oh, Caitlin. Don't you know how many times I've wanted to help you? Don't you think I know why you've finally come to me?"

She swallowed hard and her fingers closed tighter around his arm. "You know about the baby?"

He stared down at her and his pallid face blanched even whiter. "Baby?" His voice was a hoarse croak. "What baby? Do you mean—?" In one movement he pulled the red cloak from her shoulders and swept her apron aside. With the intimate touch of a lover he trailed his hand down her belly, his palm curving to the distorted contour.

Caitlin's pulse quickened, and she felt her face going red with a rush of emotion that had more to do with shame than passion.

"When did you—why didn't you tell me sooner? My God, Caitlin, didn't you think I had a right to know that you're carrying my child?" His hand cupped her chin and forced her to look up at him. The amazement, the joy in his eyes cut her worse than any accusation. She had to tell him.

"Mason, I—" Before she could finish, he pulled her into his arms.

"If I'd only known that was why you were staying away, I would have come after you. But I thought it was because of McKevett. I thought you hated me for sending him out of the country. I never dreamed . . ."

Caitlin felt a tenderness in his hands as they caressed her hair and back that she had never felt before. The aloofness was gone, his guard was down, and his heart was open to her for the first time. And she knew why. He was overjoyed to think that he had fathered a child, and that joy had released a flood of emotion in him that freed him to love.

She would have preferred that he were angry, that he had cursed or struck her. Then it would have been easier to tell him the truth. "Mason, please, I—"

"Sh . . ." He pressed his finger across her lips. "You don't have to beg, Caitlin. You know that I'd never let you go hungry, whether you were with child or not. I'll take care of you and the baby. You'll live here with me and to hell with what the villagers think. They'll be too busy trying to stay alive to worry about morality in the months ahead. And when the child is older, I'll send him to England for an education. Don't worry. I'll take care of everything."

Caitlin said nothing as she grappled with the most difficult decision of her life. If she told him now, he would hate her. After opening his heart to her, after offering to care for her and the child, he would be devastated to hear that she had been with another man and that he had played the fool.

He would hate her, and she knew Mason Armfield well enough to know that he was a formidable enemy. Her pub was on Armfield's land, and if he wanted he could evict her. On the other hand, if she didn't tell him, if she let him go on believing that this child was his, he would provide not only food and shelter for the baby, but a bright future in England that she alone could never provide.

In Lios na Capaill her son or daughter would be shunned as the landlord's bastard, and Caitlin had lived on the fringe of polite society too long to wish that fate on any child of hers. There was only one decision a mother could make, and Caitlin made it.

"It's thankful I am to you, Mason," she said, stepping closer into his embrace. "I'll be forever in your debt."

When he smiled, she realized that gratitude was all he had ever wanted from her—and her indebtedness. He had won. She had bought her life and that of her child's, and the price had been her independence. She would never again be able to hold her head up and say, "Caitlin O'Leary owes no man, and no man owns her."

He dipped his head and kissed her. She returned the kiss, a gesture of thankfulness, not passion. His hands moved over her and she cringed beneath his touch.

Caitlin knew that she would sleep in his bed tonight. He would expect it, and she owed him. She would touch him because she had to, not because she chose to. And for the first time in her life, Caitlin O'Leary felt like a whore.

Chapter Seventeen

Caitlin ran her finger down her son's cheek and wondered that anything on earth could be so soft. "Ah, Bridget, isn't he the loveliest baby ye've ever seen?" she said to the ancient midwife who shuffled at the foot of the bed gathering the soiled sheets and towels into a pile.

Bridget's shriveled face split with a toothless grin. "Every sheep thinks 'tis her lamb that's the whitest," she said with sage wisdom. Then she leaned over the bed, took the child, who was only minutes old, into her arms and squinted down at him owlishly. "But I must admit he is a fine one. And a big lad, too. Just look at the size of him."

Caitlin sighed and fell back against the goose down pillows. "Aye, he seemed as big as a colt coming through. Who would have thought it would be so much work bringing a soul into the world?"

Bridget chuckled as she bundled the baby in a soft linen towel. "And you had an easy time of it at that. You're built for having babes, Miss O'Leary. Ye should have two dozen before you're through." Her wise old face sobered. "Though now's a bad time to have any extra mouths to feed, what with folks eatin' the grasses and brambles to stay alive."

Taking in the bedroom with its carved, four-posted bed, mirrored armoire, and silver candlesticks, Bridget reconsidered. "Though I don't suppose that yer hard put to find a morsel of food here in His Honor's bedchamber."

The unspoken criticism stung Caitlin deeply. She had always liked old Bridget, and it hurt to be judged by someone she admired. " 'Tisn't His Honor's bedchamber," she said in feeble defense. " 'Tis me own."

Bridget looked down at the child in her arms. "But this is his babe?"

Caitlin said nothing, but stared down at the bloodstained linen sheets at the foot of her bed.

"I'll go clean him up a bit," the midwife replied as she left the room with her precious bundle.

Caitlin closed her eyes and winced against the pain in her body, and worse yet, the one in her spirit. She ached for Michael, longed to have him there beside her, holding her hand, sharing the joy of their son. But Michael was a world away, and he didn't even know that he had a son, a big healthy boy with eyes as green as his own.

"Oh, Michael, come back to me," she whispered, sending her heart across the sea to him.

Like the wrong answer to her summons, the door opened and Armfield stepped into the room. He entered tentatively, almost reverently, unlike his usual direct manner. "May I come in now?"

She was surprised to hear the shyness in his voice. "Yes, of course. It's all over."

He walked to her bedside, his eyes scanning the empty cradle beside the bed. "Is the baby all right? I hear a cry and—"

"The baby is fine. A strong, lusty lad. Bridget is giving him his first bath."

The joy that lit his scarred face broke her heart. "A son. That's wonderful, Caitlin!" He cast an anxious glance at the bloody sheets, winced and looked as though he might be ill. "Are you—are you all right? Are you in pain?"

She smiled weakly. "Not nearly so much as a while ago. I'm just tired."

Bridget returned with the baby wrapped in a fresh blanket. With great ceremony she laid him in the cradle and turned to the landlord, her hands on her hips. "Ye've a fine son there, yer honor. May he bring much happiness to ye and yer home, and ye owe me a half-crown." She held out a bony hand.

He raised one eyebrow and the corner of his mouth twisted upward. "Now, Bridget, you wouldn't try to take advantage of an Englishman, would you? Surely you don't charge your fellow Irishmen that much, or there would be far less of them in the world. At that price, they couldn't afford to be born."

"I charge a man what he can pay," she said, her chin nearly touching her long nose when she spoke. "And I don't figure it's goin' to hurt you none to fork over a half-crown."

"Well, let me see what you've brought me first, and then we'll decide what you'll be paid."

Caitlin caught her breath as he walked over to the cradle and lifted the blanket away from the child's face. Would he see the resemblance? Surely it would be as obvious to him as it was to her.

He studied the child for what seemed like an eternity, then he looked at her with affection shining in his eyes. It was the first time she had ever seen such an expression on his face. He said nothing to her, but turned back to the midwife. "You've done a fine job, madam," he said, fishing in his pocket for a coin. "Here's a crown for you. And may you find some food to buy with it. If you can't, you may trade it for whatever you like in my kitchen. Tell the cook to give you your money's worth."

Her fingers clutched the coin as though she were afraid he would snatch it back. "Thank you, yer honor. God bless you, sir." She scurried from the room, her treasure clasped tightly in her hand.

When she had closed the door behind her, Armfield turned and walked back to Caitlin's bedside. He stood quietly, looking down on her for a long time, then he reached out and touched her. With only one fingertip he stroked her cheek, but it was the most intimate touch he had ever given her. It brought tears to her eyes, tears of shame.

"Thank you, Caitlin," he said, wiping away the tear that spilled onto her cheek. "He's a fine child. I'm very proud of my new son."

"Please, don't thank me, Mason." She turned her face away from him and buried it in the pillow. " 'Tis me should be thanking you. I'd have starved sure if you hadn't taken me in and cared for me these long winter months."

"You don't owe me anything, Caitlin." He walked over to the child and lifted the baby from the cradle. "This fine boy is more than enough payment for ..."

Through her tears Caitlin saw Mason looking down at the baby. She saw him hold the child close to his chest for a moment. Then he quickly laid him back down. Something had changed; Caitlin could feel it in the air. Did he know?

She knew he was staring at her, but she couldn't bring herself to look up at him.

Finally, he cleared his throat and said, "I'll go now. You need some rest. We'll discuss the child's future after you've slept."

A moment later he was gone, and Caitlin was left alone with her new son and her fears.

"I was born in this cottage. Me father built it himself, and me mother died here, may she rest in peace, and you can't throw us out when our rent's paid in full."

Sean stood in the doorway of his humble byre cottage, his left arm wrapped tightly around his young wife who shivered at his side.

Constable Sheldon reached into his coat pocket and pulled out an official looking bit of paper. Sean couldn't read, but he knew an eviction notice when he saw one. Heaven knows, there had been plenty of them circulating the county these past few months. He felt Judy sag against him as the realization hit them both. Tonight they would be homeless, and Sean Sullivan had never felt less a man.

Behind the constable stood a company of his best officers, and behind them sat Travis Larcher on his fine bay gelding.

Sean's eyes searched the constable's, but the soldier who had hunted and hanged desperate criminals avoided his gaze and stared at the ground.

"Are ye truly going to throw me out of the only home I've never known, Sheldon?" Sean asked, keeping his voice low so that Larcher wouldn't hear. "Look at my Judy ... she's with child. What kind of man throws a woman with child out of her home?"

The constable cleared his throat and hardened his face. "I have to follow my orders, to uphold the law."

'It's a cruel law that condemns the innocent to death

without a hearing. We'll die if you throw us out, man. What have we done to deserve death?" Sean knew it was pointless to argue. Words of reason were pitiful weapons in the face of blind oppression, but they were his only defense.

"What's the delay here?" Larcher asked, venturing toward the head of the pack. The officers on foot moved aside to let him pass. But once his back was to them, their eyes sliced into him with hate and contempt. "Get them out of there and pull this rat heap down. We have other calls to make. I want this property cleared of them and their Irish stink by sundown. The land is to be plowed tomorrow morning. Get on with it."

The constable turned back to Sean. "Bring your belongings out of the house now."

"No, please—" Judy's hand went protectively to her swollen belly. "My baby will come any day now, and if we've no roof over our heads—"

"You should have thought of that before you let that boar of yours go rutting on you," Larcher said with a lascivious smirk as his watery eyes swept her slight figure. "You Irish breed like hogs and then you expect us to take care of your litters."

Sean caught his breath as rage seared him, hot as a forge oven. He took one step toward the landlord, his fists clenched, his blue eyes blazing. The constable and two of his men quickly stepped between them.

Judy ran up behind him and grabbed his arm. "Sean, don't. It doesn't matter what he says. We're only poor, dumb animals to him. He doesn't know us."

Sean, the peacemaker, stood, his face white with fury. "Ye'll die, Your Honor," he said with deadly quiet. "Ye'll die slowly and in great pain, with your blood in your throat. *Om theanga-sa, go ngaibheadh se' chugat-sa!* By my tongue, may it get you."

Larcher stared down at the young Irishman, his rheumy eyes wide, his mouth open. Finally he closed it and glanced around wildly. "Did you hear that?" he asked the constable and his men. "He threatened me! That bloody Irishman just threatened to kill me. Arrest him this instant!"

Judy stepped between her husband and the constable. "He wasn't threatening you, Your Honor," she said with a gentle humility that didn't show in her eyes. "He cursed you. Surely there's no law against cursing. After all, you Englishmen don't believe in such heathen pishogue."

The constable smiled wryly. "She has a point there, Your Honor. Shall we go ahead with tumbling this cottage so we can get on to the next?"

Larcher pulled a lace handkerchief from his pocket and swabbed his sweaty forehead before he decided to let the curse pass. "Yes, burn it and make sure no stone is left standing," he said, turning his horse's head away from the cottage.

"But their belongings—" the constable objected.

"Damn it, I said burn it now!" Larcher shouted over his shoulder as he galloped away.

Sean didn't want to watch, but he couldn't pull himself away. He and Judy stood at the edge of the woods as the men shoved dried furze bushes into the windows and doors of the tiny cottage and lit the kindling.

In moments the flames were licking at the new roof that he and Kevin had thatched just before his and Judy's wedding.

Judy stood at his side, her small chin held high and her back straight. Most women would be hysterical to see their home burned before their eyes. She was good stock, his Judy. Larcher's insult to her still stung Sean like an adder's venom and poisoned his spirit.

He watched as Larcher directed the men to pound the walls with battering rams until they fell, the flaming thatch raining down inside the broken shell. The black smoke floated across the field to burn their eyes and parch their throats.

Sean put his arms around Judy and pulled her against him, feeling the bulk of their child between them. "We're going to be all right, lass," he said, patting her dark hair. "We'll get through this somehow, I promise ye."

"I know," she said without hesitation. "I know."

"I'm sorry about your mother's china, darlin'," he whispered, holding her even closer.

She nodded and buried her face against his shirt. It was only then that she began to softly cry.

"I'm telling you, gentlemen, if you don't reappoint the Central Board of Health and take action immediately, there will be corpses littering your fine streets this summer. You'll be carting them off by the wagonful with no where to bury them. If you think the starving hordes that are descending on this city now are loathsome, wait until those pathetic crowds are plague-infected."

Lord Hamilton tapped his spectacles impatiently on the burled oak tabletop and cast a bored and somewhat disgusted look at his colleagues who sat, straight-backed and equally bored, around the conference table. "Mason, really, this is the fourth time in six months you have come to Dublin, predicting this coming of the Black Plague. We have tried to be patient with you, but God knows, you do try this council's patience."

"Try your patience?" Mason's gray eyes glittered with anger. "Forgive me if my long-windedness here this afternoon has interfered with your card games or your visits to your mistresses, but we are speaking of a national disgrace. Do you know how many fever wards you people have set up in the length and breadth of this country? Does anyone here know?"

The six council members stared down at their finely manicured fingertips, up at the scrolled ceiling, then out the window at the dark River Liffey that flowed through the heart of Dublin.

"I'm sure that *you* know exactly how many there are, Mason," Lord Hamilton replied wearily. "And I'm equally sure that you intend to tell us."

"Twenty-one. In the whole bloody country there are twenty-one fever wards, and most of those are here in this city."

"And does that number include your estate in Lios na Capaill?" Hamilton asked with an underlying note of sarcasm. "We understand that you have converted the first floor of your house into a fever ward. Is that true?"

Mason's jaw tightened. "It is true, but that has no bearing on this matter—"

"We also hear that you are living with an Irish peasant woman and she has borne you a son. Is that why you suddenly have this heartrending mission to save the Irish?"

Mason's eyes narrowed and every man present felt the chill of that gray ice. "The woman who lives with me is nursing the sick night and day, saving lives at the risk of her own. I'll not have her integrity questioned by this council, which clearly cannot see where its duty lies."

Lord Hamilton rose to his feet and lifted his chin so high it threatened the placement of the powdered wig on his head. "This council does not need to have its duty defined by you, sir, and frankly, we find it surprising that you would defend a people who murdered your good lady and destroyed your face."

Mason winced internally, but although every eye in the room was trained on him, no one saw his pain as the memory cut through him as sharp and vivid as though it were happening even then.

"Some of us learn from our mistakes," he said quietly and without emotion. He glanced around the room at the pompous, overfed faces. "And, obviously, some of us don't. History has shown us that famine is quickly followed by an even worse calamity ... fevers." Mason turned on his heel and walked to the door. With his hand on the crystal knob, he paused and said over his shoulder, "If you don't use your God-given power to avoid this catastrophe, may God spare your loved ones. And may He smite you all."

Caitlin moved from pallet to pallet, making one last check of her wards before going upstairs to catch an hour or two of stupefied sleep. She had given up long ago trying to provide beds for the sick. The mattresses were quickly soiled and ruined, and straw pallets had been put into service. The cases could be ripped open, the straw burned, and the cloth boiled in lye along with the filthied sheets in one of the many kettles that bubbled night and day over fires in the courtyard.

Armfield House no longer resembled the grand estate of a year ago when it had housed only its reclusive lord. Outside the kitchen door stood the perpetual line of emaciated figures who shivered in the bitter cold and waited, sometimes for hours, for a bowl of the soup that simmered on every hearth on the ground floor. The soup contained the careful rationings of the estate's summer crop of vegetables, along with anything else

Lord Armfield was able to purchase on his frequent trips into Cork and Dublin.

Shortly after his speech before the council in January, the Central Board of Health had been reappointed and over three hundred fever hospitals had been built.

But, as Caitlin surveyed the scores of victims, covering the floor of the enormous dining room, she wondered if the hospitals had made any difference at all. It was like trying to bail out the mighty sea. All spring, summer and fall she had nursed the sick brought in by family and friends who were terrified of the highly contagious fevers, too frightened to care for their own relatives.

A few stayed to minister to their kin and helped with the others as well. For those, Caitlin was truly grateful. As for the others, she tried not to judge them, tried not to be bitter when those who had shunned her for bearing a child out of wedlock put their own babies into her arms and ran, afraid of the deadly diseases. This was no time to nurse grudges. There were too many of the sick to nurse, and she simply didn't have the strength to hate or question.

As she leaned over the last child in the long line, she found that the girl had stopped breathing. The little body that had been twitching an hour before, lay still now. When Caitlin placed her hand on the child's forehead she found it cool for the first time in days.

She should be sad. The little girl deserved to have at least one person grieve her passing. But Caitlin had no more grief to offer; it had all been used up like the fresh summer vegetables. The only emotion she felt as she looked down on the dead child was that of quiet relief. The girl's face was relaxed. She looked as though she had fallen asleep in the arms of some benevolent saint, and no one looking at her now would have believed the hell she had endured these past few days.

With a sigh, Caitlin knelt to lift the frail body and take it outside to the men who would lay it on the cart beside the others and carry the corpse out to the cemetery they had started last winter for children who had no one to claim their bodies. There were six hundred graves there now and only God knew how many there would be before this nightmare was over.

"I'll take her out," a quiet voice said, as gentle hands pulled Caitlin to her feet.

She was surprised to see Mason in the sick room. He was spending his wealth buying food and supplies for the fevered and starving. He spent his every waking moment finding food, interceding on behalf of the tenants and their landlords, and petitioning the various councils and private charities in Dublin and abroad. But he seldom came into these rooms.

Caitlin could hardly blame him. What sane person would choose to spend a moment in this stinking, vermin-infested, disease-ridden environment? God knows, she wouldn't be here except she couldn't leave. These were her people who were dying, and she couldn't turn them away.

She didn't believe that it was the stench or the threat of disease that kept Mason away. Although he had never said so in so many words, she knew that he simply couldn't bear to see the suffering. It took a certain kind of strength to take in that much pain and not go mad. And for all his power and confidence, she knew that Mason simply didn't have that kind of strength. But she didn't judge him, either. There was no point.

"Go on upstairs, Caitlin," he said. "Your son needs you, and you have to get some rest before you collapse. I'll be up soon."

She nodded and turned to go up the stairs, but before she was halfway up she heard a banging on the front door. She waited to see if someone else would open it, but when no one did, she answered the knock herself.

"Father Murphy," she said wearily. The good father was a frequent caller these days. "I see you have another one for us. Come on in."

But the stricken look on his face told her that this was no stranger he had found on the road. The person whom he held in his arms wrapped in a tattered blanket was someone he loved.

"Father, who is it?" She lifted back the blanket edge and peered down into the face that was swollen and jaundiced, the dreaded symptoms of Yellow Fever. "My God," she breathed. " 'Tis Michael's own mother."

"Hush, Sorcha. Close your eyes now and try to rest, dear." Caitlin wet the towel again in the bucket at her feet and wiped the woman's brow. Sorcha tossed her head and mumbled deliriously as she had for the past three nights.

"Paddy ... he's hurting Michael. Patrick don't—don't you touch that lad. Leave him alone, I say." She began sobbing, but no tears fell. The fever had burned all the tears out of her.

"Sh ... Michael is safe. Paddy's dead. He can't hurt Michael anymore." Caitlin had listened to these ravings all night and she didn't know if the woman's condition was improving because she could talk now, or if the fever had driven her completely insane.

"Paddy—he'll get me yet," she muttered. "Must pray. Pray every night. Keep grass away from his gravestone. Must pray every night."

Caitlin shook her head, unable to believe what she was hearing. So, that way why Sorcha McKevett had spent all those nights there by her husband's grave. She hadn't been grieving after all. She had been trying to appease the spirit of a man who had brutalized her and her son.

"Michael did it," Sorcha whispered through cracked lips, her dark eyes glowing with fevered madness as she reached up and plucked at Caitlin's sleeve.

"What did Michael do?' Caitlin asked, almost afraid of what she was going to hear.

"Michael kilt Paddy. He burned him. Michael burned Paddy up."

Something caught in Caitlin's throat and choked her. This woman was crazy. She had always been crazy and now she was sick as well. There was no reason to believe anything she said, but Caitlin believed her. For some reason she knew that Sorcha, mad as she was, was speaking the truth. It hadn't been the hurricane that had killed Patrick McKevett after all. Michael had murdered him. Caitlin felt no shock or outrage, only pity for the young boy who had been abused once too often. And her heart broke for the man she loved who had carried his dark secret for so long.

She glanced around the room, but there was no one well enough to listen or care about another's deliriums. "Sorcha, you must be quiet, dear. You shouldn't say such things aloud."

"Burned him. Michael burned him.. He's burning me too. I'm burning." Her eyes were wild and the strength in the hand that clutched at Caitlin's arm was amazing. "The fire. I'm burning!" she screamed, rising up off the pallet.

"There's no fire. 'Tis only the fever you feel. Lie back there now. Please, Mrs. McKevett."

The woman, frail and sick as she was, fought against Caitlin. She rose from the pallet, arms flailing at the imaginary flames. "Fire! The house is on fire!" she cried as she ran across the room toward the window. "Get out! Paddy, Michael, get out!"

Caitlin ran after her and made a flying leap to grab the woman just before she hurled herself against the glass. They both landed on the floor in a heap, Caitlin's body over Sorcha's, her arms wrapped tightly around the woman's waist. But all the strength had gone out of Sorcha, and she lay quietly sobbing in Caitlin's arms.

Caitlin sat up and gathered her to her chest as she had the hundreds of children who had come under her care in the past months. "There, there," she whispered, smoothing the woman's thin hair, which was coming out in patches. "The fire is out now and you're safe. Michael's safe. Everyone is safe now."

Sorcha lifted her head and looked around the room with unfocused eyes. "Is Michael here?"

"No, Michael had to go away for a while. But he'll be back soon, I promise, and I'll take care of you until he comes."

The two women sat on the floor, holding each other, until Sorcha finally drifted into a troubled sleep.

For a long time Caitlin sat and watched her sleep, wondering at her own words. When she had said that Michael would return soon, it had been her heart speaking. Caitlin wondered if her heart knew something that she didn't.

"How is Sorcha McKevett?" Mason asked as he stood beside the cradle and looked down at the sleeping infant.

"She's dying." Caitlin poured water from the china

pitcher into the vanity bowl, scooped up a bit of the soft soap from a smaller bowl and began to scrub her hands vigorously. "She's having her third bout with the Yellow Fever, and each time she gets weaker. I think the next one will kill her sure."

"I can't believe that the world will miss her very much. She's a bitter woman without a kind word for anyone."

Caitlin dried her hands on a towel and walked over to the cradle. "A load of pain and suffering has knocked on Sorcha's door," she offered in defense of a woman she had never thought much of herself.

"Suffering has visited us all," he said, still looking down on the baby. "Stephen's growing so fast that he's nearly too big for that cradle. We'll have to move him to a bed soon."

Caitlin wondered what Mason was thinking as he watched the baby sleep. Since he had taken the child in his arms that first day and laid him back down, he had never touched him. Why?

She studied his face carefully for any signs of recognition. Did he know that it was Michael's baby? Fear coiled inside her belly every time she considered the implications. He couldn't know. If he had guessed, she and little Stephen would have been thrown out long ago.

But every night during these past four months Mason had come here to her bedchamber instead of summoning her to his. He stood over the cradle, watched the baby and planned for the child's education and welfare as any father would. He had even named the boy after his own father.

But he never touched the baby, and that made Caitlin sad. A son should be held by a man, bonded to a male who loved him. Every child needed a man's love and protection, and her mother's heart grieved for her son's loss.

Michael would hold you, little one, she thought as she looked down on the baby with his curling auburn hair and tiny hands with their long, sensitive fingers that were so like his father's. *If Michael McKevett knew that you were his son, he would take you in his arms and never let you go.*

She lifted the baby from the cradle and carried him to a rocking chair close to the fireplace. Mason sat in his usual leather, wing-backed chair across from her, a ledger in his lap. By the light of a tabletop kerosene lamp, he added columns of figures.

Caitlin unbuttoned the row of tiny pearls down the front of her dress, untied her chemise and offered her breast to the infant, who attacked it with vigorous sucking. She felt Mason's eyes on her and looked up only to see him glance quickly back down at his ledger.

"You've been wearing that dress a lot lately," he said with a gruffness in his voice that she guessed came from embarrassment. "In fact, these past few weeks I've only seen you in that one and the blue calico. Where are the clothes I gave you?"

Caitlin squirmed uncomfortably. He had given her his wife's wardrobe after the baby had been born, and with working so much, eating so little, and nursing the baby, the clothes were no longer tight on her. "You said they were me own. Were they or not?"

"They were," he replied without inflection.

"So they were mine to do with as I pleased?"

"They were yours to *wear* as you pleased."

She felt her face growing hot. "I see."

"Caitlin, did you give away your clothes?"

"You gave them to me and I gave them to some people who had nothin' to wear. Nothin' at all. Would

339

you have me keep a wardrobe full of lovely clothes for meself alone when others are naked in the cold?''

He looked at her for a long time, and she couldn't tell if he was angry or not. Sometimes it was hard even for her to guess what was going on behind those gray eyes.

Finally he shook his head and returned to his ledger. ''I suppose I'll just have to be careful what I give you in the future.'' A thought struck him, and he looked up quickly. ''The jewels . . . they aren't yours. I only allow you to wear them, and you'd better not give any of them away.''

She winced at his accusatory tone. ''I'd not give away your lady's emeralds,'' she said defensively. Then she shrugged. ''What would these poor souls do with a necklace, anyway? It would hardly keep them warm and they couldn't eat it, though they'd be sure to try.''

They sat in silence as they did every night. Mason with his ledger; Caitlin with the baby. Each night she couldn't help thinking that if she were with Michael, they would be sharing one world together. They would be a family, a real family.

When she looked down at the child at her breast, she felt very close to Michael, though he was many miles away. And she ached for him, for the quiet strength that he radiated. There had always been a bond between them, a bond that distance couldn't break. And though she loved Mason, felt terribly grateful to him, and slept beside him every night, there was no such bond between them. Though they sat in the same room, they lived in separate worlds, and Caitlin felt alone, achingly alone.

''What are you thinking about?'' he asked abruptly.

The question startled her. He never asked what was in her mind or her heart. She was surprised that he would even wonder, let alone ask. She searched her mind for a lie, but found none. "I was thinking of Michael."

Her answer didn't surprise him; she could see that. "Well, what about him?"

She stood and walked over to the cradle. As she laid the sleeping baby down, she thought of how to put her feelings into words he would understand, words he would accept. There were things she had to say to him, but she was risking her life and her baby's to say them.

She rebuttoned her bodice as she walked back to the fireplace. But instead of sitting in the rocker, she knelt on the floor in front of his chair and laid her hands on his knees. "Michael's mother is dying," she said. "She cries and begs for him every time the fever takes her. And I just heard that Sean Sullivan and his wife, Judy, were evicted. They're living in a horrible cave up on Carrantuohill. Larcher told Kevin O'Brien that if he took them in, he'd evict him too. I hear that since the famine hit old Kevin isn't himself, just sits around like a scarecrow all day, and his family is going down fast." She stopped to draw a long breath. "If Michael were here, he could save his family. A man should be with his loved ones when they're in such trouble as this."

She watched Mason's eyes for a flicker of compassion but saw nothing behind that icy veil. "What are you saying, Caitlin? Are you telling me that I should feel guilty for sending Michael McKevett, a coldblooded murderer, out of Ireland?"

Michael wasn't a coldblooded killer, and they both knew it. Any man in his position would have done the same thing, Caitlin reasoned, but she decided it was best not to defend Michael too staunchly. She was walking on treacherous ground as it was. "No, I know that you did what you thought was best for everyone under the circumstances, but—"

"But what?" he asked, his voice deadly quiet.

She moved her hands up his thighs and felt the muscles tense beneath her touch. "I wish that you would think on it again. You've always been a just and fair man, Mason, and I can't believe you feel good about separating a man from his family. You're the only one who can bring him home. You could send him a message and tell him that he can come back ..." Her words trailed away as she watched the carefully guarded mask slip away from his face.

Fury took its place. His hands moved up to her shoulders and dug into her flesh as he pulled her toward him. "God damn you, Caitlin. You know why I sent him away. Don't you?"

She nodded her head and swallowed the knot that was choking her. "Aye, 'twas because of me."

He pushed her away from him and she fell backward onto the floor. "How much is enough, Caitlin O'Leary? What else will you ask of me before you're done?" He stood and began to pace like a caged wolf. "I've fed and clothed you and your son. I've turned my house into a hospital and soup kitchen to save your people. I've spent the fortune that has been in my family for hundreds of years." He picked up the ledger and slammed it down on the floor beside her. "Do you realize I've spent almost every penny I have trying to save your damned Irish?"

Sitting up, she wrapped her arms around her knees to stop their shaking. She had never seen Mason this way before—out of control. Her mind reeled at the revelation that he did, indeed, harbor passions of his own.

"What you've done here with Armfield House," she said, "you've done for yourself as well as for me. You

342

couldn't stand by and let innocent men and women die, not to mention the babes. You allowed it to happen once before, and you couldn't just let it happen again while it was in your power to stop it."

She rose from the floor and tentatively approached him. After a hesitation, she placed her hand on his shoulder. *I shouldn't be doing this,* she thought. *I mustn't press him now.* But she was afraid that if she didn't ask him now, she would never be able to summon the courage again. And she had to ask for Michael's sake.

"If you send for him," she said, "if you tell him that it's safe for him to come home, I swear to you on me mother's and father's graves that I'll not try to see him. I'll discourage him if he comes around. I promise you that I'll not betray your trust in me."

"You already have, Caitlin," he said, his anger fading, giving way to sadness.

He walked over to the cradle and looked down at the baby for a long time. Then he said, "I'll send for Michael. You're right about one thing—I haven't been at ease with my decision to exile him. McKevett is an honorable man and his family needs him if they're to survive this hell. But I'll tell you one thing, Caitlin. If I do this, and the two of you betray me after all I've done for you—I'll see you both dead."

Chapter Eighteen

"What do you mean you couldn't find him?" Mason glanced around his drawing room at the patients who lined the floor from one wall to the other. But they were beyond caring. Lost in their private agonies, they had no curiosity about an argument between the landlord and his steward. Mason lowered his voice and leaned closer to the man. "Damn it, Tom, I never would have sent you personally to deal with this matter if it hadn't been of utmost importance."

"I know, yer honor," Tom Banks replied in a broad Kerry accent. One drooping corner of his brown moustache twitched with nervousness as he faced his master's anger. "We picked up ol' Michael's trail right away. Wasn't hard to find a man with a wheel of flyin' horses. But when we got to the end of the trail, he wasn't to be found."

"What is that supposed to mean?"

"He's left England. Gone. Disappeared entirely, he has."

"How can you be so sure?"

Tom propped his boot on the marble hearth and leaned his elbow on the mantel. At the landlord's disapproving scowl he lowered his foot and stood to attention. "Well, Yer Honor, I followed his trail, like I said, and I wound up at this pub in Chipping Campden. They remembered Michael well because he's such a big fellow and with those wonderful horses of his—"

"Go on."

"Michael came in there about a week ago, and they were all talking about the blight. He'd heard that some of the potatoes had failed, but he didn't know that it was so terrible. Seems a lot of folks in England think it's no great loss, but word's gettin' around. When they told Michael that almost all the potatoes are bad this year and that people are dyin' like flies from the hunger and the fevers, he jumped up and ran out of there, cussin' up a whirlwind. They said he was after coming back home as quick as he could. I suppose he's probably back on Irish soil by now. Pullin' that wagon will slow him down a bit, but he's bound to be here soon."

Mason bent down to stir the fire with a poker, his fingers tight around the iron rod, his face set in stern lines. A mixture of rage and admiration swirled through him. Those were the feelings that most often assailed him when he thought of Michael McKevett. How dare that bloody Irishman come back to Ireland without his permission. He should have the bastard hanged the moment he crossed the county line.

But despite his anger and frustration at having his plans altered, Mason couldn't help but harbor a grudging respect for a man who would risk the gallows to be with his family in a crisis.

Mason heard a groan from the corner of the room and the terrible, gagging sounds of vomiting—a sound that he would never become accustomed to, just as he would never accept the horrible sights and odors of these fevered miserables. This time it was Sorcha

McKevett retching as though her body were trying to turn itself inside out. In seconds Caitlin had hurried into the room and was on her knees beside the woman, holding her head and murmuring soothing words.

The landlord turned back to his servant and whispered, "You'll mention this to no one, Tom, no one at all. As far as anyone here in Ireland is concerned, you found Michael McKevett there in England and summoned him home yourself. Do you understand?"

Tom's eyes followed Armfield's gaze. Both men watched as Caitlin tried to comfort a delirious Sorcha who was begging for her son and cursing him with the same breath.

"I'll not tell a soul, Yer Honor," Tom assured him. "Not a livin' soul."

Michael drove his wagon filled with bright dreams through the nightmare landscape of what had once been his beloved Erin, but was now a living hell.

When his ship had pulled into Cobh Harbor, Michael had thought that the accounts of the famine he had heard in Chipping Campden had been exaggerated. The harbor was filled with ships that overflowed with cattle and grain. He had breathed a sigh of relief at the sight. How could Ireland be starving when there was so much food to export?

But his consolation had been short-lived. The moment he had driven his wagon off the ship, he had seen a legion of constabulary guarding the quays from more beggars than he had seen in his entire life. Everywhere he looked the tattered, emaciated creatures held out their hands in pathetic supplication, only to be driven back by the police armed with muskets and whips.

The streets of Cork had been even worse. The city

had always had its share of beggars, but never so many, so desperate. Hordes of the starving homeless roamed the streets, searching vainly for food and shelter.

As Michael drove past the corpses that lay neglected and decaying on the sidewalks and in gutters, fear twisted and churned deep in his guts. The accounts were true after all. This blight was a bad one, much worse than the crop failures of 1837 or even 1839.

As he left Cork and turned his horse west toward Killarney, Michael told himself that the cities had to be the worst. The countryside would be better.

But he had been wrong. Very wrong.

The deeper he drove into the rural areas of West Cork, the more horrors he saw. A grim procession of living skeletons thronged the main road to Killarney— ragged, dirty starvelings whose empty eyes stared out of waxen faces. Michael hadn't known there were so many people in all of Ireland as he saw traveling that road those three days. They staggered along, a mindless, dispirited army of cadavers in search of food, while herds of fat, healthy livestock and wagons bulging with grain were being driven down the middle of the road. The starving multitudes obediently moved aside to let them pass.

Michael couldn't comprehend this insanity. Who would export food from a country that was starving? How could that be?

The corpses of men, women and children lay strewn along the road and in the ditches, shriveled, grotesque things that bore no resemblance to the lively, spirited people Michael had left behind when he had gone away to England.

On the roadside to his left, Michael saw a flock of crows picking at a dead child's body. He drove on, keeping his eyes straight ahead as he had driven by the

347

other horrors the past three days. The first time he had seen a dead child, Michael's mind had crawled deep into a dark cave, refusing to face the ghastly reality. But the fear that had started in the pit of his stomach was growing with every mile.

As he drove along, he searched every hollow-cheeked face he passed to see if it was someone he loved.

That could be Danny, he thought every time he saw a red-haired child with spindle-legs and a bloated stomach. His heart stood still, afraid that it was Daniel, afraid that it wasn't. *The boy could be lying in a ditch somewhere, dying,* he thought. *He may have starved or frozen to death while I was away in England with plenty to eat and warm clothes to wear.* Michael shoved the thought to the back of his mind, but the guilt and the fear of what he would find at home were becoming unbearable.

Ahead he saw another wagon coming toward him. This one was loaded down with barley. As it lumbered down the road, none of the peasants tried to grab any of the grain inside the wagon, but when it had passed they gathered the loose grains that fell to the ground as the wagon jolted over the bumpy road.

When Michael's wagon met the other, he saw that the driver was an Irishman. Michael hailed him, and they both pulled their horses to a halt.

The driver was lean and lank, but he seemed healthy enough compared to the poor wretches on the road.

Michael climbed down from his wagon and walked over to the man. "Where are ye from?" he asked.

"I drive for Lord Carleton of Tralee," he replied in a voice that sounded like the echo of an empty barrel.

Something in the Irishman's face made Michael question his earlier assumption that the man was healthy. His eyes had a strange blankness about them that looked as though a part of him had died. Michael had seen a few men in his day who had gone mental, and this man had the same look about him.

"Did you come through Lios na Capaill on yer way?" Michael asked.

"Lios na Capaill?" he repeated and shook his head as though in a daze. "No. I don't think so."

"Have you heard how the folks there are?" Michael asked.

"No. Haven't heard about that village. Some towns are better than others. Others are—" He paused and wiped his hand across his face as though trying to blot out what he had seen. "Other villages are dead. Every soul dead or dying. I drove through Terracoulter yesterday morning and I saw ... oh, Jaysus ... the village was deserted, not a living person in the street, only corpses. Piles of corpses in the cottages with the living lying there among the dead, and them too weak to move."

The driver took a deep breath and crossed himself. "I saw a young mother lying dead with her babe in her arms. The wee one had ... had gnawed on her breast before he died." He shuddered, and Michael's mind backed deeper into its cave. He couldn't think about that young mother right now. If he did, he'd surely go mad.

The Irishman continued, the words spilling out of him. "In one cottage I saw two frozen bodies and the rats—the rats were eatin' those bodies, they were. God in heaven, I'll never forget the sight."

Michael's heart sickened. Terracoulter was only ten miles west of Lios na Capaill. He had to get home. He had to know. But there was one thing he had to do before moving on.

"Where are you taking this grain?" he asked as he

349

stepped up onto the running board and peered over the sides of the wagon at the barley.

"To Cork. 'Tis going out of Cobh Harbor in four days."

Michael studied the driver from his battered hat to his boots, sizing him up. He wasn't a small man, but he wasn't all that big either, and Michael saw no sign of a weapon. Apparently, the English thought the Irish too weak and downtrodden to consider them a threat to their shipment.

Michael looked down at the peasants who were crawling on the ground, gathering the grain. "No, I don't think so," he said quietly. For the first time since he had stepped off the ship, Michael felt alive. By God, someone had to do something for these people, and he was thankful that he was healthy and strong enough to do it.

"I beg your pardon?" the driver asked.

"I said, I don't think so. This barley was grown on Irish soil by the labor of Irish hands. It'll go into Irish stomachs, not be shipped abroad to pay some Saxon's gambling debts."

Michael swung himself onto the wagon and climbed on top of the pile of grain. Bracing himself with one hand on the back of the driver's bench, he kicked the sideboard with his heavy brogue. Wood splintered as the boards gave way, and the barley spilled like golden rain onto the ground. In seconds the peasants were scrambling for it, and there was plenty for all.

"What the bloody hell do you think yer doin' there?" the driver shouted as he climbed into the wagon bed and grabbed at Michael, who was throwing the grain overboard with both hands. "Yer robbing His Honor's barley! That's a crime and a sin!"

Michael paused and looked at the Irishman as though he were, indeed, insane. "How can you say that, man, after all you've seen? How can it be a sin to feed hungry children? Look at these people, for God's sake! Think about that dead village, and tell me where the crime and sin is here."

The driver looked down at his fellow countrymen and their wives and children who were diving into the life-giving grain, and tears filled his eyes. "But what will I tell His Honor? How will I explain this?"

Michael smiled grimly and laid his huge hand on the man's shoulder. "Tell him you were robbed by a big, desperate Kerry man who threatened to kill you if you didn't hand it over."

"But you didn't threaten me."

Michael looked down at the children who were shoveling the barley into their mouths that were stained green from eating grass. "No, I didn't. But make no mistake, I would have killed you to give these children food. And it might have been a crime, but it wouldn't have been a sin."

Michael left the distraught driver with his empty wagon and hurried back to his own. As he drove away, he cast one departing look over his shoulder at the multitude who had been saved from starvation for at least a few more days. He felt a surge of happiness, of pride and fulfillment, but it didn't last long. He thought of Terracoulter, the dead village, only a few miles from Lios na Capaill. He had helped some of these poor souls, but would he be able to save his own family?

He thought of Oisin who had stayed in the Land of the Ever Young for three hundred years and had returned to find Ireland changed and everyone he loved dead. Michael was afraid that, like Oisin, he had waited too long.

* * *

The first thing Caitlin noticed when she entered the O'Briens' yard was that there was no smoke issuing from the forge chimney. For as far back as she could remember, Kevin O'Brien had worked that forge everyday except Sunday, and even then the fire had been banked, ready to flare anew on Monday morning.

The next thing she noticed was the absence of fowl in the yard, which had always been overrun with chickens, geese and guineas. Kevin O'Brien's blacksmith trade had always assured him a solid position in the village economy. While a smith would never be as rich as a landowner, he would never be as poor as the simple farmer ... and there was always plenty of fowl in his yard. Except in times such as these, when everything that could be slaughtered for food had been killed and eaten long ago. Even at Armfield House there had been no meat for many months.

Caitlin knocked on the door and waited. When she heard no reply, she opened the door a crack and looked inside. Kevin O'Brien sat on a three-legged stool beside the fire, and it occurred to Caitlin that, except for the hours spent in her pub, this was the first time she had ever seen the smith idle. "Mr. O'Brien, 'tis Caitlin O'Leary. May I come in?"

Kevin didn't answer her, only stared into the fire. So she ventured inside. "I've come to have a word with Annie," she said. "Is she about?"

He didn't look up, but he nodded vaguely toward the loft. Caitlin turned to see Annie coming down the ladder, her skirts gathered primly around her and disapproval scrawled across her pinched face. She was much thinner than the last time Caitlin had seen her, as everyone was these days, and Annie looked much older than her twenty-two years.

"What would the likes of you have to say to me, and why are you here in my house?" she demanded in a tone that set Caitlin's strained nerves on edge.

"I came to give you news of your mother-in-law," she said. "If you care, that is."

A flicker of concern almost erased the indignation on Annie's face, but not quite. "She's not ... not ..."

"No, not yet. But I believe she's at the end. I've nursed her day and night these past few weeks and she's having her fourth relapse now. Like the others, about the time we think they're on their way, they come down with it again—the high fever, the shaking and the vomiting. I haven't been able to keep any water in her for nearly three days, and that's not good."

Annie shrugged frail shoulders and cast a searching look at Kevin, who said nothing, though Caitlin could tell by the tilt of his head that he was listening. "Aye. And what would you have me do? We can't bring her back here. It wouldn't be proper for her, an unmarried widow, and me father, a widower himself, to be livin' under the same roof."

Caitlin tried to rein in her temper, but she was so tired, too tired to make the effort. "That's a ridiculous pile of horse shit. Do you really think anyone would suspect that poor ol' Sorcha would seduce your father into her death bed? For heaven's sake, the woman is burning up with fever, raving out of her mind and retching up her guts. Do you really think she's someone a man would want to bed?" Caitlin looked down at Annie McKevett and saw the face of every villager who had left a loved one on her doorstep to nurse. The anger and contempt that had been simmering for months boiled over and flowed onto Annie.

"If you don't want to take the trouble to nurse your mother-in-law, Annie McKevett, just say so. Don't try to hide behind the laws of God. I suspect He'll get tired of you doin' that and kick you in the arse one fine day. And if He doesn't, I might do the job meself."

To Caitlin's surprise, Annie's indignation disappeared. Her face crumpled and she began to cry. "But . . . but you don't understand. I've loved Sorcha for years and years. I've taken care of her—and her daft as a goose—for ever so long. I've bandaged her poor hands and dragged her out of that awful graveyard. But we're afraid to take her in. We're afraid of the fever, of dying. I don't want me little brother, Daniel, to catch the fever, or me father. And we don't have food enough for ourselves, let alone for Sorcha as well." She walked over to the pot on the fire and lifted the lid, showing nothing but water and a few cabbage leaves that smelled more rotten than edible.

Caitlin felt her anger melting away before she was ready to let it go. She was too exhausted to be angry. "Then would you come with me yourself, Annie? She's begging for you or Michael. She's going to die any time now and she wants to be in the arms of someone she loves. Surely you owe her that much. You owe it to Michael."

"Don't you tell me what I owe my husband, Caitlin O'Leary." Annie's eyes glittered with a fever that was so like Sorcha's delirium, Caitlin wondered for a moment if the woman were mad. "Michael ran away and left me, left us all in our time of need. If Sorcha dies without the comfort of her son's arms, 'tis on his head and not me own. Get out of my house now and don't you come back where ye aren't welcome."

Caitlin left without a backward glance at Kevin O'Brien. It broke her heart to see him, a man who had been so vibrant and strong, now an empty shell. This calamity had changed them forever. Tragedy had brought out the hidden sides of them all. Those who had been truly strong were now like steel that had been tried in the furnace, while the weak had crumbled. And those like Annie McKevett, who had harbored the seeds of hate in their hearts, had reaped a bitter harvest.

Walking down the road back to Armfield House, Caitlin passed the empty, tumbled cottages and the desperate knots of people huddled and dying in the ditches. Where was the sound of the piper, she wondered, and where were the bright dreams they had cherished? Where had all the songs gone and the children's laughter?

For the first time since Michael had left, Caitlin was glad that he was gone. She wouldn't have wanted him to see his beloved Erin weeping for her children ... with no hope ... and no joy.

But there was hope; a tiny spark still burned in one heart, a heart too young and full of love to know that hope had died in Ireland.

Danny O'Brien sat, chisel in hand, and stared up at the wooden horse he had been carving for over a year. He stared at it for the better part of an hour before he thought of yet another thing he could do to it. There was room for one more small flower on the edge of the saddle blanket. Just one more.

Surely the horse would be finished then. He simply couldn't think of another thing to do. The spark of hope flared into a blaze, and the boy attacked the horse with vigorous but careful strokes. One more flower. A few more petals. Then surely ... surely, Michael would be home.

* * *

God, let them be alive. Please, let them all be alive.
Michael threw open the front door of Kevin's cottage
and rushed inside, expecting to find the same horrible,
rotting corpses that he had seen along the roadside.
But what he saw instead was his wife in the arms of
another man.

"Would you like to tell me what you're doin' there
with me woman?" His deep voice filled the room, and
Annie and Father Brolin jumped apart as though God
himself had spoken from the heavens. "You'd best tell
me quick before I murder ye."

"Michael!" Annie's face turned as pale as a banshee's nightgown, and her mouth opened wide, then
snapped shut.

Michael wasn't disappointed that she showed no joy
at seeing him. God knows, he felt none at seeing her
again. The thought did sadden him a bit. A man should
be happy to see his wife after fourteen months away.

The priest quickly recovered his composure as he
straightened his collar and donned an aggrieved expression. "I was comforting your wife in her time of sorrow."

"I'll thank you to leave that job to meself." As Michael stepped between them and the priest moved well
out of arm's reach, Michael remembered the last time
he had seen the good father; he had been lying on the
floor, holding his jaw after it had collided with Michael's fist. It was a memory that gave Michael pleasure
to recall, just as it pleased him to look into the father's
bright blue eyes and know that the priest was remembering too.

"Just why is it yer in need of comforting, Annie?"
Michael asked, turning toward his wife. He saw the tears
in her eyes and he thought of Daniel and the children
on the road. Fear shot through him, and he forgot all
about the priest. "Is it Danny? Is the lad well?"

356

" 'Tisn't Danny," she said. "The good father just came by to give us the word ... your mother ... 'tis your mother, Michael, who's dead of the fever. She died just this morning."

Michael steeled himself against the pain that shot through him. He wouldn't allow it to hurt now, not yet. He would keep the pain, like a terrible hound, at bay for as long as possible. After the nightmare of his journey, his mind couldn't take in this sorrow and remain sane. "Where is she?" he asked, his voice as empty as the faces of the starvelings along the road.

"Her body is at Armfield House," the priest replied.

"Armfield House? What was she doing there?"

Annie shuffled her bare feet on the slate floor. "She ... ah ... she went there because of the fever. They've set up a fine fever ward in His Honor's big house. That Caitlin O'Leary has been living there with His Honor— had a baby by him, she did—and she's running this hospital for the fevered."

"My mother died in Armfield House?" As the realization washed through him, Michael felt the beast shake the bars of its cage. What kind of mockery was this that his mother would die in the house of the man who had exiled him? "Why wasn't she here? Why weren't you taking care of her yourself, Annie?"

Father Brolin stepped forward. "Now, listen, son—"

"I am not your son, and you'll keep a shut mouth on this matter, priest," Michael said, lifting a clenched fist. "Ye've caused grief enough in my marriage. Now explain to me if ye can, Annie, why my mother died in an Englishman's house instead of in the arms of the ones she loved."

Annie's small face blushed scarlet with anger and her blue eyes narrowed as she shook her finger in his face. "Yer the fine one to be accusing me of not caring for your mama. Yer the one who ran away and left us all here to

357

starve to death. She'd been askin' for you for weeks and weeks, begging and crying for her only son to be at her side when she expired. But where were you, Michael McKevett, when she died with your name on her lips?"

Michael didn't answer her. There was nothing to say. So he turned and left the cottage as quickly as he could, before he did something terrible, before he struck Annie or the priest and removed those self-righteous sneers from their faces.

He knew that he couldn't keep the pain at bay much longer and he didn't want them to see it, didn't want them to enjoy his grief, as he was sure they would. God, what had he ever done to Annie to make her hate him so much?

He was walking across the yard toward the barn, leading his horse by her harness when he realized that he hadn't seen Kevin, Sean, or Judy inside the house. For all he knew, they were dead too. Mother of Mercy, when would this nightmare be over?

Daniel felt the tiny wooden rosebud with his fingertip and found it perfectly smooth. He let the sanded paper drop to the barn's straw-covered floor as he stood back and surveyed his workmanship. The horse was truly finished this time. It had to be. There wasn't another thing he could think of to do to it.

So many times before Danny had thought that the horse was done. He had finished some part of it with joy, thinking that the job was finally completed. But as he waited, day after day, for Michael's return he had gone back to the horse, looking for something that could be improved, yet one more thing that might be keeping Michael away. And he had always found something, some little something.

But now, he couldn't think of one thing left to do as

his eyes ran over the saddle with its intricate stitching, the mane with the hairs defined, the roses and lilies that circled the horse's neck with every petal and leaf detailed. And on the horse's rump were straps with merry little bells like those he had seen on Lady Kenmare's mount when she had ridden through Lios na Capaill on her way to Killarney three summers ago.

When Danny looked at the horse, he couldn't believe that he had carved it himself. It was as lovely as Michael's horses, even lovelier in its own way. But, looking at it now, Danny wasn't sure where the beautiful creature had come from.

It was as though the horse had come out of a dream, a dream that had gone through his head and come into the world through the carving. He remembered Michael saying something about carving dreams, but he couldn't remember what it was now. Michael had been gone such a terribly long time that it was getting harder and harder for Danny even to remember what his friend looked like.

Danny wondered where on God's big earth Michael was now, and he wondered if Michael was as unhappy as everyone else in his life. Sean and Judy were living up in that terrible cave, and he hadn't seen them for months. His father just sat on the stool and stared into the fire as though his mind had deserted him entirely. And Annie did nothing but cry the live-long day or complain that she was hungry.

Danny was hungry too. In fact, he couldn't remember a time when he hadn't been hungry. But he didn't cry about it or complain. He had carved, night and day, to finish the horse. As soon as he finished the horse Michael would come. He had promised—and the horse was done.

* * *

Michael entered the barn and stopped in his tracks, frozen by the sight that greeted him. Against the far wall a little red-haired boy stood, his arms around the neck of a glorious wooden stallion. The lantern light lit the boy's hair, setting it aglow with copper fire. The lad was taller than he had been and thinner, and there was a haggard gauntness about his face. But the child's eyes shone with the pride of a master craftsman, and Michael knew that pride. Though it had been a long time since he had felt it, the look on the boy's face reminded him of the glory.

"Daniel."

The word was scarcely a whisper, but the boy heard it. He turned, and the expression on his face was one of pure rapture as he flew into Michael's arms. " 'Tis all done, Michael. I finished him today and I knew you'd come back. Annie said I was daft and you'd never come back just because I was carvin' an old, stupid horse, but I knew you'd come back because you promised."

As Michael crushed the child to him, he felt a ripping in his chest, an explosion of the emotions that had been building since he had stepped off that ship and into a nightmare. He held Danny in his arms and looked at the beautiful horse. His dream hadn't died after all. This child's love and faith had kept it alive.

Tears ran down Michael's cheeks, wetting them both. And Michael knew that if he lived to be a hundred years old, he would remember this as the saddest and the happiest day of his life.

Chapter Nineteen

Caitlin stood, shivering, at the edge of the cemetery, well-hidden behind a blackthorn hedge. In the graveyard a small circle of mourners had gathered around a newly dug grave, and at the head of that grave stood Father Murphy, looking more bent and weary than Caitlin had ever seen him.

But she hadn't come to see Father Murphy or to pay her respects to Sorcha McKevett. She had come for one reason only, to catch a glimpse of Michael.

He stood, his head bare to the falling rain and his broad shoulders slumped. From her hiding place she couldn't see his face, but she felt his grief, and she longed to share his sorrow with him.

At his side were Annie, Daniel and Kevin. The boy's hand reached up for Michael's, and Caitlin watched as he pulled the child to his side and patted the lad's shoulder.

She waited to see if Annie or Kevin would offer any solace, but they didn't, and Caitlin wasn't surprised. Annie wailed into a ragged bit of a handkerchief, and Kevin simply stood, staring down into the grave in the same vacant way that he stared into the fire.

Caitlin trembled, more from the rush of emotions that coursed through her than from the icy rain. She wanted to go to Michael, to put her arms around him, to comfort him and take away a part of his pain if she could. But she was bound by her promise to Mason. She shouldn't even be here. If Mason found out, he would be furious and rightly so. But when she had heard Michael was in town, she had to come. She had to see with her own eyes that he was truly alive and well.

Hungrily she drank in the sight of him. In a country where everyone was starving or about to, the sight of a strong, healthy man was a welcome one. Looking at him now, she could almost believe that he could make a difference in this terrible time. If any man could save his family from starvation, it would be Michael Mc-Kevett. He didn't have Mason's wealth, but he had a strength about him and a fierce protectiveness for those he loved. She couldn't help wondering if she was still someone he loved.

She saw him bend down, scoop a handful of dirt and throw it down onto the lowered coffin, and her heart reached out to him across the distance. *Michael, I love you.* The message was silent, but powerful. So powerful that she wasn't surprised when he turned and looked directly at her.

She quickly pulled back behind the hedge, gathered her cloak around her and ran all the way back to Armfield House. If she dared to stop, she would surely go back to him, and they would both be damned.

He saw her—just a glimpse of red among the brush. Then she was gone. But the feeling remained, the feeling of having been touched by another person, someone who loved him, someone who cared deeply. And, having been touched, Michael didn't feel so alone as before.

He looked down into the yawning hole that had just accepted the body of his mother, and he wondered why he wasn't destroyed entirely, why he didn't hurt more than he did.

He thought of the last time he had seen her on the day he had left for England. It had been in this very spot, here beside his father's grave. Somehow he had known even then that he would never see her alive again.

Ye've finally got her, ye ol' devil, he thought as he looked down on the hated, chipped monument with its sneering cherubim. *I just hope to God that her soul's out of your reach.*

He looked up at Father Murphy and tried to listen to his words about eternal life and the soul's rewards. Perhaps his mother was in the arms of the angels rather than the clutches of Patrick McKevett.

When the words had been said, and the holy water sprinkled over the grave, Paul Gannon moved forward with his shovel in hand to cover the coffin. Annie collapsed into her father's arms, and together they left the cemetery without a word to Michael or the priest.

Danny clung to his hand. When Michael looked down into the boy's face, he saw that the child was waiting, waiting to judge the extent of Michael's sorrow before deciding how sad he, himself, should be.

Michael dropped to his knees on the muddy ground and pushed the strings of wet hair out of the boy's eyes. Even in his own grief, Michael knew that he would never have a better time to teach the boy about death.

"Are ye sad, Michael?" Danny asked as his amber eyes searched Michael's face.

"Sad, indeed. 'Tis a hard thing to lay one you love beneath the sod."

Danny nodded his understanding. "Now yer like me. Ye've no mother either."

"That's true. But all things come to an end sooner or later, even life itself. So remember that, lad. When you've got something good in your life, enjoy it, because it won't last forever. And if something bad is sittin' on your doorstep, endure it, because it will have to depart someday as well."

Danny looked around the graveyard at the multitude of freshly dug graves. "Do you think this blight will leave our doorstep someday and everything will be the same as it was before?"

Michael looked up at Father Murphy, who said nothing but stared down at the prayer book in his hands. "Surely the blight will leave someday. But Ireland will never be the same again." As he watched Paul Gannon shovel the dirt over his mother's coffin, he thought of Terracoulter's cottages filled with the dead. His eyes met the priest's, burning with green fire. "Erin will never forget the cries of her children. And she won't let England forget," he added grimly.

The old priest stepped forward and cleared his throat. "You'd best be running along home now, Daniel, and comfort your sister. Michael will be along presently after I've had a word with him."

Reluctantly, Daniel left Michael's side, and Michael stood, brushing the dirt from his knees. The last thing he wanted right then was to have a talk with the priest, something that he had avoided for the past seven years.

"I need to be getting along to me family," he said. "I've some important business to attend to, like finding something for Annie's soup pot."

Father Murphy laid a gently restraining hand on his

shoulder. "I'll not keep you long. I just wanted to tell you what a fine job you did on your mother's coffin. You must have stayed up all night building it for her."

Michael shrugged and cast a look over at the community coffin that the last mourners had left on the stone wall surrounding the graveyard. "Me mother was a good woman," he said, "and she deserved better than a coffin with a hinged bottom to drop her into the dirt. 'Tis a sorry son who couldn't provide better than that for the woman who gave him life."

The priest clucked his tongue sadly. "Aye, but many's the son these days who has one brogue in the grave himself, and that hinged coffin is the best he can do."

"Times are bad."

The priest nodded. "Times are bad."

"I should be getting along now."

"Michael, wait. There's more I want to say to you." Father Murphy paused as Paul patted the last shovelful of soil into place, muttered a consoling word to Michael and took his leave. "Your mother . . ." He spoke slowly as though choosing his words carefully. "She was an unhappy woman, even bitter, you might say."

"We mustn't speak ill of the dead," Michael reminded him.

"No, but we must speak those words that might free the living if we can. I probably knew Sorcha McKevett better than anyone. She worked for me and lived with me these past seven years, and I've heard her confessions every morning for the thirty years I've been priest of this parish. And I watched her over the years, watched and bit my tongue while she piled the weight of her own grief on your head. Michael, after all these years of listening to the joys and sorrows of hundreds of people, I've decided that people are only as happy as they want to be. And your mother, God rest her soul, didn't want to be happy. She thought that grief was her lot in life, and she embraced sorrow like it was a long, lost friend.''

Michael listened to the words that echoed what he had always felt deep in his heart, but had never allowed himself even to think, let alone voice. "Are ye saying that I couldn't make her happy because she didn't want to be?''

"That's just what I'm saying. And I'm saying it because I don't want you to go through the rest of your life grieving over her miseries. Not even your father could make her happy, though he tried."

Michael's sorrow quickly flared into anger. "He never tried to please her. He only beat her and mistreated her and—''

The priest held up his hand in surrender. "He did all those things, it's true, and I'll not deny it. But I remember times before you were born, when they were still young. He tried to please her, to be a loving husband to her, but she let him know every day how little she thought of him, of his drinking and him not going to confession as often as she thought he should. Patrick McKevett was a devil, I'll give you that. But your mother wasn't the saint she imagined herself to be either.''

Michael brushed the priest's hand off his shoulder. "Why are you saying these things? She loved you so, Father. She served you and—''

"So she did, and I loved her for it. But I want you to see her the way she was, a person, like you and me, capable of hurting the ones she loved. And I know that she hurt you badly, lad, over the years."

Michael bit his lip and blinked back the tears that stung his lids. "I caused her a heap of pain, too. She died calling out for me, and me not there to comfort her in her hour of need," he admitted with a half sob. "Father Brolin told me that himself yesterday." It was Michael's first confession in years, and he was surprised at how good it felt to unburden himself on the father's bent, but sturdy shoulders.

The priest's jaw tightened, and he shook his head in disgust. "Father Brolin is the holy jackass that Mary sat on. You'll forget what he said and listen to me alone. You must bury your mother's bitterness there in the grave, lad, and go on with your life."

The old priest smiled, and for the first time in years, Michael felt that maybe he was on the right side of God, or at least not on His left side.

"Away with you now," the father said, thumping him soundly on the shoulder. "And may the good God put some food in your hand or show you which direction to look for it."

Michael had searched at least a dozen caves and, though he had seen many familiar faces peering out at him from the dark interiors, he hadn't found Sean and Judy.

The road before him followed the flank of the hill and curved to the left. Below him Lough Leane glistened cold and gray, reflecting the winter sky.

Michael looked up, studied the clouds, and sniffed the air. Snow was on the way; he could smell it, taste it on the wind. He shook his head and chuckled wryly. Wasn't it enough that the children were starving? Did the snow have to fall on their bare heads as well?

This was one of the coldest winters that anyone could remember. Even old Bridget, who was as ancient as the Rock of Cashel, couldn't remember a winter so cold or snow so early.

Michael thought of Father Murphy and wondered

how a benevolent, loving God could sit up there on his throne and let the cold winds bite those ragged children he had seen on the road and the ones he had just found huddled in the caves.

Father Murphy said that they must trust God and not question that which He handed down. But Michael did question. Maybe, if it had only been adults who were suffering, there might have been a reason. Perhaps they had sinned enough to warrant this punishment. But what had the wee ones done to deserve this living death? No, Michael couldn't understand a Father God who would allow that to happen. What kind of father watched his children suffer so desperately and did nothing?

Looking over his shoulder, Michael checked the position of the sun. It would be setting behind the hills soon, and there would be no moon tonight. He had time to look at one more cave, then he would have to start back home and take up his search again tomorrow morning. But he knew that he wouldn't stop looking until he found his friend. Kevin might have let Sean and Judy down, but he wouldn't.

He saw the deep cleft in a rock set high in the cliff above him, a jagged fissure in the stone, carved over the centuries by the waters that flowed through it during heavy rains. Slipping and sliding on the thin layer of ice that crusted the side of the hill, Michael made his way carefully up to the cave entrance.

It was a small cave, only tall enough for a short man to stand and about three paces deep. But when Michael stuck his head into the narrow entrance, he saw a group of no less than a dozen people huddled together like squirrels, seeking the meager protection the damp, musty walls offered.

Michael blinked his eyes, trying to identify the faces

368

of the cave's inhabitants, but they all looked alike: haggard, dirty, starving. He heard a baby whimper weakly and smelled the pungent odor of unwashed bodies and sickness.

"Sean? Judy? Is there a Sean Sullivan within?" he asked. "I'm after finding me sister-in-law and her husband. Has anyone—"

She fell, sobbing, around his neck, clinging to him as though to life itself. He put his arms around her waist and lifted her against him. She had always been tiny, but now she was nothing but bones in a ragged dress.

"Judy . . . ah, darlin' girl. I found you at last. Where is that husband of yours and where's the baby? Tell me it's alive they are."

"Aye, we're alive but barely. Sean's out trying to get a hare for our dinner. He's a poacher these days, for sure, but what's a man to do? He'll be hanged if he's caught."

"Better hanged like a man than to starve like a dog. Where's the wee one?"

She released him long enough to reach down and take an infant from the arms of an old woman. She held the baby up for Michael's inspection.

"He's a handsome lad, sure," Michael said. "I see he has your pretty black curls. Now if he has his father's bright smile, you'll be chasin' the girls away before he's twelve."

Judy hugged the child to her and leaned against Michael. His arm went around her for support. "I don't believe he'll ever be twelve years old, Michael. I thought at first that we would make it through this winter, but now I just don't know."

"We'll all be alive to see Erin wearing her pretty Spring dress, you'll see." He took the baby from her

369

and slipped him inside his great coat. "Gather your things together, love, and let's be off."

"Things? What things? We've only the rags on our backs."

"Then come along and show me where that husband of yours is huntin' hare. We'll be home and settled in our beds before the sun's in his."

It took all of Michael's self-control not to walk over to Kevin and knock him off that three-legged stool. Neither he nor Annie had even bothered to embrace Judy, Sean and the baby when Michael had brought them home. Kevin simply muttered something about them bringing ruin on their heads, while Annie complained about having more mouths to feed.

"But I've brought food," Sean said with a helpless sideways look at Michael. He held out three hares by their hind legs to Annie.

Annie assumed the self-righteous pout that Michael had grown to hate. "I'll not have poached meat in this house. That game belongs to the landlord, and 'tis a sin to take it."

Michael could stand no more. He walked over to Sean, took the hares from his hand and flung them on the table. "The animals of the forest are Erin's, not some damned Englishman's. Annie, get over there and cook those beasts before you're a minute older." With his hand on her back he gave her a prodding shove toward the table.

The look she gave him would melt Donegal snow, but she did as she was told. "I'll cook it, but I'll not eat a bite meself," she threatened.

Michael looked down at Danny, who stood beside the table, his mouth watering at the sight of food. "That's

370

fine. Daniel will be glad to eat your portion, him a growing lad and all."

"They can't stay," Kevin said, his voice as empty as his eyes. "Larcher said that if anyone takes in someone who's been evicted, even if it's his own family, his house will be burned down around his head. They can't stay."

Sean turned to Michael, and Michael hated the fear in his friend's eyes. Since when had they all changed from men into frightened animals?

"They'll stay, and Larcher be damned," Michael said.

"Ye can't fight a landlord, lad," Kevin said.

The whimpering tone in his voice made Michael furious. He walked over to Kevin and kicked the stool out from under him. The smith landed with a thud on his backside in the ashes.

In an instant Kevin was on his feet and for the first time in months his eyes glittered with rage. He held up his clenched fists before his face, his red beard bristling. "I don't know what ye think yer about, lad, but no man knocks Kevin O'Brien on his arse without payin' the price. Up with your fists."

Michael laughed, but he didn't raise his hands. "Well, the old dog bares his teeth, I thought he was a toothless hound, sure, and the landlord had yanked his fangs, but there they are. Aren't they a fine sight?"

Sean, always the peacemaker, stepped between them. "We'll go, Michael. I won't bring calamity on this house, and I'll not have you and Kevin at each other over us."

"You and your family will stay right here under this roof where you belong," Michael said. "And we'll fight the bloody Englishman right here on our own soil." He looked over Sean's shoulder at Kevin, who was still sputtering with indignation, and he smiled. "And now that

371

we have the mighty Kevin O'Brien back to fight alongside us, how can we lose?''

Travis Larcher's horse knew its way home from Killarney, and it was a good thing because His Honor had a generous quantity of whiskey in him, and he was in no shape to navigate the dark road at midnight. He slumped over the bay's neck and muttered an obscene observation about the horse's lack of speed and its ancestry.

The animal simply snorted a white cloud into the frosty night and loped along as though aware that her rider was doing well to keep his seat even at this slow gait.

They passed through town and out the west end past the graveyard. Larcher, a superstitious man, nudged the horse impatiently, eager to have the cemetery with its freshly dug graves behind him.

It was at the far edge of the cemetery that he heard it, a faint scraping sound behind him. His hand went to the inside pocket of his jacket for his silver pistol, only to find the pocket empty of money, snuff, and weapon. Larcher had had a bad run of luck at tonight's card game.

Suddenly, out of the blackness of the night stepped an even blacker figure, a giant directly in the road ahead of him, a hulking figure wearing a hood.

"Whoa there, Yer Honor," a deep voice said. "We'd have a word with ye this fine evening." The man grabbed the bay's bridle and for some reason, the horse didn't even skitter.

"Who the bloody hell are you, and what do you want with me?" Even with the whiskey to give him courage, Larcher felt his knees go to water. He was in trouble and without a servant or constable, or even a pistol for protection.

"Let's just say that I'm a man whose family ye threw out into the cold this winter. Now that should narrow it down a bit. Though I hear ye've tumbled nearly a hundred cottages in the past five months, so ye might be guessin' for quite some time. I've brought me friends along. They'd have a word with ye, too."

From out of the brush beside the road appeared two more hooded figures. The first man, the big one, stepped up beside the horse and before Larcher knew what was about he was standing on the ground; at least, he stood as best he could with the whiskey coursing through his veins and his knees quivering with fear.

"What are you going to do with me?" he asked, afraid that they would tell him.

"Well ... we were going to kill you," the big man said, "but if we did that, we'd be no better than you. So we won't murder you this time. We're just after teaching you a lesson. Come along, Yer Honor. We've something to show ye."

The threesome half-led, half-dragged the landlord along the road, back in the direction he had come. To the graveyard.

"No!" Larcher dug his heels into the ground and found it soft and spongy. "You pointy-eared devils aren't taking me in there."

"You're already inside, sir," the hooded giant said, "and these are the graves of your tenants you're walkin' on this very minute. We thought you might want to spend just one night among them, just one night to see what they suffered before they died, and all because you threw them out into the wind and weather."

Spend the night? In this place? Even drunk, the idea terrified Larcher. He didn't like graveyards, especially

Catholic graveyards. God only knew what kind of heathen spirits lurked around these places after sundown.

"You can't be intending to leave me here. I'll freeze to death. You'll all hang for murder if you—"

"Ah, you'll not freeze, sir." The smallest of the three, the skinny one, stepped up to him and poked a finger in the landlord's side. "Ye've a barrel of lard around those ribs of yours and, judging from the stink of your breath, a goodly amount of whiskey in ye. You'll pass the night warm enough."

He saw where they were taking him, to the center of the graveyard, to the round tower.

"If you harm a hair on my head, you'll pay for this, you scoundrels." He tried to sound indignant, lordly, and outraged, but, instead, he sounded as though he were going to cry.

"A hair on his head, he says," the skinny one taunted. "He hasn't a hair on his head. I'll wager he hasn't a hair on his entire, ugly body. What do you say, lads?"

The big man threw Larcher up against the cold wall. "If you please, Your Honor, we'll ask you to take off your clothes now. There's others in greater need of them than you."

"Take off my clothes? What kind of perverted deviants are you?"

The three roared with laughter. "We've no evil intentions toward your fine body, sir," the giant said. "But we're after teaching you a lesson. We want to show you what misery you've heaped on others by throwing them out naked into the cold. Now take those clothes off and be quick about it or we'll take them off ye. And that's not a job any of us would treasure, sure."

Piece by piece Larcher removed his clothing, pausing after each garment in hope that they would be satisfied, but they insisted that he strip entirely, including his linen drawers.

"Now, won't that be a sorry sight to greet the villagers come sunrise," the thin fellow said with a chuckle as he pulled a long length of rope from inside his shirt. Larcher's heart sank to his bare feet. They were going to hang him after all.

"Aye, I've seen a handsomer belly on a sow ripe with piglets," the third man commented as he tied the rope around Larcher's left wrist. "Maybe some of those starving Catholic heathens will mistake you for a hog and butcher you for their breakfast tomorrow morning."

They passed the rope all the way around the tower and tied it securely to Larcher's right wrist. He twisted, trying to free himself, but the cold, wet stones of the tower grated against his bare back, and the ropes held tight.

"If anybody asks you who committed this foul deed against ye, just tell them 'twas the Black Oaks. Ol' Cornelius and William and Seamus themselves, resurrected from the grave." The skinny man scooped up a handful of dark mud and smeared it across the Englishman's white belly in the crude outline of a tree.

When he had finished and stepped back to survey his handiwork, the giant stepped forward. He stood so close that Larcher could feel his breath hot on his face. "And if they ask ye why the Black Oaks did this to you, you tell them it was a warning. If ye throw another family out of their home, if ye tumble one more cottage, we'll come after you again. And the next time, we won't be tying you to a tower. We're going to dig a grave right here in this very cemetery, and we're goin' to bury you in it. And we won't be taking the trouble to kill you before we bury you. Do you understand what we're after telling you here, Your Honor?"

Larcher looked around the graveyard at the silent tombstones and nodded once. A gust of frigid wind swept up the street and swirled between the stones, and the sound was like that of a woman keening.

"Listen to them, sir," his tormentor said. "Listen to the mothers crying for their children."

They left him alone then with the tombstones, the wind and the freshly dug graves. And long before dawn Larcher found that his fat didn't keep him warm on a cold, Irish night. Neither did the whiskey, nor even the fury that raged through him when his fear finally subsided.

Chapter Twenty

"Annie! What happened to your hair, girl?"

Michael couldn't believe his eyes. Annie sat, huddled on the hearth, her arms wrapped tightly around her legs and her face buried in her knees. Her beautiful hair was chopped off raggedly at her neck.

He hurried to her and dropped to his knees beside her. "Annie . . ." He shook her shoulder, forcing her to look up at him. Her eyes, nearly swollen shut from weeping, made Michael remember that day so many years before when he had tied her hair in knots. His heart went out to that innocent little girl he had loved, who was so different from the bitter woman he was married to. "What happened, darlin'? Who cut your lovely hair?"

"A . . . a . . . tinker," she sobbed. "A yellow-haired tinker."

"A damned tinker did this to you? But why?" His hands ran over her face and down her body searching for signs of attack or rape. "Did he hurt you? Did he—"

"No, he just cut my hair."

"Why?"

"Because I sold it to him."

With a flood of relief that left him weak, Michael sat down abruptly on the hearth. Then a rush of impotent anger followed. "Why the devil would you sell him your pretty hair, lass?"

Her dimpled chin trembled. "We need food, Michael," she said with a sniff. "And we've no money to buy it with."

"Ah, Annie." He pulled her into his arms and rocked her gently. "What am I to do with ye? Do you think I'd let you all starve? That's why I came back to Ireland, you know, to take care of you. You didn't need to trade your lovely hair for food."

"I didn't trade it for food," she muttered against the front of his shirt.

"Then I hope he paid you well in coin, for I'd rather have the fine gold of your hair than any English crown."

"Didn't trade it for gold either."

Something in her tone made him uneasy. She didn't sound right. She sounded weak and shaky, as though something inside her had broken. He would have preferred to hear her scolding. "Annie, what did you trade your locks for?" He stroked her poor chopped hair.

She reached into the pocket of her skirt and pulled out two long lengths of blue ribbon and held them out to him. "I was going to trade for food, but I saw the ribbons and I wanted them instead ..."

Her voice trailed away and Michael sat there staring at her as though seeing her for the first time. She had traded her hair for ribbons. Now she had blue satin ribbons, and no hair to tie them in.

Michael couldn't find his voice, so he simply hugged her while she cried. And as he held her a fear took hold of him, a new fear to add to all the others that plagued him. He would make sure that his family didn't starve, and if he was lucky he could keep them safe from the fevers.

But as Michael listened to his wife's choked sobs and he fingered the satin ribbons, he wondered what good would it do to keep their bodies alive, if they lost their minds and their spirits were broken?

The cold wind whipped the wet sheets against Caitlin's face as she tried to hang them on the line that stretched from one end of the courtyard to the other. Overhead the sun broke through the gray clouds for a moment, reminding her that she had to get the sheets on the line and dried before the wind turned them to ice.

Her hands were red from the cold and the harsh lye soap. Her eyes watered from the smoke of the campfires that dotted the courtyard and the fumes of the lye that bubbled in kettles above the flames. And her back ached from carrying the heavy baskets full of wet sheets and towels.

But no matter how hard Caitlin worked each day or how long the kettles boiled, she couldn't keep the sick clean. There were too many of them and too few hands to do the work.

She was grateful for the few volunteers, mostly those who had survived a bout of the fever and were immune. Father Murphy was there every day except Sundays, helping as best he could in between administering last rites. He had seen the need the day he had come to collect Sorcha McKevett's body, and she felt less alone with him there to offer comfort and practical assistance in the form of nursing.

And there was young Billy O'Shea. The poor lad had lost his entire family in less than a year, his father to the noose, his mother and sisters to fever. Caitlin offered him a weary smile as he brought her yet another basket full of sheets. He set it beside the basket that held little Stephen, who looked like another pile of laundry, swathed in a white blanket.

"Thank you, Billy," she said. "Why don't you rest a bit and go get yourself a bowl of soup, thin as it is?"

He nodded shyly and crossed the courtyard to stand in the long line beside the kitchen. Every day the line grew longer and the soup thinner. Caitlin dreaded the day when the line would stretch all the way through the village and they would have nothing in the pot but water. But the villagers didn't seem to care. Most of the public soup kitchens required a Catholic to renounce the church and pledge his allegiance to Protestantism. At least the soup at Armfield House could be had without sacrificing your soul.

Hearing the rumble of wagon wheels over the cobblestones, Caitlin swept a hanging sheet aside to see who it was. Her heart leaped when she saw the wagon with its merry cargo of painted horses.

Quickly she dropped the sheet back into place, hiding behind it while she took a deep breath and tried to slow the pounding of her pulse. Why was he here? Didn't he know that his life and hers depended on him staying away? She silently cursed him for intruding in her world, a world that was too complicated already. With the same breath she blessed him for giving her a glimpse of himself.

She peeped around the edge of the sheet and saw that he had climbed down from the wagon and was walking toward her. Panic rising in her throat, she reached for the basket that held Stephen and carried it over to one of the kettles. She set the child down and grabbed the paddle, busying herself by stirring the kettle that brimmed with sheets and lye.

Out of the corner of her eye she watched him as he walked up to her and stood, silently waiting for her to acknowledge his presence. Finally he reached out and took the paddle from her, his hand brushing hers with a touch that went through her body like molten fire. He began to stir the boiling pot, and both of them watched the motion of the paddle intently with feigned interest.

"I saw you in the trees," he said, "at me mother's funeral. I was glad to know you were there."

She simply nodded and stared down at the pot.

"And 'tis glad I am to be seeing you this minute," he said with a sincerity that wrenched her heart. Why did he have to be kind to her? It made her want to throw herself into his arms and bury her face against his broad chest. It made her want to kiss him and—

"Ah, Michael, you shouldn't have come here," she said, clasping her hands so tightly that her reddened knuckles turned white. "If His Honor sees you . . ."

"We'll not worry about His Honor this minute. There's only the two of us right now."

She cast a nervous glance up at the dark windows of the house. She thought she saw a movement at one of the windows, his bedchamber window. "Please, go away from here before he sees you talking to me."

Michael left the paddle in the kettle and turned to face her squarely. "I have some business here, and I'll not leave until I've finished. First I have to thank you, Caitlin, for nursing me poor mother through her last days. I hear you were the only one to stand by her, and I owe you a great debt for your kindness."

"You don't owe me anything, Michael," she said as she turned and picked up the basket with the baby. "Your mother was just one of hundreds I've nursed these past few months."

She started toward the house, but he blocked her path and took the basket from her. Her breath caught in her throat. What would happen if he knew that he was holding his son in that basket instead of laundry?

"Caitlin, I know," he said, as though reading her mind.

"You—you know what?"

"I know that you're living here with Armfield. I know that you've borne him a son." He bit his lower lip and she thought she had never seen him look so sad. "He's a lucky man, Mason Armfield is, a lucky one indeed."

As though responding to Michael's words, the baby in the blanket whimpered, then squalled loudly. Michael nearly dropped the basket. "My God, is it the wee one himself?" he asked, pulling back the blanket.

She watched breathlessly as he gazed down at the baby, and she felt a pleasure that was more like pain when he reached out and trailed one finger along the child's cheek.

"He's a fine lad, Caitlin," he said, his voice low and husky with emotion. "He has your curls."

And your green eyes, Michael, she thought. *Can't you see?*

Her heart reached out to embrace him, though her arms couldn't. He loved her child. Even thinking that she had borne this baby by another man, Michael loved it because it was hers. The warmth and affection that she saw on his face as he looked down at the baby was the emotion she had hoped to see on Mason's face all these months. But it had never been there.

"Please give that child back to its mother."

Caitlin spun around and saw Mason coming down the back steps of the house. His eyes were on her and they were as cold as the winter sky above them. Without a word, Michael handed the basket into Caitlin's arms.

Then he crossed his muscular arms over his chest and stood his ground, his feet apart and firmly planted.

"Why are you here?" Armfield asked when he stopped a pace away from Michael. The two men squared off as though for battle, and Caitlin clutched the basket protectively to her bosom.

"I came to thank Caitlin and you for nursing my mother in her illness. And I want to tell you that it's grateful I am that ye seem to have put our past differences behind. At least, I'm assuming you have, since I didn't find a rope waitin' for me when I arrived home."

"The gallows is still a possibility." Armfield said without emotion, "if you interfere with my family." He nodded his silver head briefly in the direction of Caitlin's basket.

Michael's jaw tensed, but he didn't break eye contact with the landlord. "I've no intention of tryin' to take what's yours. 'Tis clear enough to me that Caitlin has made her choice."

Caitlin knew what that admission cost Michael, and it pained her to hear him speak the words. If he only knew that the child was his, and her heart as well.

"There's another bit of business I have with you, sir, before I leave," Michael said. "I've brought back your wagon and your horse, and I thank you for the use of them."

Armfield said nothing, but Caitlin knew that he was pleased. There were few horses left in the stables these days, as he had sold most of them to keep the hospital and kitchen open.

"And" Michael continued, "I heard that you've been giving some of the men from the village jobs to help them feed their families. I'd appreciate any work ye might have for me."

Caitlin winced, knowing Mason's answer before he

spoke it. "I don't need another servant," he said. She could see that he enjoyed Michael's humiliation, and she hated him for it. "If you and your family are hungry, you can stand over there in the soup line with the rest of your neighbors."

Michael's green eyes blazed, as he fought to control his temper. "I wasn't asking for a handout, sir. I was willing to barter with ye."

"But you have nothing I want."

Michael drew a deep breath of resignation. "You want my carousel."

Armfield raised one eyebrow. "I seem to recall a time when I offered to buy it, and you told me it wasn't for sale."

"Everything's for sale in times like these. A man has to feed his family."

Caitlin despised the light of triumph that burned in Mason's gray eyes as he said, "How much?"

"Enough to feed my loved ones this winter and to plant a garden in the spring."

Armfield looked across the courtyard at the wagon full of wooden horses, the only bright spot in a dismal scene. Caitlin knew that Armfield couldn't afford to buy the carousel, that he was nearly at the end of his resources. But she knew that he couldn't pass up this chance to put Michael McKevett beneath him.

The landlord reached inside his jacket pocket and drew out a handful of coins. "This should be enough," he said as he tossed them onto the ground. They jingled as they hit the cobblestone, a merry sound that mocked the occasion.

When Michael bent over to pick up the money, Caitlin turned her face away and closed her eyes. She couldn't bear to witness his humiliation, though in that moment, he was the better man in her estimation by far. He had just sacrificed his very heart to provide for his family. It was a courageous act, one that gave him dignity even as he knelt to retrieve the landlord's money.

And Mason Armfield ... she had never entertained a contemptuous thought toward him until this moment.

When she opened her eyes, Michael was walking away, past the line at the kitchen, past the wagon that held his dreams and the work of his hands.

"That was a cruel thing you did, Mason," she said, not caring if he directed his anger toward her. "You just took what he loved most in the world. No man should do that to another."

When Mason looked at her, she was surprised to see no anger on his face, only sadness. "Why not?" He looked down at the baby in the basket and then at her. "He took what I loved." He turned his back on her and walked slowly into the house.

Caitlin watched him until he closed the door. Then she sat down on the steps, gathered her child in her arms, and, for the first time in many months, she allowed herself to cry.

Michael sat on the edge of the stone bridge, his legs dangling over the side. It was the middle of the night and all the world was asleep except him, and the frogs along the river's edge, and the full moon overhead.

Far below his feet the dark waters of the River Laune flowed deep and fast, swollen from the heavy winter rains. The night air was damp and heavy with silence. Michael listened for the sound of another living being and heard only the rushing water, the frogs croaking, and his own breathing. He had never felt so alone.

Michael was tired, too tired, it seemed, for his heart

to beat. He had no more strength, no more ideas, and no more hope.

For ten days he had scoured the county, looking for any bit of food to buy with his coins. But his money, the price of his dreams, was worthless. Every morsel of sustenance had vanished, devoured by the starving multitudes. Those who were fortunate enough to have hoarded a few supplies were long past greed and weren't in the least tempted to part with their grain or vegetables for mere gold.

Only the landlords had food, and they either shared it with their tenants or were exporting it as quickly as possible to keep it out of the hands of the "heathen parasites" who were finally doing something right— they were lying down in the fields and ditches and dying by the thousands and thousands.

Michael reached into his pocket and pulled out the handful of coins that Armfield had paid him. They glimmered like tiny golden moons against his dark palm.

Silver and gold. Many men would kill for much less than what he held in his hand. He, himself, had traded his heart for it. But what did silver and gold matter in times like these?

Michael thought of the flying horses and of the agonizing hours he had spent carving them with scarred hands that would never be as agile as they once had been. Those had been some of the most painful, but joyful, hours of his life, and he had traded it all for a handful of coins.

He thought of Annie's golden hair, her beauty and glory, lost to a tinker's shears, now adorning the pompous wig of some Englishwoman.

He thought of his mother and wondered if he had been here instead of in England, would she still be alive? If he had been holding her when she had died, would she have whispered words of forgiveness or condemnation?

He thought of Caitlin and the baby, who had her soft auburn curls. That child should have been his, not Mason Armfield's. Someday he might get over Armfield having his carousel, but he would never forgive Armfield for being the father of that beautiful baby boy.

Michael jingled the coins in his palm and watched them sparkle in the moonlight. Silver and gold. What were they worth after all?

He flung the coins into the dark waters below and watched until they sank to the bottom and out of sight.

Caitlin felt better with every step that took her farther away from Armfield House. As she walked along the river bank she breathed the fresh night air, the first sweet air she had smelled in months, and she felt free at least for an hour or so.

After leaving the sick in Father Murphy's care, she had made certain that Mason and the baby were sound asleep, then she had stolen away for a rare moment of solitude. She felt guilty leaving for even a short time, but consoled herself that she deserved a bit of time alone to think.

These past ten days had been difficult ones. She had felt Mason's eyes on her, watching, probing her thoughts. But every time she had met his gaze, he had looked away, his face a mask of indifference.

As she walked along the river bank she thought of Michael and the way his emotions always showed on his face. Whatever Michael felt—love, desire, hatred, joy, or despair—was reflected in his expressive eyes. And when Caitlin looked into his eyes, she was caught up in the passion that consumed him.

With Mason she simply wondered what was he thinking and feeling? And the wondering left her empty and drained.

Rounding the bend in the river, she saw the bridge ahead. She froze in midstep when she saw a lone figure seated on the edge of the bridge. She would have known that silhouette anywhere. No other man in Kerry was that large, or so broad of shoulder.

A bolt of fear shot through her. She should turn around and run back to Armfield House while she still could. If she met him now, here in this lonely place . . .

Yet she felt instinctively that the hand of Fate had brought them both here, and she couldn't force herself to turn away from him.

There was something about the set of his shoulders that bothered her, something in the way his back was bowed and the way he was looking down into the water that told her something was wrong. She didn't have to see his face or read his eyes to know the depth of his despair.

She watched as he stood and took off his great coat. Her anxiety rose when he removed his shirt and pulled off his brogues. The night was a cold one, and no man in his right mind would be pulling off his clothes in this weather.

Something clicked in her mind and she shook her head in disbelief. *No. Not Michael. He wouldn't—*

She started running toward the bridge, but her foot slipped on the muddy bank. She fell, wrenching her knee, but she got up and ran on, ignoring the pain. When she was nearly to the bridge, he did it. He pulled off his pants, hesitated only a moment, then dove headfirst into the dark waters.

"Michael! Oh, God," she sobbed as she tore at her

own clothes, ripping off her dress and the heavy petticoats. Wearing only her thin chemise, she plunged into the cold water and swam toward the spot beneath the bridge where he had disappeared.

Caitlin was a good swimmer, but she was in a weakened condition, and the current was strong as she fought against it. Finally, she reached the place where he had gone down, but there was no sign of him. She gulped a chestful of air, then dove beneath the water's surface. But in the darkness she couldn't see a thing.

She surfaced and cried out his name again and again. A horrible numbness claimed her limbs, and she could feel herself losing the fight against the current. Then something heavy collided with her just beneath the water. A moment later he bobbed up beside her, shaking the water from his hair.

"Caitlin, what the bloody hell—" One of his arms went around her waist, and he pulled her to him. Together they battled the dark, icy current as they fought their way to shore. They collapsed on the grassy bank, shivering violently and fighting for breath.

"Michael, you stupid fool," she sobbed through chattering teeth. She rolled toward him onto her side and hit him on his bare chest with her fist. "I could murder you for trying to do something like that." She hit him again, spending the last bit of her strength on the feeble blow.

He sat up and grabbed her wrists. "What are you talking about? What were you doing out there in that river? You could have drowned yourself, woman!"

"Drowned meself? I was tryin' to save you, horse's arse that you are." She burst into tears and pulled her hands away from his. "I saw you jump off the bridge, and I couldn't stand by and watch you kill yourself.

389

Why would you do that, Michael? Why would you do such a terrible thing?"

"Kill meself? You jumped in after me because you thought I was drownin' meself? Ah, lass—"

He pulled her into his arms and hugged her to him. Even in her confusion and anger she was aware of his wet, naked body, the touch of his bare flesh on hers.

"Caitlin, love, I wasn't after killing meself. I was discouraged and feeling poorly, so I tossed his honor's coins into the river. That was a foolhardy act, so I was diving in to collect them back again."

"You what?" His words sank slowly into her numbed brain. His eyes twinkled in the moonlight and she could see that, although he was obviously touched by her attempted rescue, he was also amused. She pulled back her fist and let him have it again, this time in the ribs. "I thought I was saving your life, you dirty cur. I jumped into that cold river because—"

He winced at the blow but his grin widened. "I'll throw meself back in if ye want me to, and you can leave me out there if it would make you happy. Just let me drown like the cur that I am."

The pitiful look on his face was her undoing. She couldn't be angry anymore, not with him sitting there grinning at her, alive and healthy, though a bit chilled. Relief washed over her like a warm tide and melted her anger. She threw her arms around his neck and laughed at herself and at him.

"Well, did you find your coins?" As she asked the question, her palm moved over the cool dampness of his chest. She could feel his heart pounding in a rhythm that matched her own. Her eyes traveled over his nakedness, and she remembered another night when he and his magnificent body had been hers alone. The

390

memory warmed her in spite of the wet chemise that clung, cold and clammy, to her skin.

"No. It was black as Toal's cloak down there. Couldn't see a bloody thing. Guess I'll have to come back tomorrow when the sun's up." His hand slid down the wet chemise to cup her breast. "Where are your clothes, Caitlin?" His voice was low and husky.

She shrugged. "Scattered down the river a bit. I took them off as I ran."

His fingertips found her hardened nipple and massaged it through the damp cloth. "You've got to get out of those wet clothes, love," he whispered. "You'll soon be sick if you don't. Wait here. I'll be right back."

She watched and savored the sight of his body glistening in the moonlight as he walked back to the bridge and gathered up his shirt, pants, and greatcoat. He returned and spread his coat on the grass. Dropping down onto it, he pulled her beside him. The desire in his eyes when he slowly peeled the wet chemise from her body went through her, leaving her weak and trembling.

He pressed her back onto the coat, covering her with his body which was growing warmer and harder by the moment. She closed her eyes, savoring the reality of the dream that had haunted her every night since they had last touched.

He kissed her, sweetly at first, then violently in a release of passion that had been pent-up too long. When he finally pulled away, they were both breathless.

She clung to him, her hands roaming hungrily over the rounded hardness of his hips. "Michael, he'll kill you if he finds out I've been with you. He told me so himself."

His lips traveled down her throat to her breast. "Sh . . ." he said. His tongue swirled over the rosy crest, and she gasped with the pleasure of it. "You may be living with His Honor, but you're mine, Caitlin. It doesn't matter if you bore his child or if you sleep beside him every night. You're mine, and you know it. And that's why Mason Armfield hates me, because he knows it too."

"Michael, I can't let you do this." Sean shook his head sadly as he stared down at three tickets in his hand, passage for three to America. "I know how you got the money for these tickets, and I can't take them from you."

Michael sat down in a pile of hay in the corner of the barn. He took a knife and a length of birch from his coat pocket and began to strip away the bark. "You have no choice as I see it," he said. "You can take Judy and your baby to America, or you can stay here and we'll all starve to death together."

"Why don't you take Annie and Danny and go yourself?"

"Ah, Annie wouldn't go. She's afraid of the sea. And Kevin wouldn't let me take Daniel. Besides, I don't think I could bear to leave dear Erin again."

"I don't think it's old Erin yer so attached to," Sean said, sinking down into the straw beside him. "I think it's a certain landlord's red-haired tallywoman."

Michael looked up from his carving, his green eyes flashing. "You'll keep a shut mouth about matters ye know nothing about, Sean Sullivan."

Sean simply smiled his slow, easy smile. Michael had never raised his hand to him, and Sean wasn't afraid of his temper. "There's no denyin' it, man. Yer smitten, through and through. Everybody knows it. I think Annie herself knows it."

They heard the barn door creak, and when they

looked up, Annie was standing there wearing a look that made Michael's heart sink. She had surely heard it all. Nothing else would have brought that pinched grimace to her white face.

"Michael, ye must come into the house," she said.

"I'm busy, Annie." He returned to his whittling. "I'll come in when I'm ready."

"Ye must come in," she repeated. " 'Tis Daniel. His headaches's getting worse and his face is turnin' dark. He's retching, and he's hot as an oven. I think he's got the black fever."

Chapter Twenty-one

Somehow Caitlin knew, even before she answered the urgent summons at the door, that it was Michael. And she knew that he was in trouble.

"Caitlin, it's Danny. He's got the fever. Ye must help me, please." Michael stood in the doorway, holding the boy in his arms.

She ushered them inside and led them into the dining room that was lined with straw pallets, most of which were empty. The fevers were finally beginning to subside in Lios na Capaill, since most of the population had already emigrated, died of starvation, or developed an immunity.

"Lay him over there." She pointed to a pallet in the corner. "And let me have a look at him."

Michael did as she said and stood quietly as she examined the child. It was the black fever, surely. The boy's freckled face was stained dark blue, and his skin was hot and dry. His big amber eyes stared up at her vacantly, seeing past her into his own world of solitary suffering.

"Will he die?" Michael asked when she straightened up and faced him. "Tell me. I must know."

She saw the fear in his eyes, the same stark terror she had seen in the faces of hundreds of fathers and mothers. She wanted to tell him what he wanted to hear. She longed to assure him that the child would be fine, but it would be even crueler to deceive him. So, she told him the same thing she had told them. "I don't know. We'll do what we can for him and pray for the best. Some live, some die. I'd say it's about half and half."

He winced as though her words had cut him. "What can I do?" he asked in a thick, choked voice. "Please tell me how to save him."

"We have to cool him down if we can," she said. "You take his shirt off, and I'll get some water to bathe him with."

When she returned a moment later with the bucket of water and a clean cloth, she saw Michael sitting on the pallet, holding the boy in his arms. Michael looked so vulnerable, such a big, strong man, yet so helpless. She had to give him something to do to help this child who meant so much to him.

"Here," she said, "bathe his face and chest with this cool water. Try to draw some of the heat out of his body."

Michael did as he was told, and Caitlin watched quietly. She would have offered to help, but she knew that this was something that Michael needed to do himself.

"There, lad, just be easy," he murmured. "We'll take good care of you and you'll be well before you know it."

The boy looked up at Michael, and he seemed to comprehend what he had said. Then he breathed a deep sigh and closed his eyes.

Caitlin heard the familiar, light footsteps behind her as Mason walked into the dining room. She turned to face him and steeled herself against the inevitable confrontation.

"I thought I made it clear to you, McKevett, that you are not welcome in my home," he said. He stood with arms akimbo, looking very much the part of the English landlord in his silver linen coat and ruffled cravat. Though the fine coat did look a bit threadbare, and it occurred to Caitlin that this coat was the only one she had seen him wearing lately. Could it be that he, too, had given away his clothes to those in need?

Michael laid the folded cloth across the boy's forehead and stood to face the lord of the house. "I understand why you don't want me under your roof, Your Honor," he said, choosing his words with care. "But I ask you to reconsider. This is Kevin O'Brien's only son, Daniel. He's as fine a lad as ever walked the green earth, and he deserves better than to die at this tender age. I want to save his life, but I don't know how. Caitlin here knows what must be done to save him, and I beg you to let her do that."

Caitlin saw no sign of humiliation in Michael's face as he pleaded. His desperation was much greater than the day he had sold his carrousel. He was far beyond such things as pride.

"Then leave the child here and let Caitlin attend him," Armfield said. "We'll let you know if he lives or dies."

Michael shook his head. "I can't leave him, Your Honor. Me mother already died without her son at her side because you sent me away. And this lad is dearer than life to me, like my own son. You have a fine son of your own now. Surely you wouldn't leave him if he were courtin' death."

Caitlin held her breath as she watched the changing

emotions play across Mason's face. It was impossible to tell what the man was thinking, what he would say next.

Michael stepped closer to Armfield, his eyes never leaving the landlord's face. "Your Honor, I know that you hate me and I know why. But you've already taken everything I have. You have my carousel. You have the woman I love and her baby. Please, don't take this child's life out of hate. You're too good a man to do such a thing as that."

Armfield looked down at the boy, then at Caitlin. She begged him silently with her eyes.

"Yes," he said at last. "I don't suppose I hate even you that much."

From his vigil beside Daniel's pallet Michael watched with a quiet sense of pride and affection as Caitlin moved among the sick, bathing the fevered bodies, comforting the dying and performing even the meanest of tasks without complaint. No other woman he knew was strong enough in body, mind and spirit to do what she was doing hour after hour, day after day. No man, either, for that matter.

He watched her every move, but without the simmering passion that he had always felt in her presence. When she bent over Daniel and laid her cool palm on his hot brow, when she helped Michael change the soiled bedding, and when she instructed him on how to bathe Danny and how to coax water down his parched throat, one drop at a time, Michael felt a tremendous love for her. But he felt none of that desperate longing to bed her. Bedding was the last thing on either of their minds these days.

During the long hours of nursing the boy, and at times like this when he watched her caring for the others, Michael could feel a bond growing between the two of them, a bond stronger than any that could be forged on a mattress or a moonlit river bank.

His heart reached across the room to embrace her, to express silently his admiration and love for her. She looked up from the old woman she was feeding and smiled, returning the unspoken caress.

"How is the lad this afternoon?" Father Murphy seemed to appear out of nowhere. If he had seen the exchange between them, he didn't seem to mind. His blue eyes were smiling and full of concern as he bent over Daniel, who slept on, unconscious of the attention he was receiving.

"He had a bad night," Michael replied wearily. "It's been five days now and that rash has spread all over his body just as Caitlin said it would."

"Does she think he'll live?"

"She doesn't know yet. She says she's seen worse than him pull through, and better than him die. 'Tis as long as it's broad right now, I suppose."

"If there's anything I can do, let me know."

Michael glanced surreptitiously around the room. Caitlin had gone into the parlor, and the other patients were asleep or so deep in their own misery that they weren't listening to what was going on around them. "Father, I've been wanting to talk to you if you have the time."

The old priest knelt stiffly on the floor beside Michael, tucking his skirts around his knees. "Yes, my son, what is it?"

"I wanted to ask you if—" Michael's voice knotted up in his throat and he had to wait a minute before he could continue. "I was wondering if all the trouble I've been having is because of a sin that I committed long ago."

"It's certainly possible, son. Sometimes the Good Shepherd chastises us severely to bring us back to Himself when we've strayed from the path. Is that what you think has been happening to you?"

"I don't know. I was just wondering if God would punish someone as innocent as this child here because of something I did years ago. 'Tis something I've forgiven myself for, but I've never confessed it before God and man. Could that be why this child is sick?"

The priest stroked his cheek thoughtfully, his fingers rasping over the white stubble of unshaven whiskers. "I should think that rather than punishing you by making the boy ill, the good God is trying to get your attention, trying to tell you that it's time to cleanse your soul of this sin that's weighing you down."

Michael thought on this carefully, and it seemed to make sense. "If I were to confess this sin that's between me and God, do ye think He'd listen to me prayers then? I can tell He doesn't pay me any mind at all now."

"I'm sure it would help. I can listen to your confession now, if you're ready to make it."

Michael looked down at Danny, at his parched lips and fever-blushed face. He looked at the tiny hands and thought of the beautiful wooden horse in Kevin's barn. "I would like to do that, Father. I should have come to you long ago, but it seemed such a terrible sin that I couldn't bear to think of it, let alone speak of it. But now my eyes have seen so many horrors—it changes the way a man looks at things." He took a deep breath and closed his eyes. "Bless me, Father, for I have sinned. I murdered me father with me own hand."

* * *

399

"My head hurts so bad, Michael," Danny whispered as he reached out to grasp Michael's hand, but he was too weak even to raise his arm.

Taking the child in his arms, Michael held him close and tried to communicate some comfort, to impart some of his own strength and health into the frail body. The moment he touched the child, Michael's heart lurched. He was terribly hot, much hotter than before and he was limp, as limp as a dead rabbit in a snare.

Michael looked out the window into the darkness of the predawn hours. This was when it happened most often. Caitlin had said so, and he had seen it happen over and over during the past week. They died just before sunrise.

"Sh-h-h-," he said, smoothing those precious red curls with his scarred palm. "Ye mustn't talk now. I know it hurts, lad, I know."

Michael caught a glimpse of Father Murphy's black skirt at the doorway. He gently laid the child back on the pallet and hurried to the door. "Father, come quick." With a firm grasp on the priest's forearm he pulled him to Danny's side. "Ye must pray for him, Father. I'm afraid he's slippin' off. Pray for him straight away."

As the priest kissed his stole and began his prayers, Michael stood by, fighting down his panic. After a moment Michael realized with horror that Father Murphy was administering last rites. "No. That's not the prayers I meant!" He dropped down onto his knees beside the priest. "I want you to pray that he won't die. Ask God to let him live."

The priest shook his head and sighed. "We can't dictate to God, my son. His will must be done here, and 'tis our duty to accept His will."

"Accept this child's death? No! I'll not accept as

sweet a soul as this one dyin' so young. If you won't pray for his life, away with ye."

"I must pray for his soul, Michael—"

"Ye'll do no such thing." Michael scooped the boy into his arms and held him away from the father. "You can't have him yet, priest. While he lives and breathes, he's mine. And if you won't pray for him, I will."

Reluctantly, the priest left the room and Michael sat down on the pallet, cradling the limp body in his arms.

After a time Danny opened his eyes and stared up at Michael, a look of wonder on his face. "I can see her. I can see her this very minute," he whispered.

"Who, lad? Who is it you see?"

"Princess Niav. I see her coming up out of the water."

"What's she doin', lad?"

"She wants me to come with her on her white stallion. She's waving to me."

Michael's arms tightened around the boy as the knife of his fear cut deeper. "Don't go with her, Danny. Tell her to go away."

"But she's going to take me away . . . to the Land of the Ever Young. She says I'll feel better there. My head won't hurt anymore."

"No, tell her you're going to stay here with me. Don't go with her."

Daniel's eyes widened, and Michael knew that he was seeing that enchanted land more clearly than Michael ever had in his fantasies. "There's flying horses everywhere," Danny said, his voice stronger now. "And a hundred lights, and music, loud and sweet. It's lovely, Michael. So lovely."

"Danny, don't—"

Michael watched as the soft brown eyes closed. The small body in his arms shuddered once, then went limp.

Slowly he laid the boy down on the pallet and sat, looking at him for a long moment. Then Michael's body began to shake. He shook as though his heart were being torn out of his chest by a cruel hand. The Hand of God. The beast inside roared out its pain, and the sound shattered the silence of the house.

Upstairs Caitlin heard the cry and seconds later she was flying down the staircase. She ran into the dining room and saw Michael sitting on the floor, his knees drawn up to his chest, his face buried in his hands. He was sobbing.

"Michael! What is it?" But she knew there was only one reason why he would be crying. She hurried to the pallet and pressed her fingertips to the boy's throat, searching for a pulse.

"He's dead," Michael said, raising his eyes to hers. "I confessed my sin, and God let him die, anyway."

She bent over and put her ear to the boy's chest, then she wiped the beads of sweat away from his forehead, cooler now than it had been for days. "Michael," she said, her voice choked with compassion. "Yer a terrible nurse if ye can't tell the dead from the living. Danny's not dead. He's in a deep sleep, and his fever's broken. 'Tis a good sign. I think he'll live after all."

Caitlin walked out the back door with a basket of sheets under one arm and a basket holding baby Stephen under the other. The early morning sun hung red in a gray sky, and its feeble glow did little to warm the frosty air.

Michael was sitting on the back porch with his knees apart, his elbows resting on his thighs and his head bowed. He stood when he saw her and took the basket of sheets. Together they walked to the nearest empty kettle, and he dumped them into the boiling water.

"I was thinking that it's been five days now since Danny turned the corner," he said, stirring the kettle with the wooden paddle. "If you think he's strong enough, I'll take him home today."

"He's strong enough," she said. "And you can rest easy about him now. He'll not get the Black Fever again. They never do when they've had it as bad as he."

"That's good to know." He looked down into the basket that held the baby. "You must be careful that this little lad doesn't get sick. That would be a sad day, indeed."

She smiled, pleased at his concern. "I am careful. I keep him upstairs away from the sick ones and I bring him out here in the fresh air as often as I can. I'm going to miss you, Michael," she said suddenly. "It's been good to be able to see you every day. Though I'm glad the boy's well now."

"Caitlin ..." He looked around the courtyard and saw no one. The house's few servants were still asleep, and the kitchen didn't open the soup line now until late afternoon. He stepped closer to her and put his hand on her shoulder. "It seems that every day my debt to you grows. I'll never be able to repay your kindness to me and my family."

She looked down into the basket at the baby with his curling auburn hair and green eyes. "You've given me more than enough already."

"I love you, lass." His eyes met hers, and she felt a tugging as though he were pulling her to him, into himself. "I loved you before this, and I love you even more now. How am I going to live without you?"

She blinked back the tears that seemed always near the surface these days. "I don't know, maybe someday—" She swallowed the words, knowing that once her hope was spoken aloud it would torment her even more. There was no hope. He was married, and she . . .

"I'd better be going now," he said.

"Yes, you'd best be off."

He leaned over and kissed her once on the cheek. When he walked away from her she felt her heart reaching out to him, but her heart alone wasn't strong enough to hold him.

She turned to go back into the house, but as she climbed the back steps she heard someone coming up behind her, pounding up the stairs with heavy footsteps.

"I saw that!" A woman's voice, shrill and indignant, assaulted her ears. Annie stood several steps below her, her hands on her hips and red spots of fury in her wan cheeks. "I came over here to see what was going on between you and my husband, and I saw him kiss you with me own eyes."

Caitlin sighed deeply. She was too tired for this, much too tired to be nice to a shrew like Annie McKevett. "And such a kiss it was," she said sarcastically. "Lasted all of two heartbeats and on the cheek at that." She thought of their nights together in her pub and on the river bank, and she wondered what Annie would say if she had seen the caresses they had exchanged on those occasions. "Run along home now, Annie, and tend your little brother, who, since you ask, is going to be fine."

A flicker of relief crossed Annie's face, but her indignation quickly returned. "I'm glad to hear about Daniel, but that doesn't change the fact that you have been—doing things—with my husband, you wicked, sinful . . ." She sought the words desperately. " . . . loose woman."

Caitlin slowly set the basket containing Stephen on

the porch and walked down the steps to stand in front of Annie. She towered over the smaller woman, Annie's nose nearly in her bosom. "The word yer lookin' for is 'whore.' Come on, you can say it. If you can accuse another of being such a thing, you can at least let the word pass your virgin lips."

Annie's face turned an ugly mottled purple as she stood there opening and closing her mouth like a netted salmon. "Aye, that's what you are," she said at last. "Yer a dirty whore, going around stealin' other women's husbands, and yer a landlord's tallywoman besides. You don't deserve to live, you and that Englishman's bastard son of yours."

Caitlin heard the crack of her palm across Annie's face before she even knew that she had struck her. Annie lost her balance and fell backward, sitting down hard on the stone steps. A bright red handprint blossomed on her cheek.

Fetching the baby from his basket, Caitlin returned to Annie and held the child under Annie's nose, which oozed a small trickle of blood. She wasn't finished with her yet. Her anger wasn't going to be appeased with one blow. "Look again, Annie McKevett," she said. "Look at my bastard son and tell me who fathered him."

The instant the realization hit Annie, her blue eyes widened and the air gushed out of her in one harsh gasp. "Michael. He's Michael's."

"That's right. And Michael doesn't even know." She leaned down until their faces were nearly touching. "Why don't you tell him, Annie? You love to bear tales. Why don't you run home this minute and tell Michael what a sinful, adulterous husband he is? Tell him that he's fathered a bastard by a landlord's whore."

If Caitlin had seen anyone else hurting as Annie

405

McKevett was at that moment, her heart would have gone out to them. But she was too angry to feel any pity for this woman.

Annie jumped up from her seat on the steps, clasped her hand over her mouth and gagged. Then she turned and ran across the courtyard as though the Devil were lighting a fire on the hem of her skirt.

"You won't tell Michael," Caitlin called after her. "Because if you do, he'll leave you, sure. And you hate him too much to set him free."

"Oh, Father Brolin, 'twas the worst moment of me life. Ye'll never know what it's like to have a woman such as that stand there so proud and haughty and tell you she's been with your husband. And then she told me that bastard of hers was Michael's own babe and then she hit me. She had me down there on the ground and she was beatin' me black and blue. 'Twas terrible, Father. Simply terrible. May she burn in hell . . . in hell itself, Father."

Annie's shoulders convulsed with sobs as she collapsed into a chair beside the fire in the rectory's kitchen. She had been fortunate enough to catch Father Brolin alone and had poured her griefs and woes into his sympathetic ear. The priest reached over to pat her, and she sobbed even harder.

"There, there," he said in his gentle way that always made her feel better. If only Michael would comfort her that way. If only Michael were a good, holy man like Father Brolin, she thought. But then, if Michael had been holy, he wouldn't have bedded that awful woman and that baby in the basket would have been the landlord's like everyone in the village thought. Every time she thought of them together, of the sinful things they

406

must have done to each other, she wanted to kill them both. She also felt this strange tingling in the pit of her stomach. She was feeling it right now with the father's gentle hand on her shoulder and his kind voice in her ear.

"Have you ever heard such a disgusting thing in all your days?" she asked him as he knelt beside her chair.

He thought carefully, then nodded. "I've heard worse than that," he admitted, "much worse. But it is a terrible sin your husband has committed," he added quickly when the corners of her mouth pulled down and her lower lip protruded. "And I know how you must be suffering."

"Oh, Father," she said with a sniff, "you always understand. What a wonderful man you are."

He blessed her with his most benevolent smile. "You're one of my favorite parishioners. You're a fine woman, Annie McKevett, a fine and rare woman. And that husband of yours has no idea what a treasure he has, or he would treat you better."

His words were balm to her wounded spirit. So, there was a man in this world, after all, who could appreciate her. And he was a such a handsome man with such lovely blue eyes. With the sun shining through the window on his blond hair, he looked almost like an angel. The tingling in her stomach moved lower into more intimate parts of her body.

His hand moved up to stroke her head, and she realized that he was looking at her cropped hair. Suddenly, she wished he couldn't see her. She didn't want him to think that she was ugly, not when she thought he was so beautiful.

"What happened to your lovely hair, Annie?" His voice was deep and she could hear his concern for her.

"I had to sell it, Father. Michael made me sell it to a tinker so that we could buy a bit of bread."

"Oh, Annie . . . I'm so sorry. That man should be horsewhipped. I wish you weren't married to him."

"You do?" Annie caught her breath as she searched his blue eyes. What did he mean by that? Something in the way he was looking at her made her think that maybe he was wishing that she weren't married and he weren't a priest.

Still kneeling beside her chair, he leaned toward her and put both his hands on her shoulders. "Yes, I do. You deserve better than Michael McKevett. You deserve a man who would cherish you and love you, who would hold you in his arms and—"

She couldn't bear it any longer. She threw her arms around his neck and slid off the chair to kneel in front of him. But Annie's gesture was impulsive and clumsy and the priest fell backward onto the floor with her on top of him, her arms still locked around his neck.

"I love you too, Father," she cried. "I didn't know it until just this minute, but 'tis you I love. 'Tis you I've always loved." The tingling spread like fire through her body. All she saw was a pair of startled blue eyes as she lowered her head and pressed her lips to his.

For one brief, blissful moment she felt him returning the kiss. Then he jammed both of his hands between their chests and shoved her off him. She tumbled sideways and rolled across the floor until she slammed into the china press, rattling the dishes and pans and cracking her ribs soundly.

"What the devil do you think you're doing, woman?" he shouted, wiping his mouth with the back of his hand. He sat up and shook his head as though trying to clear it. "What kind of blasphemy is this, you trying to kiss a priest?"

Annie scrambled up from the floor and held her hand to her bruised ribs. She was hurt, confused and angry. "The same blasphemy as a priest kissin' back, I'd say," she returned. "You said you loved me, that you wanted to hold me."

"I didn't."

"You did."

"That's not what I said at all. I said that I—"

"You're no better than that rotten husband of mine." Tears streamed down her cheeks, and she was shaking all over, her hands clenched at her sides. "You don't want me either. I loved you and Michael, but neither of you wanted me. Damn you, I say! I hate you both." She hung her head as hysterical sobs overtook her.

She heard him rise from the floor and walk over to her. As furious as she was at him, she thought that maybe, just maybe, he was going to apologize and take her in his arms. And Annie couldn't decide what she was going to do if he did.

His hand closed around her arm, but this time there was nothing gentle or affectionate about his touch. His fingers bit into her flesh as he propelled her toward the door. "You'd better get out of here right now, Annie McKevett," he said as he opened the door and shoved her outside. "And don't you ever speak of this to anyone, or I'll tell them how you tried to seduce a priest. Now away with you."

He slammed the door in her face and left her standing there alone in the icy rain. As hailstones pelted her bare head, Annie McKevett wondered what more could possibly happen to her before this miserable day was over.

Chapter Twenty-two

The rain turned to snow, and the road and meadows quickly disappeared beneath a glittering cloak of white. The only spot of color on the narrow road between the rectory and the village was the bright red caravan that belonged to Liam Donnelly, the tinker.

The caravan was Liam's pride and joy, a gay little wagon with a rounded roof that was bright blue with yellow stripes adorning its sides. On the top of the caravan perched a tiny chimney, the flue for the small oven inside which kept Liam warm while the caravan's sturdy sides sheltered him against the blast of the storm that had descended, as most of this winter's storms, without warning.

Liam checked the pot that bubbled on the oven's iron lid and found the water boiling. With great ceremony he took down an ornately decorated tin from an overhead shelf. From a drawer beside the oven he removed a delicate silver tea ball, filled it with the fragrant mixture from the tin, and dropped it into the boiling water.

Liam Donnelly was a tinker, a traveling man, a tinsmith by trade and a damn good one. He dabbled in other trade as well . . . a horse now and again, a bit of cloth for the ladies and pretty combs and ribbons for their hair. And lately, he had discovered a new way to earn a coin or two. He bought hair from the Irish lasses and sold it in Dublin and Cork to the English ladies for wigs.

The tinker had been accused on many occasions of being a rascal who found things before they were lost, of selling goods for more than they were worth, and of leading more than one tender maiden astray. And while he had done all of those things at one time or another, Liam Donnelly was happy with himself and his lot in life. He had seen more of the world than a dozen of the villagers who accused him, and he had more tales to tell than a bard.

While his tea steeped in the pot, Liam went to the caravan's one small window and looked out into the storm. To his surprise he saw a lone figure struggling down the road, and with Liam's sharp eye it didn't take long for him to see that it was a woman.

He threw on his greatcoat and plunged out into the weather after her. Two minutes later he had her inside the wagon, sitting on his rug with a cup of hot tea in her hands.

"That's the finest cup of tea to be had in the length and breadth of Ireland," he announced proudly, pouring himself a cup as well. "All the way from China it is. Straight from the Emperor's own cupboard."

The young woman didn't seem to be impressed. She just sat there, holding the cup between hands that were blue and shaking. Liam began to regret that he had given her the fine bone china cup, afraid that she might drop it at any minute.

He reached over and pushed the hood of her cloak back from her face, and that was when he recognized her. "Ah, so we meet again," he said, looking at her short, blond hair. He remembered her well, because he had thought it such a pity to take the girl's only beauty. She might have been prettier with a bit of flesh on her gaunt face and the bloom of roses in her cheeks. But now she looked like the very Devil. She had been crying, her nose was red, and the expression on her face was one of pure misery.

"What are ye doin' out in this storm, lass?" he asked. "Your husband will be worried to death and out lookin' for you, sure."

She sniffed loudly and wiped her eyes with the back of her hand. "My husband doesn't give a tinker's damn—begging your pardon—for me, and he'd not look for me if I was gone a year and a day. He'd just fancy himself lucky to have me gone."

Liam tucked that information away in the part of his brain used for seducing young ladies. "Is that why yer crying? Because that husband of yours doesn't care about you?"

She nodded and took a long gulp of the hot tea.

"Well, I used to have a wife, but we were poorly mated. She didn't care about me either, scolded me night and day, she did. But I made her sorry for how she'd treated me."

She looked up from her tea, and he could see that he had her full attention. "How did you do that?"

Liam grinned broadly, showing a row of jagged teeth that had met the fists of too many jealous husbands. "I bedded her sister."

The girl blushed violently and looked down into her tea. "That was an awful thing to do. You should be ashamed."

"Should I?" Liam thought carefully. "Maybe you're

412

right. But haven't you ever done anything you were ashamed of?''

Her blue eyes instantly puddled with tears that rolled down her cheeks and dripped into the tea. Liam wasn't sure exactly what she had done or with whom, but she was certainly ashamed. He felt ashamed for embarrassing her.

He pulled a handkerchief from his pocket and held it out to her. "Here, dry your eyes, girl, and stop that crying. I'd rather see a goose go barefoot than to see a woman weep."

But she didn't stop crying. She buried her face in his handkerchief and sobbed loudly—terrible, wracking sobs that seemed to tear her small body apart.

Liam quickly rescued his china tea cup, then sat down on the rug beside her. He put his arm around her shoulders and shook her gently. "Stop that, girl. You'll hurt yourself, sure, if you keep squallin' like that. If you stop your crying I'll give you a present." He reached behind them into a large trunk and pulled out the length of golden hair that he had taken from her. "Here. 'Tis your very own hair that I haven't sold yet. You can pin it here on your head like the English ladies do and then you won't be so ugly and maybe that husband of yours will have a kind word for you."

She lifted her face from the handkerchief, took one look at the hair and screamed. It was the most miserable shriek that Liam, who had slaughtered pigs with his father as a child, had ever heard. She fell face down on the floor of the caravan, beat the rug with her fists and kicked it wildly with her tiny feet.

Liam tossed the hank of hair behind the chest and threw himself down on the rug beside her. He wrapped his arms and legs around her, trying to hold her still.

"Girl, stop that! You're going to rip something if you don't settle down."

She struggled against him, but feebly. At last she gave up the fight and lay quietly in his arms, still crying. "Do—do you think I'm ugly?" she sobbed against the front of his shirt.

He looked down at her and grinned. "Aye, terrible ugly," he said, his tone more gentle than his words. "But that's just because you're unhappy. Any woman looks bad when she's unhappy. Now if you had a smile, even a little one, right here ..." His fingertip traced the bow of her upper lip. "Just a little smile and you'd look much better."

As he had anticipated, she rewarded him with the faintest of shy grins. Liam had played this game many times, and he knew each move well.

"What's your name, girl?" he asked as he tightened his arm around her waist.

"Me name's Annie," she breathed. "What's yours?" Her tears had ceased and her eyes were on his lips as he lowered his head to hers.

"I'm Ryan Garvey." Liam had learned long ago never to use his true name when playing this game. "And I'm very pleased to meet you, Miss Annie."

He kissed her, and he knew by the way she accepted the kiss that she wouldn't be one he would remember forever, like that fiery black-haired beauty last summer in Dungarvan. But she was willing ... and that was enough for Liam Donnelly.

Annie stood outside the horseshoe-shaped door of her father's forge and took a deep breath, trying to gather the courage to step inside. She couldn't remember a time in her life, until now, that she had ever been afraid of her father. Kevin O'Brien had a temper to be sure, but it seldom boiled over its pot and never onto his children. But then, she had never come to him with such a terrible problem before, and if there had been anyone else in the wide world she could have gone to, she would not have been there at the forge door.

She cast her eyes heavenward for a moment, crossed her chest, and stepped inside.

The fire in the oven lit the dark interior of the forge with an eerie red glow. The smell of smoke, ash dust, hot metal and masculine sweat filled her nostrils, scents that Annie had always loved and associated with her father.

Kevin stood at his anvil for the first time in months, pounding away on a hot iron rod. At the sound of her closing the door, he quickly hid the rod behind his back. When he saw it was only his daughter, he resumed his pounding.

"Is that a pike you're working on, Da?" she asked fearfully. It was against the law for a smith to fashion pikes, the age-old weapons of Irish peasant insurrection.

"It is, indeed," he said, "and you're not to tell a soul about it."

"But why are you making a pike?"

"I've made a dozen of them this past week. A man never knows when he'll need a weapon in times such as these."

He thrust the rod into the cooling bath. Clouds of steam rose around him, adding to the moisture that trickled down his face, neck and bare chest. Like every other Irishman in Lios na Capaill, Kevin was much thinner than he had been in years, but his fine muscles were still toned, his body like that of a much younger man's. Only the increasing silver in his red hair betrayed the fact that he was a grandfather.

Annie clenched her hands tightly in front of her apron and tried to stop trembling. She also tried to remember the speech she had memorized. But now that she stood face to face with him, every prepared word went out of her head.

"Da, I've somethin' I must say to you," she said. "But you must promise that you won't hit me or scold me when I tell you."

"I've never hit a child of mine in me whole life and I'm not likely to start now. What is it, girl?"

"I'm going to bear a child."

Kevin dropped the pike on the hard-packed dirt floor. The clatter made her jump. "Yer what?"

"I'm with child, Da, but you promised you wouldn't scold."

"I promised I wouldn't beat you. I said nothing about scolding. Now what kind of foolishness has that Michael been up to? He knew what old Bridget said about you havin' another babe. It could kill you sure. I'll beat that husband of yours for this, I will."

As Annie watched her father's face go livid, his massive hands clenching into fists, she knew that the worst was yet to come. "But, Da, it wasn't Michael who did it to me," she said in the high squeak of a mouse caught in the cat's jaws.

Kevin's eyes flashed with a fire that paid tribute to his ancestor, Brian Boru. "What are ye sayin', girl?" His voice was quiet and threatening. "Are you telling me that you've been with another besides your own husband?"

"Ah . . . yes . . . but I didn't mean to do it."

He stepped up to her and grabbed her by the upper arms. "The act that brings a babe into the world isn't likely done by mistake, girl. It's not like spilling a crock o' milk."

"I know . . . I mean . . . he forced me."

Kevin's florid face went white. He released his grip on her, and she nearly fell to the floor. "What man forced you, Annie? Tell me now."

Annie had never seen her father look this way, not even when her mother had died or on the Night of the Big Wind when his home had been destroyed. He looked as though he were going to murder someone this very minute, and she was the only one in sight. If she told him that she had been with a lowly tinker . . .

" 'Twas the priest, Da. The good father himself did it to me there in the rectory when I went to him for consolation one day."

She saw the disbelief in his eyes and thought for a moment that her falsehood had backfired on her.

"Do you really expect me to believe that old Father Murphy got you with child, Annie? Surely that's not what you're sayin'."

She laughed a tense, shaky giggle. "No, of course it wasn't the old father. 'Twas Father Brolin. He's the one who forced me to . . . you know . . . there on the floor of the rectory."

The only sound in the room was the crackling of the fire in the oven and the sound of Kevin's harsh breath as he stood, looking down at his daughter, who stared back at him with guileless blue eyes. Her expression resembled that of a wounded deer.

Kevin took his shirt from the hook on the wall and slipped it on. Taking down his coat as well, he headed for the door.

"What are you going to do, Da? Yer not after murdering him, are you?"

"I'll not endanger me soul by killing a priest," the smith said, "but I'm going to bash his head and break his arm, sure."

She ran to him and stepped between him and the door. "He said if I told anyone that it was he who did it, he would say that I encouraged him, and I didn't. Don't listen to his lies, Da. Tell me you won't let him say bad things about me."

"Don't worry, lass," he said, pushing her aside. "If he tells any lies against you, I'll not break one of his arms. I'll break them both."

Father Murphy took a bag of Indian corn from the barrel behind the door and pressed it into Tomas Kiley's hand. "That's not much pay for your bonesetting services, son, but it's all I have to offer you," he said as he ushered Tomas out the door.

"That's fine, Father, just fine. I only hope the young father manages to stay astride his horse better in the future. 'Tis a shame to see him in such pain."

"Yes, a terrible shame," the priest muttered as he closed the door and turned to face Father Brolin, who sat in the straight-backed chair beside the fire, an ugly cut across his forehead, his eyes black as turf soot, and both arms bound to his sides. "It's a shame that Kevin didn't break your neck as well," he added dryly.

He walked over to the younger priest and fixed him with a baleful glare. Brolin was in no condition to stare him down, so he dropped his gaze to the floor.

"You know, son," Father Murphy said with a philosophical tone, "I've never liked you. Couldn't stand the sight of you from the moment I laid eyes on you. I should have sent you on your way when I caught you holding that silly girl in your arms. I almost tossed you out on your ear when I heard that you were charging those poor starving souls for blessing their pitiful potatoes, which rotted, anyway. You can't even offer up an effective prayer, it seems."

The younger priest winced, but continued to stare at the floor as though memorizing the lay of the stones.

"But this ..." Father Murphy continued his barrage. "Breaking your vow of celibacy with a member of your own flock. You disgrace yourself, you disgrace me, and all the priests before us who shed their blood so that we could practice our faith on this soil. I'm sorry I lived to see this day."

Father Brolin couldn't contain his anger any longer. It spewed forth like the spring torrent over Torc Fall. "Surely you don't believe what that woman said. She's lying. She is, I swear."

"Oh, I'm sure she lied about the fact that you attacked her. Not even you would ravish a woman, and she certainly wasn't one who would have to be forced. She's been in love with you for years, and you knew it. You enjoyed her attentions and encouraged her. I'm sure what happened between the two of you was as much her fault as yours."

"But nothing happened, I tell you. I don't know who fathered her baby, but I swear it wasn't me."

"Enough of this!" The priest's roar echoed through the rectory. "I've said all I intend to say. I want you out of my sight and out of my parish before the sun sets, or, I swear by the Holy Saints, I'll do you harm myself."

"But—but, Father, surely you don't mean that. How can I travel now? Look at me, for heaven's sake."

The priest perused his battered body from head to toe. "You can travel," he said. " 'Tis your arms that's broken. Not your legs."

* * *

Caitlin opened the door of the O'Brien's barn and stepped inside the dark, musty interior. The old byre was silent, the horse, the cow and her calf long gone. Across Ireland most barns were silent this winter.

But this stable had at least one horse in it, a wooden horse. In the far end, beneath a gleaming lantern, Michael and Daniel carved intently on a glorious carousel stallion, Michael at the head, Daniel on the saddle ornamentation. Caitlin stood in the shadows and watched in quiet wonder for a time before letting her presence be known.

"You see, Danny, lad," Michael was saying, "these are horrible times we live in now, times that break men's spirits and destroy their dreams. Dreams are fragile things, as fragile as a man's heart. And they must be handled very carefully and kept alive in times like these. There's so much ugliness around us, that we must try to bring some beauty into the world if we can."

Daniel stood back and surveyed their work with a critical eye, the lantern light glittering in his copper curls. Caitlin's heart whispered a prayer of gratitude that this lad had survived. Of all the children who had died in her arms, she was deeply thankful that Daniel O'Brien hadn't been one of them.

"Well . . ." Danny said, "this is a lovely horse to be sure. Do you think we'll ever have another carousel, Michael?"

When Michael looked up from his work to answer the boy, he saw Caitlin standing there. Their eyes met and, as usual, she felt the tug of the bond between them. "We'll have another carousel someday, Danny," he replied. "I promise you that. And Princess Niav's enchanted stallions will soar again." He laid down his chisel and walked over to Caitlin. Taking her hand, he led her into the golden circle of lantern light. "And the fairest lasses from Kerry to Donegal will come to ride our horses, Daniel. And when we're finished riding, we'll dance the night away ..." He took Caitlin in his arms and waltzed her across the hay-strewn floor. "... and the good times will be here again with food and drink for everyone. And Erin will hear the laughter of her children, instead of their crying. Won't it be grand?"

He stopped dancing, but he still held her in his arms, gazing down at her with the light of hope dancing in his green eyes. She wanted to smile back at him, wanted to hope and dream with him about better times, but she couldn't. Not tonight. Not when she knew what heart-breaking news she had come to share.

Looking down at Daniel, she saw the first smile she had seen on any child's face in months. She hated the fact that she would be the one to shatter his world once again.

"Caitlin, what is it?" Michael's voice was tense as though he already suspected. "Why have you come out here tonight?"

She hung her head and bit her lip. She could have let one of Mason's servants deliver the news to the O'Briens, but she had wanted to do the deed herself, and Mason had consented. "I've some bad news for you, very bad indeed. A friend of His Honor's came by Armfield House this afternoon. The gentleman's name is Trenton. Do you know him, Michael?"

A dark shadow crossed Michael's face as his smile died. "I know the name. He's the gentleman who owns the ship, Morning Glory." Michael's face turned pale in the lamp light. "'Twas the boat I put Sean and Judy and their babe on to sail to America. Why?"

"Sir Trenton told His Honor that there was a terrible outbreak of fever aboard the ship and ... Michael, Judy's gone. She died at sea. I'm so very sorry."

421

They heard a gasping sob and turned to see Daniel drive his chisel deep into the side of the wooden stallion. Then he buried his face against its neck and sobbed wildly.

Michael rushed to him, picked the child up in his arms, and held him close. Caitlin couldn't stop her own tears as they flooded her eyes and fell down her face. Was there no end to the suffering? When would it be enough? Everyone was saying, "It's always the darkest before the dawn," but how dark could the night get and how long could it last before daybreak?

Caitlin's gaze met Michael's over the child's shoulder and, although he said nothing, she watched his eyes and saw a part of him die. He had sold his dream to buy life and freedom for his loved ones. Even that sacrifice had been doomed.

"I remember the night before young Judy Sullivan went to America," old Bridget said, around the stem of her clay pipe held tightly between her toothless gums. "I kissed her goodbye and wished her well. Little good it did her. May she be dead a year before the Devil hears of it, and may God be good to her."

"God be good to her," intoned the mourners who had gathered in the O'Briens' kitchen for the wake.

Once, wakes had been novelties, social occasions where sorrow was well-mixed with generous portions of potent liquor, good food, pungent tobacco and vigorous dancing. But these days there were too many wakes and not enough souls to attend them, not to mention the lack of food and drink.

Paul and his brother, Eoin, had brought a pint of whiskey, two pints of ale, and a jug half-full of poteen. It was hardly enough to send a soul into the far-beyond with honor, but it was enough to dull the pain of those left behind. There was tobacco enough for one pipe, and it had been offered to Bridget out of respect for her age.

Michael sat on the hearth, his legs crossed before him, staring into the fire. Daniel sat beside him, clinging to his hand as though he expected Michael to be snatched away as cruelly and as suddenly as the sister he had loved.

Starvation had taken the village's three professional mourners, women known the county wide for their ear-splitting keening. But Judy Sullivan was being mourned handsomely by her older sister, Annie, who sat on the edge of the outshot bed, rocking to and fro, her head in her hands, shrieking so loudly that she could be heard at both ends of the village.

"She was a fair one with a gentle spirit was my Judy," Kevin said from his seat at the table beside the Gannon brothers and young Billy O'Shea. They had all danced a jig in Judy's honor to the tune of Billy's pipe, but their hearts weren't in it. So they had settled down to drink the beverages at hand. "To look upon her smile was to see the sun itself shining warm on your face. But I'll never see her smile again."

"Aye, there's no returning from the grave," Paul sighed, hoisting the pint of ale.

Kevin's broad shoulders began to shake and he covered his face with a tattered bit of handkerchief. "Who would have thought that I'd live to see the death of one of me own children? 'Tis the worst misery a man can suffer, lads, the worst."

Eoin shook his head in agreement, having lost a son and two daughters to the fever. "It's a great sorrow to see the young ones go before ye." he said. "You cannot tell which skin will hang from the rafter first, the old sheep's or the lamb's.''

Michael sat quietly, saying nothing, slowly draining the jug of poteen. Daniel laid his head over on Michael's knee and sobbed. As Michael stroked his curls, trying to impart some comfort to the child, he thought of Judy, her dark glossy hair and bright eyes. He couldn't bear to think of her dead and buried in the cold sea. Judy wouldn't have wanted that. She would have wanted to be laid beneath the green sod with daisies at her head, cradled in Erin's bosom forever.

He thought of his friend, Sean, and wondered how he was coping with his loss. Michael tried to imagine what it would be like for a man to lose his wife. He looked over at Annie and listened to her hysterical sobs, and he couldn't picture it at all. But Michael did know the pain of losing the woman he truly loved. And Sean had loved Judy truly. Michael thought on that for a while, and his heart ached for his friend.

''If it weren't for Travis Larcher, me darlin' daughter would still be alive and walking the earth.'' The liquor was slowly turning Kevin's grief to anger. ''He threw those children out of their own home and burned it to the ground. They'd never left Ireland if they'd had a roof over their heads. 'Tis His Honor's fault entirely.''

''Cursed landlord,'' Paul swore. ''May vultures gouge his eyes out, may madness take him, and his entrails fall out.''

''But may he still live till everyone's sick at the sight of him,'' young Billy added.

''Aw . . . I'd rather see him dead, food for the worms. I fancy him dead this very night.'' Kevin blew his nose loudly into his kerchief. ''What do you say, lads? Shall we don our black hoods and pay his honor a call in my Judy's honor?''

"Aye, let's do it." Paul rose to his feet, or at least he tried to, but none of them had enjoyed such a quantity of drink in the past year and the liquor was hitting him hard. He sat down on the floor, missing the chair entirely.

"There's nothing to be gained by killing the man tonight," Michael said. His voice was low but resonant with authority. Every eye turned his way.

"Nothing but revenge," Kevin reminded him.

"Revenge makes a thin soup. And if we go after him without a plan, with nothing to gain and in our cups, we'll be kilt ourselves. I can't see how that will bring honor to Judy or anyone else."

They nodded solemnly, accepting his wisdom.

"We'll strike a blow for Judy," Michael said, lifting his jug of poteen, "but we'll wait until the time is right. We're Irishmen, and if there's one virtue we Irish have, it's patience. We'll wait. And when we make our move, we'll have something to show for our pains, and a fine legacy for Judy Sullivan."

The mourners eventually left, Daniel fell asleep, and Michael laid him in his outshot bed before making his way cautiously up the ladder to the loft bedroom. With the poteen flowing through his blood, he was in a delicate condition.

Only Annie and Kevin remained in the kitchen. Kevin banked the fire, taking care not to fall into the ashes. Kevin's condition was as delicate as Michael's.

"So, girl," he said, "have you told that husband of yours about the baby yet?"

Annie pressed her hand to her abdomen and grimaced. "No, I haven't. I can't tell Michael. He'll beat me, sure, if I do."

"Ah, Michael wouldn't raise a hand to you. Though he might not fall for that story of yours as quickly as I did. Michael has a suspicious nature. He's not as gullible where you're concerned as meself.''

Annie swelled like a river frog. "What are you speaking of? Are you sayin' you don't believe me anymore?''

Kevin replaced the poker and shovel in their stand and sank down on the hearth. "I've seen a lot of scoundrels and liars in me time, Annie, and that priest was a scoundrel sure. But a man seldom lies when he's gettin' his limbs broke, and he said all along that he never forced you. I don't know what game you're playing, love, but you should have a better story to tell your husband than you told your father. You'd best make Michael believe that child is his own.''

She sat down on the hearth and stretched her hands toward the fire. "But how can I do that, Da? He hasn't touched me since he came back to Ireland. He'll know it can't be his.''

Kevin reached for the bottle of whiskey, tilted it and let the last drop slide down his throat. He stared into the fire with red, tear-swollen eyes that were as empty as his soul. Kevin O'Brien was a man who had lost too much, too quickly, and he would never be the same again.

"Use your brain, girl,'' he said. "Michael's snoring away up there this minute. He's never had a head for poteen. Tomorrow morning he'll not remember a thing that happened tonight. If he wakes to find you beside him, it shouldn't be too hard for you to convince him that the two of you came together in the night. You're a woman, Annie, and a woman can convince her man that the sun rises in the west if she sets her mind to it.''

Annie's hand returned to her belly. "But the baby will be here in seven months. He'll know it's too soon.''

Kevin sighed with exasperation. "Don't be stupid, girl, if ye can help it. Babies come early all the time."

"You want me to lie to me own husband, Da? That's a mortal sin."

He gave her a scornful look that seared her to the core. "So is rutting with a priest on a rectory floor, but it seems ye weren't above that." He ignored the look of anguish on her face and raked his fingers through his hair that was almost completely gray now. "You've got yourself in a devil of a fix, girl, but you'll do whatever you must to hold on to your man. Because I'll tell you this . . ." He closed his eyes and tears squeezed out from beneath his lids. ". . . I've lost my Judy and I can't bear to lose Michael too. I couldn't stand it, Annie. So you get your arse up that ladder and do what you have to do."

Her father's sharp words stung long after Annie had removed her dress and underclothes and slipped into the bed next to Michael, who was, indeed, dead to the world. She wept silently for over an hour until, finally, she had no tears left. The room was cold, almost as cold as her heart. She could feel the warmth radiating from Michael's body only inches from hers, an inviting warmth. With Judy gone forever and her father distancing himself from her, Annie had never felt so alone.

Instinctively she moved toward Michael and for the first time in their marriage, her bare body touched the length of his. She had never experienced the comfort of such intimate contact and for a moment her loneliness disappeared. She felt a tenderness toward this man who was her husband, an affection that she hadn't felt since before their wedding night.

Shyly she wrapped her arms around his waist and snuggled against him, convincing herself all the while that she was only doing this to strengthen her argument

427

if he should deny that they had been together in the morning.

At her embrace he stirred and, to her surprise, he rolled over on his side and put his arm around her as well. Annie was overwhelmed by the joy that rushed through her. She could almost imagine, there in the warm circle of his arms, that they loved each other as a husband and wife should.

His hand moved up her back to her head where it lingered, tenderly stroking the back of her hair. He moaned softly and muttered something that sounded like an endearment, but his speech was slurred and she couldn't quite understand him.

"What did you say, Michael?" she asked breathlessly, afraid to break the spell.

"Your hair—" he said. "Soft—pretty."

Her hair? How could he think her hair pretty now that it was all chopped off? She felt a rush of gratitude that he would say such a thing, but gratitude was quickly followed by guilt. She thought of how she had allowed that man, that dreadful tinker, to touch her, to do unspeakable things to her. She thought of how she and Kevin had plotted to deceive Michael in the morning and her guilt doubled.

"Do you really think I'm pretty, Michael?" she asked, hardly daring to believe that he harbored any good will toward her at all. "Do you truly like my hair?"

"Love you," he murmured, pressing his lips to her forehead. "Love your hair. Soft. Red . . . fire."

Rage coursed hot through her as she pushed him away and rolled to the other side of the bed. Suddenly Annie found that she did have more tears after all, scalding tears.

Gratitude vanished along with her guilt and all of her tender feelings. She would have no problem with

428

her conscience tomorrow morning when she lied to Michael and tried to convince him that he had held her. She would enjoy making a fool of him.

Annie was furious, not just with Michael, but with herself as well. Just because his body had been warm, just because she had felt scared and alone, she had forgotten. For those few blissful moments, Annie had allowed herself to forget how very much she hated him.

Chapter Twenty-three

As Caitlin walked through the nearly empty house she felt a temporary sense of relief, like the lull between storms. Spring and summer had brought a decline in the number of fever patients. In winter, people huddled together in ditches, work houses and abandoned cottages, and that closeness encouraged the spread of the diseases. It was now September and, although cold weather was on its way, Caitlin knew that the house wouldn't be as full as it had been the last two winters. There simply weren't that many people left in Lios na Capaill. Most of them had died, wandered away in search of food, or emigrated.

The rooms were now bare of more than just people; the furnishings were almost completely gone. Piece by piece the elegant furniture had disappeared over the past two years, and she had never asked Mason where it had gone. She didn't have to ask; she knew. Mason's furniture, along with the rest of his wealth, had gone into the soup pots that boiled day and night in the kitchen.

Caitlin had rationed herself long ago to one small bowl of soup a day, and she felt guilty taking even that.

But she had a baby to nurse and to deny herself would only starve the child. So, she went to the kitchen for her evening portion.

When she stepped through the door, she saw Mason, sitting on a stool, eating a bowl of the soup that was nothing more than water and a handful of the almost inedible Indian corn that was being distributed by the English relief committees.

Mason was wearing a threadbare linen shirt that was unbuttoned down the front. She had noticed that after he had scolded her for giving her clothes away, he too had worn only this shirt at home and another one that was a bit better when he traveled.

Seeing him now with his shirt open, Caitlin was astonished at the change in his body. Since the birth of her baby, he hadn't insisted that she come to his bed, and she hadn't volunteered. She was shocked to see his bare chest for the first time in many months and to discover how thin he had become. She had always assumed that as lord of the manor, he ate as much as he wanted. But apparently he had been denying himself even more than she. The realization filled her with a sadness and warmth that she hadn't felt toward him in a long time.

"Ah, Mason . . ." she murmured as she knelt beside his stool. "I thought you were taking care of yourself, but just look at you. Yer thin as a tin whistle."

His eyes avoided hers, and she could see that he was embarrassed to have her see him in his depleted condition. "I'm fine, Caitlin," he said, setting the empty bowl on the floor. "But I'm grateful for your concern."

In a gesture of tenderness, she reached out and laid her hand on his chest. She thought of how strong and healthy he had been, and her heart ached. Mason Armfield, like his mansion, was empty; every last drop had

431

been poured out. In that moment Caitlin fully realized the price he had paid to fight the effects of the famine. It had cost him everything.

Her hand slid down his bare midriff, and she felt every rib distinctly against her palm. He watched her silently, but his eyes told her that he was, indeed, grateful for her attention. She placed a tender kiss on his cheek, the first in a long time. "I love you, Mason," she said, and they both knew exactly what she meant. There was no passion in her love. But they were friends, a man and woman who were bonded forever because they had walked through hell and back together.

Hearing a movement behind her, she turned to see Michael standing in the kitchen doorway, his green eyes blazing with jealousy. "You sent for me, Your Honor?" he said, his voice tight with anger.

Caitlin quickly removed her hands from Mason's body, a gesture that both men noted.

Armfield met the fire in Michael's eyes with gray ice. "Yes, wait for me in the library. I'll be with you in a moment."

Michael nodded curtly, spun on his heel and left them alone again. When Caitlin turned back to Mason and looked into his eyes, she saw no trace of his affection for her, only his hatred for Michael McKevett.

Michael fought to control his temper as he tried to banish the thought from his mind of Caitlin's hands on Armfield's bare chest. If he thought about it too long, he would kill the man. The beast inside seemed to come and go from its cage at will these days. The famine had done that. Starvation and deprivation brought out the animal in any civilized man.

Besides, he had problems of his own these days, trying to find enough food to keep his family alive and worrying about Annie. Every day her belly grew and his guilt and fear along with it. He'd never forgive himself for getting her with child again, even if he didn't remember doing it.

As he waited in the library, he thought of the last time he had been in this room. The furnishings had been opulent in those days, but all that remained now was the tiny, awkwardly designed desk that Armfield himself had built.

"No one would even bid on it at the Dublin auction," Armfield said as he walked into the room and saw Michael eyeing the desk. "I suppose you were right about the faulty workmanship."

Michael simply shrugged and said nothing as Armfield walked over to the desk and sat down.

"I would offer you a chair," the landlord said, "but as you see, I haven't any left."

"Why did you send for me, sir?" Michael asked quickly. He didn't want to think about the sacrifices Armfield had made for the Irish. It diluted his hatred.

"I want to inquire about your family. How are they?"

Michael knew that Armfield didn't give a damn about his family, but he answered the question with as much civility as he could summon. "We've kept body and soul together. That's more than most can say."

"By poaching the game in my forests," Armfield added with a searching look. "I've seen your rabbit snares, McKevett."

"Aye, ye've seen them and ye've robbed them from time to time, sir," he replied dryly.

Armfield smiled and nodded. "I've done that too. I just want you to know that even though I haven't had you hanged for poaching, I've known all along that it was you doing it."

"Thank you for your generosity, sir," Michael replied, his voice tinged with sarcasm.

"You're welcome. And I'm going to help you in another way. I have some information that would be quite valuable if turned over to the right man. And I believe that you are that man."

Michael lifted one eyebrow. "And what information is that, sir?"

"Travis Larcher has reaped a bountiful oat harvest this season, as you may know. But what you may not know is that he plans to export it in a few days."

"That's no surprise. He exports everything as quickly as he can. He's afraid the bloody Irish might take it away from him."

"Now why would he be afraid of that?" Armfield's smile broadened. "Could it be because of all the unfortunate things that have happened to him this year? Like finding himself tied naked to the round tower? Or discovering halfway down a hill that the brakes on his wagon had been greased and ending up in Killarney Lough? Or maybe it was when he found two of his outbuildings leveled when there hadn't been even a hint of wind during the night."

Michael shrugged. "Aye, His Honor's been having a run of bad luck lately. And his luck is likely to get worse yet if he doesn't resolve to repent his evil doings."

"That's what I thought." Armfield nodded his approval. "So, if I were to tell you exactly when Larcher's wagon is going to be leaving with the oats, do you suppose you could do something with that information? Especially if I were to assure you that Larcher is quite complacent these days with the population so sparse, and he will probably only have one or two guards riding along."

"I would like to have that information," Michael re-

434

plied carefully. "I would also like to know why yer tellin' me this. What's in it for you?"

"Two things. I want your assurance that I'll receive half of the shipment."

"I've no objection to givin' you half. After all, you'll be feeding my neighbors with it." He lifted one eyebrow suspiciously. "But what's the second thing you want?"

Armfield's jaw tensed and his eyes lit with a gleam that surprised Michael, who had never seen much emotion on the scarred face. "Travis Larcher will be riding along with the shipment. He's leaving Ireland, returning to England to stay. I don't want that man to leave this island alive. I want your word that he will be killed during the raid."

"That's a strange request from an Englishman," Michael observed, taken aback. "Do you mind telling me why you want him dead?"

Armfield rose from his desk and walked over to the window. He folded his long, thin hands behind his back, and it was a while before he answered. "I went to see Larcher this morning. I told him that I was in desperate need of money, and I offered him Armfield House for a ridiculously low sum, but he declined my offer. He told me in no uncertain terms that he wasn't interested in owning a lice-infested, run-down, fever ward. And then he showed me the door."

When Armfield turned back to him, Michael saw in his eyes the shame, the defeat. He tried to think of something to say, but no words came to mind.

"I offered Larcher the only thing in this world that I own, the only thing that truly matters to me," Armfield continued, "and he humiliated me. Can you imagine that?"

Michael nodded solemnly. "I know how you felt, sir. I know exactly how you felt."

Their eyes met in silent understanding. Armfield was the first to look away. "Yes, I suppose you do."

"Have you sold the carousel, sir?" Michael asked, afraid of the answer.

"No. I haven't sold the carousel or my wife's jewels. There must be a few things that simply aren't for sale." He turned back to the window. "So, do I have your word that Travis Larcher will be killed in that raid?"

Michael thought of Judy and Sean. He thought of all the children, their wasted bodies lying frozen in the ditches and fields. "Aye, you have me word on it, sir. We'll take the wagon, and Larcher will die."

The door creaked loudly from disuse as Caitlin stepped inside her pub for the first time in over a year. She had stayed away for as long as she could, afraid to face the remains of the life that she had given up, the life that had vanished along with over two million people. But it was time to come back now, time to share it all with her son.

"This was your grandfar's pub, Stephen," she told the child in her arms, a strong, healthy lad, twenty months old. "I wish he could have lived to see you. My, but he would have been proud of you."

Caitlin closed the door and walked across the dark interior, lit only by the red glow of the sunset that streamed through the three mullioned windows. The rushes on the floor were dirty and well-trod. Here and there lay a ragged bit of blanket, a broken glass, a crusty dish—remnants of the many souls who had taken refuge inside these sturdy walls. Caitlin didn't mind, in spite of the filth. She was glad that someone had used the pub and hoped that perhaps it had saved some lives.

The boy in her arms squirmed to be put down, but she held him tightly rather than allow him to play on the dirty floor. "Just look at this bar, Stephen. Your grandfar would roll over in his grave to see such a disgrace." She quickly peeled the apron from around her waist and scrubbed the dust away until it shone brightly, as it had in the days and years before the famine.

She took the child around the room and pointed out the rush-lights, the tables and chairs that her great-grandfather had built, and the fancy iron crane in the fireplace, built by Kevin O'Brien's father. "That hearth warmed many a cold, thirsty traveler over the generations, lad," she told the boy who listened intently as though absorbing her every word. "And you should have heard the tales told in this room. They'd singe your ears and bring a tear to your eye, sure. I'll tell them all to you someday, when you're older. You may be away in England, getting an Englishman's education, but your mother will not let you forget that you're an O'Leary, not at all, at all."

She carried him into the bedroom, and her heart ached to see the old bed. The fine feather-ticking was gone now, but the iron bedstead remained, enough to remind her of the night with Michael. "And on that bed, Stephen, was where you were conceived. I'll tell you about that, too, when you're older, and I hope you'll understand. Some would say that what we did was a sin, but I'll tell you lad, no man and woman ever loved each other better than we loved that night. 'Tis no wonder you're a beautiful child, conceived on a night such as that."

The feelings overwhelmed her, and she had to leave

the room. She stood quietly, looking around the pub. For some reason she couldn't explain, she felt that this would be the last time she would see it. Somehow she knew that if she ever visited this place again, it would be in spirit and memory.

With her child cuddled against her ribs, Caitlin stepped outside the pub and closed the door on her childhood and her happiest memories. A gust of chilly September wind swept down the street and set the sign above the door to swinging. She held the baby up over her head and he reached out with eager, curious hands to touch the carved horse and the elaborate lettering.

"Your father carved that sign himself," she said, cuddling the child warmly against her breasts. "Maybe if the spirits will it, you'll have the gift of carving, too. I'll put the tools in your hands as soon as it's safe, and we'll see."

The creak of the rusted chain filled her with a longing for the man who had carved that sign with its graceful, rearing stallion, and a sorrow for a time of innocence and joy that was gone forever. After the horror of the past two years, Caitlin knew she would never feel that happy or safe again.

She left the pub and walked down the street toward the bridge and Armfield House. Dry, dead leaves swirled across her path, and the sight of them only added to her melancholy. Another winter was on its way. The spring and summer had been too short. She wasn't ready to give up the sunshine just yet.

Up ahead, a movement caught her eye. Someone was coming out of the barracks. A woman heavy with child. It was Annie McKevett. Caitlin had heard that she was expecting, but she still felt a surge of jealousy at seeing her. She couldn't imagine that Michael had been with her . . . and yet . . .

Annie glanced her way, and the two women were close enough for Caitlin to see the look of horror and guilt that crossed Annie's face when she recognized her.

What reason did Annie have to feel guilty or afraid? she wondered. But then, what reason did Annie McKevett have for going to the constable?

There was something suspicious in the way the woman slunk away into the woods behind the barracks, her cloak shielding her face.

An uneasiness crept through Caitlin, an illogical, but strong premonition that something terrible was going to happen.

There was only one reason why someone would steal into a barracks. Only one kind of Irishman sought out the constable and afterward crept away into the forest. And that was an informer.

After looking all through the house for Mason, Caitlin found him at last. He was in the carpentry shop where Michael had spent so many hours carving his horses and doing restoration work on the house.

Mason was carving, too. Caitlin caught a glimpse of something that looked like a misshapen pony, but the instant he saw her, Mason threw a sheet over it.

"What do you want?" he said gruffly, as though embarrassed by her intrusion.

Ordinarily she would have been surprised to see Mason carving. She had never known him to have an interest in wood. Under different circumstances she would have been curious, but this evening she had other things on her mind, unsettling things.

"Can you think of any reason why Annie McKevett would call on the constable this evening, then sneak off into the woods wearing a guilty look on her face?" she asked abruptly. The expression of deep concern that creased his brow confirmed her worst suspicions. He knew something about this after all.

"No *good* reason," he replied.

"Why did you send for Michael the other day?"

One corner of his mouth twitched, but there was no twinkle of amusement in his eyes. "I had some information that I thought would be valuable in the hands of the right Irishman. And Michael seemed the only one resourceful enough to take advantage of this special knowledge."

"What did you tell him?" She didn't like the feeling that was sweeping through her. Something was terribly wrong. She knew it, and judging from the cat-and-mouse look on Mason's face, he knew it, too. "What information did you give Michael?"

Mason laid his chisel down with great deliberation before answering. "I told him that Travis Larcher would be transporting a shipment of oats from his estate to Cobh. I told him when and by what route, and I encouraged him to hijack the load. I might add that he didn't require much encouragement."

"Does Annie McKevett know about this robbery?"

Mason shrugged. "If Michael or Kevin or any of the others were foolish enough to discuss the details in her presence, I suppose she knows." He walked over to the window and stared out on the moonlit courtyard. "And if you saw her sneaking out of the barracks this evening I'd wager that she shared her knowledge with the constable."

"But why would she do such a thing?" Caitlin couldn't imagine how a wife could betray her husband. It was unthinkable, even for Annie.

Mason turned to face her, and his eyes searched hers thoroughly before he answered. "Mrs. McKevett is jealous, and jealousy can make a person bitter. Jealousy is a powerful emotion, Caitlin. It can make you want to hurt the ones you love. It can even make you wish them dead."

She shivered at the coldness in his voice and the depth of pain in his words. Had she really hurt him that badly? "When is the raid to happen?" she asked, turning the conversation away from the two of them.

"At the break of dawn."

"At dawn? Mother of Mercy! We must warn Michael and the others. We must tell them that Annie's informed against them. You do know where they are, don't you?"

He nodded once. "I know."

"Then let's go straight away before it's too late." Even as she spoke the words she watched his face harden and she knew what his response would be.

"I gave him the information. He chose to act on it. I wouldn't deliberately send Michael McKevett to his death, but if his foolish wife informs on him and he dies because of her betrayal, so be it."

"You can't mean that." Caitlin reached for him and grasped the front of his shirt with desperate hands. "You're a good, decent man, Mason. Look at what you've done here at Armfield House. You've sacrificed everything you have to save lives. I can't believe you'd let an innocent man and his friends die because of jealousy."

His long fingers circled her wrists and squeezed until her hands went numb. "I want to be rid of Michael McKevett, Caitlin. I want him out of my life and out of yours."

He meant it. He was going to let Michael die, and she couldn't stop it from happening. The strength went out of her legs, and she sank to her knees in front of him. "Mason, please . . . if you'll just do this, I'll never ask you for another thing as long as I live. At least tell me where he is so that I can warn him."

He shook his head as he backed away from her toward the door. There was no mask covering his emotions; she saw only raw pain. "Get up, Caitlin. For God's sake, you've always been such a proud woman. I can't stand to see you on your knees. You'd never humble yourself like that for me."

"You're wrong," she said as sobs tore at her throat. "I'd plead for the life of anyone I love. I love Michael. It's true. But I love you too, Mason, and I can't believe you're going to do this. You'll not be rid of Michael by letting him die. You'll think of him every day for the rest of your life and you'll feel the pain of this night over and over again."

He shook his head violently. "No! I'll not save him this time, Caitlin." He yanked the door open and stepped outside. "Not even for you."

She heard the tread of his boots on the cobblestones as he crossed the courtyard. If she didn't stop him now, Michael would die. There was one last weapon she could use against Mason. Only a woman who had been a man's friend and lover would have such a weapon at her disposal, a woman who had slept beside him and listened as he shared his heart with her.

She sprang to her feet and ran out the door. She caught him on the backsteps of the house.

"You've already spent everything you have to pay penance for your past sins. You have nothing left. What will you sacrifice to atone for killing Michael McKevett?" she said, clinging to his hands. "If you think it's hard to look at your scarred face in the mirror or in a still pond now, just wait until tomorrow morning."

* * *

"I'm only going to ask you one more time, and if you don't tell me, I'm going to kill you, sure." Caitlin leaned over Annie, who cowered in the corner of the O'Briens' kitchen. Daniel watched wide-eyed from his outshot bed. "Where are Michael and the lads planning to take the shipment? You told the constable, and, by God, you'll tell me if I have to beat it out of you."

To emphasize her point, Caitlin grabbed a handful of Annie's hair, which had grown long enough for her to get a firm grip. Annie squealed and tried to squirm away. "Ow—yer hurtin' me!" she howled. "And me a woman with child."

Caitlin yanked harder. "I know that the Black Oaks are planning to rob old Larcher of his oats, and I know you turned them in. Now you tell me exactly what you told the constable and what he told you."

Annie's eyes rolled backward in her head and she slid to the floor in a heap.

Daniel jumped off his bed and hurried to his sister's side. "Annie, tell her. Tell her so she can help Michael," he begged. With one finger he lifted Annie's right eyelid and peered at her intently. "She's not really fainted," he said, shaking his sister's shoulder. "She does this all the time. Annie, open your eyes and tell her where Michael is."

Caitlin grabbed the woman around the waist and hauled her to her feet. Then she pinned her shoulders to the wall and shouted in her face, "Where are they? Damn you, Annie—where?"

"They're waitin' for His Honor at the bottom of McGill's Gap. There's a bunch of rocks there for them to hide behind."

"When?"

"Larcher's supposed to be leavin' with the shipment

at first light of dawn. They'll be looking for him to come through the gap shortly after that.''

"Did you tell the constable all of this?"

When Annie nodded, Caitlin wanted to hit her. And if Annie hadn't been with child she would have done just that. "What did the constable say when you told him? What are his plans?''

"He said he was going to warn Larcher. He's going to be riding with the wagons, he and one of his men. They'll have guns.''

Caitlin looked down at Danny who, despite his youth, understood exactly what was going on.

"Ye informed on Michael?" the child asked with horrified disbelief. "Ye want him to get kilt?''

"Yes!'' Annie's eyes glittered with madness. "He's a murderer and a whoremonger, and I want him dead.''

"And how about the others with him?" Caitlin asked. "Did you stop to think that you're betraying them as well?''

"There's only the Gannon brothers and they're no better than Michael himself, always drinking and chasing women.''

Caitlin's eyes narrowed as she studied Annie, trying to comprehend how anyone could be so foolish. "Where is your father, Annie?" she asked, keeping her voice low and even.

"He's working in the forge.''

"Is he now? I don't think so. When I passed the forge on the way here there was no smoke comin' from the chimney.''

"He's there, I tell you. I saw him there only this afternoon and he was making some—''

Annie's face went white and Caitlin thought that she might truly faint. "What was he making?''

"Pikes. He was putting the point to some pikes. Oh,

Holy Jaysus . . . I thought he was finished with the Black Oaks. I didn't think he'd go with them on something as awful as—''

"That's what's wrong with you," Caitlin interjected. "You don't think at all. I hope for Kevin's sake he isn't with them, and I hope that I can get to Michael in time to warn him. You'd better pray that I do, Annie, because if Michael dies, you'll die. Men aren't the only ones who can commit murder, you know. If Michael dies because of you, I'll wait until after your babe is born, and then, I swear, I'll kill you meself.''

Every night since Mason had bought the carousel from Michael McKevett he had come out to the carpenter's shop, drawn by something he didn't understand, but something he couldn't deny. And tonight, as he stepped over the threshold into the moonlit room, he felt it again—the attraction that had become an obsession.

Silver light streamed through the shop's two windows, bathing the room and its carved occupants in a dreamy wash of moonshine.

Mason had spent many pleasant hours here in this room before he had purchased the carousel, hours of secret carpentry and carving. He had never been satisfied with his results, but he had enjoyed the pastime that took him out of his own empty world where gentlemen used only their wits and never their hands, except for the occasional game of cards.

But since the carousel had filled this room, the shop had changed. He had noticed the difference the first night he had come down here to inspect his new acquisition. He had stepped inside the room and had found the air charged with a strange vibrancy that seemed to radiate from these animals that weren't flesh and blood, but somehow, weren't merely wood either.

He felt it again tonight more strongly than ever as he closed the door behind him, sealing himself in the room with this eerie power that he felt but couldn't comprehend.

Mason never touched the horses. He only looked at them. He had the uneasy feeling that if he touched them, he would be changed forever, as though they would steal his soul away, or at least alter it somehow. It was a foolish notion, of course, brought on by having lived on this strange island where superstition and mysticism were part of the land he walked, the water he drank and the air he breathed. Mason was long overdue for a trip back to England to straighten out his logic. He was a Saxon in danger of becoming a Celt if he wasn't careful.

He walked along the row of horses, the armored stallion and his small herd of mares. He paused beside the pretty little mare with the necklace of roses. Mason admired the stallion, but this pony tugged at his heart in a way that he found most unsettling, especially tonight.

As always her soft brown eyes seemed to follow him, to look into his with gentle wisdom, understanding, even acceptance. But tonight Mason didn't welcome her delicate beauty or her gentleness. It mocked him, condemned him. The man who had created this beautiful creature was going to die—and he was going to let him.

Mason turned to leave the room, but he couldn't move. He was held by that intangible force that seemed to roll out of the horses in waves that swept over him and made his legs weak and shaky. He turned back to the mare, and his hand, as though by its own volition, reached out to touch her.

He laid his palm against the heavily muscled, but graceful, neck. The horse was warm, not cold as he had

446

expected. And for a moment he fancied that he could feel the pulsing of life through the wood, as vibrant and vital as the man who had patiently carved, sanded and painted the animal.

Mason knew that it was Michael McKevett he was sensing in the mare. The deep, secret core of a man translated into wood.

Then Mason felt something that he had never experienced before. A tingling warmth spread from the spot where his palm touched the mare, up his arm, into his shoulder and throughout his body. In that moment he felt a tie between himself and McKevett that was stronger than anything he had ever felt with any other person in his life, stronger than when he had held his dying wife in his arms, more intimate than his most private moments with Caitlin.

Shaking his head, Mason tried to regain control of his logic, of his emotions, but logic had no place in a moonlit room filled with dreams. And Mason had no time to evaluate this strange, Celtic experience with his Saxon mind. It would be dawn in less than an hour.

He left the wooden horses and the shop and ran across the cobblestone courtyard to the barn where he saddled and mounted the white stallion, his one remaining horse.

He turned the stallion's head toward McGill's Gap and raced across the dark fields into the night.

Chapter Twenty-four

Caitlin was halfway to the gap when she realized that she wasn't going to be able to run the entire distance. Her legs shook with fatigue and her ribs ached as she gulped in the chilly damp air of early morning.

A dreary dawn was stealing over the mountain tops and a soft rain misted her face, collecting on her eyelashes and cooling her flushed cheeks. The red cloak she had pulled around her shoulders was heavy with rain, and the cold, morning dew had long ago soaked through the worn soles of her shoes, numbing her feet.

She tried to slow to a walk, but when she did, her imagination brought horrible pictures to mind, the image of Michael and the others lying dead because she hadn't arrived moments earlier.

The picture brought new life to her legs, and she ran on, ignoring the pain in her side and the trembling of her limbs. Finally she reached the lower end of the gap, the end closest to Lios na Capaill. This was where it was supposed to happen. According to Annie, Michael and the others should be somewhere around here.

The gap was a sharp defile separating the Macgillycuddy Reeks from the Tomies Mountains. Awesome cliffs rose on either side of the narrow road that wound through the valley. And from those cliffs protruded massive boulders, some of which looked as though they were suspended in midair and the merest breath would dislodge them.

But there was no wind in the gap this morning, not even enough to stir the heavy fog that lay in patches, a cold, gray, shroud that absorbed all sound, even the small rustlings of the birds in the furze.

Caitlin was aware of her footsteps and the sound of her own breathing as she walked slowly through the gap, straining her eyes to see any movement in the rocks above her on either side.

But with all her listening and careful watching, she still didn't hear him when he made his move. And she didn't see the man wearing the black hood until he grabbed her from behind, his heavily muscled arm around her waist, his other hand clamped firmly over her mouth.

She struggled against him as he dragged her behind a large boulder and spun her around to face him.

The mask unnerved her more than she could have imagined. If it hadn't been for those green eyes blazing at her from the ragged holes in the hood, she would never have believed this was the man she loved. "Michael," she gasped, "you nearly scared the life from me."

"Never mind that," he said, his voice hoarse and raspy. "What the devil are you doing here, woman?"

"Your Honor, I truly wish you would reconsider and stay at home. With only one officer at my disposal I can hardly guarantee your safety." Constable Sheldon and Travis Larcher stood watching as Larcher's driver hitched the team to the wagon, which looked ready to burst its sideboards with a bountiful harvest of oats.

Larcher stood beside his bay mare with a traveling satchel in his hand, a freshly starched cravat at his throat, and a grim, but determined, look on his round face. He reached into the breastpocket of his brocade waistcoat and pulled out the tiny golden snuff box that was never far away from his red nose.

"I'm going," he said, snorting a pinch of the contents. "And I'll not discuss the matter with you any further. Those bloody Black Oaks have made my life a living hell these past few months, and I intend to see them pay for their heinous crimes. If they don't see me riding along with this shipment, they'll suspect that something is amiss and they won't attack."

The constable chewed the end of his thin black moustache carefully as he took stock of his troops. It didn't take long; there was only himself, his one officer and Larcher's driver, a wizened old Irishman with one bad eye that was no more than an empty socket. "Is your driver armed?" he asked doubtfully.

"Certainly not. He's a stupid old Irishman. He wouldn't know what to do with a gun if you put it in his hand."

The constable caught the quick sideways glance from that one eye and thought that if anyone were stupid, it was Larcher. Even a landlord couldn't insult the Irish the way Larcher had all these years and expect never to pay the price. Hatred could build in even the gentlest heart under such abuse. Sheldon immediately discounted the driver. He'd be no help at all in a confrontation. He could hardly be expected to risk his life for a master such as Larcher.

"By the way, where are the rest of your men?" Larcher asked, replacing the snuff box and blowing his nose loudly in a linen handkerchief with fine, Irish lace trim. "Surely you need more troops than this to enforce the Queen's law."

"Some of them died of fever. Some deserted. It seems they couldn't stomach certain duties that had been imposed on them lately, like throwing women and children out into the cold and burning their homes to the ground, or protecting wagons of grain from the starving multitudes."

Larcher flushed until his cheeks matched his nose. "The Black Oaks aren't starving children. They're ruthless criminals. You know what they've done to me . . ." His voice trailed away at the memory, and the crimson on his face deepened to a mottled purple.

The constable stifled a grin. "Yes, we all know about the terrible crime they committed against your . . . person, sir."

"Then, as an English officer of the law, you should understand my position on this matter." Larcher mounted his bay and adjusted his cravat as though it were the breastplate of his armor. "My ship is leaving Cobh in three days, and I swear upon my honor as a gentleman and a servant of the Queen, I'll not leave this country until those bastards are dead."

"Are you sure you want to do this, Caitlin? Ye've done enough already just by warnin' us." Michael and four other hooded men stood in a half-circle around Caitlin behind a pile of stones at the top of a cliff.

She looked beyond them to the narrow road below that funneled into an even narrower passage between two large rock formations. "Aye. I'm in it with you," she said, "but do you think it will be enough, moving the ambush from the bottom of the gap up to the entrance?''

'' 'Twill have to do,'' Michael said. ''If they're expecting us at the end of the gap, we'll have a bit of advantage surprisin' them here. If Lady Luck is in an Irish mood today, maybe it will be enough.''

Michael's voice was tight and strained, and although Caitlin couldn't see his face for the black cloth, she knew that he was deeply hurt and outraged over Annie's betrayal. He had taken the news calmly enough, far too calmly, and it worried her.

''Can you move that rock then, ma'am?'' Paul Gannon asked.

''Aye, the whole plan will go down river if ye find ye can't budge it,'' Kevin added.

''We'll do it together, we will,'' Eoin Gannon replied, putting his arm around Caitlin's shoulders in a gesture that made her feel truly a part of this strange circle.

She walked over to the largest stone and leaned her weight gingerly on the pike that Michael had wedged beneath the rock to dislodge it partially. She felt the stone move ever so slightly, but enough. ''Aye. No trouble at all,'' she said as she watched Eoin do the same with his stone. ''I'll be proud to strike a blow for old Erin.''

When Caitlin saw the pride shining in Michael's green eyes as he looked down at her, she felt a rush of joy and a sense of being a part of something that mattered. Finally, they would have a measure of revenge against the powers that had abused and murdered so many innocents. And, just as importantly, they would have lifesaving food to share with others.

Michael looked up at the sky, noting the sliver of sunlight that was just beginning to show above the purple mountain tops. ''Let's go, lads. It's time for us to get into position. His Honor should be calling on us very soon now."

Constable Sheldon shuddered as sweat puddled in his arm pits and trickled down his ribs—cold, nervous sweat. He had a bad feeling about this morning, an uneasiness that increased with every passing minute.

Even the weather was Irish today, drizzling mist and heavy fog that made it impossible to see the road even a hundred feet ahead. As they neared the gap he felt the hair prickle along the back of his neck. That wasn't a good sign either. After years on the battlefields and in her majesty's service, Constable Sheldon had found his hackles most reliable in predicting trouble ahead.

He had thought that he was finished with the Black Oaks when he had hanged O'Shea and Quirke. He wasn't sure who was continuing the tradition of terrorism, but he had his suspicions. At first he had thought it was Rory Doona, but Rory hadn't been seen in the county for such a long time that Sheldon had finally decided that the scoundrel must be dead.

There was only one man in the village with the strength and wit to lead a gang to commit the crimes they had perpetrated on Travis Larcher, and that was Michael McKevett.

There was a simmering rage in those green eyes that made Sheldon hope it wasn't McKevett he was dealing with today. He didn't want to find himself on the receiving end of that fury. And Sheldon had to admit that there was yet another reason why he didn't want to fight McKevett; he simply liked the man and didn't want to have to kill him.

"Damn this fog," he muttered to his officer, Robert Murchison, who sat on the wagon seat next to Larcher's driver. Like Sheldon himself, Murchison had exchanged his uniform for the ragged clothes of an Irish farm hand. "Can't see a bloody thing up ahead."

"Maybe it'll be clearer at the end of the gap," Murchison said.

"I hope so."

Constable Sheldon intercepted a scornful look from Larcher, who rode his bay on the right side of the wagon. "I don't know what you're so worried about," Larcher said offhandedly. "They're just some stupid Irishmen, probably the three who attacked me that night. They aren't armed and—"

"Don't be so quick to assume that just because they don't have guns, they won't be armed. An Irishman can make a weapon of a potato if he's in a fighting mood."

Larcher sniffed his contempt and Sheldon wondered at his complacency. The landlord had suffered extreme humiliation when the town had wakened to the glorious sight of His Honor's naked body tied to the round tower. Not only had the peasants found his nudity highly amusing, but none had bothered to untie him. If the constable himself had not ridden by late that afternoon, His Honor might have found his vulnerable private parts exposed to yet another night of freezing temperatures.

Apparently Larcher's hatred had robbed him of his common sense. Any sane man would have felt the normal pangs of anxiety riding headfirst into an ambush.

The constable's horse heard it before he did and cocked its ears; then it was audible to all, a faint scraping sound from the cliff above their heads. Sheldon reached for his gun. Through an opening in the veil of fog he saw a patch of bright red. "Up there!" he shouted. "In the rocks!" He took aim, but just as he was going to pull the trigger, the fog closed and he saw nothing. He fired anyway. The sound ripped through the silence of the gap.

Then another sound filled the canyon, a deep roar like thunder reverberating off the cliffs. The ground below them shook as the wall of stone to their right crumbled and rained down around them, blocking the road ahead. The horses screamed and reared. Larcher fell to the ground and the driver had his hands full with the team as the horses bucked and tried to tear loose from their harnesses.

Sheldon caught the movement out of the corner of his eye, the blurred image of a man in a black hood with his arm raised. A split-second later the arm descended and the constable heard a cracking sound. He saw the pain, bright and glittering, as it shot through his head. His body convulsed and his finger squeezed the trigger again.

He felt himself falling off the horse and hitting the ground, the shot still ringing in his ears, then he heard nothing at all. A thick, warm blanket of darkness enveloped him.

From the bottom end of the gap Mason heard the rumbling of the avalanche, and he knew that he was searching in the wrong place. He whirled his horse toward the top of the pass. He shouted and kneed the animal so hard that it leapt beneath him and raced down the narrow road. But even as he rode, Mason heard the shots and he wondered if he was too late after all.

With a blackthorn shillelagh in hand, Michael stood over the unconscious constable. He picked the gun up from the ground where it had fallen. The barrel was hot, and it felt strange against his palm, foreign some-how. It was the first time Michael had ever held a gun, and he didn't like the feel of it, so he tossed it onto the ground several yards away.

The victory had been an easy one. Too easy, Michael decided when he looked around at his comrades who had dispatched their appointed foes as quickly as he.

Billy O'Shea knelt over the inert form of Murchison, who lay in the back of the wagon atop the heap of oats. A large bruise was already rising on his forehead, in-flicted by the rock that Billy held in his right hand. A primitive weapon, perhaps, but effective.

The Irish driver rolled about on the ground, holding his shins and howling in misery. Paul Gannon walked a circle around his victim, pike in hand, a self-satisfied swagger to his step. The one-eyed Irishman would live, but he would long remember the day when the Black Oaks had whacked him across the shins with a pike handle.

But Travis Larcher's situation was more desperate. He sat on the ground where his horse had thrown him, and Kevin stood over him, holding a foot-long butcher knife to his throat. Larcher's eyes widened with terror as Kevin waved the knife menacingly.

"So, lads," Michael said as he left the constable and walked around the wagon to stand between Paul and Kevin. "We did it. We have the oats and, best of all—" he looked down at the helpless landlord—"we have you, sir."

Larcher cast a pathetic look toward Murchison and the constable, neither of whom had budged.

"They won't be helpin' you now," Kevin said. "You're on your own, Your Honor. It's just you and your beloved tenants, face to face."

"But it's not face to face," Larcher complained in a shaking tenor. "I can't even see your faces for those hideous masks. Aren't you going to let me know who you are before you kill me?"

"Aye, you'll see our faces, sir," Michael said, peeling off his hood. "We wouldn't want you to depart this world without knowing who was sending you on your way."

One by one the others removed their masks, and Larcher quivered with hate and fear as each face was revealed. "I knew it was you, Kevin O'Brien. You're still nursing a grudge because I evicted that worthless son-in-law of yours."

Kevin's ruddy face blanched, and the knife moved inches closer to Larcher's throat. "Sean Sullivan is a fine young man, and me daughter, Judy, was a treasure. She died because of you, Larcher. And that's why these lads agreed to give me the honor of bein' the one to slit your throat."

Larcher's mouth opened and closed several times, but nothing came out. He seemed to sense that nothing he could say would save his life this time.

"Say your prayers, sir," Kevin told him, his blue eyes blazing with hate. "Let your Maker know you'll be callin' at his doorstep any minute now."

Michael held his breath, as did every other man present. The only sound was that of Larcher's whimpering moan and Kevin's harsh breath as he prepared himself to assassinate the object of so many Irishmen's hatred.

But just as Kevin's arm tensed to slice the knife through the landlord's jugular, they heard another sound—the fast, staccato beat of horse's hooves. A second later a figure exploded out of the thick curtain of fog. It was Armfield on his white stallion, his eyes red and wild, his cloak streaming out behind him. He charged directly into the middle of the startled men, who stared at him as though he were a manifestation of the Grim Reaper himself.

Every eye was turned on Armfield, and no one saw Larcher's hand when it slid into his breastpocket and pulled out the tiny silver pistol. He pointed the gun at Kevin's chest and fired.

The pistol's small bullet did an incredible amount of damage. Before the sound died away a large red hole had blossomed on the front of Kevin's shirt. He crumpled and fell to the ground, where he lay as still and silent as a tumbled oak.

"No!" Michael cried as he grabbed the pike from Paul and lunged at Larcher.

He lifted the pike to hurl it and in that instant he saw Larcher's gun pointed at his head. Staring Death in the face, Michael prepared to die.

Then it hit him, Armfield's stallion rammed its shoulder against him, knocking him to the ground. Michael heard the shot and he saw Armfield fall off his horse. Michael scrambled to his feet and hurled the pike with the speed and accuracy of a man who had hunted his food all winter.

The pike speared Larcher's thick body and pinned him to the ground, gargling and choking on his own blood.

"God Almighty! They're all dead!" Paul said. His words echoed the terrible thought that was running through Michael's dazed mind as he looked at Kevin, Armfield and Larcher. What had happened? His brain was too stunned to take it all in at once.

He ran to Kevin and knelt beside him. Michael knew, even before he pressed his hand to the man's chest, that there would be no heartbeat. It was his heart's blood that was staining the grass and rocks beneath him. There could be no life left in that hulk of a man.

Michael felt his own heart burst as he gathered the heavy, limp body in his arms, the only thing left of the man who had been his father. This time Michael couldn't hold back the grief; the shock of it drove the pain deep into his brain.

As though from far away he heard Caitlin and Eoin scrambling down the cliff. He scarcely heard Caitlin's incoherent cry as she ran to Armfield's side and dropped to her knees beside him.

Carefully, Michael laid Kevin's body down, pillowing his head on a tuft of grass. Then he slowly walked over to Armfield.

The landlord wasn't dead yet but Michael had seen enough belly wounds to know that this one was fatal. He knelt beside Caitlin, and in a gesture that neither man would have anticipated, Michael took Armfield's hand between his own. "I thank you, sir," he said, realizing how inadequate the words must sound to a dying man. "Why did you take that bullet for me?"

Armfield smiled his familiar, wry smile and chuckled. The movement caused him to cough up a horrible clot of blood. "I wouldn't have if I'd had more time to think about it," he said in a low, liquid whisper. "Just seemed like the right thing to do at the time."

Michael felt a rush of warmth and gratitude that he hadn't felt since the night in Caitlin's pub when she had bandaged his hands and lied to Armfield to save him.

Michael didn't have time to express his thoughts and feelings. From beside the wagon he heard a muffled groan and a scuffling. He turned to see that Sheldon had regained consciousness and had struggled to his feet. Young Billy had seen the constable too and had scrambled to get the gun that Michael had tossed aside.

Billy aimed the gun at the constable with a shaking

hand and shouted, "That's far enough, sir! You just hold that ground where you stand, if you want to live."

Sheldon took one careful step toward the young man, his hand outstretched. "Give me the gun, boy, " he said in a wheedling tone. "You don't know how to use it and you'll only hurt yourself if you try."

"Don't let him have it, Billy, " Michael said as he edged slowly around the back of the wagon. He couldn't rush the constable. Sheldon was closer to Billy than Michael was to the constable. Sheldon could reach the gun before Michael could grab him, and Michael wasn't sure from the look of fear and uncertainty in Billy's eyes whether or not the young man could shoot. Billy's hand shook violently, and the gun barrel bobbed up and down like a fisherman's line.

"You kilt me father," he said, a dry sob in his voice. "I watched you hang him, and he never did nothin' wrong to deserve it."

The constable stepped closer. Michael cast a helpless look at the two Gannon brothers, but they were even farther away than he.

"Your father was a convicted criminal, boy. It was my duty to hang him," Sheldon said. "You wouldn't kill a man for doing his duty. Would you?"

Billy was too overcome by his emotions to speak, so Michael answered for him. "And I suppose it was your duty to tumble all those cottages and throw those poor, starving people out into the snow?"

"A true soldier never questions his orders," Sheldon replied, without taking his eyes off Billy's face.

"I'd think now would be a fine time for you to question what you're doing. We're not after stealin' a shipment of gold here, just food for starving children. No decent man would interfere with that, duty or no duty."

Michael saw a fleeting look of self-doubt cross the

constable's face and he pressed his point. "If you'll give us your word that you'll forget what you saw here today, we'll let you go. But if you don't turn your back and walk away this minute, someone else is going to die."

Michael saw the struggle on Sheldon's face as his eyes darted from the gun, to Larcher's lifeless body, to the wagon full of grain. And Michael knew the instant he made his decision. The constable was, first and foremost, a soldier.

Sheldon took one more step toward Billy. Whimpering like a frightened puppy, Billy screwed his eyes tightly closed and fired.

The constable's body spun around once, then folded in half and dropped to the ground. Michael ran to the boy and grabbed the gun from his hand. Billy hurried to the constable where he lay face down in the dirt. He turned the body over, and they all saw the permanently surprised look on the constable's face.

Billy stared at the body and the blood that poured from the wound in the neck for a long time. Then he turned to Michael. His eyes, so like his father's, were filled with tears. "I kilt him," he said, his voice quivering. He dropped to his knees beside the corpse and covered his face with his hands. "Oh, Mother of Mercy, I kilt a man, sure."

Michael looked around at the scene that resembled a battlefield where no one had won. So many dead. Kevin, Larcher, Constable Sheldon, and Armfield dying.

He walked over to young Billy and put his hand on the lad's shoulder. "Ye'll grow accustomed to the idea with time. It sounds cruel, but ye'll find a way to live with it . . . I know."

Chapter Twenty-five

"Does it hurt so bad now?" Caitlin asked, trying to fight back her own tears as she removed the bloodied cloth from the ugly wound in Mason's belly and replaced it with a clean one that soon became as red as the first. How could any man have survived the loss of so much blood, not to mention the long ride home in a wagon full of oats?

"It's better now," he said weakly, his face as white as the linens beneath him. "Thank you for bringing me to my own bed."

"It was the least the lads could do for you," she said as she slowly slid onto the mattress beside him, being careful not to jar him. "You did a fine thing today, Mason, a noble thing, putting yourself between Michael and harm that way."

Mason closed his eyes and for a moment she thought that he had slipped into unconsciousness. Then he opened them again, took a deep breath and said, "There are some things I must ask you to do for me, Caitlin, very important things."

"Aye, anything at all. What is it?"

"The carousel ... give it back to Michael. I never

should have taken it from him. Tell him I knew that the handful of coins wasn't payment enough but it was all I had at the time. If I'd had more, I would have given it to him.''

Caitlin blinked back the hot tears that stung her eyes and nodded. "I will. I'll tell him."

"And there's something I want to give you."

"I don't want anything, Mason," she protested, reaching for his hand. "I just want you to get well and—"

He smiled his old rueful smile. "I can't give you that, my love." It was the first time he had ever called her his love. Why did it have to be now? she wondered. Would it have made any difference if he had said it before? She didn't think so. "I want you to have my wife's jewelry, the emerald necklace. It's the only thing I haven't sold."

She shook her head. "I don't want her necklace. What would I do with it?"

"You can trade it to my friend, Trenton, for passage to America. He's always admired those stones. But be sure that he puts you on a first-class vessel. Don't get on one of those coffin ships." He took a deep breath and shuddered. She could see how much strength he was expending just trying to speak. "The necklace is worth a great deal," he continued. "At least enough for passage for you and Michael and his son."

"His son?"

"Yes, his son." Mason's gray eyes met hers, and she felt her heart wrench. He knew that Stephen wasn't his after all.

"How long have you known?"

He cast a longing glance toward the small trundle bed in the corner of the bedchamber. "Since I held him in my arms. A man knows ... when he holds a child in his arms . . ." His voice trailed away and she felt a change in him, as though a part of him had left her.

"Mason?"

When he didn't answer she moved closer to him on the bed and slid her arm beneath his neck, cradling his silver head against her bosom. He was still breathing, but barely. She thought of all the times she had held him like this and of the times he had comforted her. Michael was the man her heart had chosen, but Mason had been her closest friend over the years. And he was slipping away from her even as she clutched him tighter.

"Thank you, Mason," she whispered. "I'll tell Stephen about you when he's older. I'll never forget what you did for me and my son." She bent her head to press a kiss to his cheek. "And I'll always love you."

Caitlin never knew if he heard her words, but she took comfort in knowing that the last thing Mason Armfield felt on this earth was the arms of a friend holding him close, and the healing kiss of a lover on his scarred cheek.

Michael sat on a stool before the fire with Daniel at his feet. The boy clung to Michael's leg, crying softly, but his weeping could scarcely be heard above his sister's wailing in the downstairs bedroom.

When Michael had carried the heavy body of Kevin O'Brien through the cottage door an hour before, he had wanted to kill the person responsible. And he would have done just that, if Annie had been a man, and not a woman nearly bursting with child.

But Michael hadn't even had the opportunity to say all the scorching words that had burned within his brain. The instant Annie had seen her father's dead body, she

464

had gone insane with grief. And nothing Michael could have said or done to her would have inflicted the kind of pain that she was experiencing this very minute as she knelt beside her father's bed, clinging to his limp hand and pleading with him not to be dead because of her.

As Michael listened to her outpouring of sorrow, he realized once and for all that whatever love he had felt for her was gone. He wasn't enjoying her grief, though it occurred to him that perhaps he had reason to. And to his surprise, he didn't despise her. Michael realized then that the opposite of love wasn't hate after all; it was apathy, this hollow, complete detachment from all feeling.

"Who murdered me father?" Danny asked, looking up at Michael with red-rimmed eyes. "I want to know who kilt him."

" 'Twas Lord Larcher."

Danny nodded his head as though not surprised. "And did you kill Lord Larcher, Michael?"

"I did. I ran him through with your da's very own pike that he made himself there in his forge. His Honor died a painful death there on Kevin O'Brien's pike."

"Good. I'm glad you kilt him." The boy stared into the fire as though watching the entire battle in the flames. "I wish I'd been there. I would have murdered Old Larcher meself."

Michael placed a gentle hand on the child's shoulder. "There's no joy in taking another man's life, lad. But sometimes it must be done."

The boy was quiet for a long time as he considered Michael's words. "Now I don't have a father or a mother," he said, and Michael heard the fear in his voice.

He reached down and scooped the child into his arms.

"You have me, Danny. I've been your brother all these years, and I'll be your father any time you need one. When you've grown big and strong, I'll be your friend. Either way, you'll not be alone. Not ever."

Danny threw his arms around Michael's neck and buried his face on his friend's broad shoulder.

Suddenly a scream tore through the cottage, not a shriek of grief, but of horror and pain. Michael leaped to his feet, Daniel still in his arms, and raced to the bedroom door. Annie met him there, her eyes enormous in her white face, her arms clutching her swollen belly.

On the floor beneath her skirt a dark pool of red was quickly forming. "Michael, help me," she gasped, bending double.

Michael set Daniel on his feet and lifted her in his arms. As he laid her gently on the outshot bed, Michael couldn't believe that it was happening again. This baby, too, was coming into the world, not with a flood of water as it should, but in a gush of blood.

Michael bore down on the saw with all his might and it bit deeply into the board he was cutting, but the sound still didn't drown out the screams coming from the house. He and Daniel had been banished from the cottage hours before by old Bridget and Father Murphy, who assisted her these days when there was no woman to help with a difficult birth.

"Away with ye both," Bridget had said with a wave of her gnarled hand. "Yer only in me way. If you want to be of some help, Michael, go carry a rock, the biggest one ye can find, around the house a time or two. It helps take the burden off the wife if the husband carries a rock around the cottage."

That was a ridiculous bit of pishoque, of course, designed to keep well-meaning husbands out from under the midwife's feet. But Michael had carried the rock, an enormous one, around the cottage more times than he could remember, until he had been bone-weary. But Annie still screamed.

So he had come out to the barn with Daniel to build a coffin for Kevin. This coffin wasn't going to be as fancy as Sorcha McKevett's had been. Michael simply didn't have the time. There wasn't even time for a decent wake, and that grieved Michael. Kevin deserved a fine wake to send him on his way. But Michael had to get the body into the ground before anyone saw the gunshot wound in his chest.

Of course, the authorities would figure it out sooner or later, but by then the Oaks, including Michael, would be gone from Kerry, possibly from Ireland.

It was impossible for Michael to make any plans at this point. God only knew when Annie would be able to travel, and the baby . . . Michael knew that this baby was going to die just as his little daughter had died. It was simply too early for the child to be born.

Daniel sat in the corner on a pile of straw, patiently sanding the board that would be the top of his father's coffin. He sniffed occasionally and wiped his eyes on his sleeve, but neither he nor Michael spoke as they worked. They only cringed every time they heard a shriek from the house.

As the hours passed the screams became weaker. Michael cursed himself over and over when he thought of the night of Judy's wake. Like a selfish fool he had taken her, or at least she said he had, and there was no reason to doubt her—she had the belly to prove it.

He laid down his hammer and looked up to see Father Murphy standing in the doorway of the barn. The priest's face was ashen and Michael had never seen him looking so old. "You have a son, Michael," he said without emotion.

"He's alive then?" Michael couldn't allow himself to hope. Surely nothing good could happen on the day Kevin O'Brien had died.

"The baby had some rough treatment, but he seems to have weathered it well enough."

Daniel laid his sanded paper aside and rose from his seat in the hay. "How's me sister?" he asked.

Father Murphy didn't answer him directly, but turned back to Michael. "You'd better come right away. Annie's asking to have a word with you."

Michael's eyes wouldn't meet the priest's when he said, "I've nothing to say to my wife just now. I want to see my son, but not Annie."

Father Murphy grabbed his forearm in a grip that couldn't be ignored. "I know how you feel, lad. She told me all about how she informed against you and got her father killed. But she has some things to say to you, and damn it, lad, you need to hear them. You won't get the chance again, Michael. Annie's dying."

The first thing Michael saw when he stepped into the bedroom was blood everywhere. The smell of it nauseated him. He closed his eyes and shuddered. Surely he had seen enough blood and death for one day.

He opened his eyes and looked around the room for his newborn son, but Bridget had the baby wrapped in a sheet and was carrying him into the kitchen. She wore a tired, defeated expression on her wizened face, and she wouldn't look Michael in the eye as she left.

He walked over to Annie's bedside and sat down on the edge of the bed. She looked as though she were dead already, her hair hanging in limp strings across her face, and her face had an odd, blue tinge to it. She held out her hand to him and, reluctantly, he took it.

"I'm afraid to die, Michael," she said, gripping his hand as though he could keep her from slipping over the edge.

"Maybe you won't die," he said, knowing that he lied. She had the same look about her that Armfield had worn that morning.

"I know I will. I feel it," she said weakly. "Father Murphy and Bridget know it, too, I can see it in their eyes. I can see it in yours, too."

He reached over to brush the lank hair away from her cheeks. "Sh ... Annie. Just lie still and don't try to talk."

But that was too much to ask of Annie McKevett, even on her death bed. "I'm afraid I'm going to go to hell, Michael, because of all the wicked things I've done."

"Don't fret, love," he said, his words more comforting than his tone. "I'm sure the good father can fix it all for you."

"But he says I must make peace with you. I don't want to die knowing that you hate me, Michael. I can't bear the thought."

Something in her voice reached his heart and a bit of the ice that encased it melted. "I don't hate you, Annie," he said, speaking the truth.

"But you should. I've done such terrible things to you."

He pressed the back of her hand against his cheek and shivered at the coldness of it. "I haven't been very kind to you, either. 'Tis no wonder you hate me."

"But I don't. I love you, Michael. I always have. But I was so jealous. Every time I thought about how you touched Caitlin that night by the river, I went crazy with jealousy. You don't know what it's like to be so jealous that you want to see someone dead."

Yes, I do, he thought. *I wished Mason Armfield dead, and by now he surely is.* "I understand, Annie. Truly, I do."

She squeezed his hand, but her grip was feeble. "Then tell me you forgive me. Please, I want to hear you say it."

He stroked her cheek tenderly with his fingertips. "I forgive you, Annie. Can you forgive me for not loving you as I should have?"

She began to cry, but they were soft, silent tears. "I think you've always loved me the best you could." She sniffed and for the first time since Michael could remember, he watched her fight back her tears. "Have you seen the baby?" she asked.

"Not yet. Who does he look like?"

She opened her mouth to say something, then closed it as though changing her mind. Finally she said, "He's fair and has blond hair and blue eyes."

"Then he looks like his mother. He's sure to be a handsome lad, indeed. What would you like his name to be?"

She closed her eyes and he thought that perhaps she hadn't heard him. "Ryan," she said softly. "Ryan McKevett."

Michael was surprised. No one among their family or friends bore the name Ryan, but he was glad to grant her request. "Ryan it is, then."

Father Murphy appeared at the door with a bottle of holy water in one hand and his satin stole in the other. After one look at Annie he said, "I think you'd better go now, son, and leave her to me."

Michael started to rise, but Annie clung to his hand.

"Will you kiss me goodbye?" she asked. "Please, Michael."

He bent over her and softly kissed her forehead, then her cheek. She smiled up at him and for moment she looked like the little girl whom he had loved in another lifetime, before the blight, before all the bitterness; she looked like Princess Niav of the Golden Hair. So he kissed her lips as well. "Goodbye, Annie darlin'," he said. Then he left the room as quickly as he could, before she could see the tears in his eyes.

No sooner had he stepped into the kitchen and closed the bedroom door than Bridget appeared and thrust the bundle into his arms. "There ye are," she announced. "He's a fine, healthy lad." She looked down at her bare feet and wiggled her brown toes as she worked her toothless mouth, trying to force out her next words. "I'm sorry about your missus. But, ye know, I told you young people not to go makin' any more babies, but ye don't listen. I can't stand to lose a mother. You know, Kevin's young wife, Deirdre, was the only one I ever lost until the hunger came. Now I lose mother and child both sometimes. 'Tis a sorrow to me heart, I can tell ye."

Michael wasn't listening to her. He had unwrapped the baby and was examining his strong limbs and hands. His fair coloring was Annie's, to be sure, but his features were neither hers nor Michael's. As he held the child close to his chest he wondered why he didn't feel that same bonding love that he had felt when he had held the poor, lifeless form of his baby girl. Something was different this time. He decided that it must be because of all the tragedy that had occurred in the past few hours.

"He's a big, stout child," Michael said proudly, "considering how early he came."

"Early? That babe's not early. In fact, I'd say that he's a couple of weeks late."

"Late?"

"Surely. Look at how long his fingernails are, and his skin is peelin' up. That's a sign that they've been cookin' in the kettle too long. Besides, look at the size of him. That's the biggest baby I've delivered since the blight hit us. Annie must have got her dates mixed up."

As Michael stared down at the child in his arms, his guilt began to fall away and a suspicion started to build in him. A terrible suspicion that might explain why he didn't feel a tie to this baby. "Yes," he said. "I suppose Annie got something confused."

Caitlin left the cold marble vault and walked across the cemetery to where Michael stood in the evening shadow of the round tower, holding a baby wrapped in a thin blanket in his arms. At his feet were two freshly dug graves. An ornate iron cross, the work of a master blacksmith, marked the head of one of the graves, a simple wooden cross the other. She stood quietly beside him, holding Stephen against her side with one arm. Her other hand she placed on Michael's shoulder. The simple gesture conveyed her sympathy more than any words.

"Lord Armfield?" he asked.

"Gone," she replied. "The Gannon brothers just helped me lay him to rest over there in the Armfield vault."

"I'm sorry. Mason Armfield was a good man. I owe him me life."

"We both do," she said. "Paul told me about Annie.... Is that your new son?"

An expression crossed Michael's face that confused Caitlin. "He's Annie's baby."

She was surprised by the sadness in his eyes when he looked down at the child. Knowing the way Michael cherished little ones, she had expected that he would be joyful to have his own at last.

"He looks like Annie," she said, lifting the blanket edge so that she could more clearly see his tiny face. "And he's big and strong."

"Yes, but I don't know for how long. I have to find a wet nurse for him. The women around here don't have milk enough to feed their own wee ones, let alone take on the nursing of another."

Caitlin watched as the newborn's face crinkled into a grimace, and he let out a lusty, hungry bellow. She looked down at her own son. He was hardly fat on the milk she produced with only one bowl of thin soup a day, but he was alive and healthy. She had seen so many babies die these past two years. She couldn't see this newborn die before he had even had a chance to live.

"I have milk," she said. "I was just thinking of weaning little Stephen here. 'Tis happy I'd be to nurse that wee lad for you."

Michael's gaze trailed slowly over her full breasts, but there was no passion in his eyes, only quiet love. "Why would you do that, Caitlin?" he asked, his voice soft and low.

"Because the babe's hungry ... and because he's yours."

Michael's face quickly hardened, and she wondered what she had said to bring that pain into his eyes. "I'm not sure that he is mine. In fact, I'm almost certain that he isn't. God knows whose he is. Probably that damned priest's."

473

Caitlin wondered at this revelation, but she decided not to ask.

"He's a babe who needs milk and love," she reminded him. "Every little one deserves that much, no matter who sired him."

Michael closed his eyes, bowed his head, and hugged the child close to his heart. "I know that and it's thankful I am to have him. But when he was born I thought I finally had a child of me own. That's all I've ever really wanted."

Caitlin bit her lower lip, feeling the sharp edge of his pain. The time had come to tell him. "I know," she said as she reached out with one arm and took the newborn from him. In the same movement she handed Stephen into his arms. "Mason told me that a man can tell his own child when he holds him in his arms. And he knew that this baby wasn't his." She took a deep breath, and she could have sworn that her very heart stood still. "Don't you know your own son, Michael, when you hold him in your arms?"

"My son?" he whispered. Michael stared down at the child as though seeing him for the first time. Caitlin watched as Michael's green eyes met his son's, which were greener still. He reached up to touch the baby's short, auburn curls, but the boy caught his finger in his small fist and squeezed, laughing a joyous, baby laugh. "Mother of Mercy, why didn't I see it before? Just look at him and feel that grip. He's a woodcarver, sure."

"Or maybe a blacksmith."

Michael glanced down at the grave with its iron marker. "No, a woodcarver. He'll carve flying horses, he will. Glorious horses—you'll see."

Tears flooded his eyes as he reached for her and hugged her as best he could with two babies between them. "Why didn't you tell me, lass?"

"I didn't see any way that the two of you could be together, and I didn't want you to be tormented by the thought of having a son who couldn't be a part of your life."

He nodded his understanding. "But we can all be together now. There's nothin' to keep us apart any longer, if that's what you want."

"That's all I've ever wanted."

Michael sighed deeply with regret. "But we must leave this place. Even if we hadn't robbed that wagon, we would have had to leave. There's no hope for the children if we stay. I've known it since the moment I came back, but I couldn't accept it until now. If it were only meself, I'd rather stay and die here in Ireland, but I have to take the children away." He bent down and kissed her lips softly. Then his eyes searched hers. "Will you leave with me, Caitlin? Do you love me enough to leave your home?"

She returned his kiss. "I'll go anywhere with you. But there's something I must tell you. Before Mason died, he told me to give you back your carousel, and he gave me his lady's jewelry. 'Tis enough to get us all to America. But are you sure you could leave Ireland, Michael? It nearly broke your heart when you left before."

Michael looked around the cemetery at the graves of his mother, his father, his wife, his father-in-law, and his baby daughter. His eyes traced the graceful, timeless lines of the round tower and the green fields that stretched away to the purple mountains.

"It will surely tear me heart out to leave old Erin," he said. "But I can't think of meself alone. We have to be sure that the young ones survive, and if we stay here, we'll be as dead as those poor people in Terracoulter.

And no father could let that happen to his children as long as it's in his power to take them away."

The ship, Bountiful, pulled away from the Cobh quay amid shouts, cheers, and tears of farewell. Cobh Harbor was accustomed to these departures. Thousands were fleeing daily aboard ships bound for England, America, and Australia. Erin's greatest resource, her children, were leaving her shores, most of them never to return.

Michael stood on the deck of the Bountiful, his family at his side. Caitlin with Annie's baby at her breast, Daniel holding Stephen.

And below, in the cargo hold, was Michael's giant wheel and his herd of enchanted horses, his dream that had come into the world through his own hands, despite their scars. His vision had survived Erin's greatest tragedy, kept alive by his determination and the faith of those he loved.

"I'm going to miss Ireland," Danny remarked plaintively as the shoreline receded from view. "Will America be pretty and green like Ireland?"

"No land is as pretty and green as Ireland," Caitlin replied with tears streaming down her cheeks.

"We'll carry old Erin with us, lad," Michael said, taking his son into his arms. "We'll take her stories, her songs and her spirit along and keep them alive there in America."

"But will the folks in America like Princess Niav's magic horses?"

"I've heard they're a people with great imagination and a love for beautiful things. I'm sure they will."

Michael slipped his arm around Caitlin's waist and kissed her tears away. She smiled up at him with love-warmed eyes, and he felt a strength in her that gave him the courage to face the most difficult moment of his life.

As the blue waters swallowed the shore, Michael knew in his heart that he was seeing Ireland for the last time. And he watched with hungry eyes as that last patch of green shore disappeared in the sea fog.